# DECELERATE
# BLUE

# DECELERATE BLUE

by Adam Rapp

artwork by Mike Cavallaro

:01

First Second
New York

First Second

Text copyright © 2017 by Adam Rapp
Illustrations copyright © 2017 by Mike Cavallaro

Published by First Second
First Second is an imprint of Roaring Brook Press,
a division of Holtzbrinck Publishing Holdings Limited Partnership
175 Fifth Avenue, New York, New York 10010

Library of Congress Control Number: 2016938577

ISBN 978-1-59643-109-6

Our books may be purchased in bulk for promotional, educational, or business use.
Please contact your local bookseller or the Macmillan Corporate and Premium Sales Department
at (800) 221-7945 ext. 5442 or by e-mail at MacmillanSpecialMarkets@macmillan.com.

First edition 2017
Book design by Scott Friedlander

Printed in China by RR Donelley Asia Printing Solutions Ltd., Dongguan City, Guangdong Province

10 9 8 7 6 5 4 3 2 1

Drawn with pencil on a variety of papers ranging from copy stock to sketch pads to Bristol board.
Inked and colored digitally using an Intuos tablet and a Cintiq 13HD graphics tablet in Adobe Photoshop,
Adobe Illustrator, and Manga Studio EX.

For Kurt Vonnegut
—A. R.


This goes out to anyone and everyone laboring in ways great or small
to make this a better, fairer, more compassionate world to live in.
—M. C.

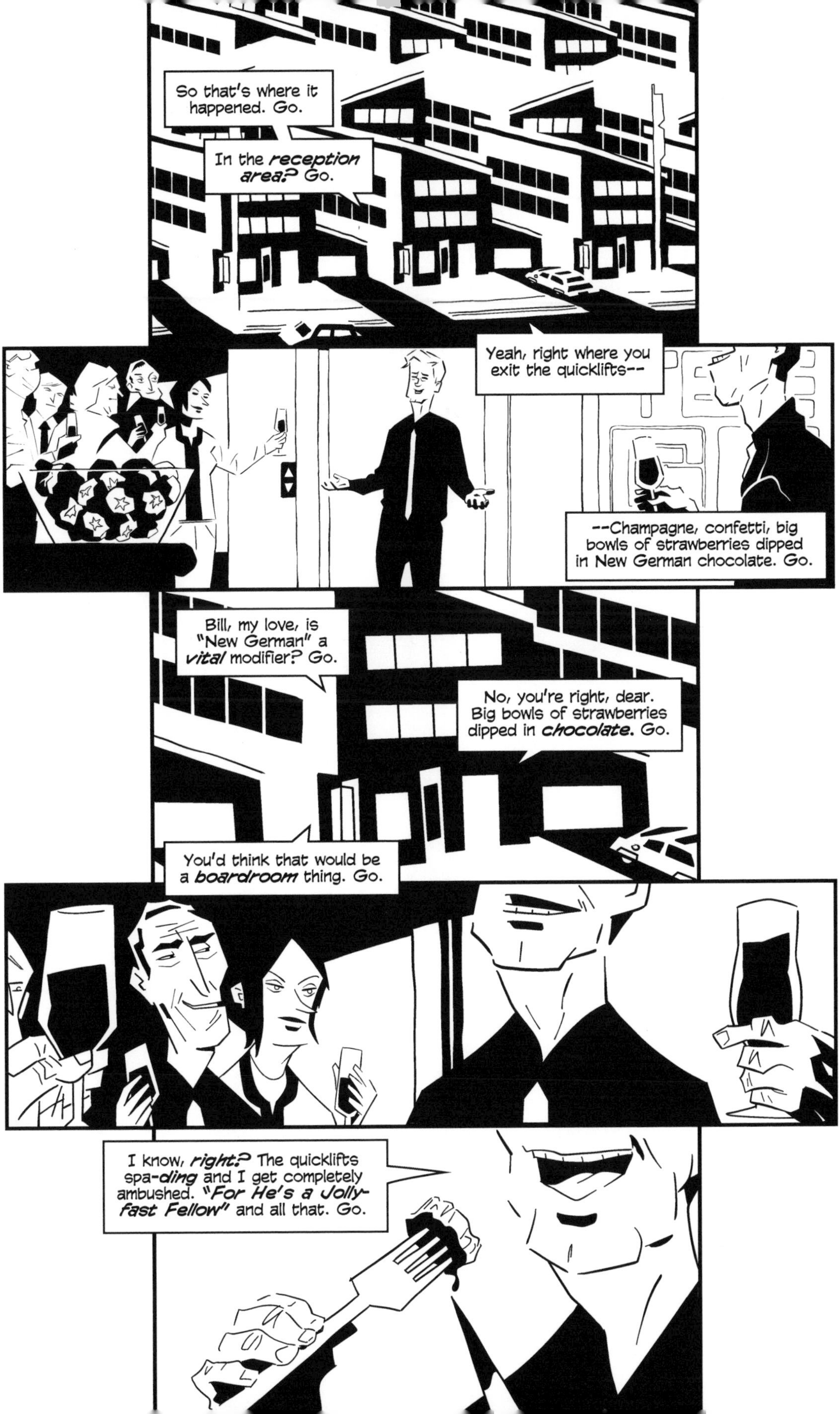
So that's where it happened. Go.
In the *reception area?* Go.
Yeah, right where you exit the quicklifts--
--Champagne, confetti, big bowls of strawberries dipped in New German chocolate. Go.
Bill, my love, is "New German" a *vital* modifier? Go.
No, you're right, dear. Big bowls of strawberries dipped in *chocolate.* Go.
You'd think that would be a *boardroom* thing. Go.
I know, *right?* The quicklifts spa-*ding* and I get completely ambushed. *"For He's a Jolly-fast Fellow"* and all that. Go.

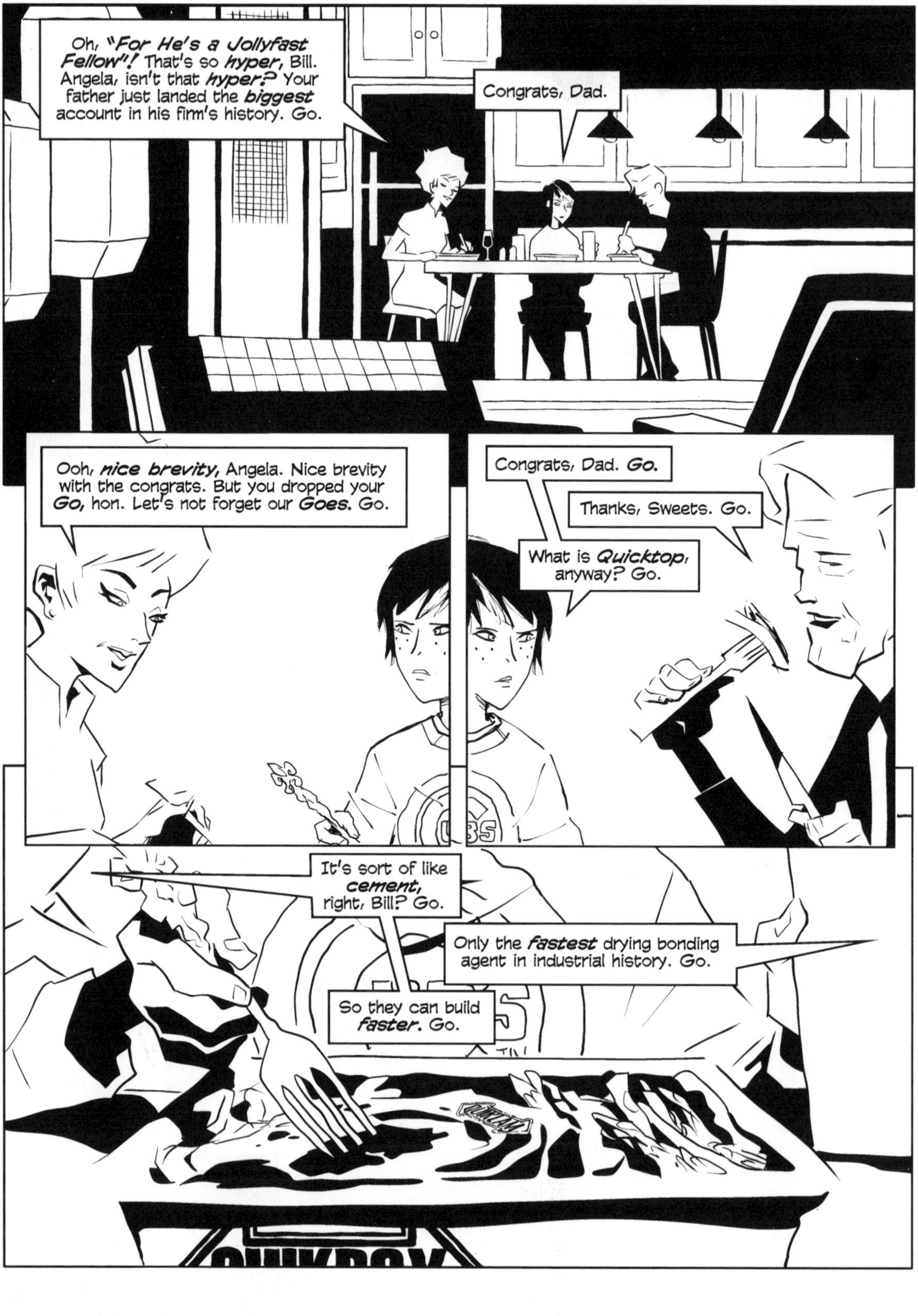
Oh, "For He's a Jollyfast Fellow"! That's so hyper, Bill. Angela, isn't that hyper? Your father just landed the biggest account in his firm's history. Go.
Congrats, Dad.
Ooh, nice brevity, Angela. Nice brevity with the congrats. But you dropped your Go, hon. Let's not forget our Goes. Go.
Congrats, Dad. Go.
Thanks, Sweets. Go.
What is Quicktop, anyway? Go.
It's sort of like cement, right, Bill? Go.
Only the fastest drying bonding agent in industrial history. Go.
So they can build faster. Go.

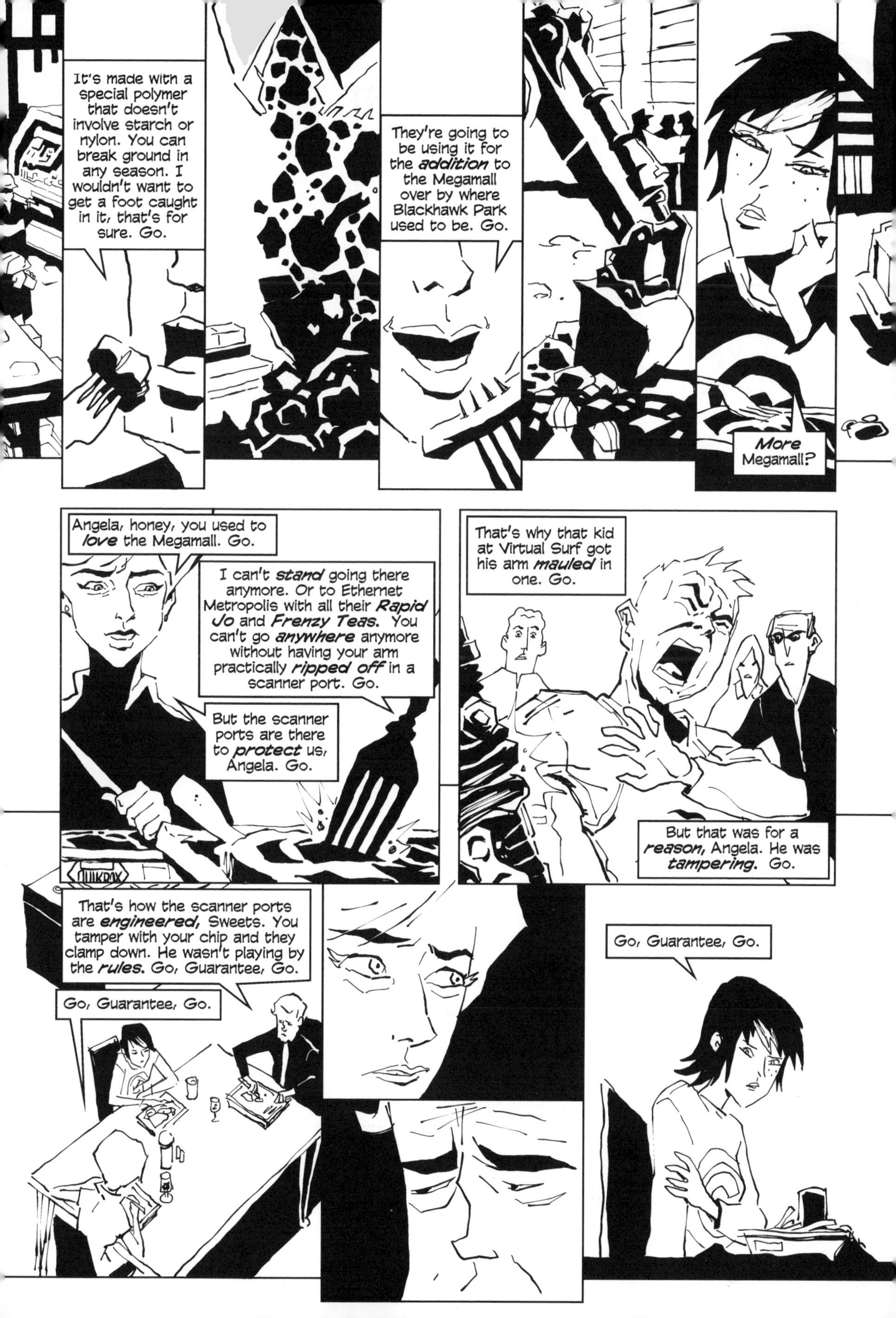
It's made with a special polymer that doesn't involve starch or nylon. You can break ground in any season. I wouldn't want to get a foot caught in it, that's for sure. Go.
They're going to be using it for the *addition* to the Megamall over by where Blackhawk Park used to be. Go.
*More* Megamall?
Angela, honey, you used to *love* the Megamall. Go.
I can't *stand* going there anymore. Or to Ethernet Metropolis with all their *Rapid Jo* and *Frenzy Teas.* You can't go *anywhere* anymore without having your arm practically *ripped off* in a scanner port. Go.
But the scanner ports are there to *protect* us, Angela. Go.
QUIKBOX
That's why that kid at Virtual Surf got his arm *mauled* in one. Go.
But that was for a *reason,* Angela. He was *tampering.* Go.
That's how the scanner ports are *engineered,* Sweets. You tamper with your chip and they clamp down. He wasn't playing by the *rules.* Go, Guarantee, Go.
Go, Guarantee, Go.
Go, Guarantee, Go.

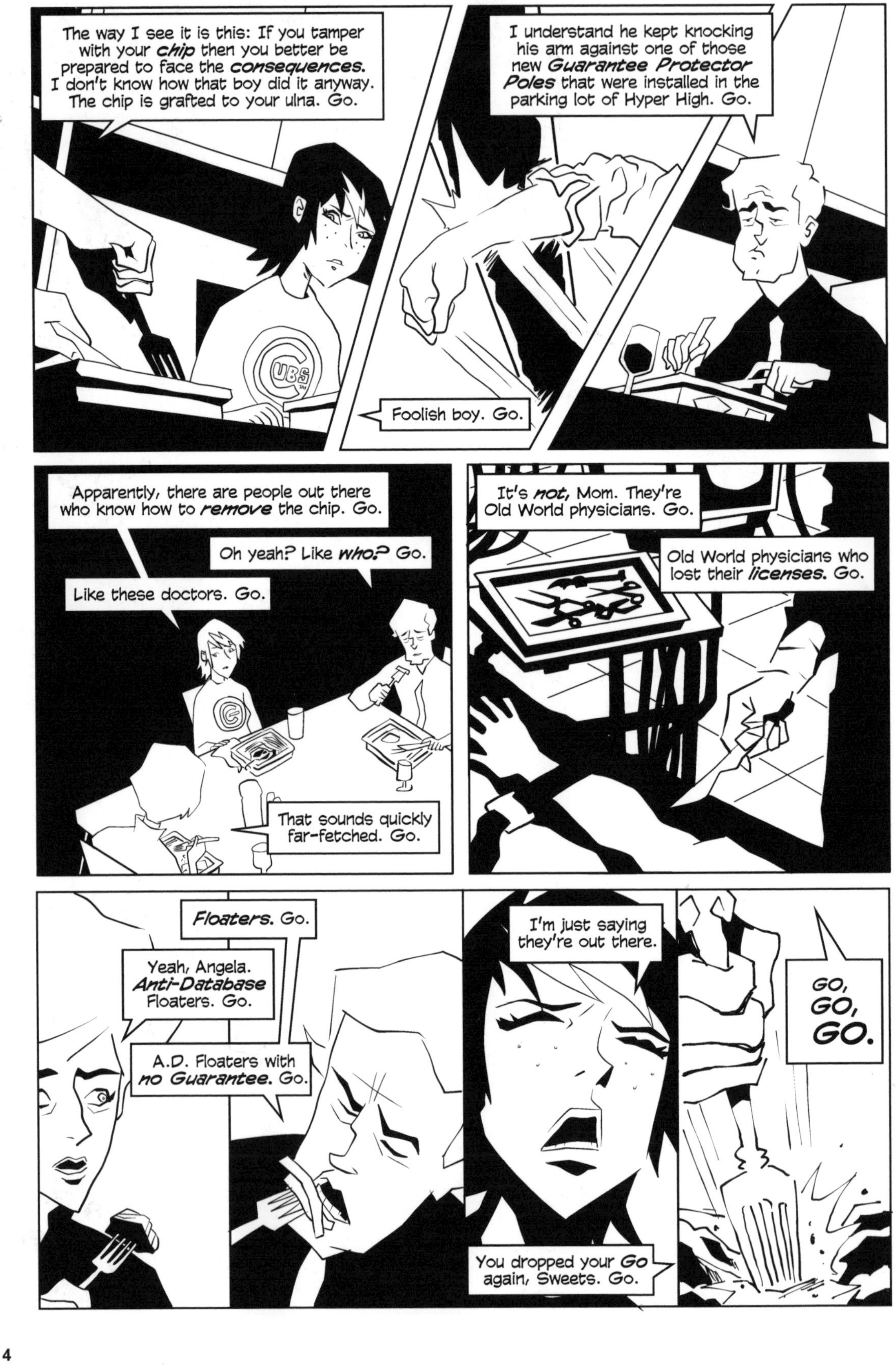
The way I see it is this: If you tamper with your chip then you better be prepared to face the consequences. I don't know how that boy did it anyway. The chip is grafted to your ulna. Go.
Foolish boy. Go.
I understand he kept knocking his arm against one of those new Guarantee Protector Poles that were installed in the parking lot of Hyper High. Go.
Apparently, there are people out there who know how to remove the chip. Go.
Oh yeah? Like who? Go.
Like these doctors. Go.
That sounds quickly far-fetched. Go.
It's not, Mom. They're Old World physicians. Go.
Old World physicians who lost their licenses. Go.
Floaters. Go.
Yeah, Angela. Anti-Database Floaters. Go.
A.D. Floaters with no Guarantee. Go.
I'm just saying they're out there.
You dropped your Go again, Sweets. Go.
GO, GO, GO.

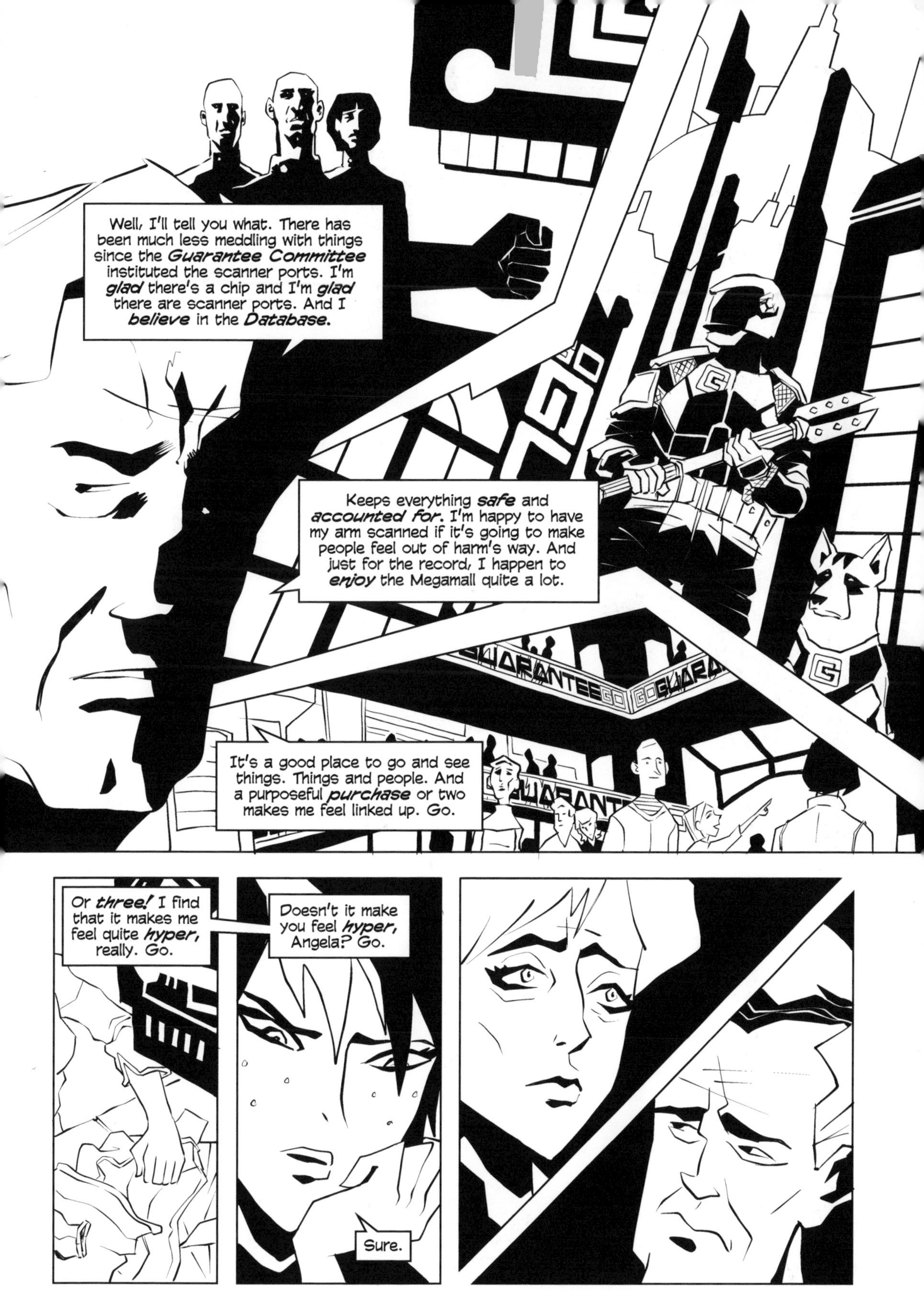
Well, I'll tell you what. There has been much less meddling with things since the *Guarantee Committee* instituted the scanner ports. I'm *glad* there's a chip and I'm *glad* there are scanner ports. And I *believe* in the *Database.*
Keeps everything *safe* and *accounted for.* I'm happy to have my arm scanned if it's going to make people feel out of harm's way. And just for the record, I happen to *enjoy* the Megamall quite a lot.
GUARANTEE GO GO GUARA
It's a good place to go and see things. Things and people. And a purposeful *purchase* or two makes me feel linked up. Go.
Or *three!* I find that it makes me feel quite *hyper,* really. Go.
Doesn't it make you feel *hyper,* Angela? Go.
Sure.

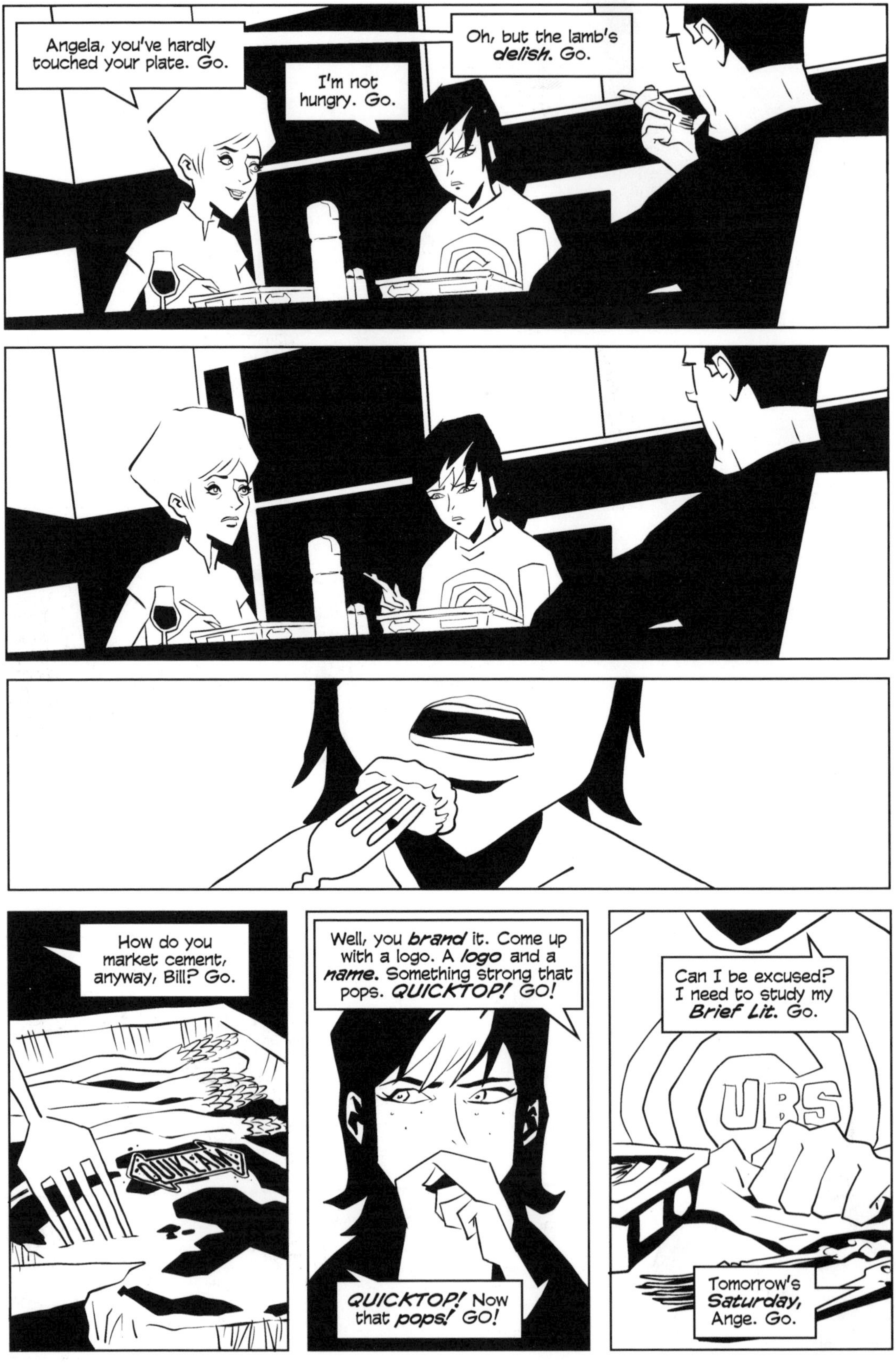
Angela, you've hardly touched your plate. Go.
I'm not hungry. Go.
Oh, but the lamb's *delish*. Go.
How do you market cement, anyway, Bill? Go.
QUIKCAN
Well, you *brand* it. Come up with a logo. A *logo* and a *name*. Something strong that pops. *QUICKTOP!* GO!
*QUICKTOP!* Now that *pops!* GO!
Can I be excused? I need to study my *Brief Lit*. Go.
UBS
Tomorrow's *Saturday*, Ange. Go.

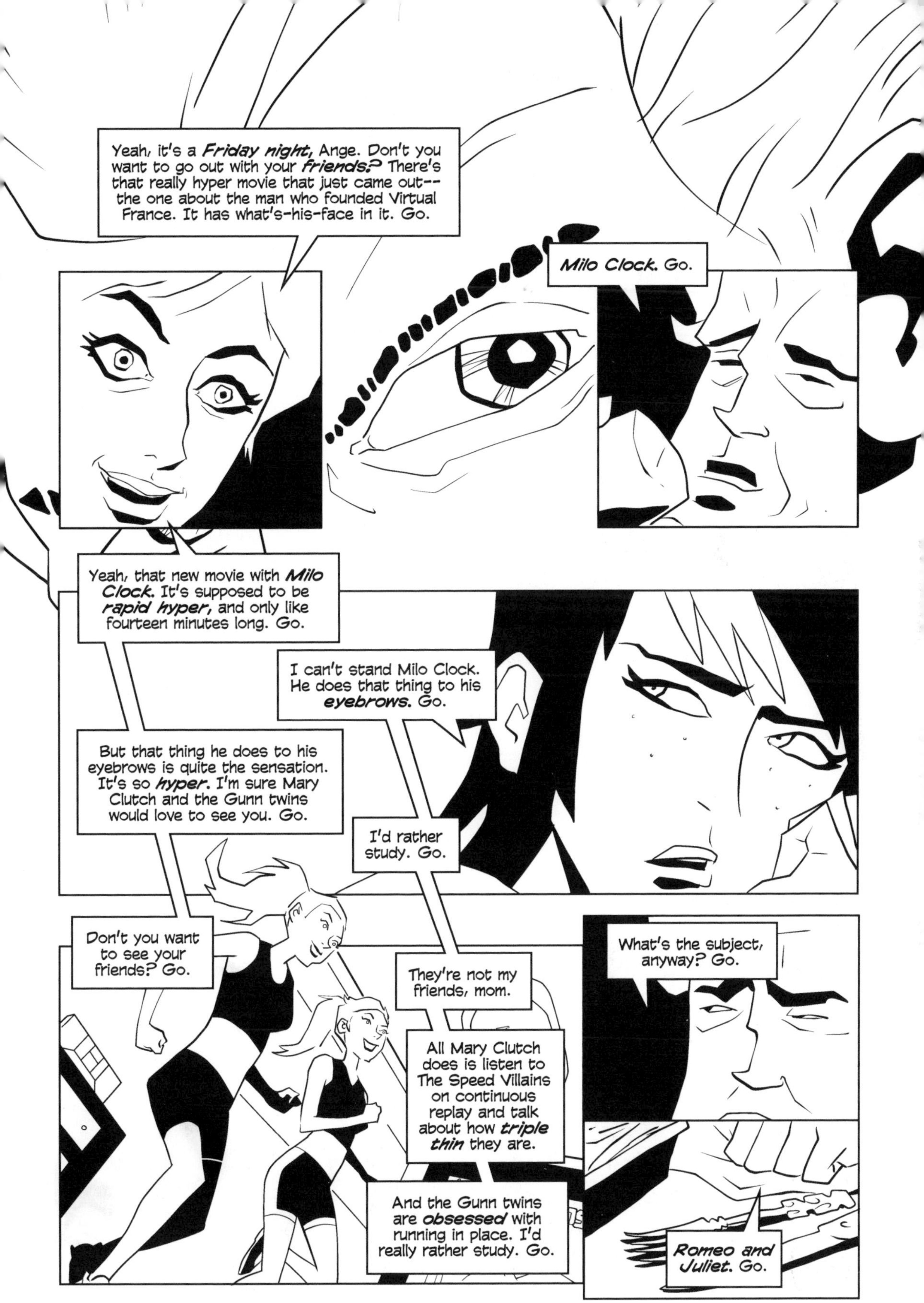
Yeah, it's a *Friday night,* Ange. Don't you want to go out with your *friends?* There's that really hyper movie that just came out--the one about the man who founded Virtual France. It has what's-his-face in it. Go.
*Milo Clock.* Go.
Yeah, that new movie with *Milo Clock.* It's supposed to be *rapid hyper,* and only like fourteen minutes long. Go.
I can't stand Milo Clock. He does that thing to his *eyebrows.* Go.
But that thing he does to his eyebrows is quite the sensation. It's so *hyper.* I'm sure Mary Clutch and the Gunn twins would love to see you. Go.
I'd rather study. Go.
Don't you want to see your friends? Go.
They're not my friends, mom.
All Mary Clutch does is listen to The Speed Villains on continuous replay and talk about how *triple thin* they are.
And the Gunn twins are *obsessed* with running in place. I'd really rather study. Go.
What's the subject, anyway? Go.
*Romeo and Juliet.* Go.

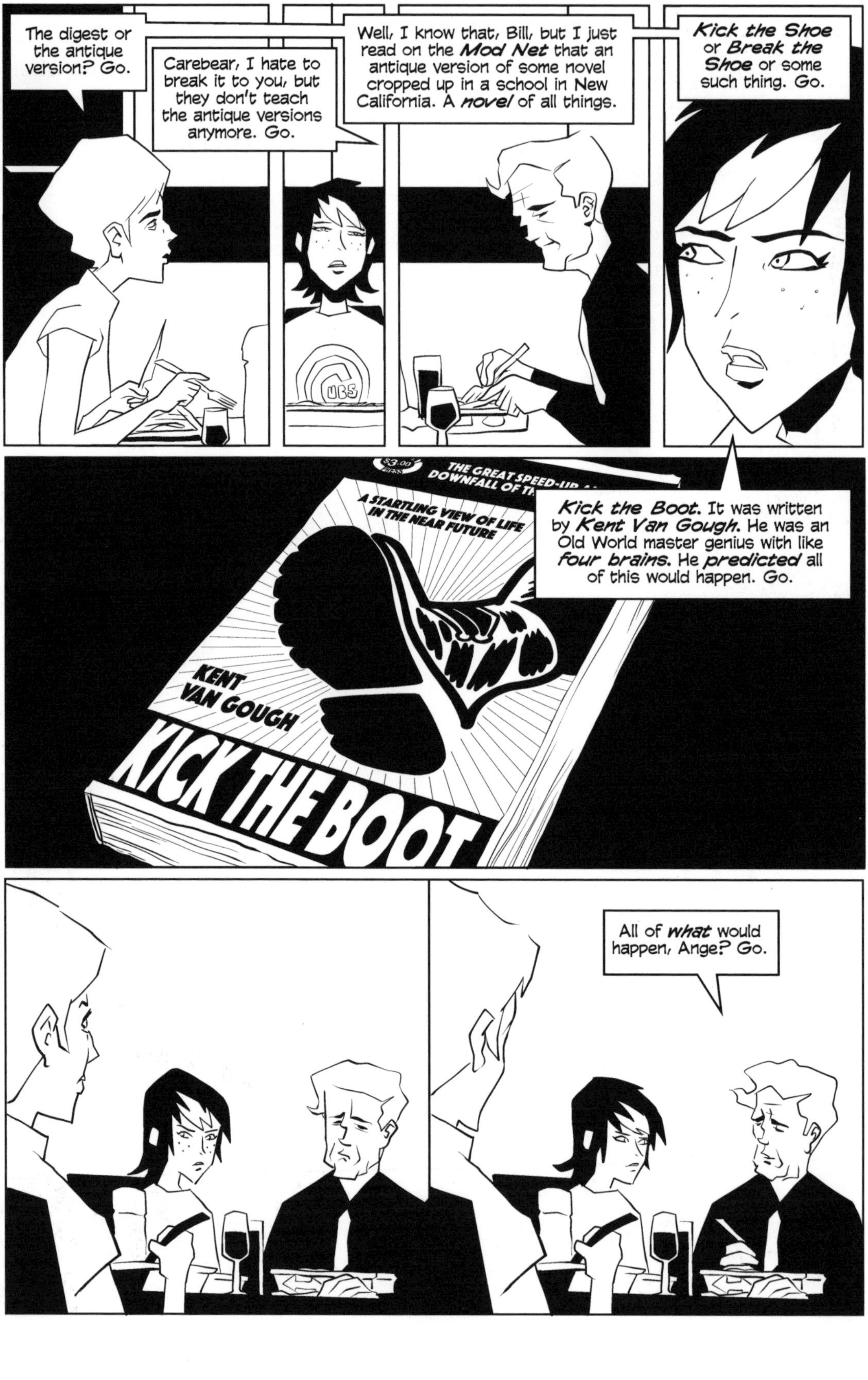

The digest or the antique version? Go.
Carebear, I hate to break it to you, but they don't teach the antique versions anymore. Go.
Well, I know that, Bill, but I just read on the *Mod Net* that an antique version of some novel cropped up in a school in New California. A *novel* of all things.
*Kick the Shoe* or *Break the Shoe* or some such thing. Go.
UBS
$3.00
THE GREAT SPEED-UP AND DOWNFALL OF TH
A STARTLING VIEW OF LIFE IN THE NEAR FUTURE
KENT VAN GOUGH
KICK THE BOOT
*Kick the Boot*. It was written by *Kent Van Gough*. He was an Old World master genius with like *four brains*. He *predicted* all of this would happen. Go.
All of *what* would happen, Ange? Go.

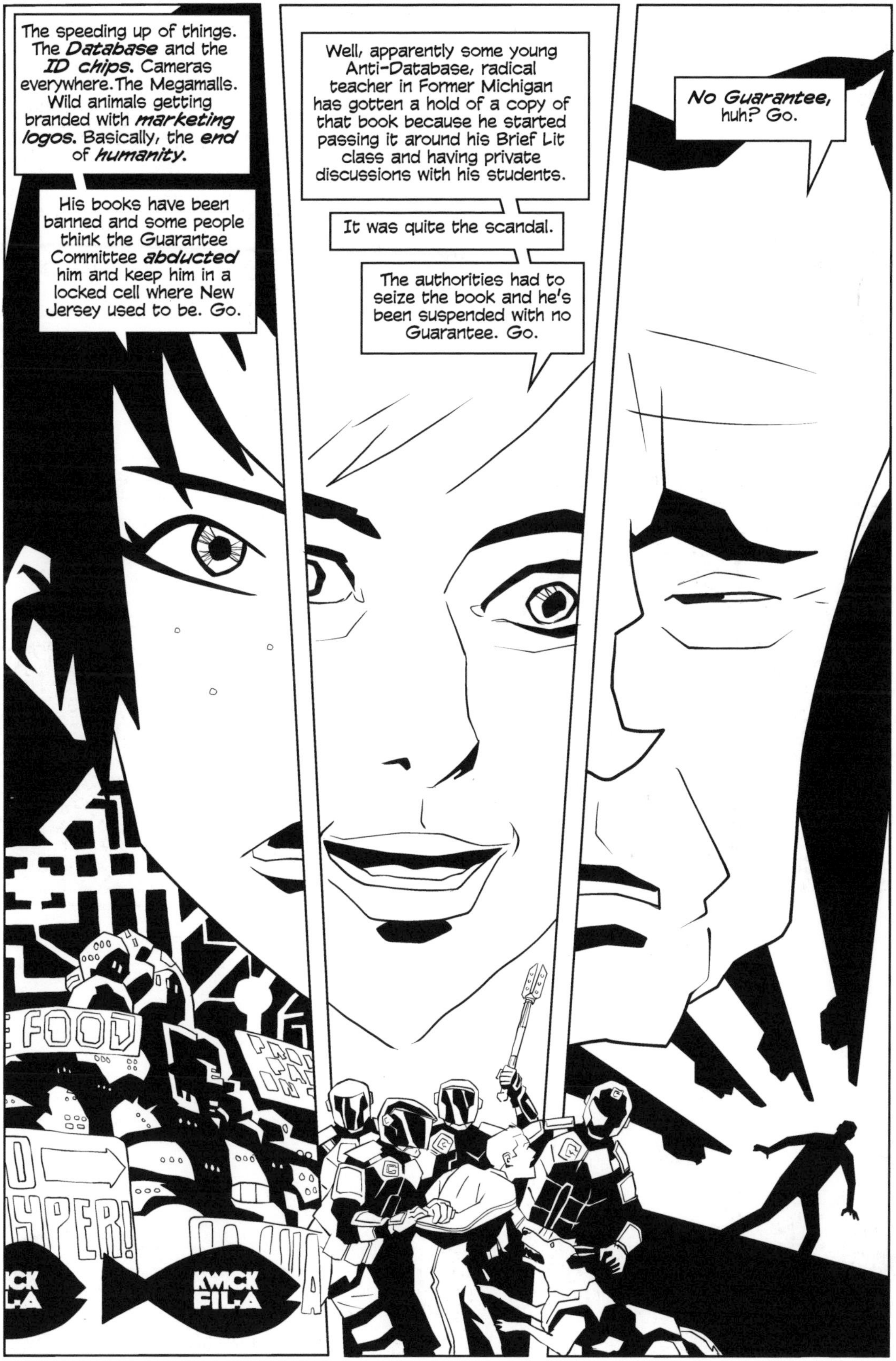
The speeding up of things. The *Database* and the *ID chips.* Cameras everywhere. The Megamalls. Wild animals getting branded with *marketing logos.* Basically, the *end* of *humanity.*
His books have been banned and some people think the Guarantee Committee *abducted* him and keep him in a locked cell where New Jersey used to be. Go.
FOOD
HYPER!
KWICK FIL-A
KWICK FIL-A
Well, apparently some young Anti-Database, radical teacher in Former Michigan has gotten a hold of a copy of that book because he started passing it around his Brief Lit class and having private discussions with his students.
It was quite the scandal.
The authorities had to seize the book and he's been suspended with no Guarantee. Go.
*No Guarantee,* huh? Go.

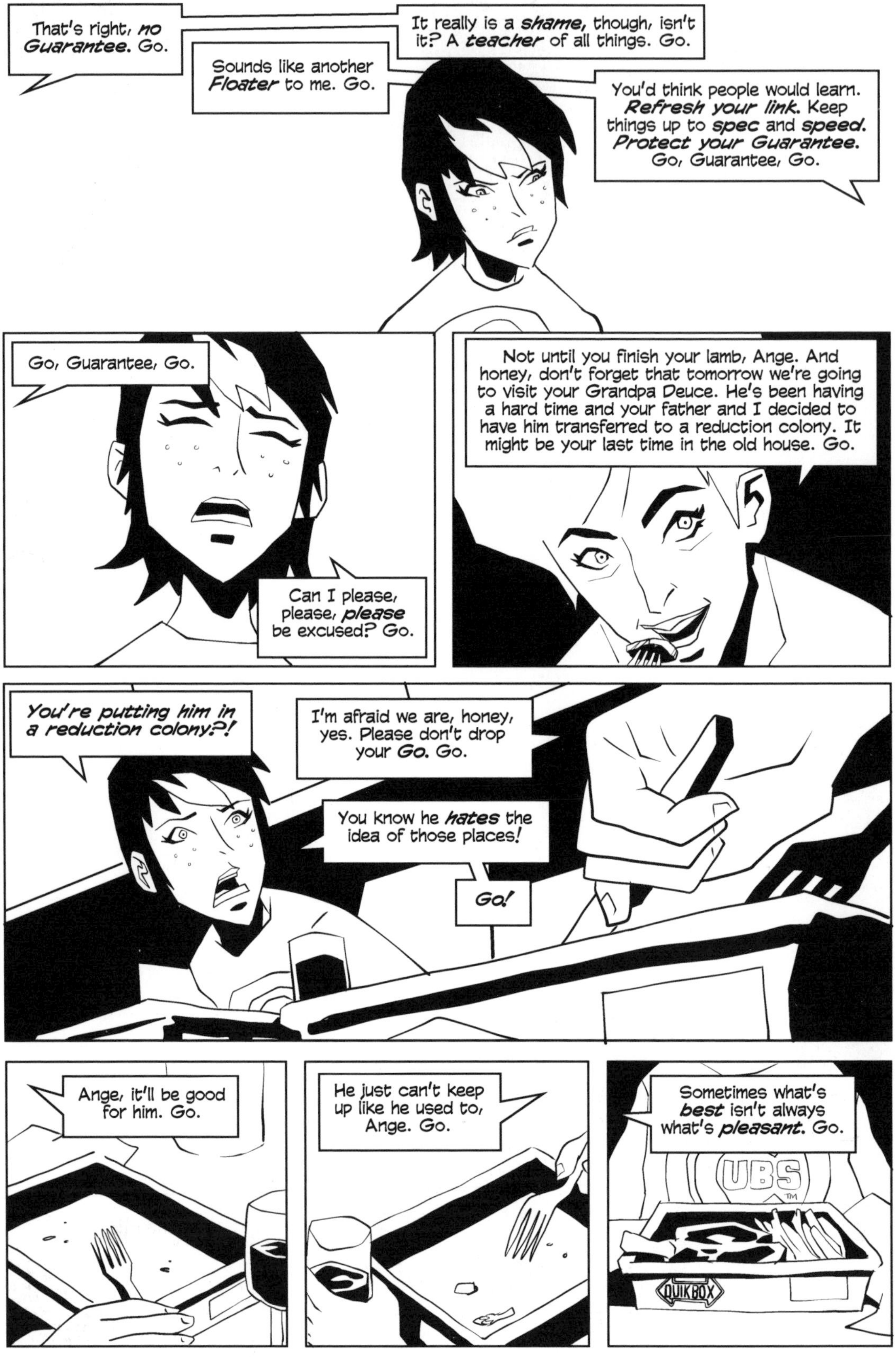

That's right, *no Guarantee.* Go.
It really is a *shame,* though, isn't it? A *teacher* of all things. Go.
Sounds like another *Floater* to me. Go.
You'd think people would learn. *Refresh your link.* Keep things up to *spec* and *speed. Protect your Guarantee.* Go, Guarantee, Go.
Go, Guarantee, Go.
Can I please, please, *please* be excused? Go.
Not until you finish your lamb, Ange. And honey, don't forget that tomorrow we're going to visit your Grandpa Deuce. He's been having a hard time and your father and I decided to have him transferred to a reduction colony. It might be your last time in the old house. Go.
*You're putting him in a reduction colony?!*
I'm afraid we are, honey, yes. Please don't drop your *Go.* Go.
You know he *hates* the idea of those places!
*Go!*
Ange, it'll be good for him. Go.
He just can't keep up like he used to, Ange. Go.
Sometimes what's *best* isn't always what's *pleasant.* Go.
UBS
QUIKBOX

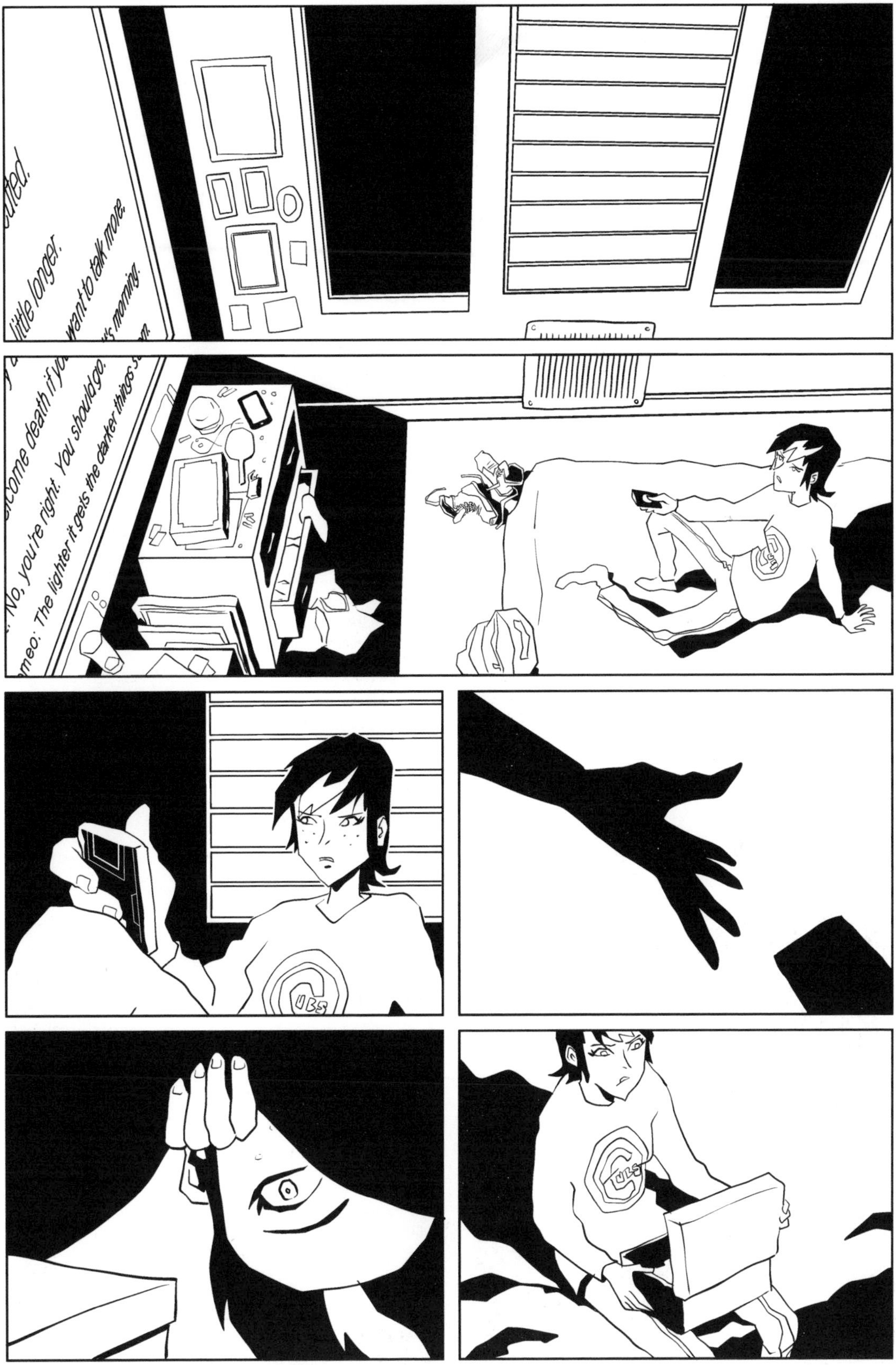

uted.
little longer.
want to talk more.
's morning.
come death if you
: No, you're right. You should go.
meo: The lighter it gets the darker things s

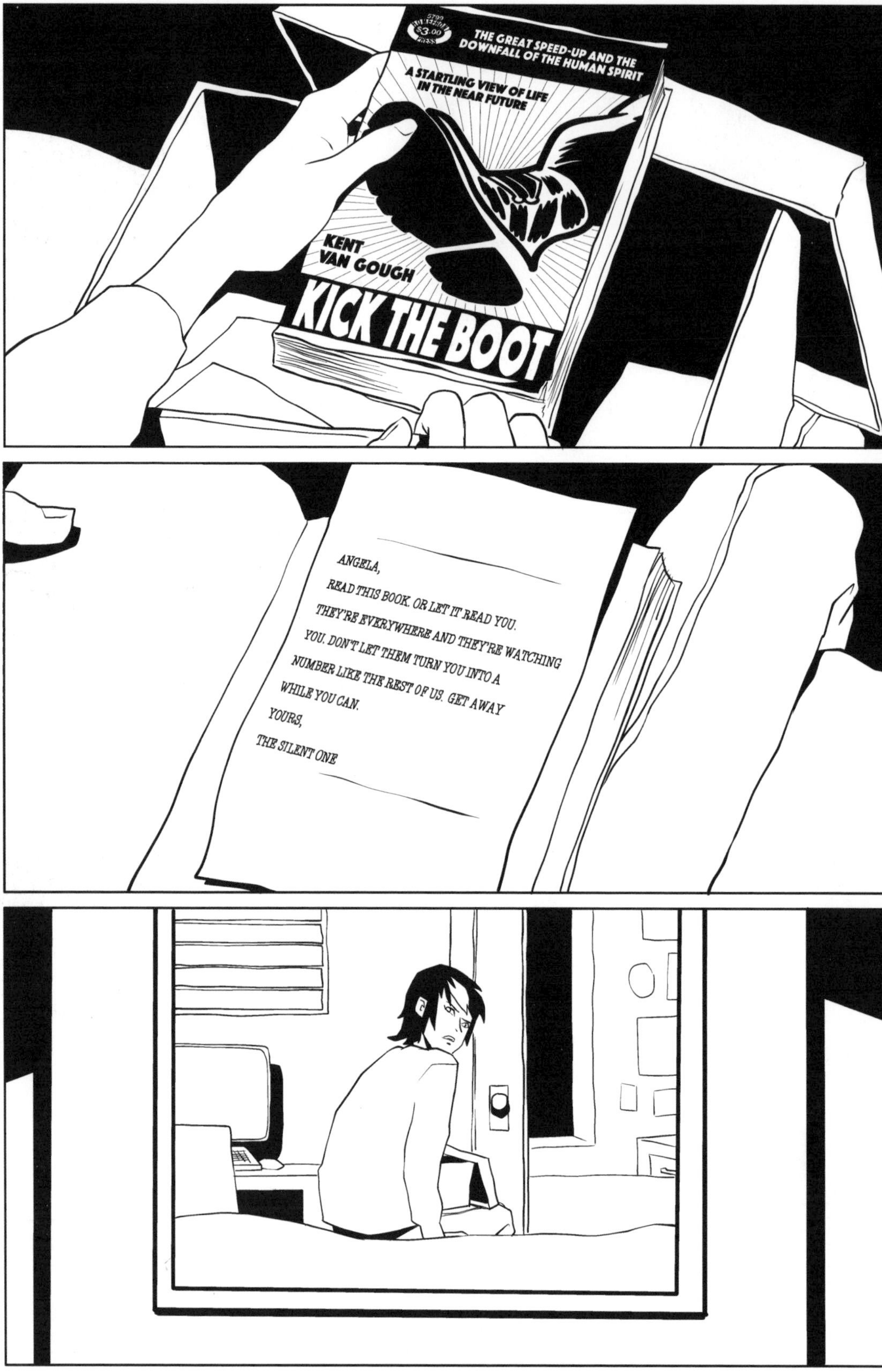
5799
$3.00
PRESS
THE GREAT SPEED-UP AND THE DOWNFALL OF THE HUMAN SPIRIT
A STARTLING VIEW OF LIFE IN THE NEAR FUTURE
KENT VAN GOUGH
KICK THE BOOT
ANGELA,
READ THIS BOOK. OR LET IT READ YOU.
THEY'RE EVERYWHERE AND THEY'RE WATCHING YOU. DON'T LET THEM TURN YOU INTO A NUMBER LIKE THE REST OF US. GET AWAY WHILE YOU CAN.
YOURS,
THE SILENT ONE

What are you looking at, honey? Go.

Why does our Guarantee Tree have that weird *box* attached to it? Go.

It's a birdhouse. Go.

I've never seen a *single bird* anywhere *near* it. Go.

Well, that's probably because they're all inside enjoying their little home. We're blessed with beautiful birds around here. I saw a *blue jay* perched on the other side of the kitchen window just the other day. Go.

It's got that *weird eye* on it.

*What* weird eye? Go.

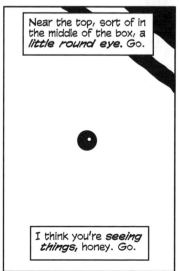

Near the top, sort of in the middle of the box, a *little round eye*. Go.

I think you're *seeing things*, honey. Go.

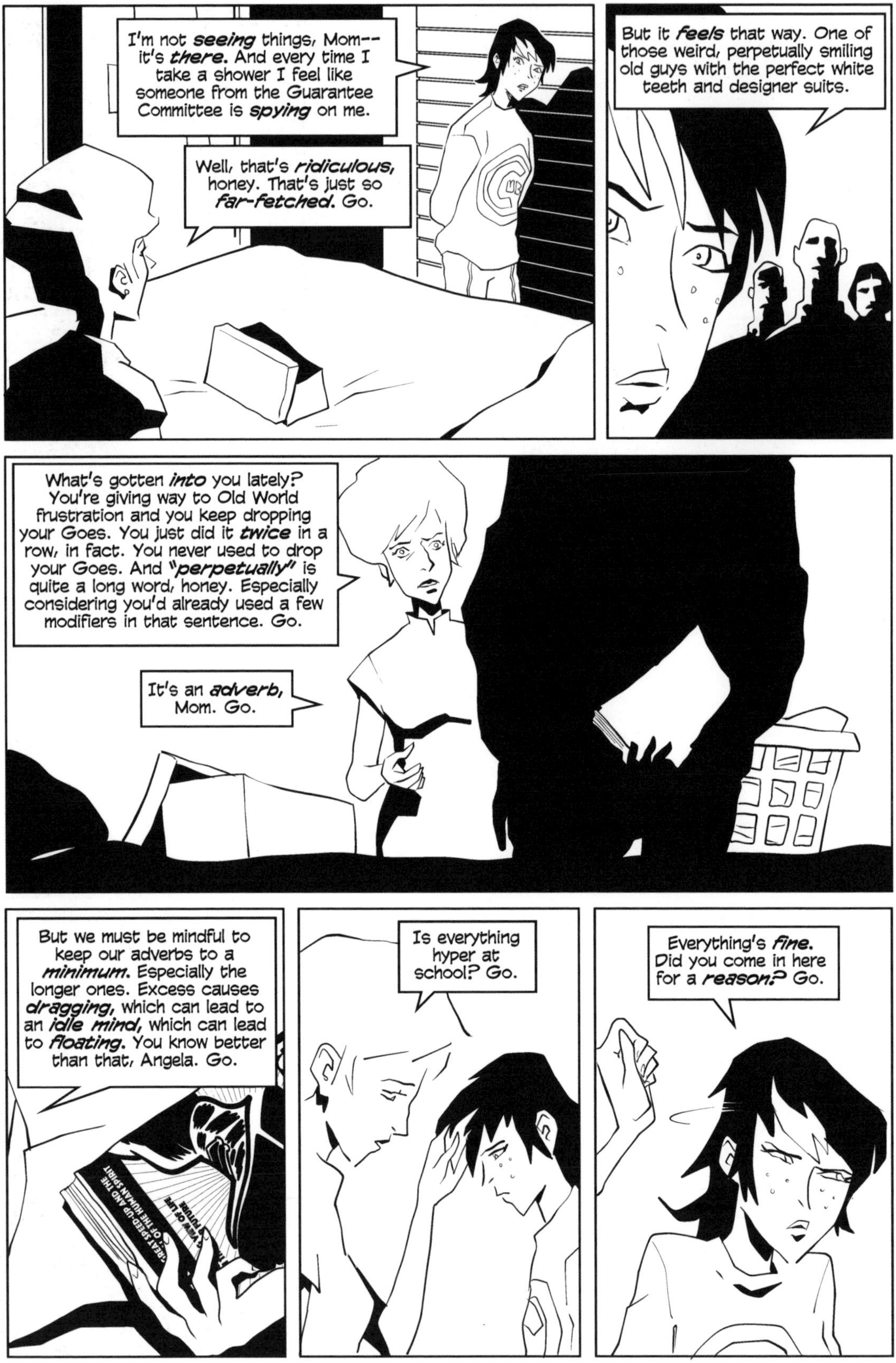
I'm not *seeing* things, Mom--it's *there.* And every time I take a shower I feel like someone from the Guarantee Committee is *spying* on me.
Well, that's *ridiculous,* honey. That's just so *far-fetched.* Go.
But it *feels* that way. One of those weird, perpetually smiling old guys with the perfect white teeth and designer suits.
What's gotten *into* you lately? You're giving way to Old World frustration and you keep dropping your Goes. You just did it *twice* in a row, in fact. You never used to drop your Goes. And "*perpetually*" is quite a long word, honey. Especially considering you'd already used a few modifiers in that sentence. Go.
It's an *adverb,* Mom. Go.
But we must be mindful to keep our adverbs to a *minimum.* Especially the longer ones. Excess causes *dragging,* which can lead to an *idle mind,* which can lead to *floating.* You know better than that, Angela. Go.
Is everything hyper at school? Go.
Everything's *fine.* Did you come in here for a *reason?* Go.

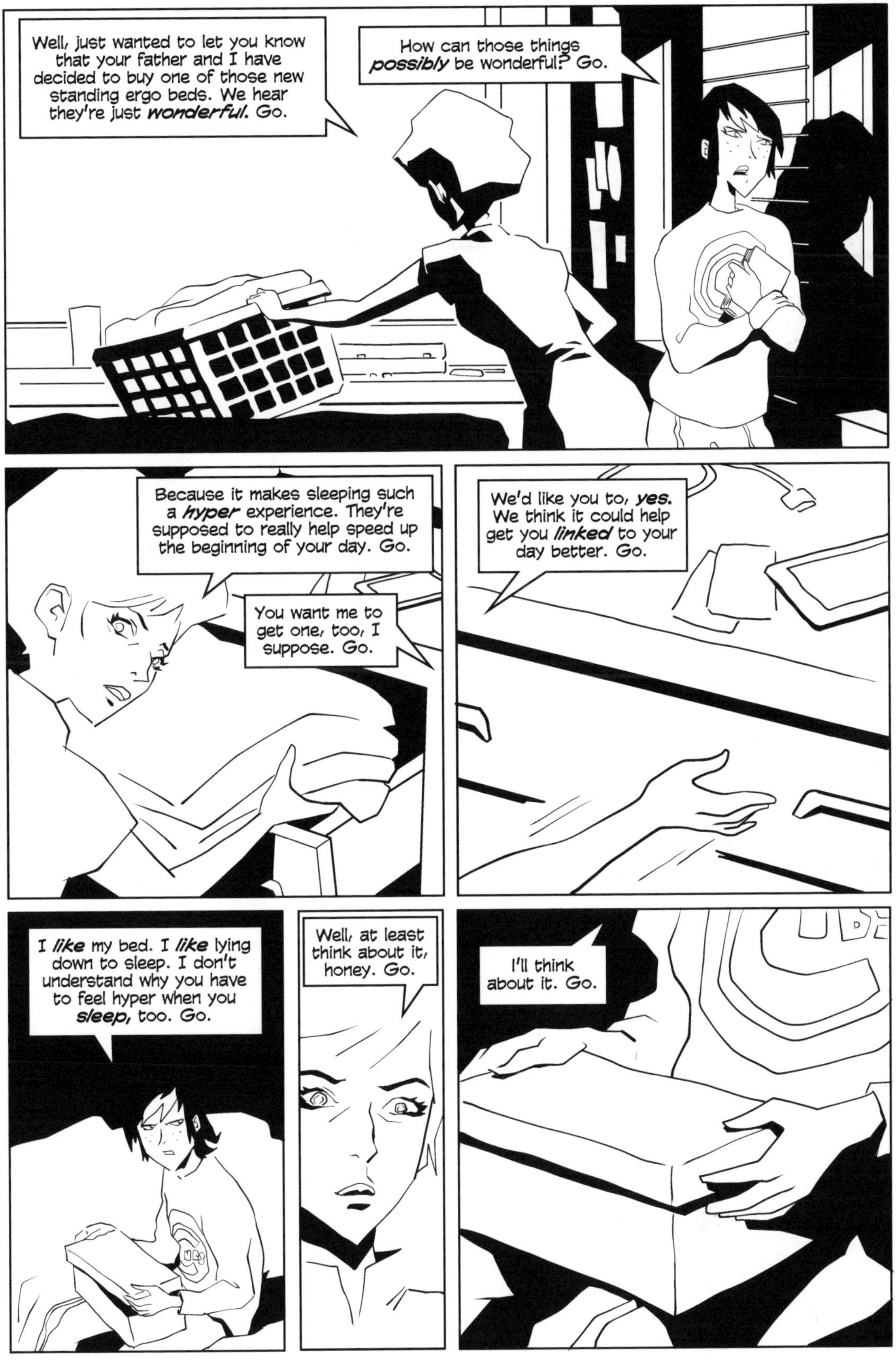
Well, just wanted to let you know that your father and I have decided to buy one of those new standing ergo beds. We hear they're just *wonderful.* Go.
How can those things *possibly* be wonderful? Go.
Because it makes sleeping such a *hyper* experience. They're supposed to really help speed up the beginning of your day. Go.
You want me to get one, too, I suppose. Go.
We'd like you to, *yes.* We think it could help get you *linked* to your day better. Go.
I *like* my bed. I *like* lying down to sleep. I don't understand why you have to feel hyper when you *sleep,* too. Go.
Well, at least think about it, honey. Go.
I'll think about it. Go.

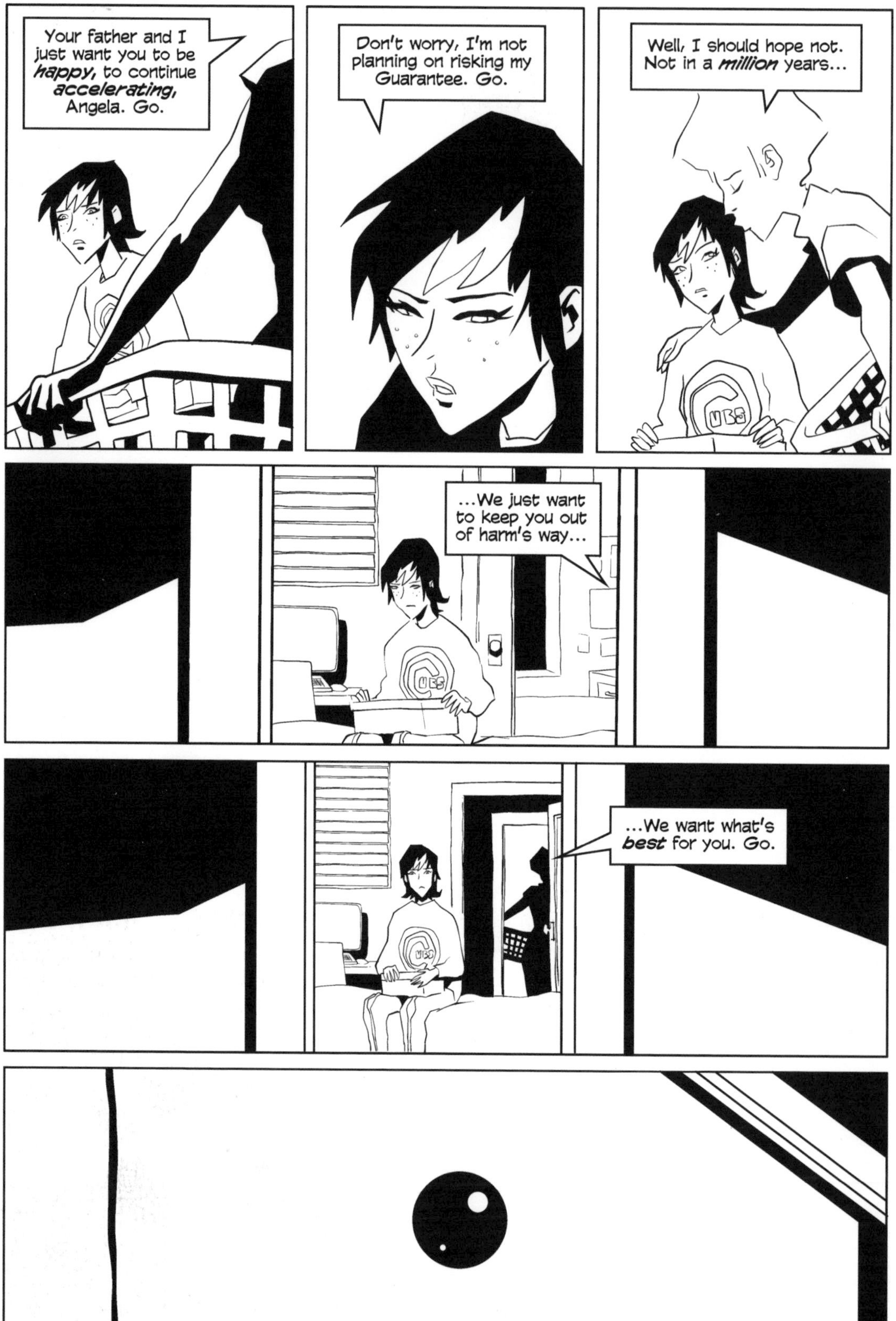
Your father and I just want you to be *happy,* to continue *accelerating,* Angela. Go.
Don't worry, I'm not planning on risking my Guarantee. Go.
Well, I should hope not. Not in a *million* years...
...We just want to keep you out of harm's way...
...We want what's *best* for you. Go.

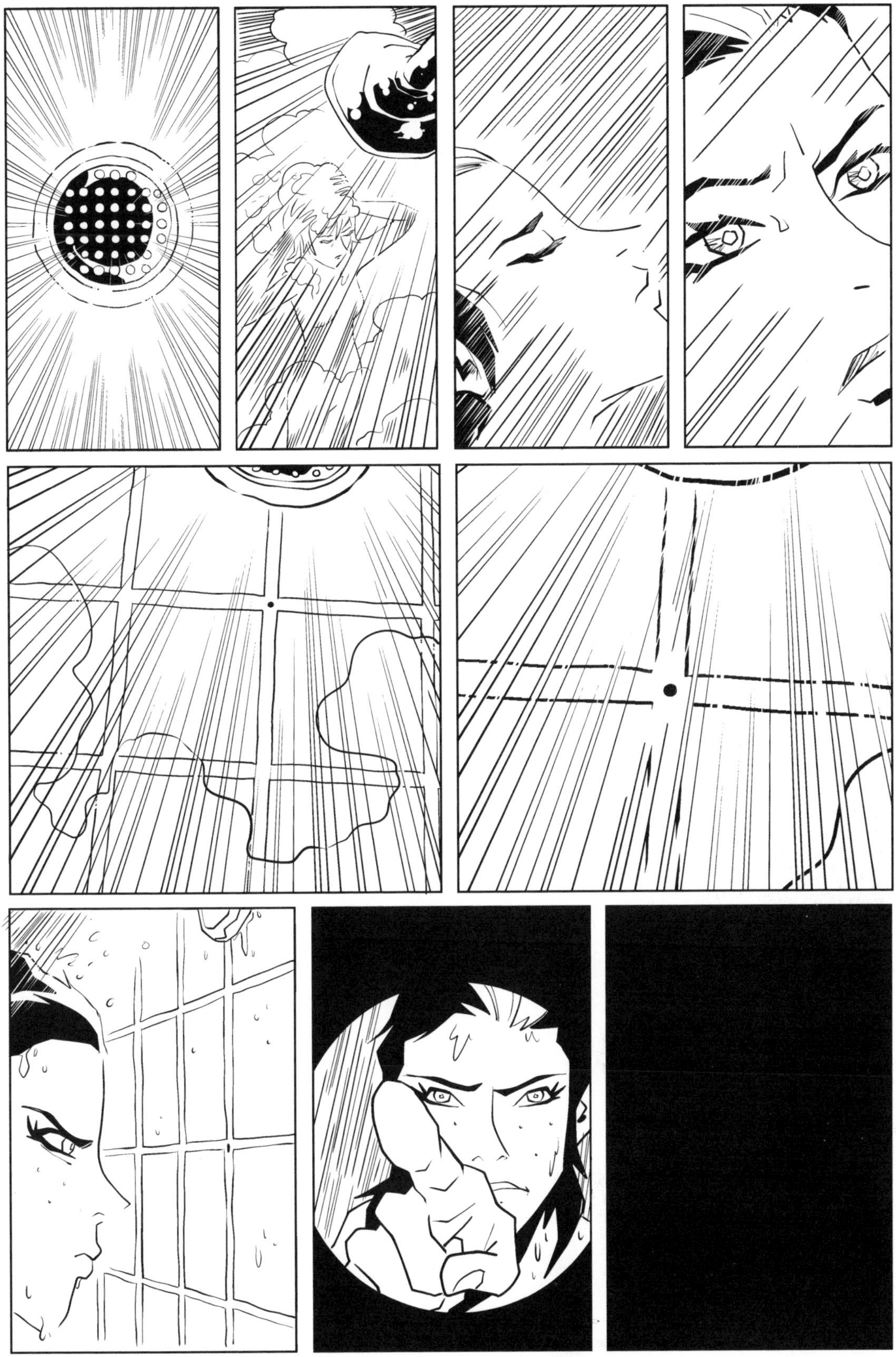

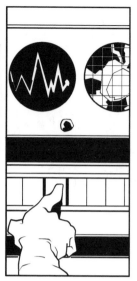

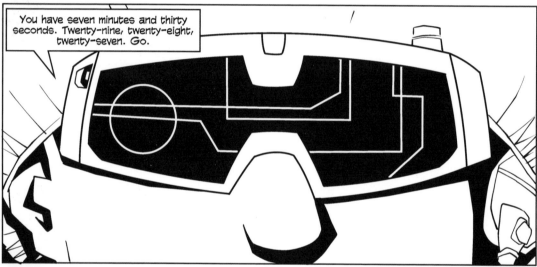

You have seven minutes and thirty seconds. Twenty-nine, twenty-eight, twenty-seven. Go.

Thanks, Nurse. Go.

Hey, Grandpa. Go.

*Angela*... When'd you get here?

About twenty minutes ago...

Mom and Dad told me they're moving you to a reduction colony. Go.

At my last checkup, I couldn't keep my heart rate up to the necessary standard. So that's when the *Committee* and all their *goons* got involved. And now I'm rigged to this godforsaken *contraption*.

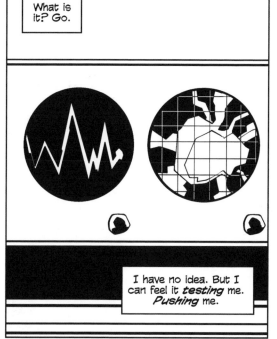

What is it? Go.

I have no idea. But I can feel it *testing* me. *Pushing* me.

I'm so sorry, Grandpa. Go.

You don't have to do your *Goes* with me, Angela. All that Guarantee stuff is just *nonsense* as far as I'm concerned.

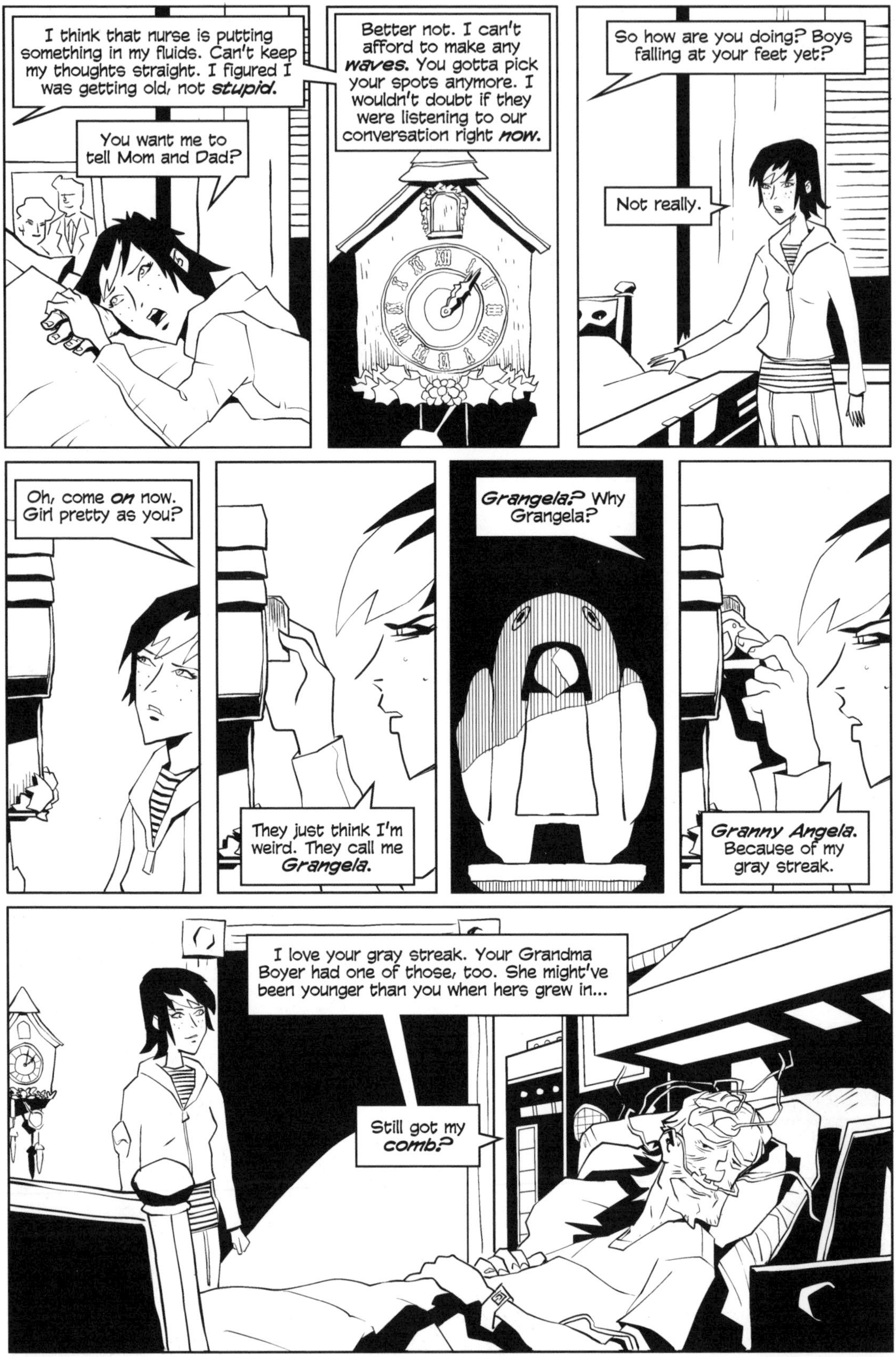
I think that nurse is putting something in my fluids. Can't keep my thoughts straight. I figured I was getting old, not *stupid*.
You want me to tell Mom and Dad?
Better not. I can't afford to make any *waves*. You gotta pick your spots anymore. I wouldn't doubt if they were listening to our conversation right *now*.
So how are you doing? Boys falling at your feet yet?
Not really.
Oh, come *on* now. Girl pretty as you?
They just think I'm weird. They call me *Grangela*.
*Grangela?* Why Grangela?
*Granny Angela*. Because of my gray streak.
I love your gray streak. Your Grandma Boyer had one of those, too. She might've been younger than you when hers grew in...
Still got my *comb?*

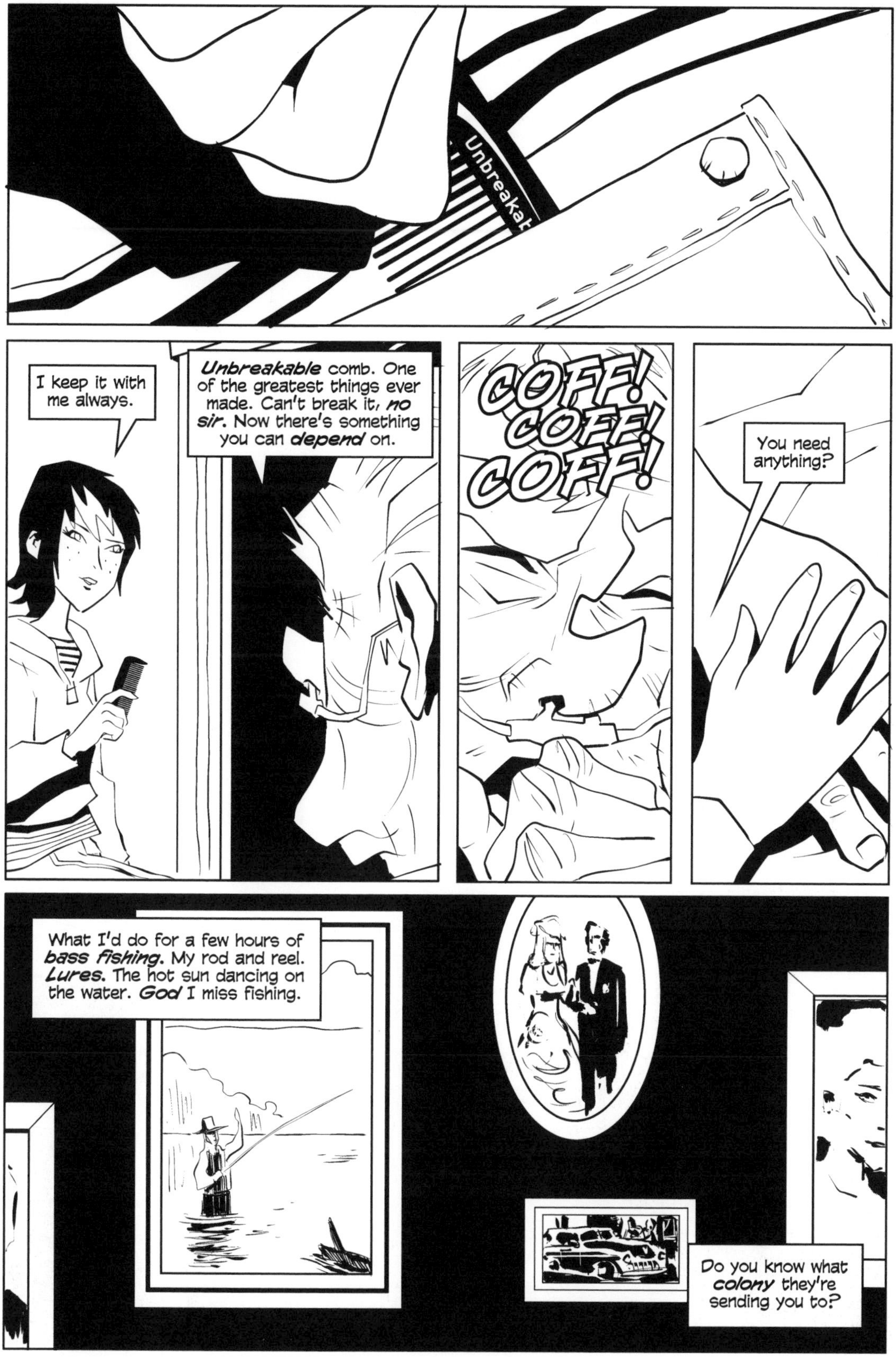
Unbreakat
I keep it with me always.
Unbreakable comb. One of the greatest things ever made. Can't break it, no sir. Now there's something you can depend on.
COFF! COFF! COFF!
You need anything?
What I'd do for a few hours of bass fishing. My rod and reel. Lures. The hot sun dancing on the water. God I miss fishing.
Do you know what colony they're sending you to?

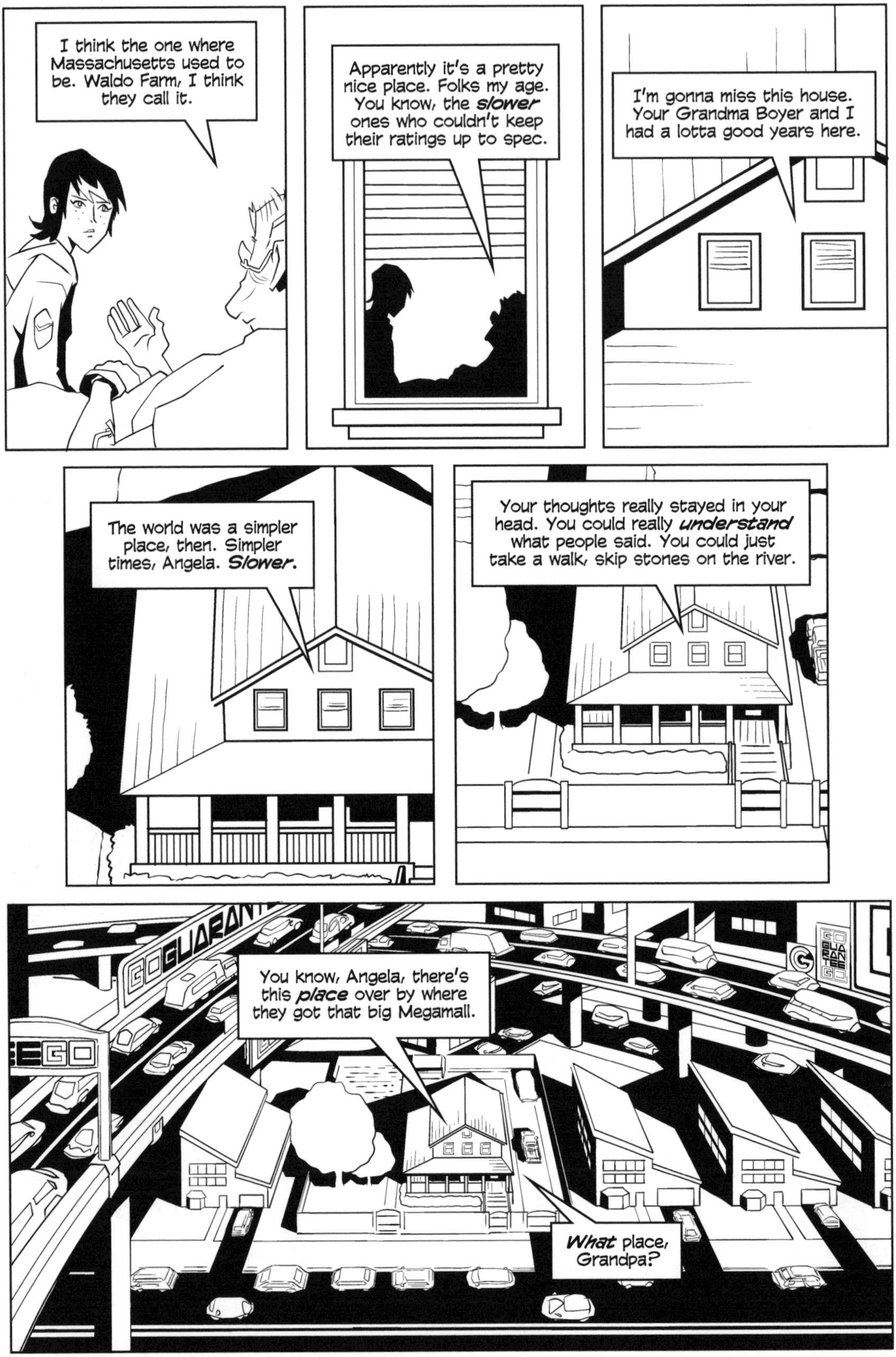
I think the one where Massachusetts used to be. Waldo Farm, I think they call it.
Apparently it's a pretty nice place. Folks my age. You know, the *slower* ones who couldn't keep their ratings up to spec.
I'm gonna miss this house. Your Grandma Boyer and I had a lotta good years here.
The world was a simpler place, then. Simpler times, Angela. *Slower*.
Your thoughts really stayed in your head. You could really *understand* what people said. You could just take a walk, skip stones on the river.
You know, Angela, there's this *place* over by where they got that big Megamall.
*What* place, Grandpa?

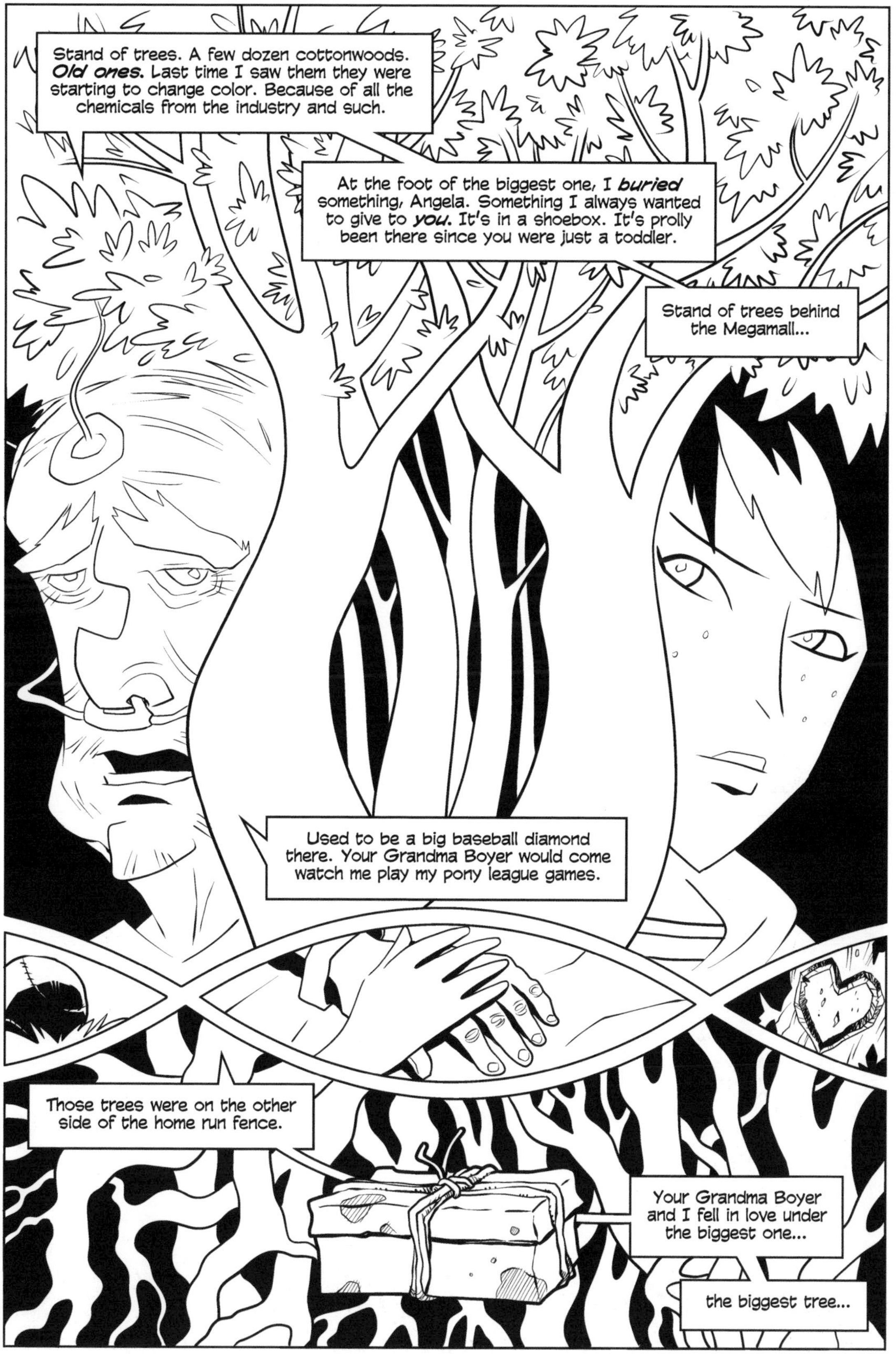
Stand of trees. A few dozen cottonwoods. Old ones. Last time I saw them they were starting to change color. Because of all the chemicals from the industry and such.
At the foot of the biggest one, I buried something, Angela. Something I always wanted to give to you. It's in a shoebox. It's prolly been there since you were just a toddler.
Stand of trees behind the Megamall...
Used to be a big baseball diamond there. Your Grandma Boyer would come watch me play my pony league games.
Those trees were on the other side of the home run fence.
Your Grandma Boyer and I fell in love under the biggest one...
the biggest tree...

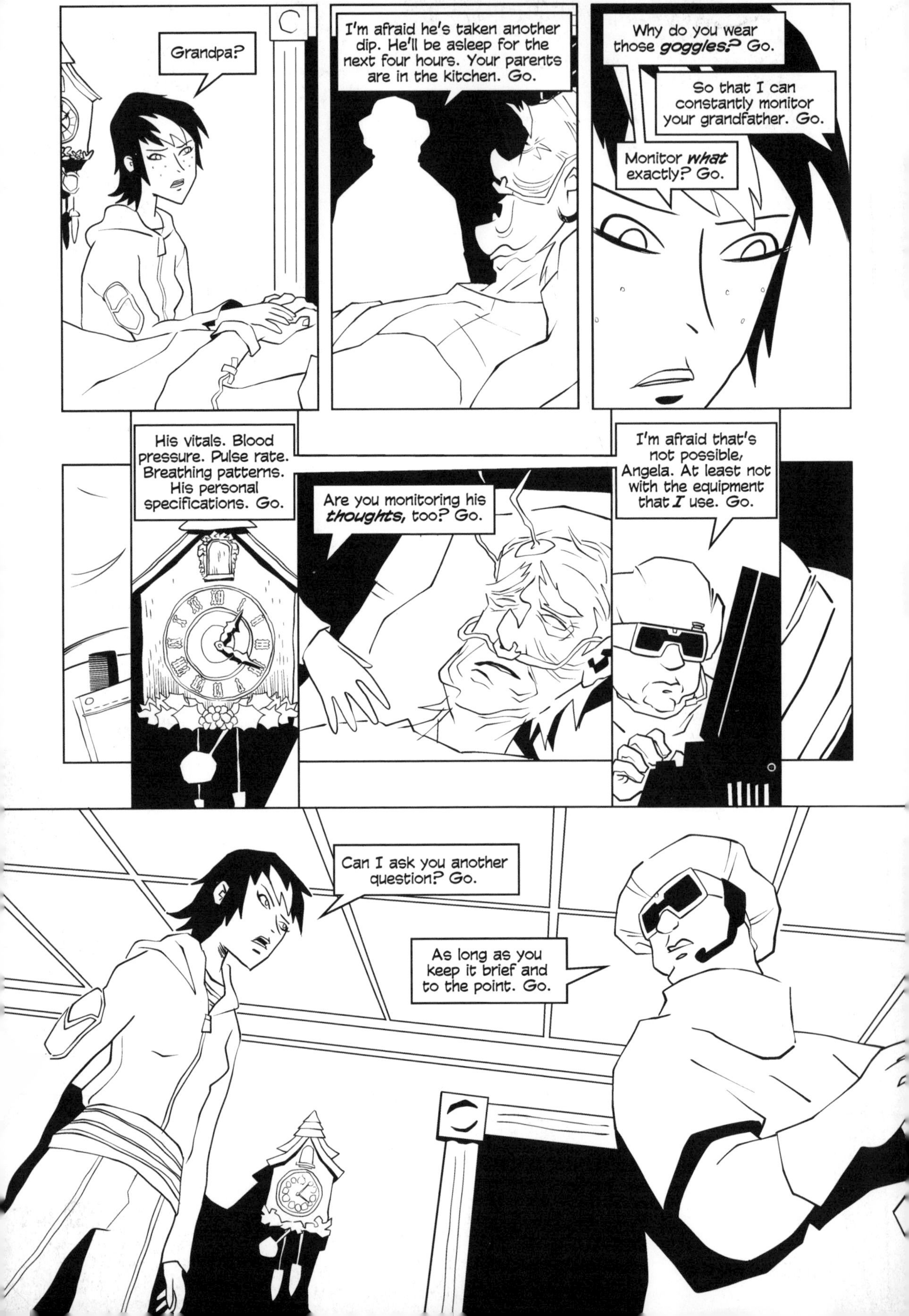
Grandpa?
I'm afraid he's taken another dip. He'll be asleep for the next four hours. Your parents are in the kitchen. Go.
Why do you wear those *goggles?* Go.
So that I can constantly monitor your grandfather. Go.
Monitor *what* exactly? Go.
His vitals. Blood pressure. Pulse rate. Breathing patterns. His personal specifications. Go.
Are you monitoring his *thoughts,* too? Go.
I'm afraid that's not possible, Angela. At least not with the equipment that *I* use. Go.
Can I ask you another question? Go.
As long as you keep it brief and to the point. Go.

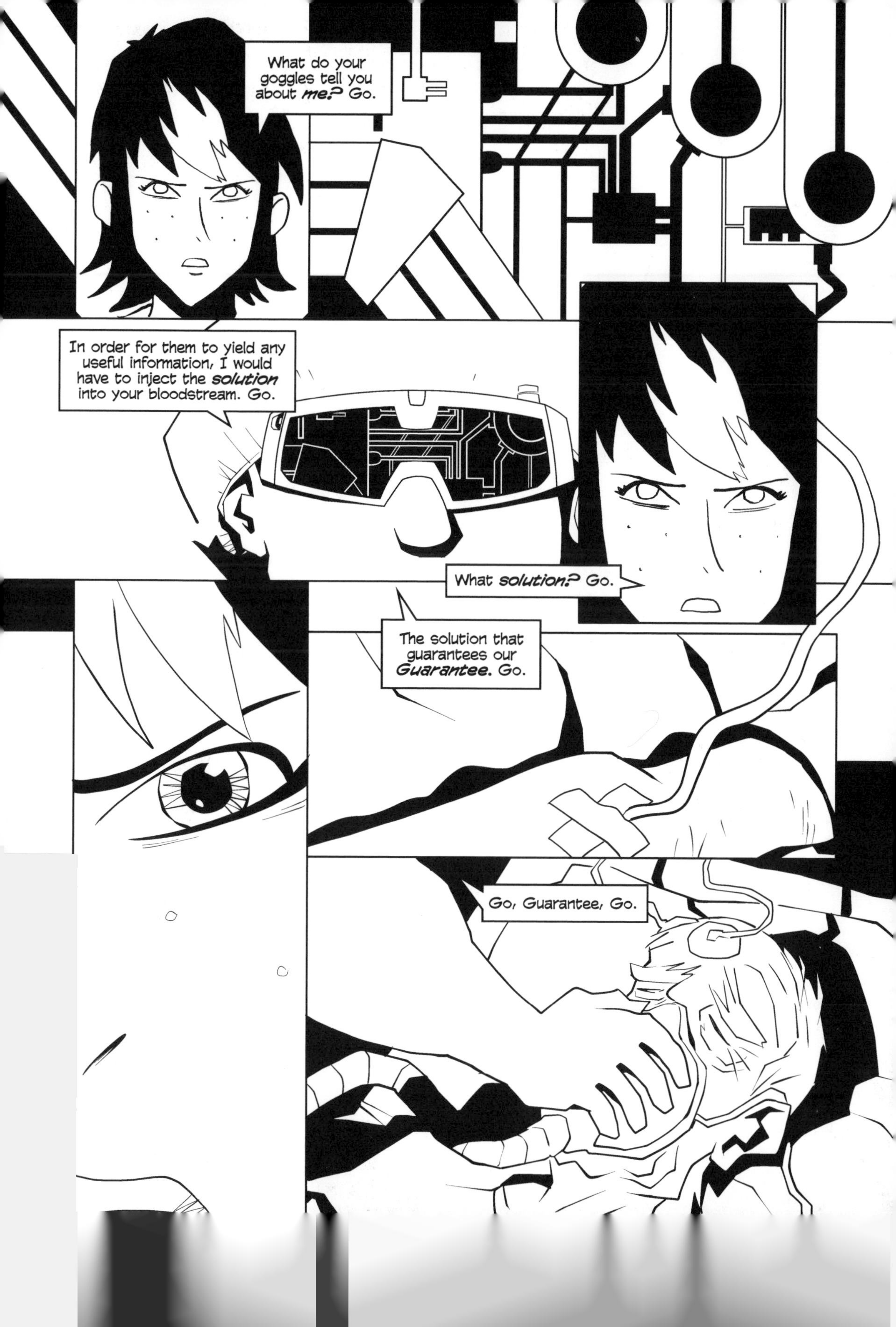
What do your goggles tell you about *me?* Go.
In order for them to yield any useful information, I would have to inject the *solution* into your bloodstream. Go.
What *solution?* Go.
The solution that guarantees our *Guarantee.* Go.
Go, Guarantee, Go.

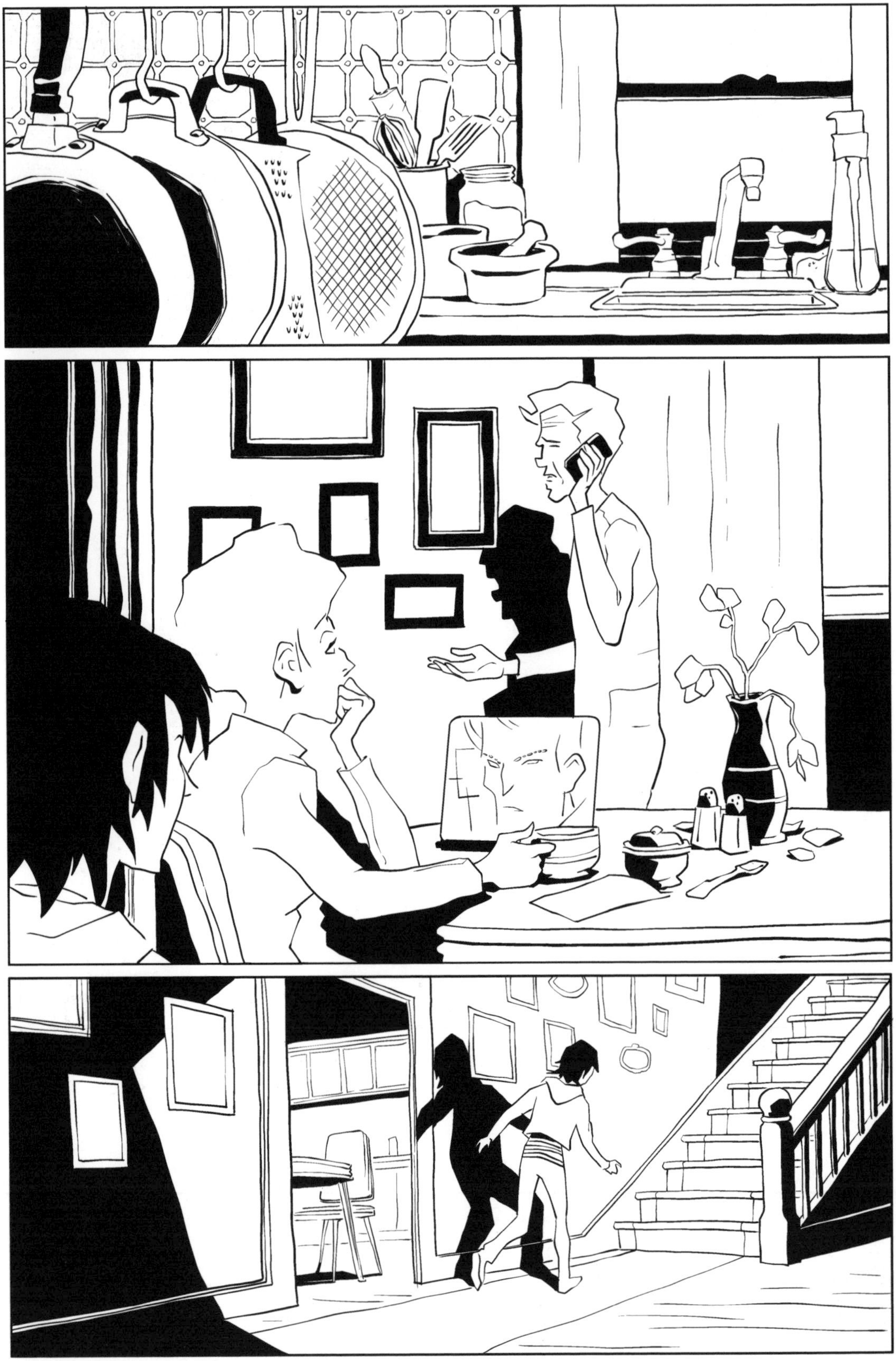

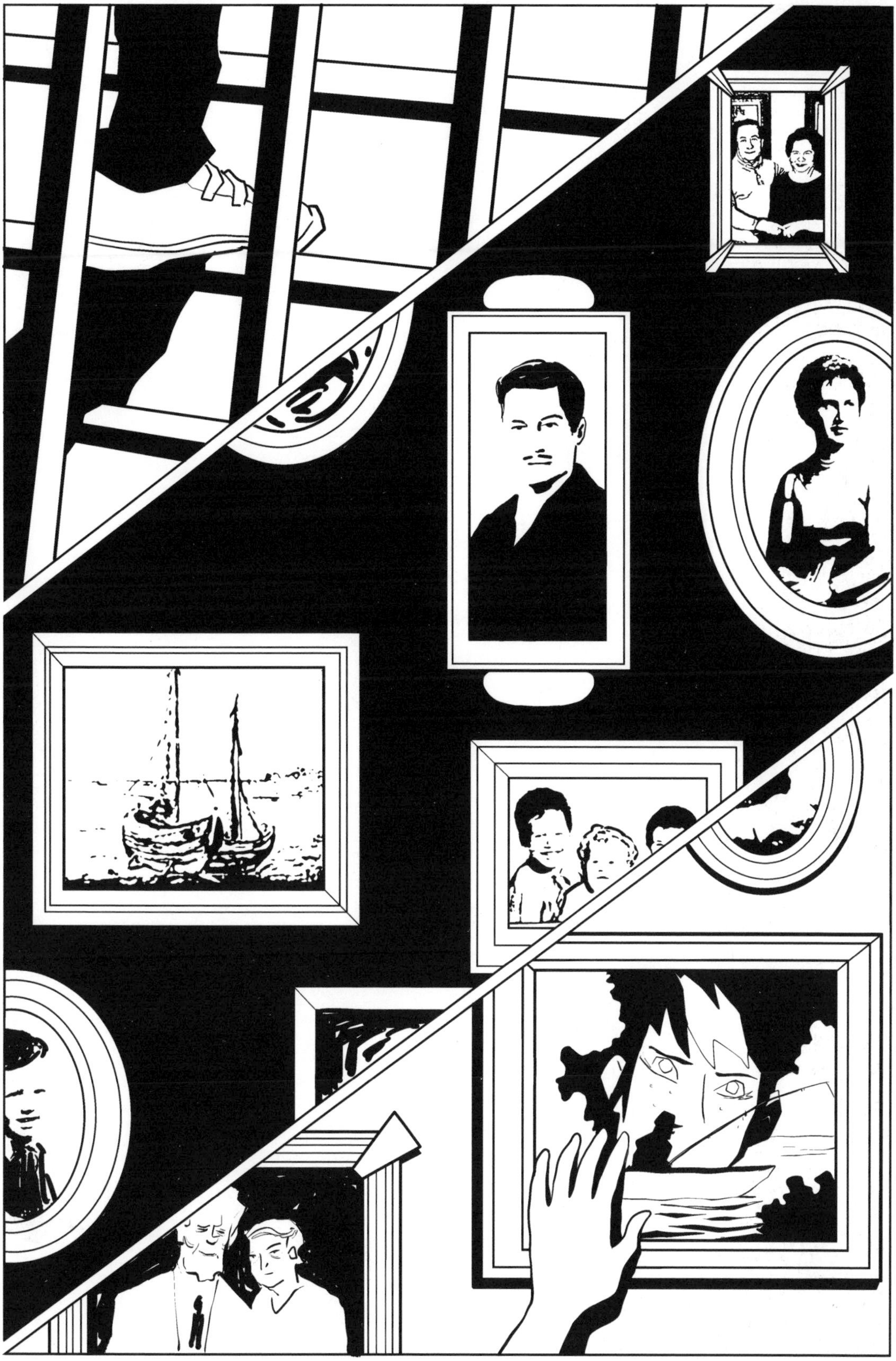

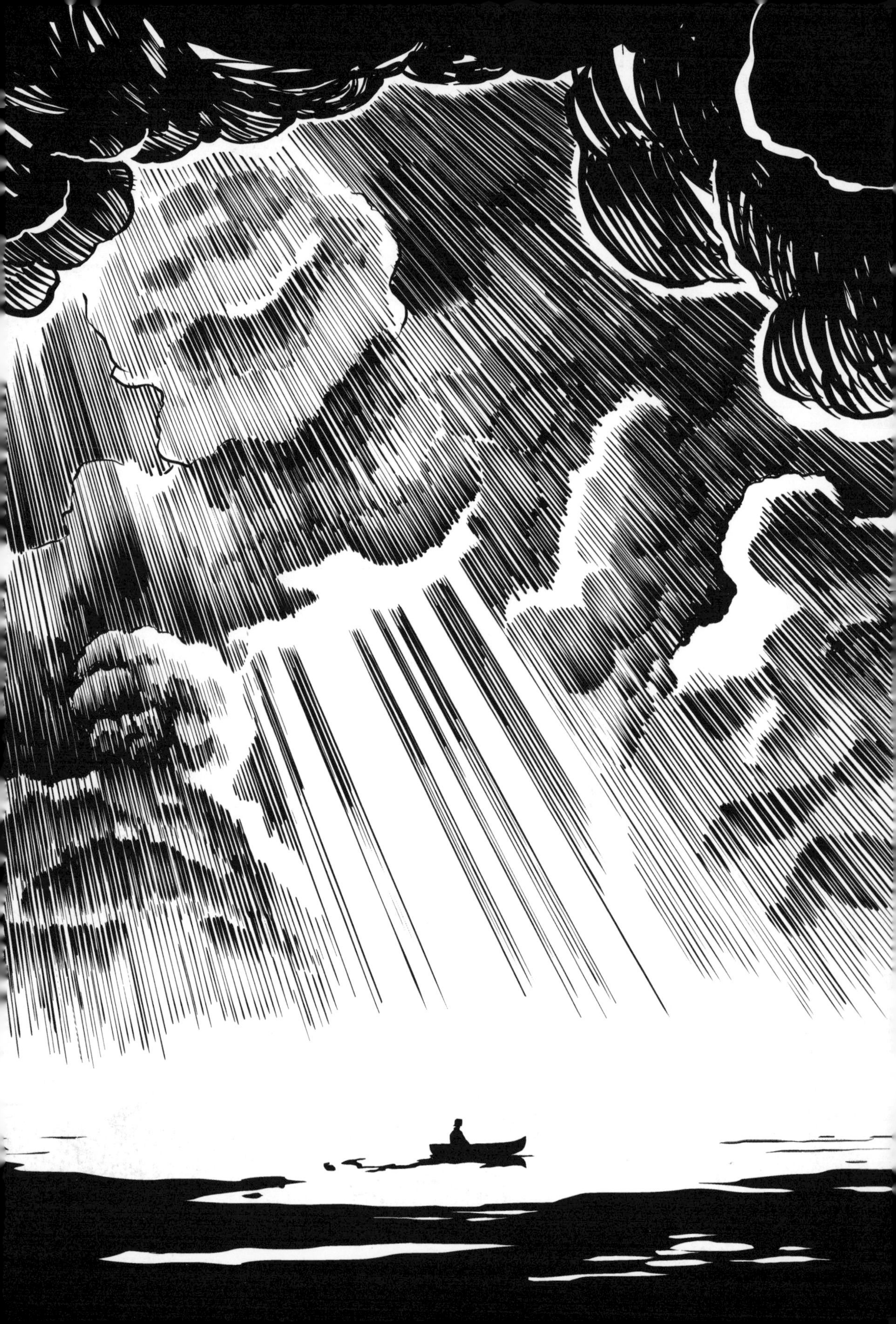

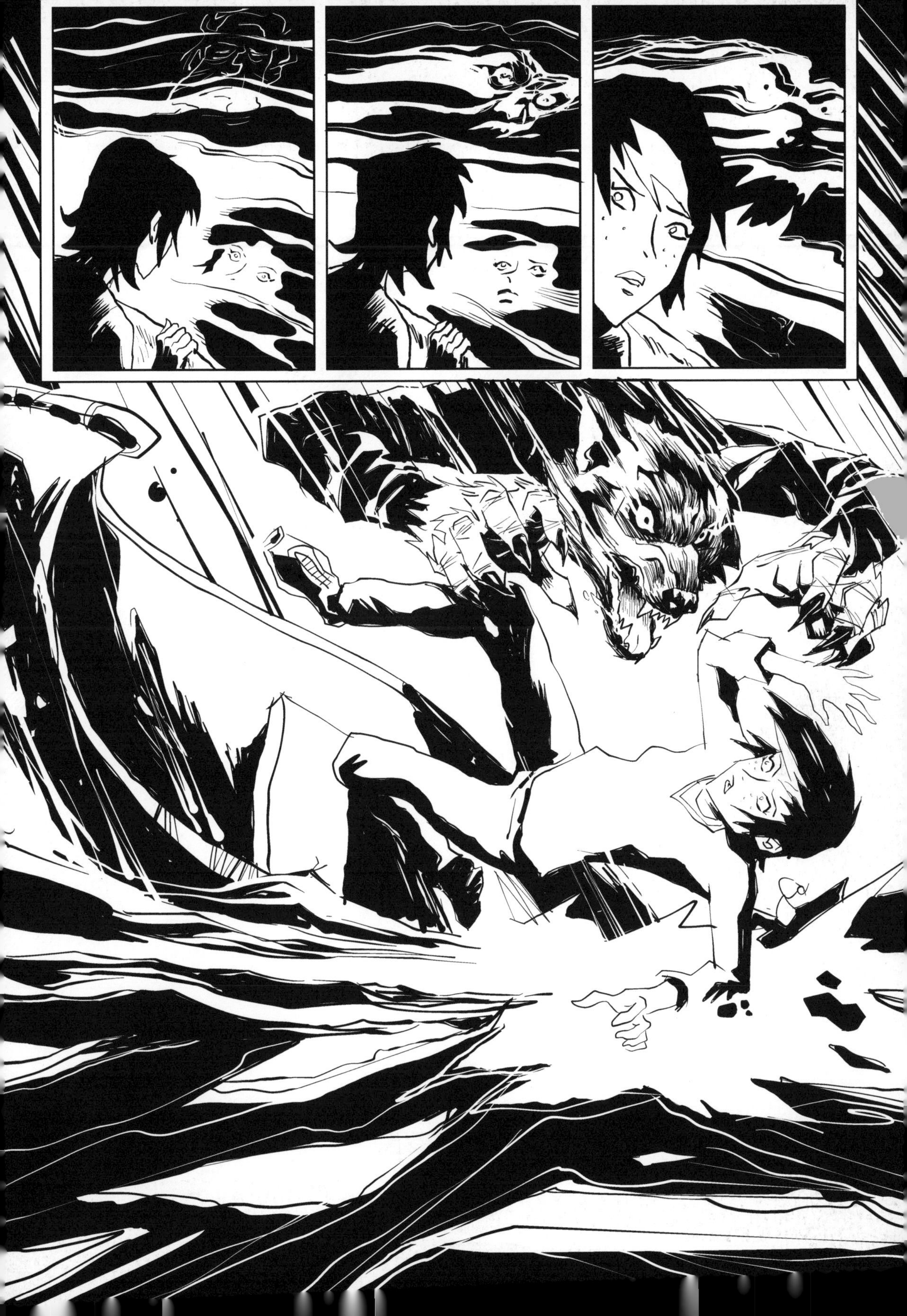

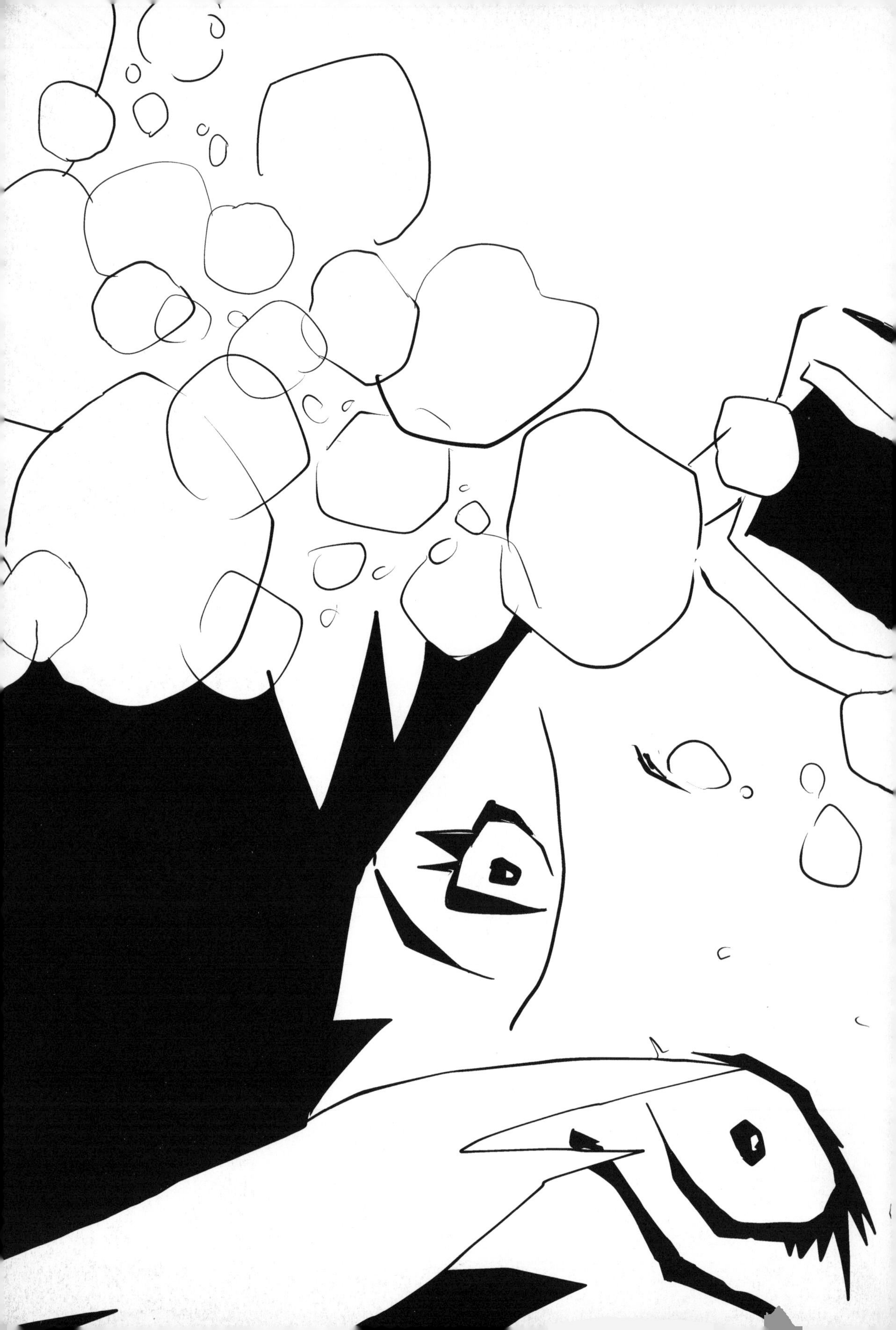

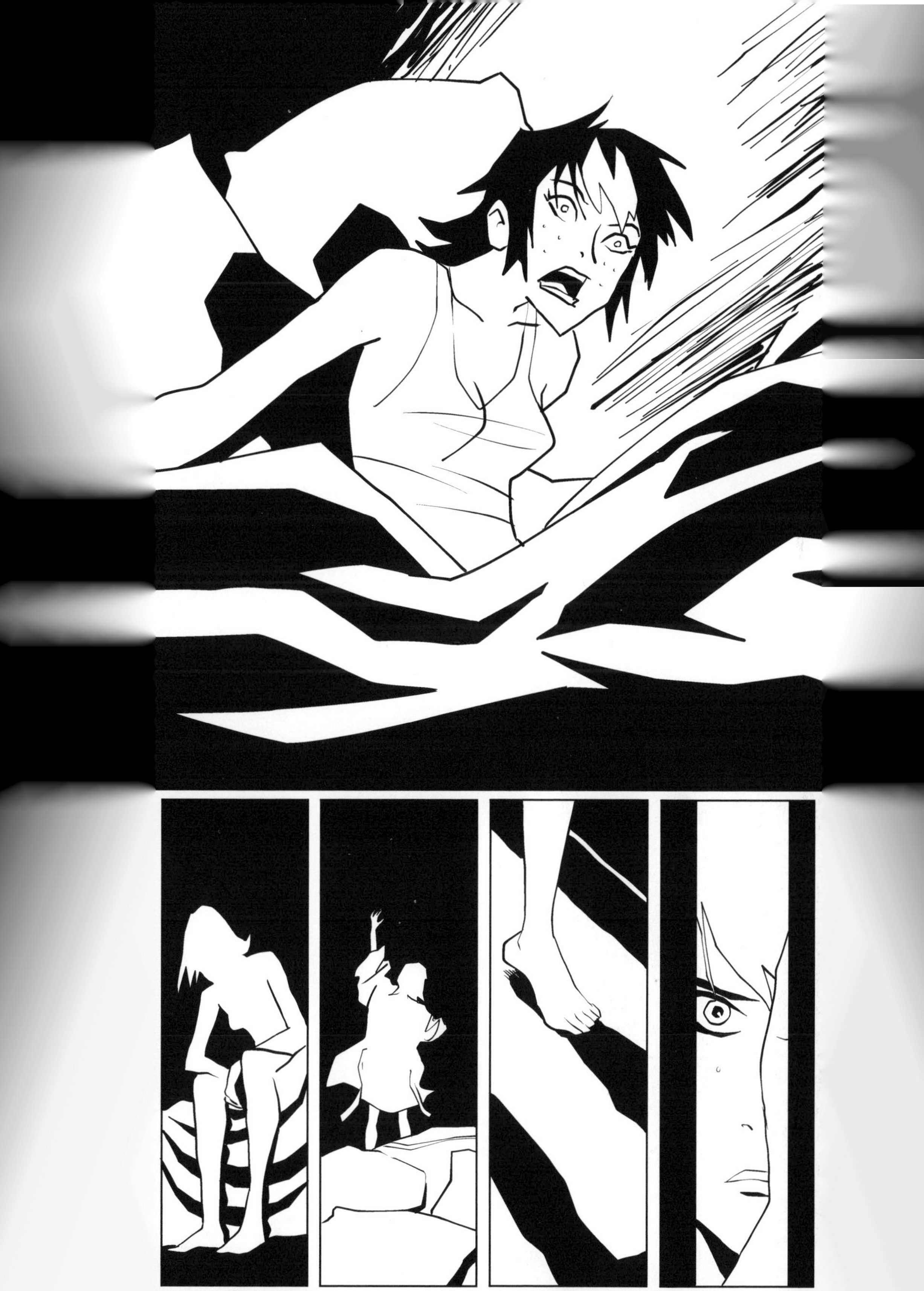

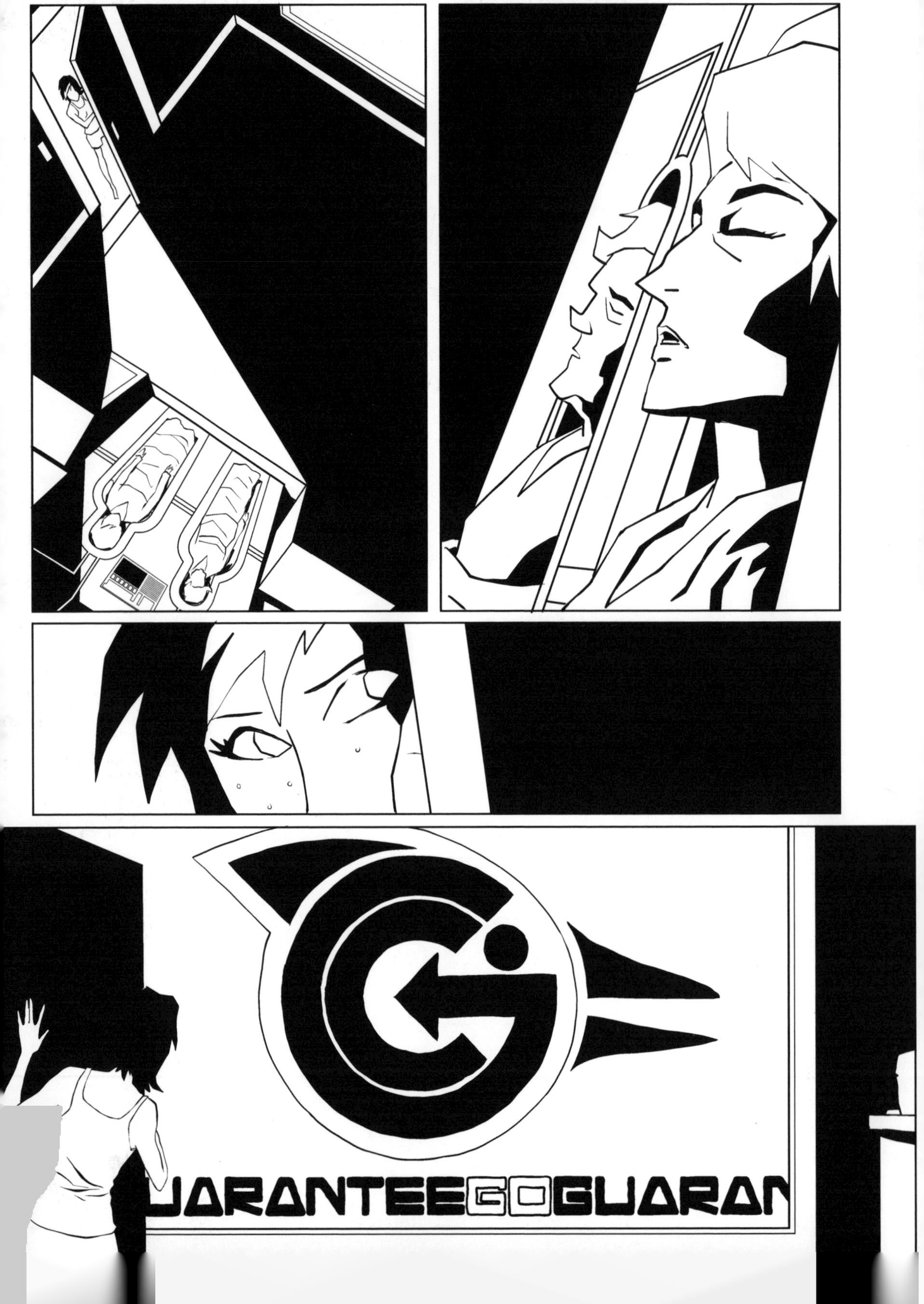
UARANTEEGOGUARAN

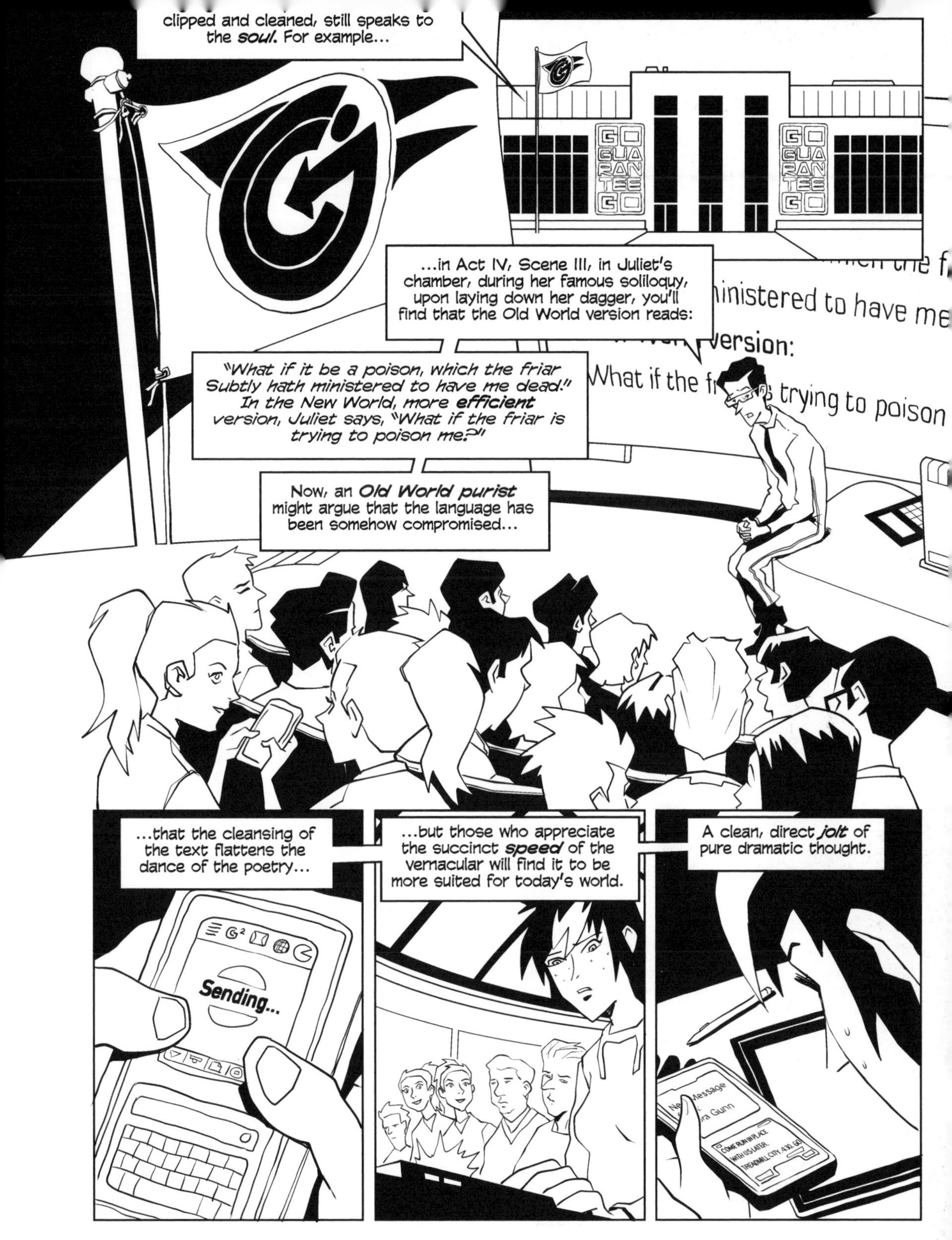
clipped and cleaned, still speaks to the *soul*. For example...
GO GUA RAN TEE GO
...in Act IV, Scene III, in Juliet's chamber, during her famous soliloquy, upon laying down her dagger, you'll find that the Old World version reads:
"What if it be a poison, which the friar Subtly hath ministered to have me dead." In the New World, more **efficient** version, Juliet says, "What if the friar is trying to poison me?"
Now, an ***Old World purist*** might argue that the language has been somehow compromised...
...that the cleansing of the text flattens the dance of the poetry...
Sending...
...but those who appreciate the succinct ***speed*** of the vernacular will find it to be more suited for today's world.
A clean, direct ***jolt*** of pure dramatic thought.
COME RUN IN PLACE WITH US LATER. TREADMILL CITY. 4:30. GO

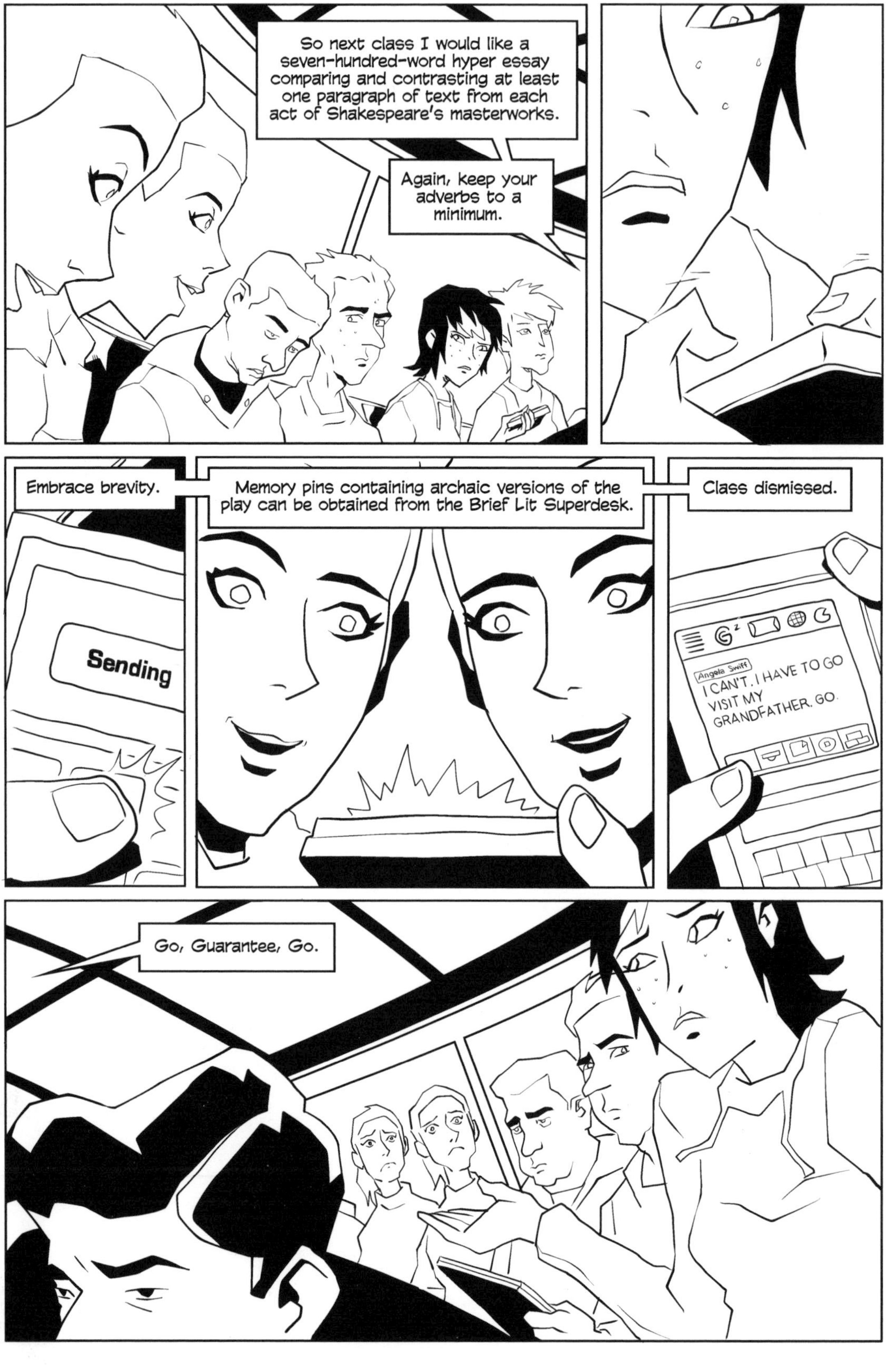
So next class I would like a seven-hundred-word hyper essay comparing and contrasting at least one paragraph of text from each act of Shakespeare's masterworks.
Again, keep your adverbs to a minimum.
Embrace brevity.
Memory pins containing archaic versions of the play can be obtained from the Brief Lit Superdesk.
Class dismissed.
Sending
Angela Swift
I CAN'T. I HAVE TO GO VISIT MY GRANDFATHER. GO.
Go, Guarantee, Go.

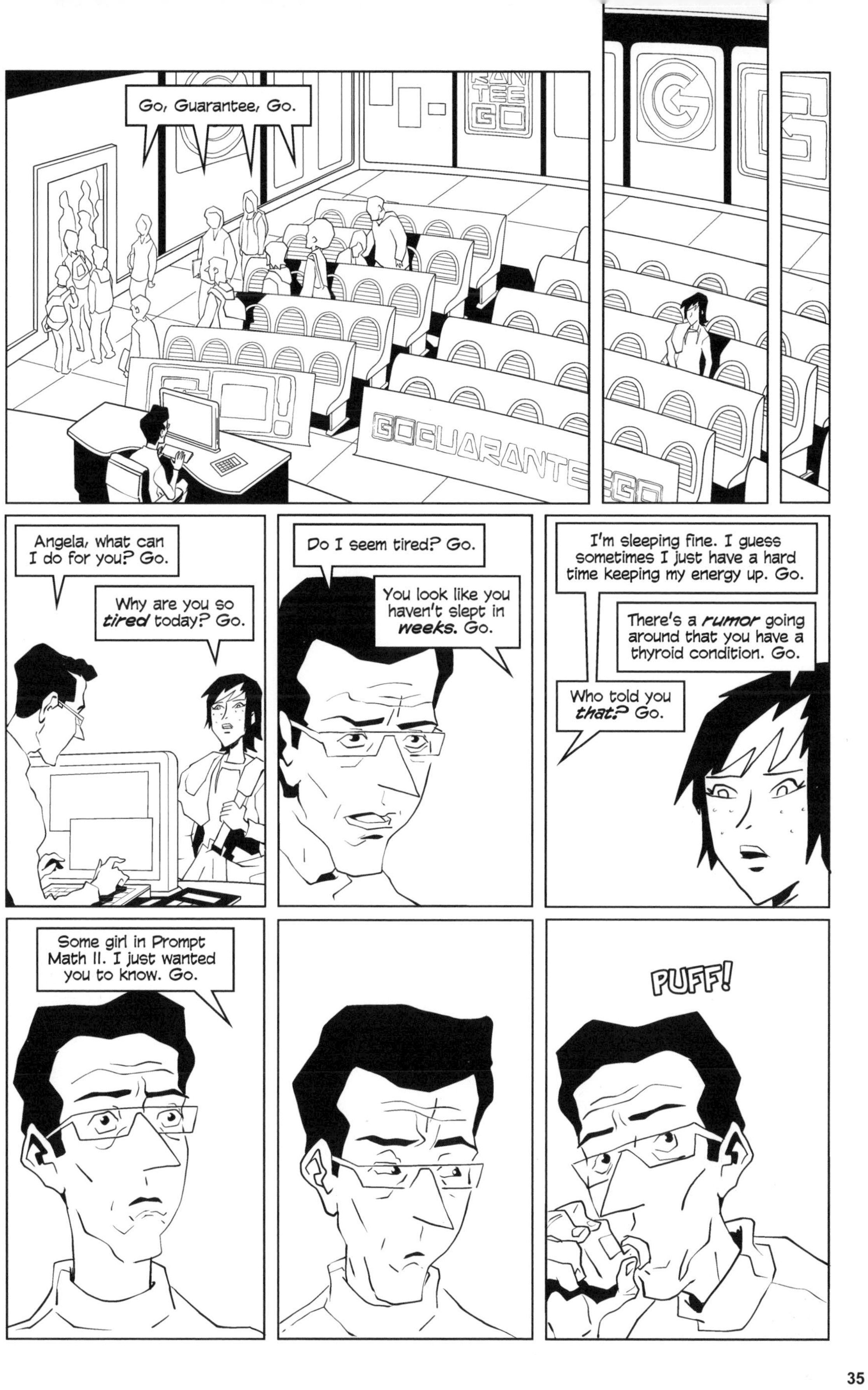

Go, Guarantee, Go.
GOGUARANTEEGO
Angela, what can I do for you? Go.
Why are you so *tired* today? Go.
Do I seem tired? Go.
You look like you haven't slept in *weeks.* Go.
I'm sleeping fine. I guess sometimes I just have a hard time keeping my energy up. Go.
There's a *rumor* going around that you have a thyroid condition. Go.
Who told you *that?* Go.
Some girl in Prompt Math II. I just wanted you to know. Go.
PUFF!

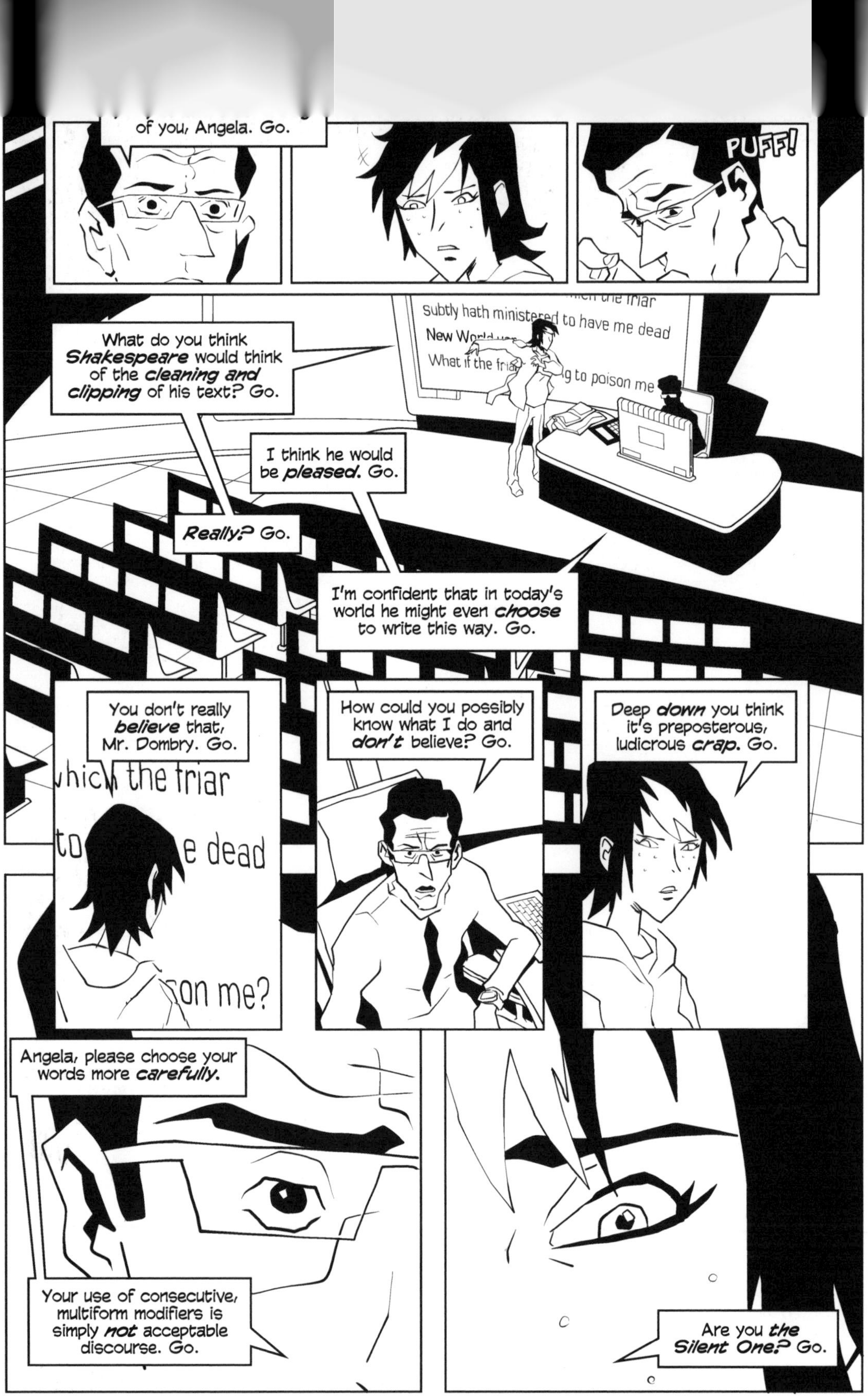
of you, Angela. Go.
PUFF!
subtly hath ministered to have me dead
What do you think *Shakespeare* would think of the *cleaning and clipping* of his text? Go.
I think he would be *pleased*. Go.
*Really?* Go.
I'm confident that in today's world he might even *choose* to write this way. Go.
You don't really *believe* that, Mr. Dombry. Go.
How could you possibly know what I do and *don't* believe? Go.
Deep *down* you think it's preposterous, ludicrous *crap*. Go.
Angela, please choose your words more *carefully*.
Your use of consecutive, multiform modifiers is simply *not* acceptable discourse. Go.
Are you *the Silent One?* Go.

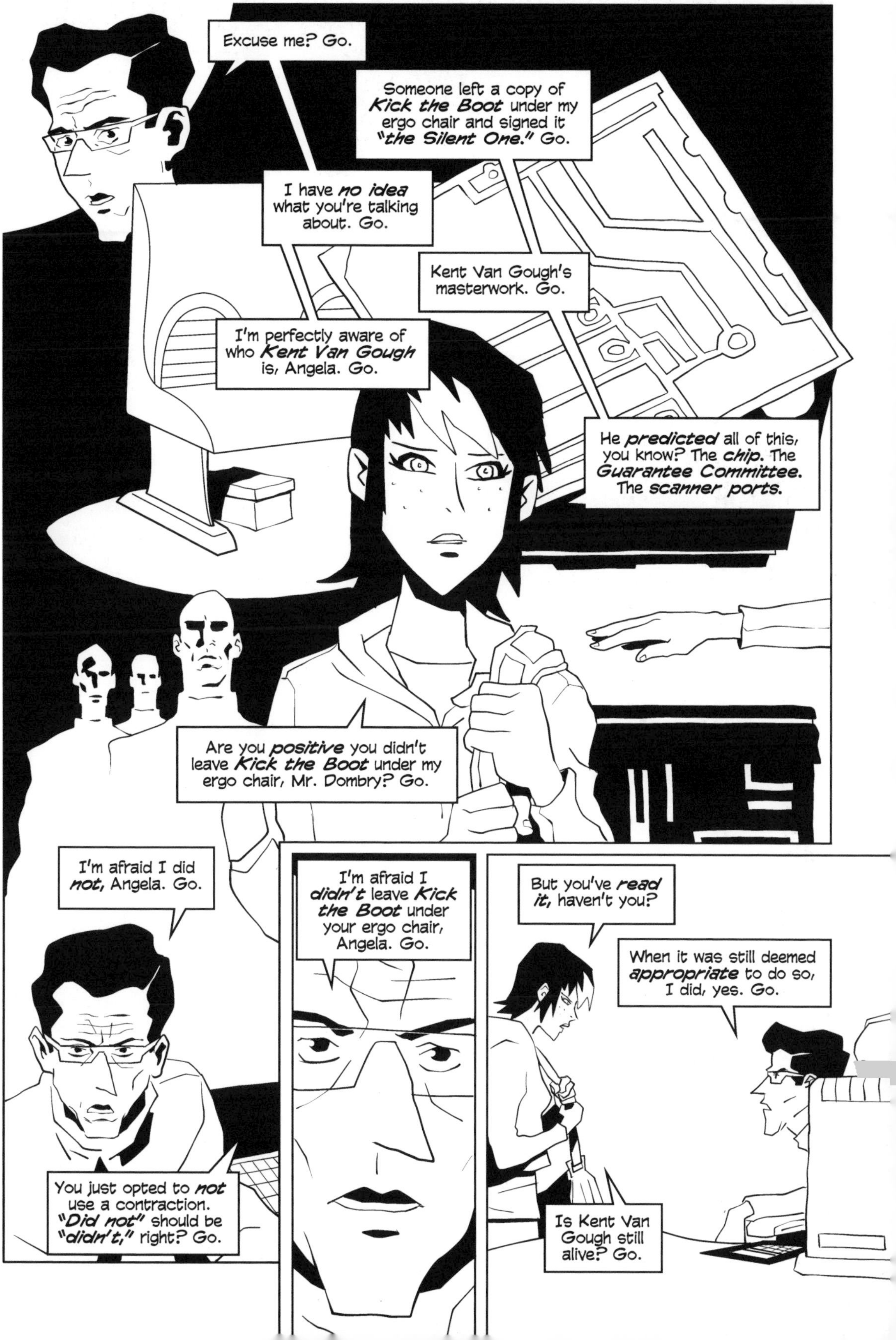

Excuse me? Go.
Someone left a copy of *Kick the Boot* under my ergo chair and signed it *"the Silent One."* Go.
I have *no idea* what you're talking about. Go.
Kent Van Gough's masterwork. Go.
I'm perfectly aware of who *Kent Van Gough* is, Angela. Go.
He *predicted* all of this, you know? The *chip*. The *Guarantee Committee*. The *scanner ports*.
Are you *positive* you didn't leave *Kick the Boot* under my ergo chair, Mr. Dombry? Go.
I'm afraid I did *not*, Angela. Go.
You just opted to *not* use a contraction. *"Did not"* should be *"didn't,"* right? Go.
I'm afraid I *didn't* leave *Kick the Boot* under your ergo chair, Angela. Go.
But you've *read it*, haven't you?
When it was still deemed *appropriate* to do so, I did, yes. Go.
Is Kent Van Gough still alive? Go.

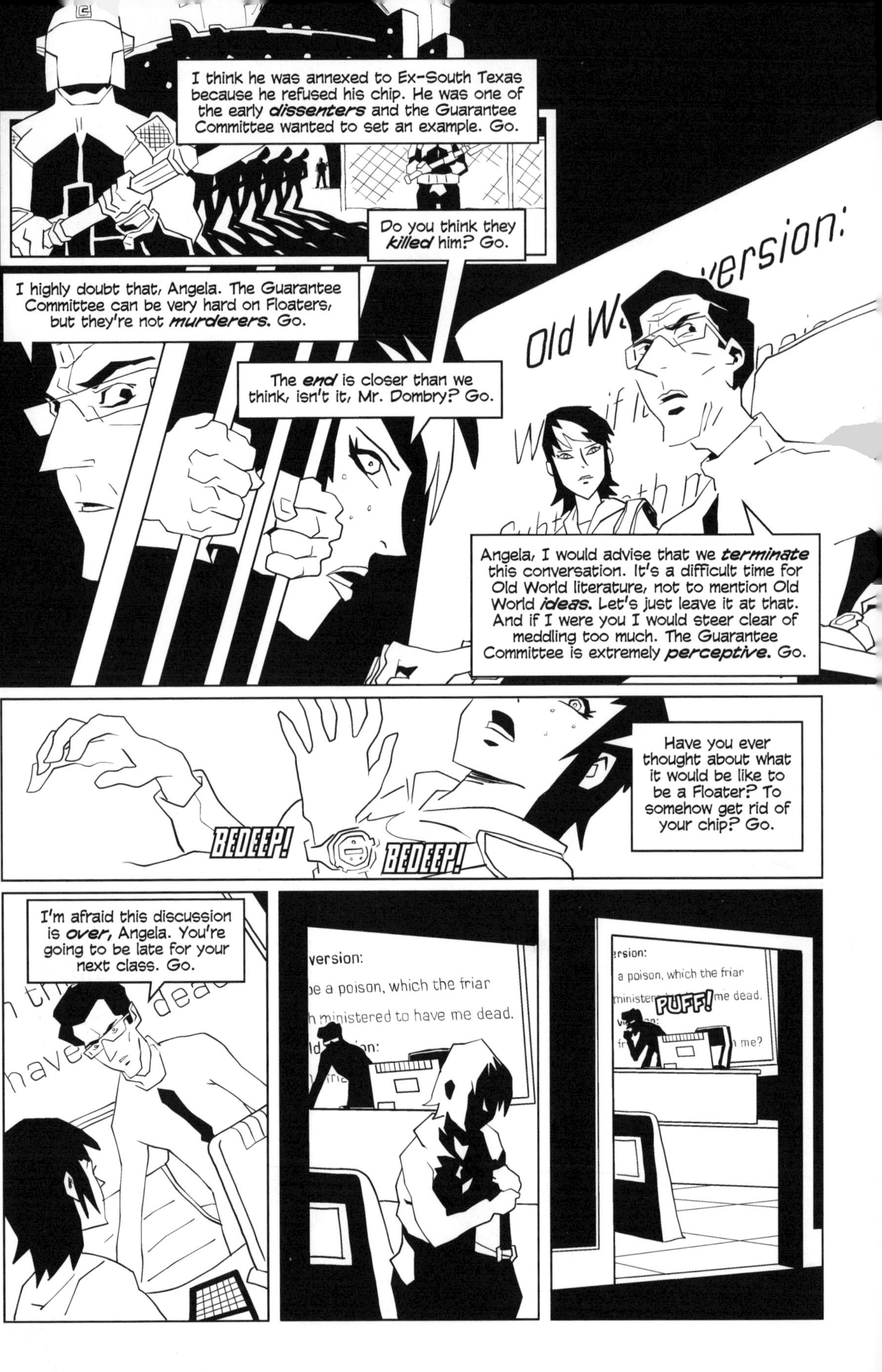
I think he was annexed to Ex-South Texas because he refused his chip. He was one of the early *dissenters* and the Guarantee Committee wanted to set an example. Go.
Do you think they *killed* him? Go.
I highly doubt that, Angela. The Guarantee Committee can be very hard on Floaters, but they're not *murderers.* Go.
The *end* is closer than we think, isn't it, Mr. Dombry? Go.
Angela, I would advise that we *terminate* this conversation. It's a difficult time for Old World literature, not to mention Old World *ideas.* Let's just leave it at that. And if I were you I would steer clear of meddling too much. The Guarantee Committee is extremely *perceptive.* Go.
Have you ever thought about what it would be like to be a Floater? To somehow get rid of your chip? Go.
BEDEEP!
BEDEEP!
I'm afraid this discussion is *over,* Angela. You're going to be late for your next class. Go.
PUFF!

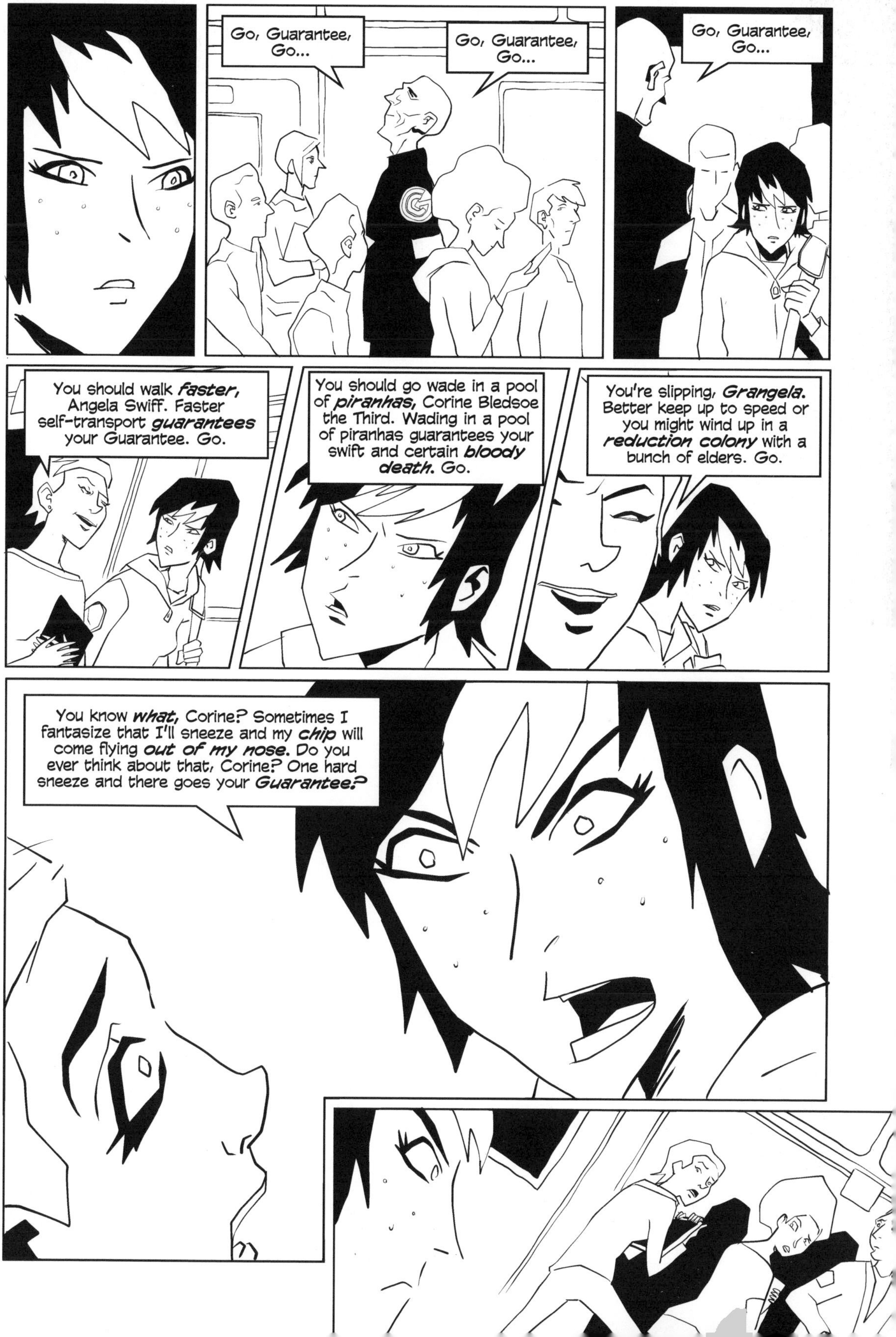
Go, Guarantee, Go...
Go, Guarantee, Go...
Go, Guarantee, Go...
You should walk *faster*, Angela Swiff. Faster self-transport *guarantees* your Guarantee. Go.
You should go wade in a pool of *piranhas*, Corine Bledsoe the Third. Wading in a pool of piranhas guarantees your swift and certain *bloody death*. Go.
You're slipping, *Grangela*. Better keep up to speed or you might wind up in a *reduction colony* with a bunch of elders. Go.
You know *what*, Corine? Sometimes I fantasize that I'll sneeze and my *chip* will come flying *out of my nose*. Do you ever think about that, Corine? One hard sneeze and there goes your *Guarantee?*

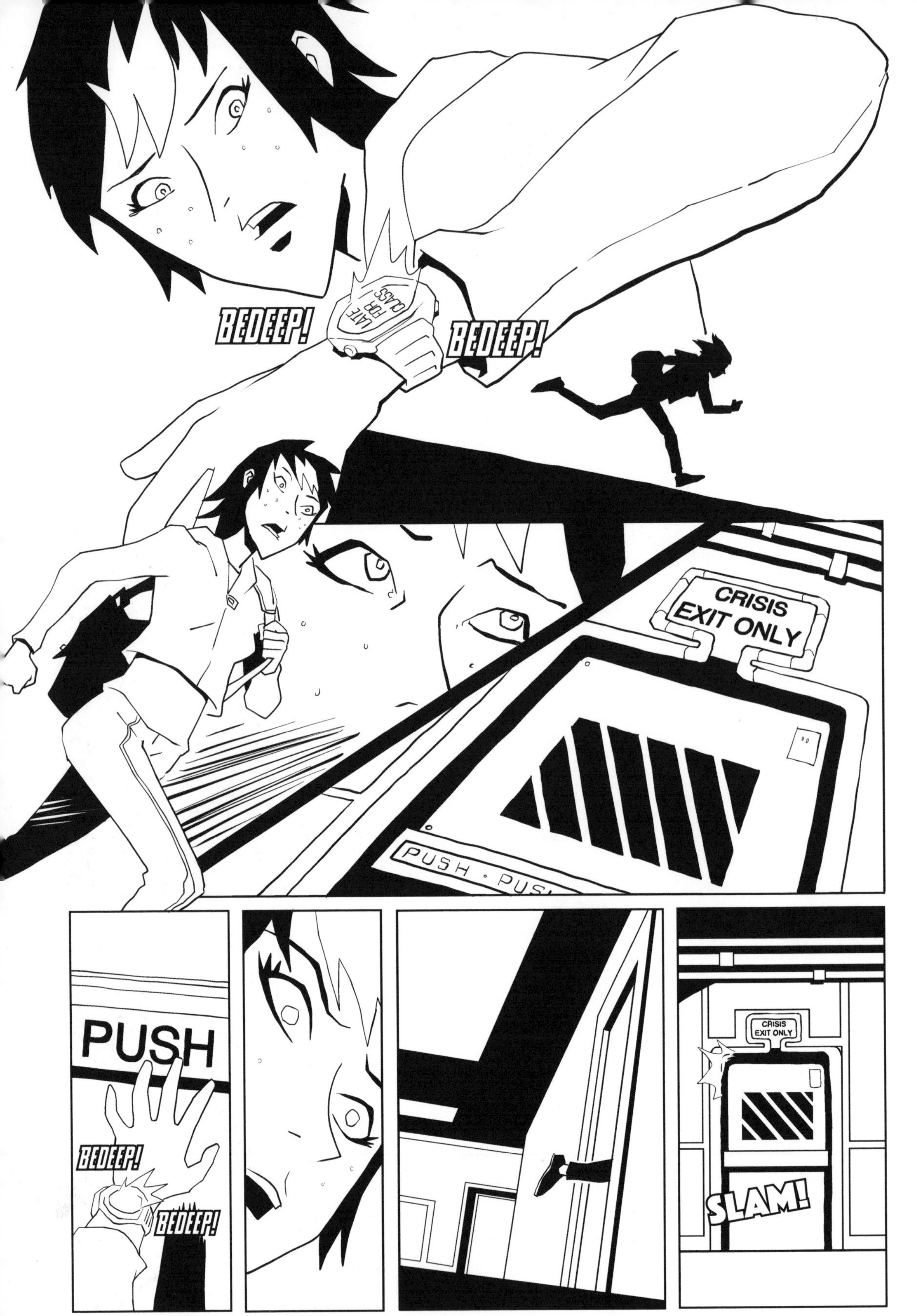
LATE FOR CLASS
BEDEEP!
BEDEEP!
CRISIS EXIT ONLY
PUSH • PUS
PUSH
BEDEEP!
BEDEEP!
CRISIS EXIT ONLY
SLAM!

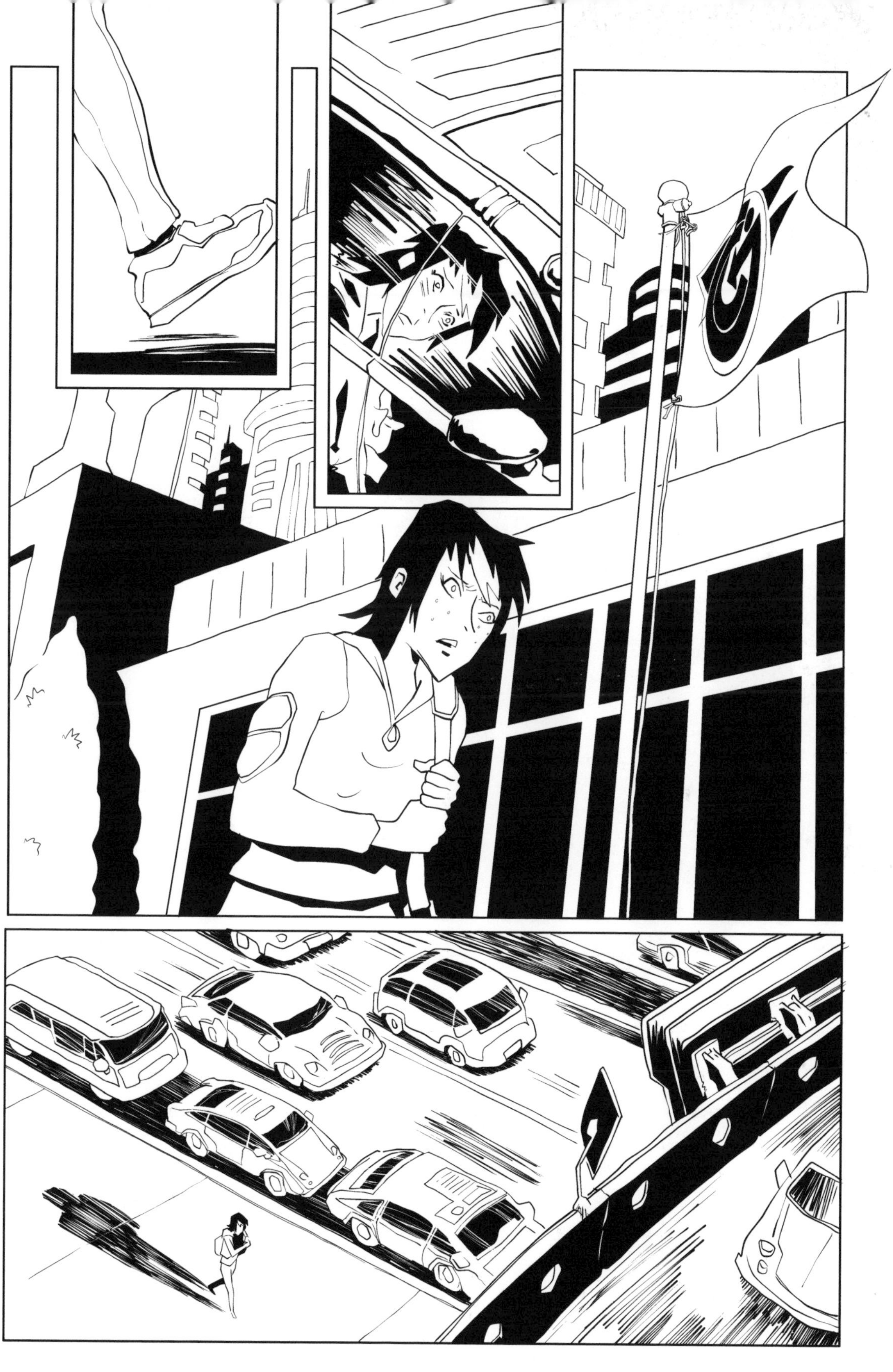

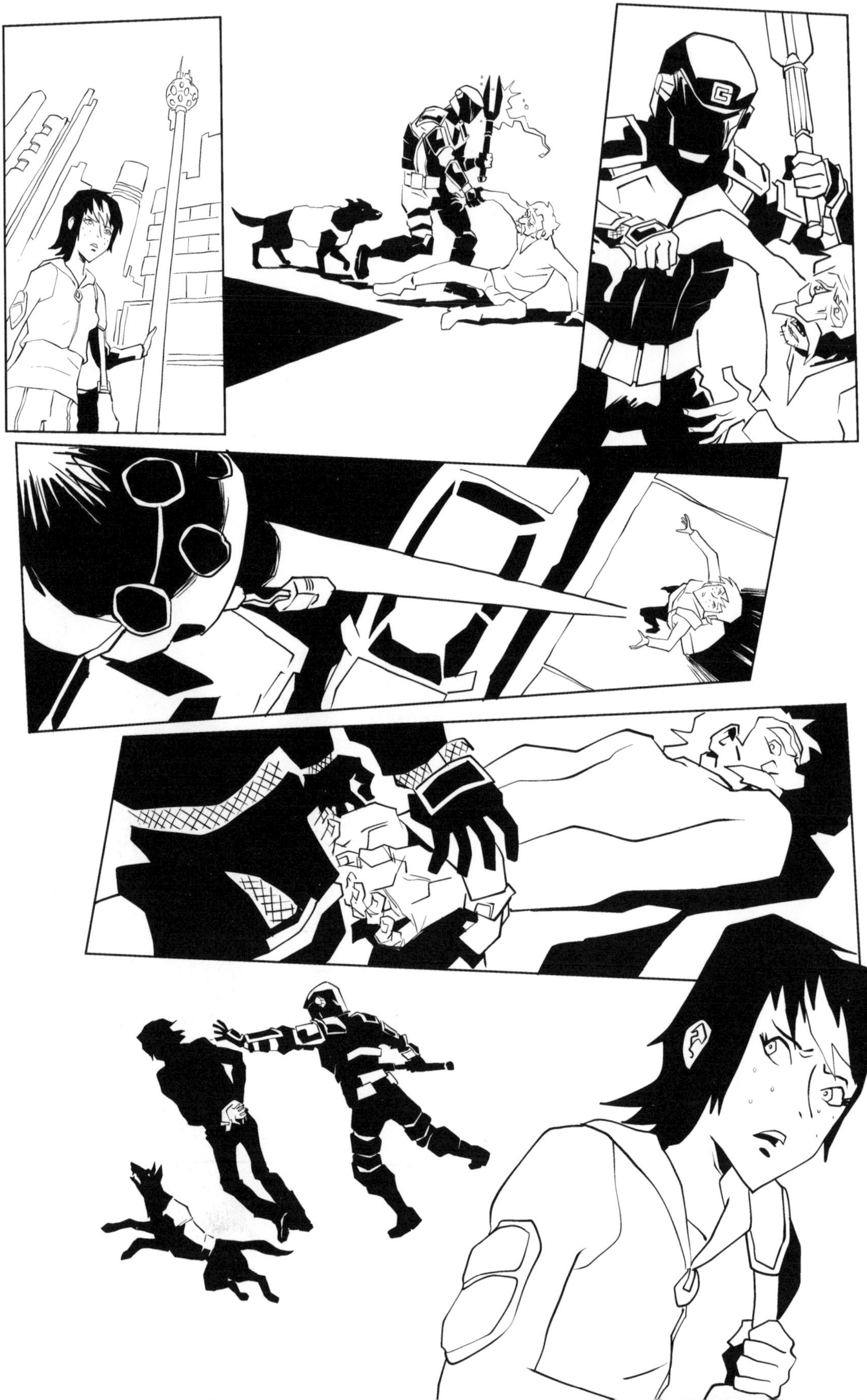

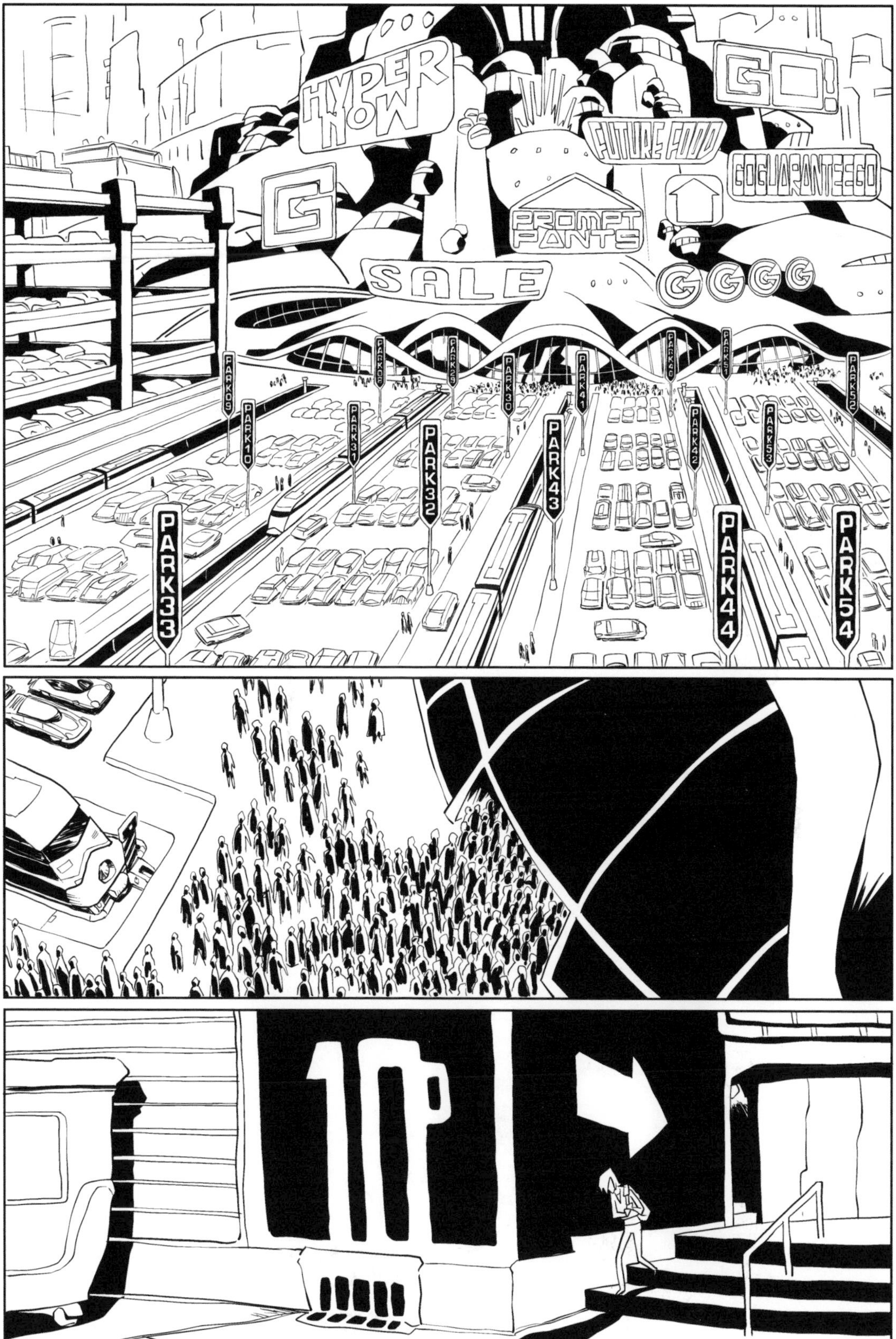
HYPER NOW
GO!
FUTURE FOOD
GOGUARANTEEGO
PROMPT PANTS
SALE
GGGG
PARK09
PARK10
PARK31
PARK32
PARK29
PARK30
PARK41
PARK43
PARK40
PARK42
PARK51
PARK53
PARK52
PARK33
PARK44
PARK54

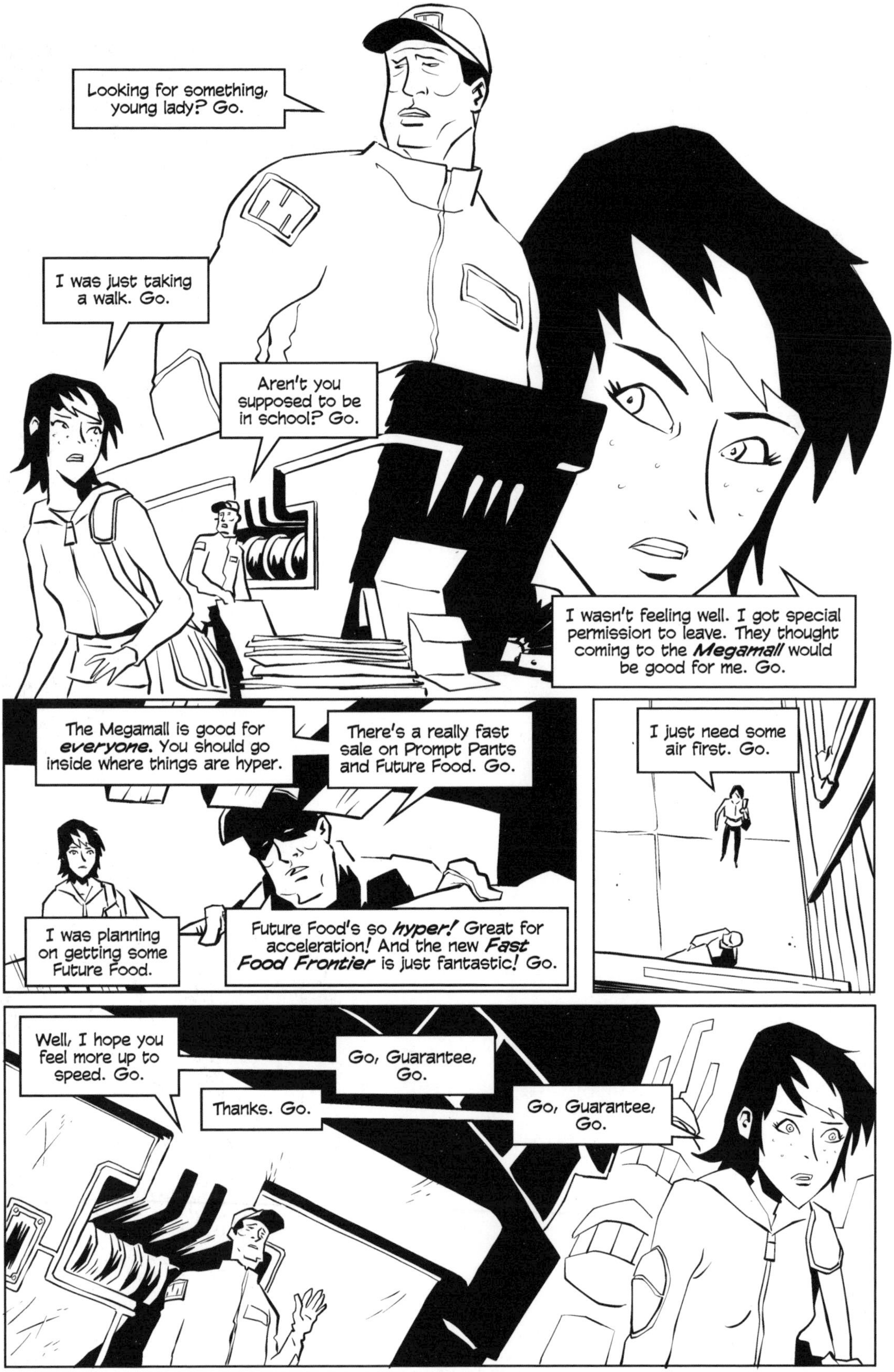
Looking for something, young lady? Go.
I was just taking a walk. Go.
Aren't you supposed to be in school? Go.
I wasn't feeling well. I got special permission to leave. They thought coming to the *Megamall* would be good for me. Go.
The Megamall is good for ***everyone.*** You should go inside where things are hyper.
There's a really fast sale on Prompt Pants and Future Food. Go.
I was planning on getting some Future Food.
Future Food's so ***hyper!*** Great for acceleration! And the new ***Fast Food Frontier*** is just fantastic! Go.
I just need some air first. Go.
Well, I hope you feel more up to speed. Go.
Go, Guarantee, Go.
Thanks. Go.
Go, Guarantee, Go.

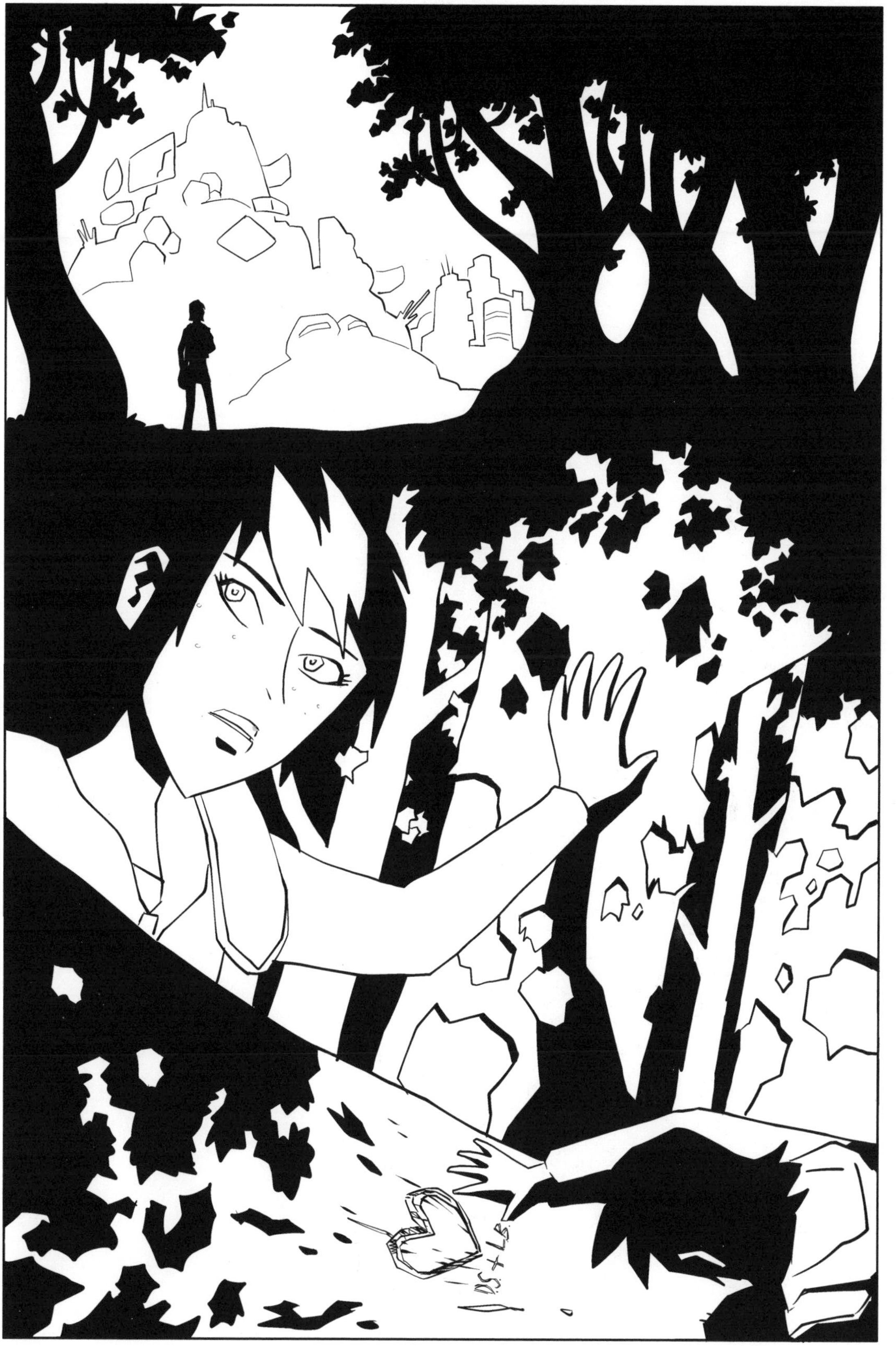
D.S. + L.B.

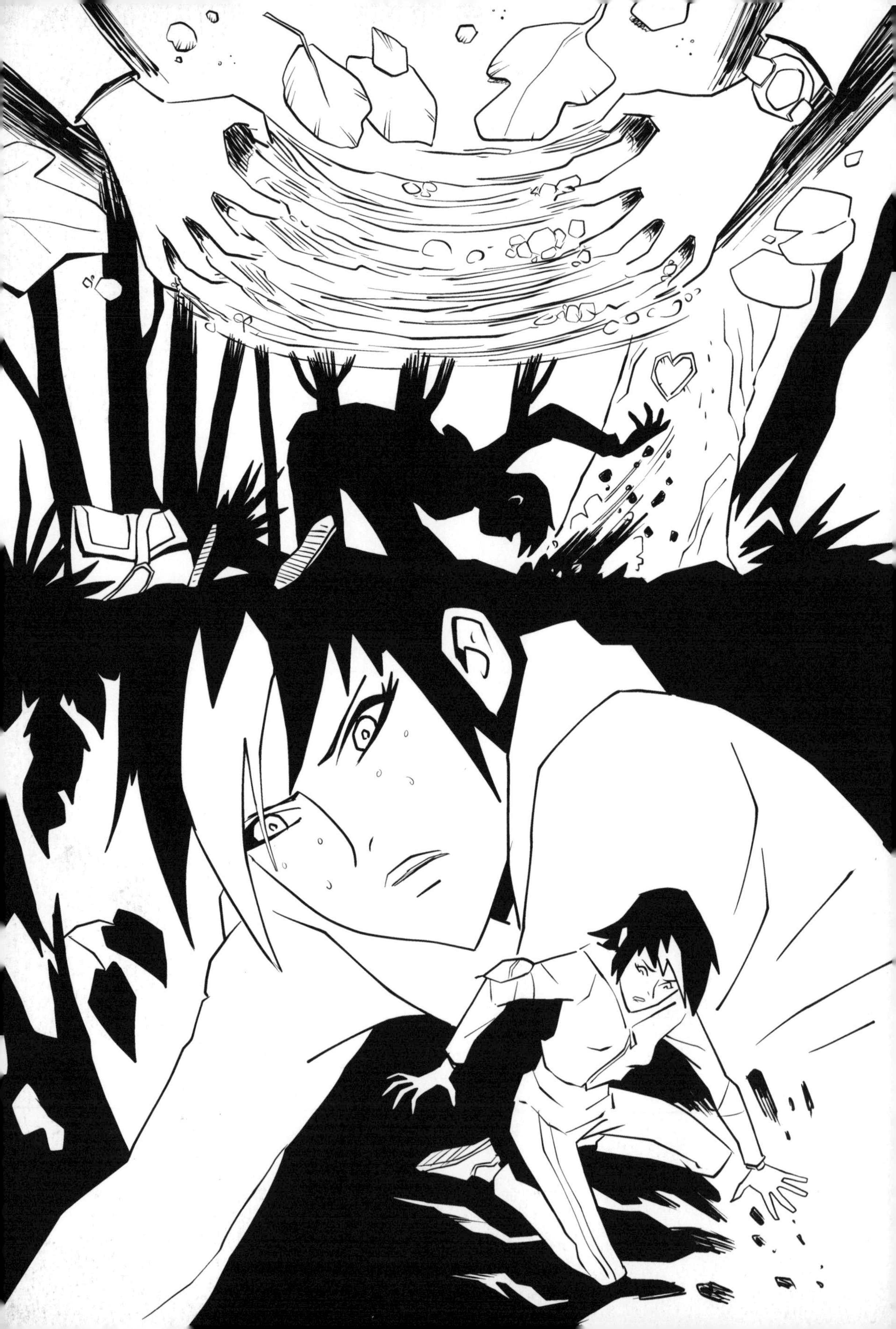

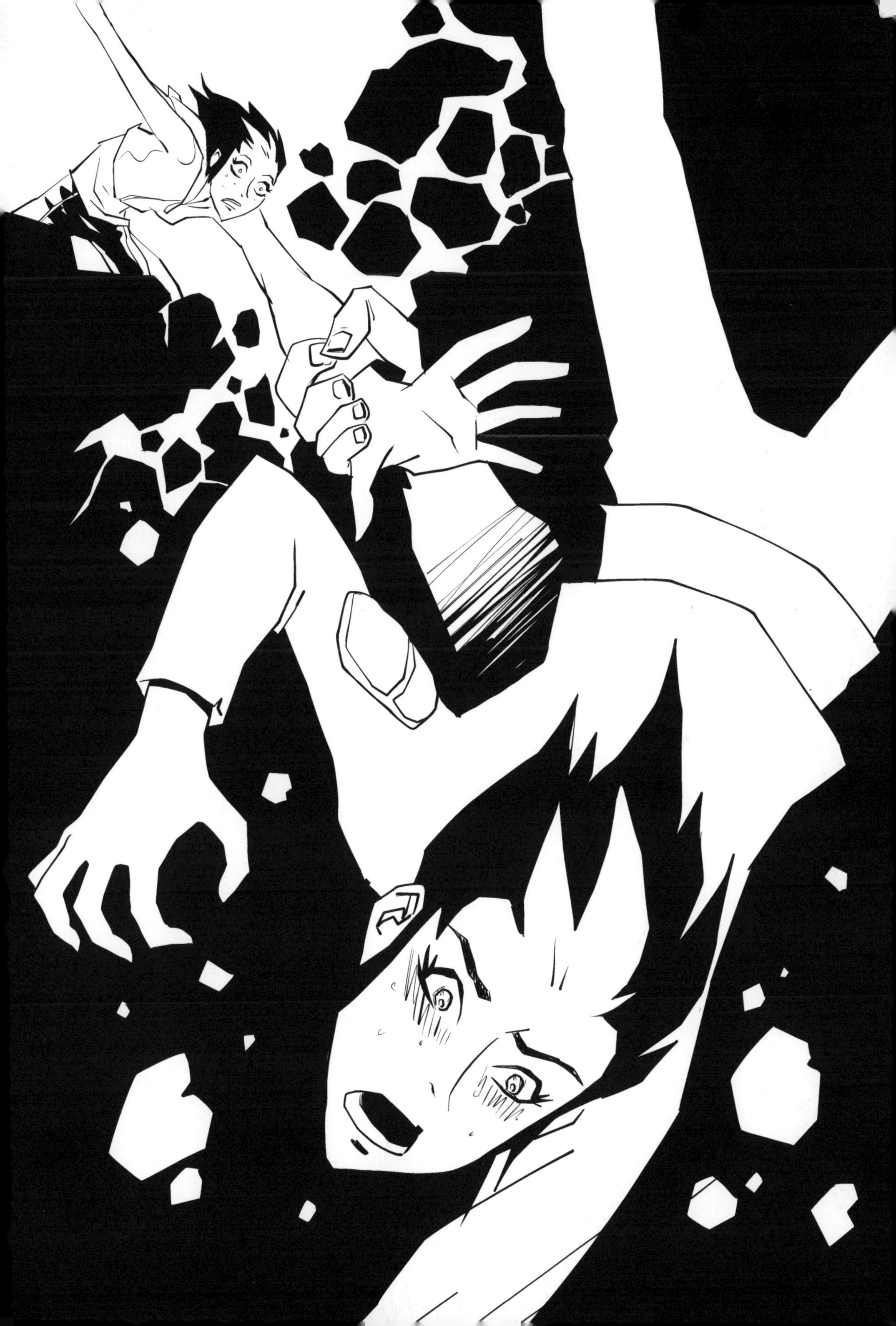

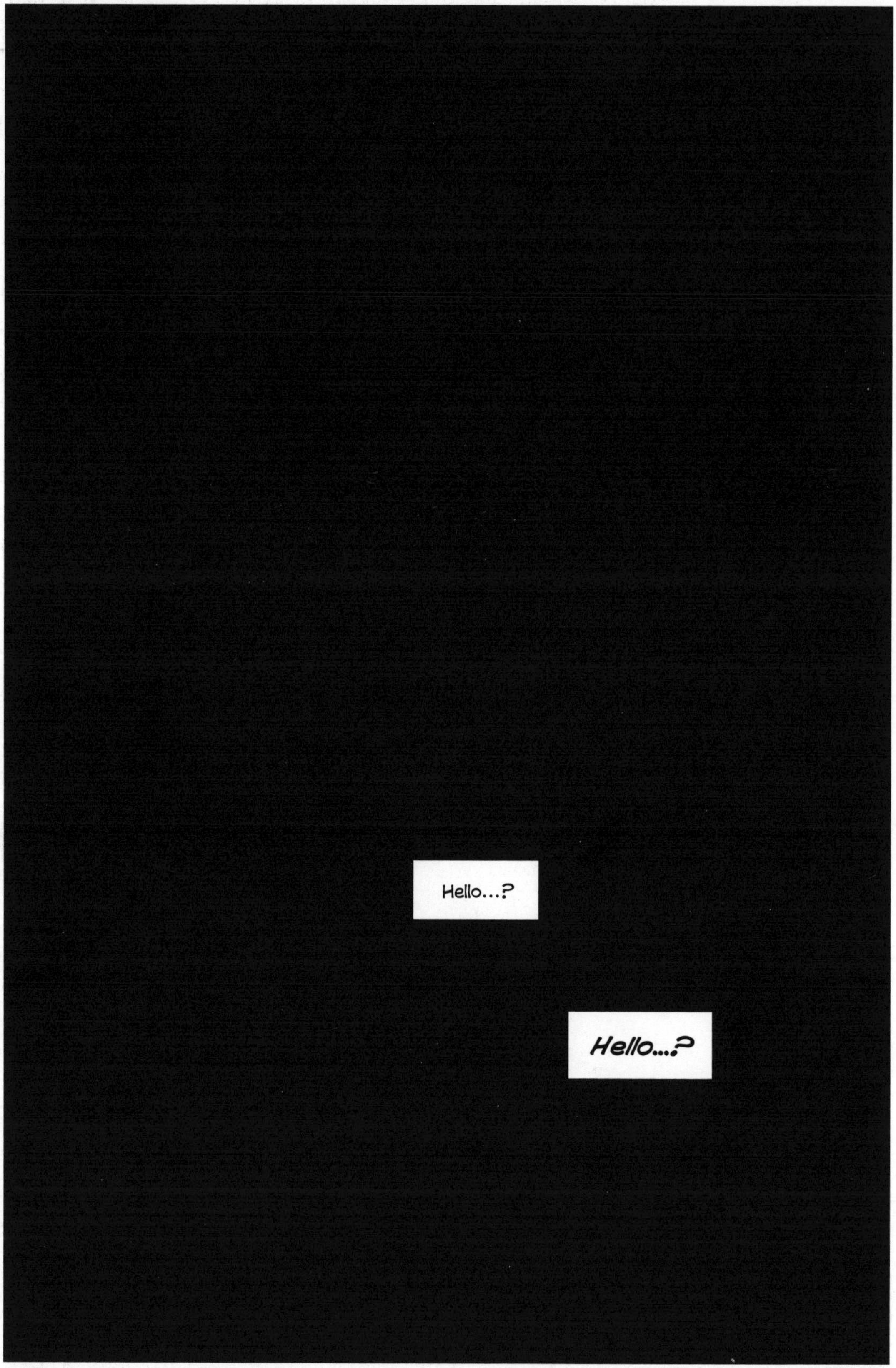
Hello...?
Hello...?

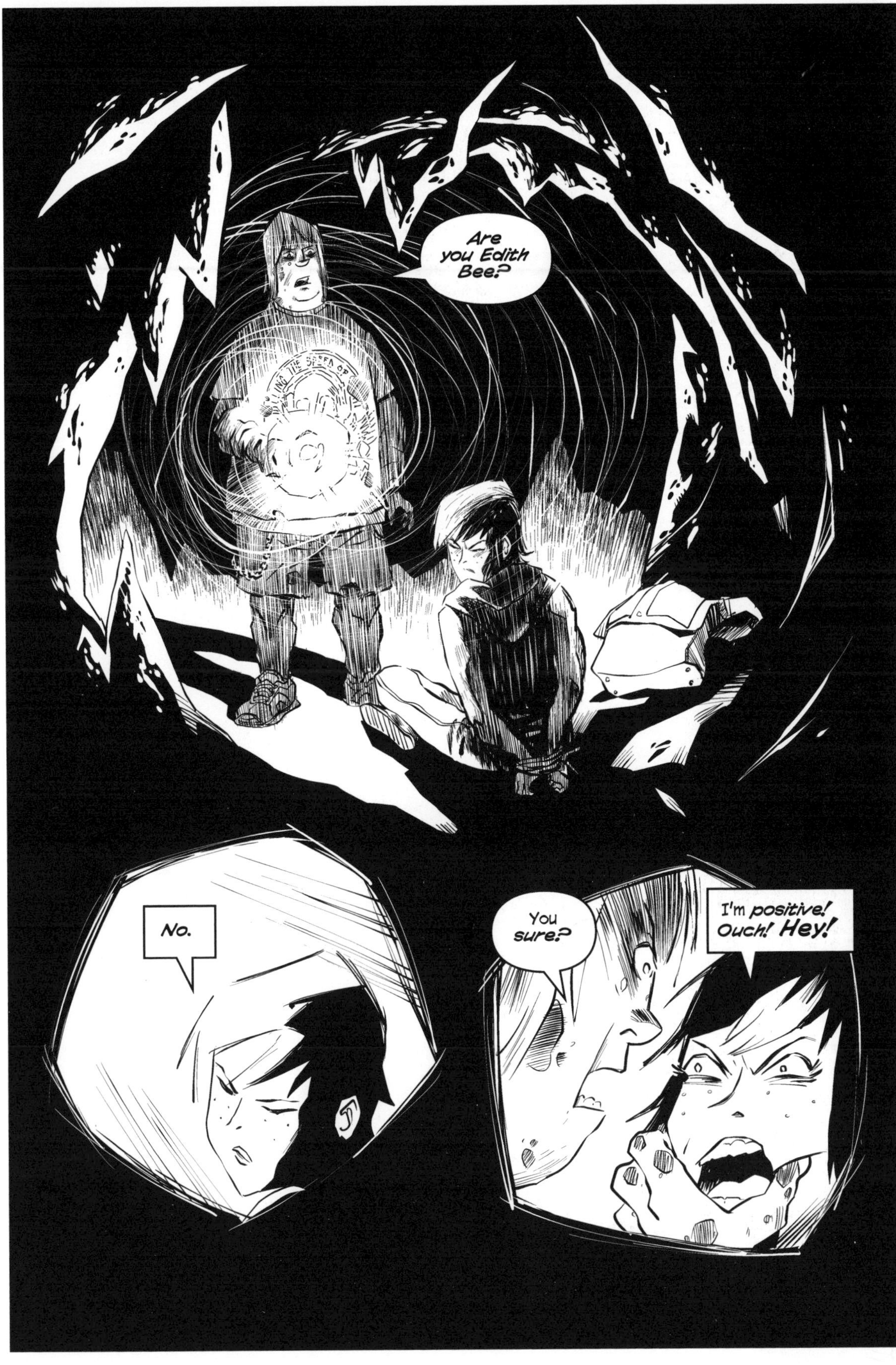
Are you Edith Bee?
No.
You sure?
I'm positive! Ouch! Hey!

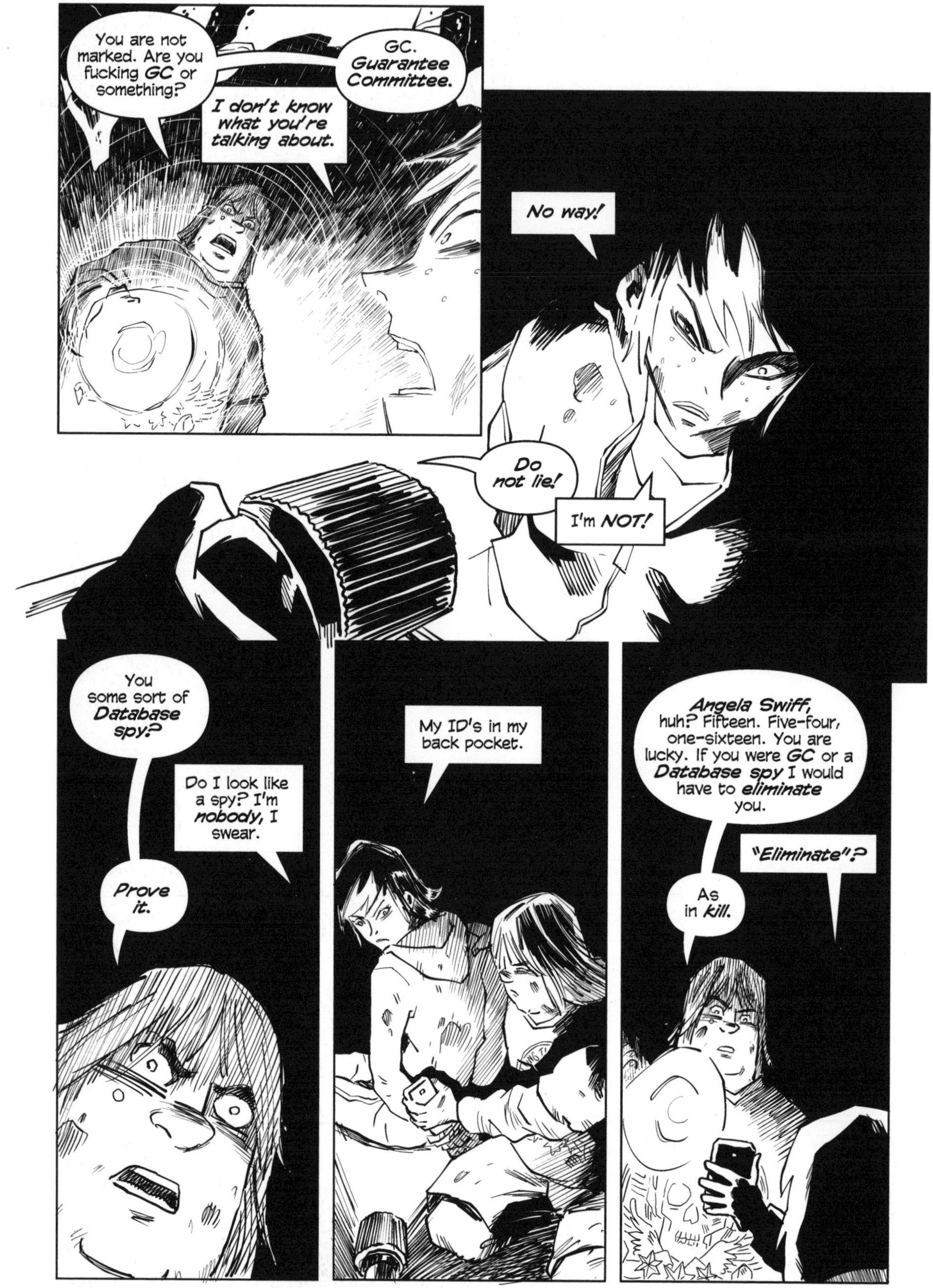

You are not marked. Are you fucking GC or something?
GC. Guarantee Committee.
I don't know what you're talking about.
No way!
Do not lie!
I'm NOT!
You some sort of Database spy?
Do I look like a spy? I'm nobody, I swear.
Prove it.
My ID's in my back pocket.
Angela Swiff, huh? Fifteen. Five-four, one-sixteen. You are lucky. If you were GC or a Database spy I would have to eliminate you.
"Eliminate"?
As in kill.

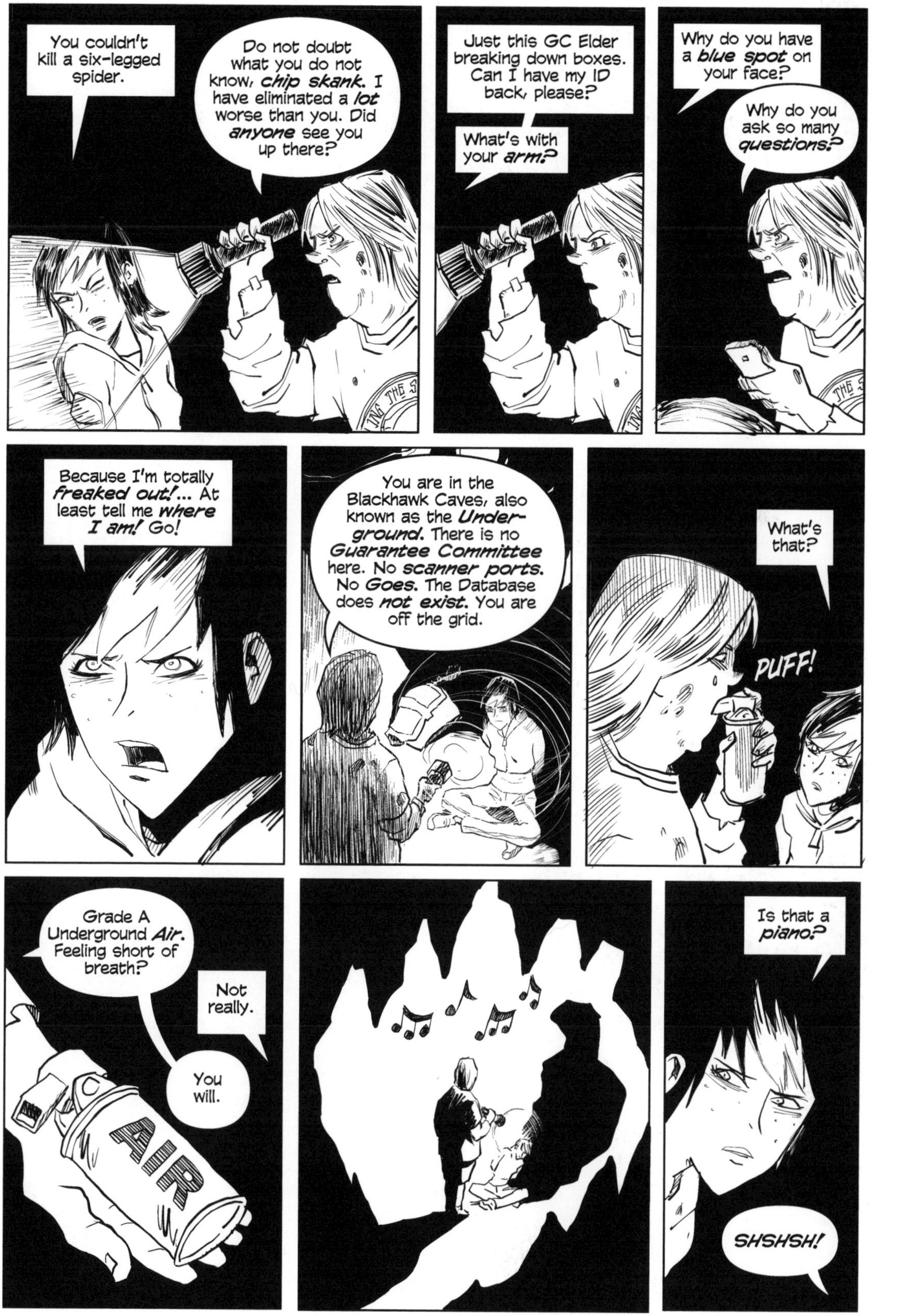
You couldn't kill a six-legged spider.
Do not doubt what you do not know, *chip skank*. I have eliminated a *lot* worse than you. Did *anyone* see you up there?
Just this GC Elder breaking down boxes. Can I have my ID back, please?
What's with your *arm?*
Why do you have a *blue spot* on your face?
Why do you ask so many *questions?*
Because I'm totally *freaked out!*... At least tell me *where I am!* Go!
You are in the Blackhawk Caves, also known as the *Underground*. There is no *Guarantee Committee* here. No *scanner ports*. No *Goes*. The Database does *not exist*. You are off the grid.
What's that?
PUFF!
Grade A Underground *Air*. Feeling short of breath?
Not really.
You will.
AIR
Is that a *piano?*
SHSHSH!

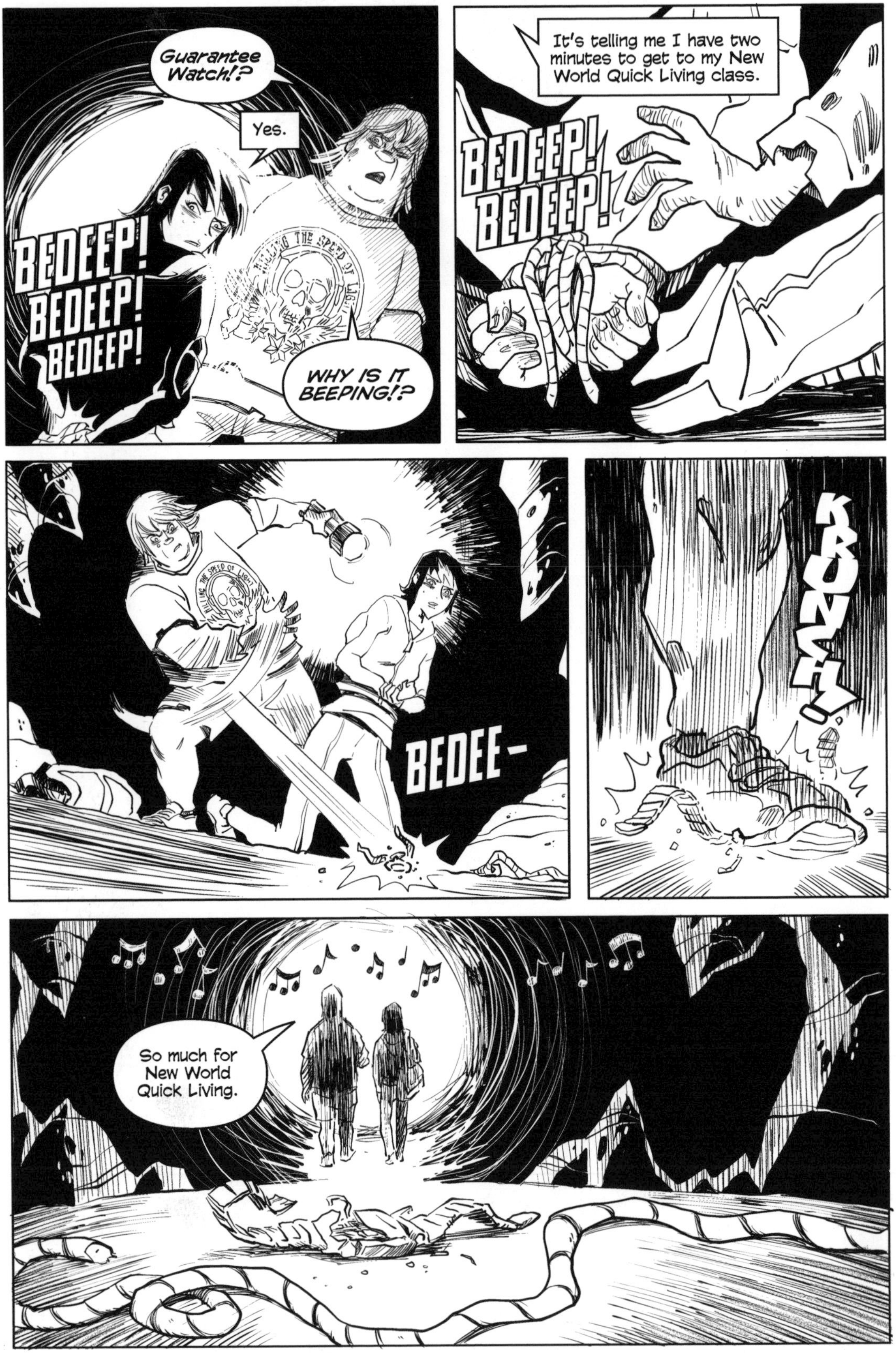
Guarantee Watch!?
Yes.
BEDEEP! BEDEEP! BEDEEP!
WHY IS IT BEEPING!?
It's telling me I have two minutes to get to my New World Quick Living class.
BEDEEP! BEDEEP!
BEDEE-
KRUNCH!
So much for New World Quick Living.

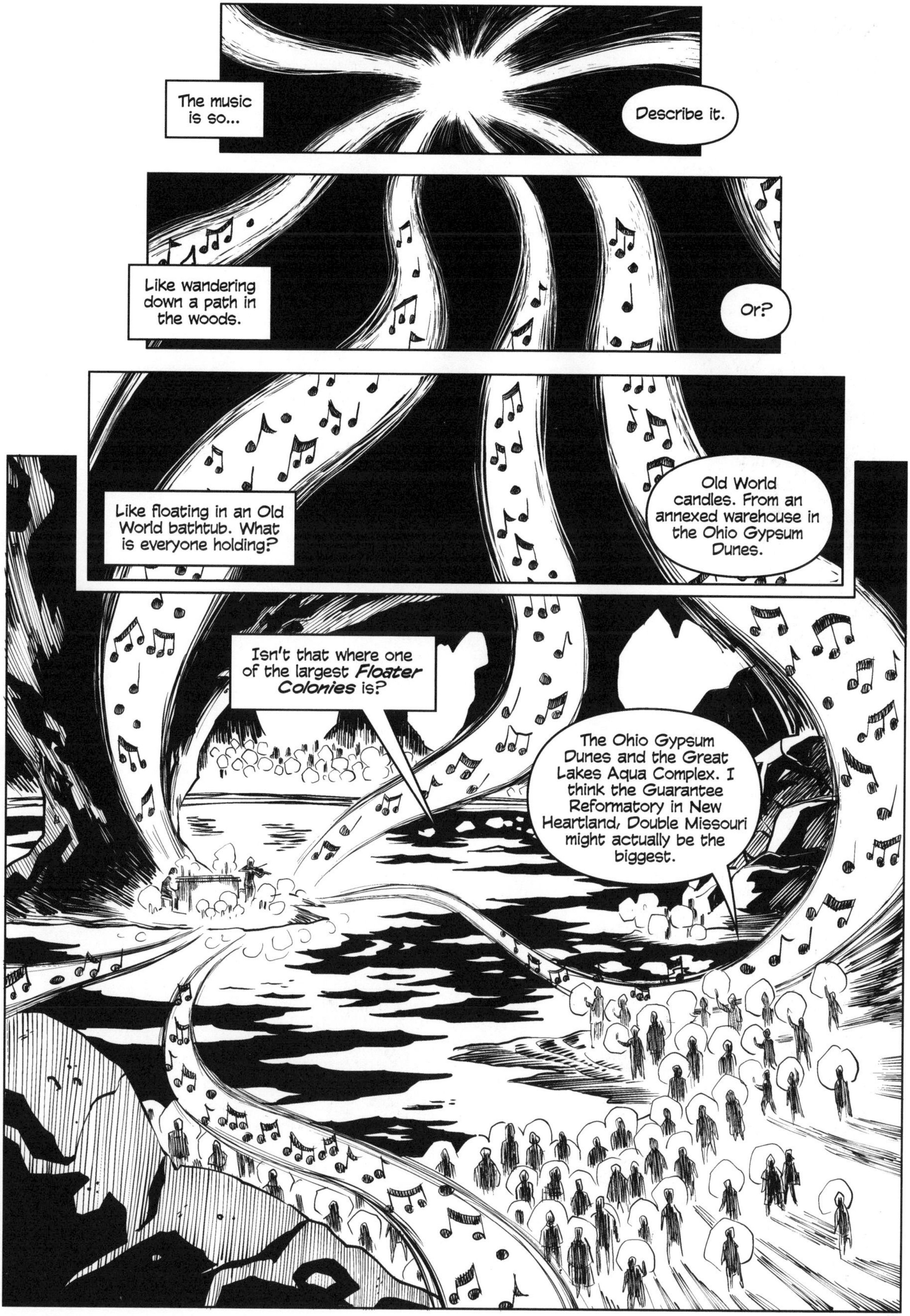
The music is so...
Describe it.
Like wandering down a path in the woods.
Or?
Like floating in an Old World bathtub. What is everyone holding?
Old World candles. From an annexed warehouse in the Ohio Gypsum Dunes.
Isn't that where one of the largest *Floater Colonies* is?
The Ohio Gypsum Dunes and the Great Lakes Aqua Complex. I think the Guarantee Reformatory in New Heartland, Double Missouri might actually be the biggest.

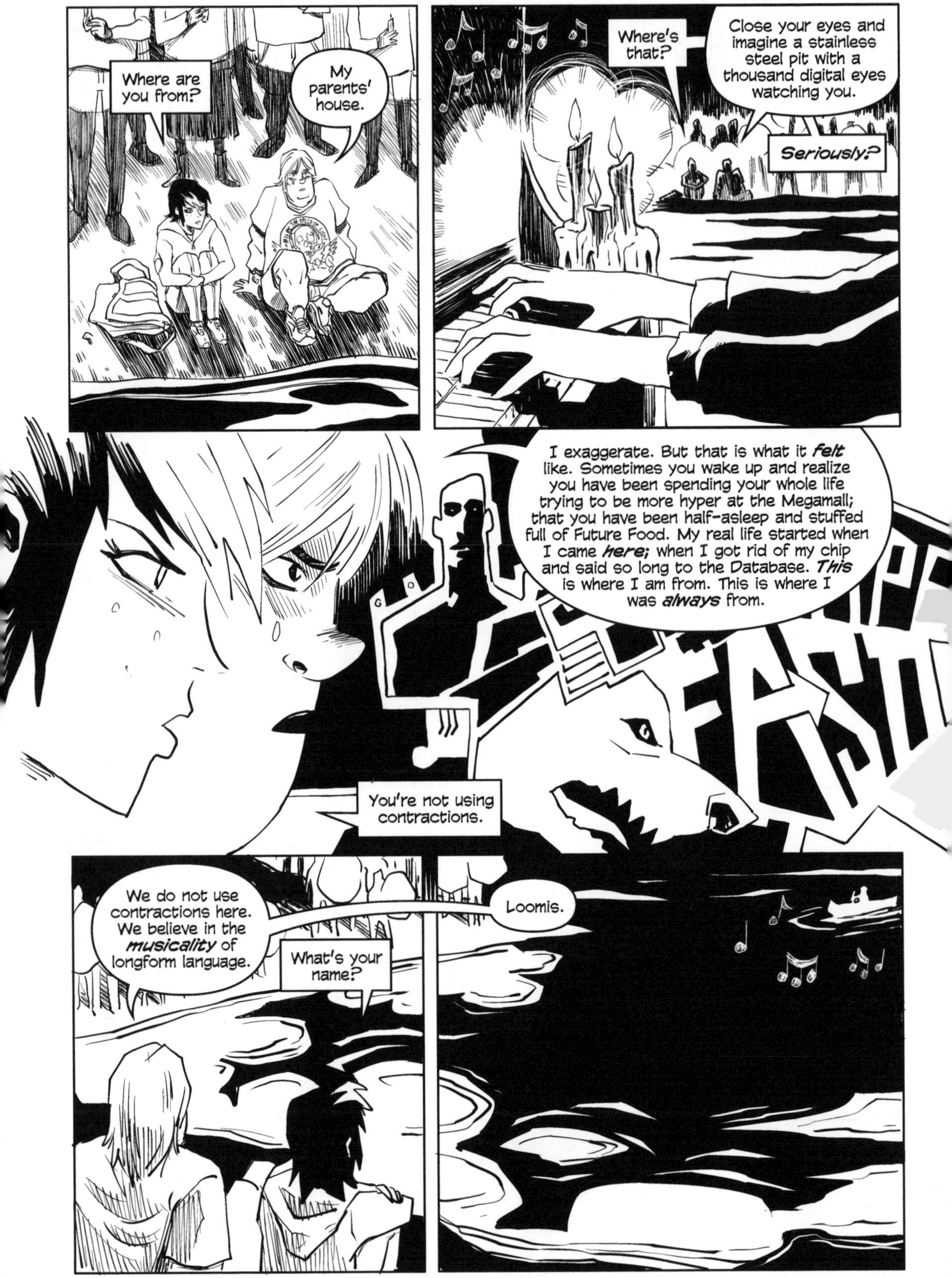

Where are you from?
My parents' house.
Where's that?
Close your eyes and imagine a stainless steel pit with a thousand digital eyes watching you.
Seriously?
I exaggerate. But that is what it *felt* like. Sometimes you wake up and realize you have been spending your whole life trying to be more hyper at the Megamall; that you have been half-asleep and stuffed full of Future Food. My real life started when I came *here;* when I got rid of my chip and said so long to the Database. *This* is where I am from. This is where I was *always* from.
You're not using contractions.
We do not use contractions here. We believe in the *musicality* of longform language.
What's your name?
Loomis.

What's going on?

There is a new member of the community. It is a piece to *decelerate* to.

To *decelerate?*

decelerate [de...

1. To decrease the...

"Decelerate" is a word that the Guarantee Committee *struck* from the New World dictionaries over twenty years ago. The opposite of *accelerate*. Related to *slowness*. How is your head?

A little funny.

Here, take some air.

PUFF!

Any better?

Much better, thanks.

Why is the music stopping?

Just *watch.*

55

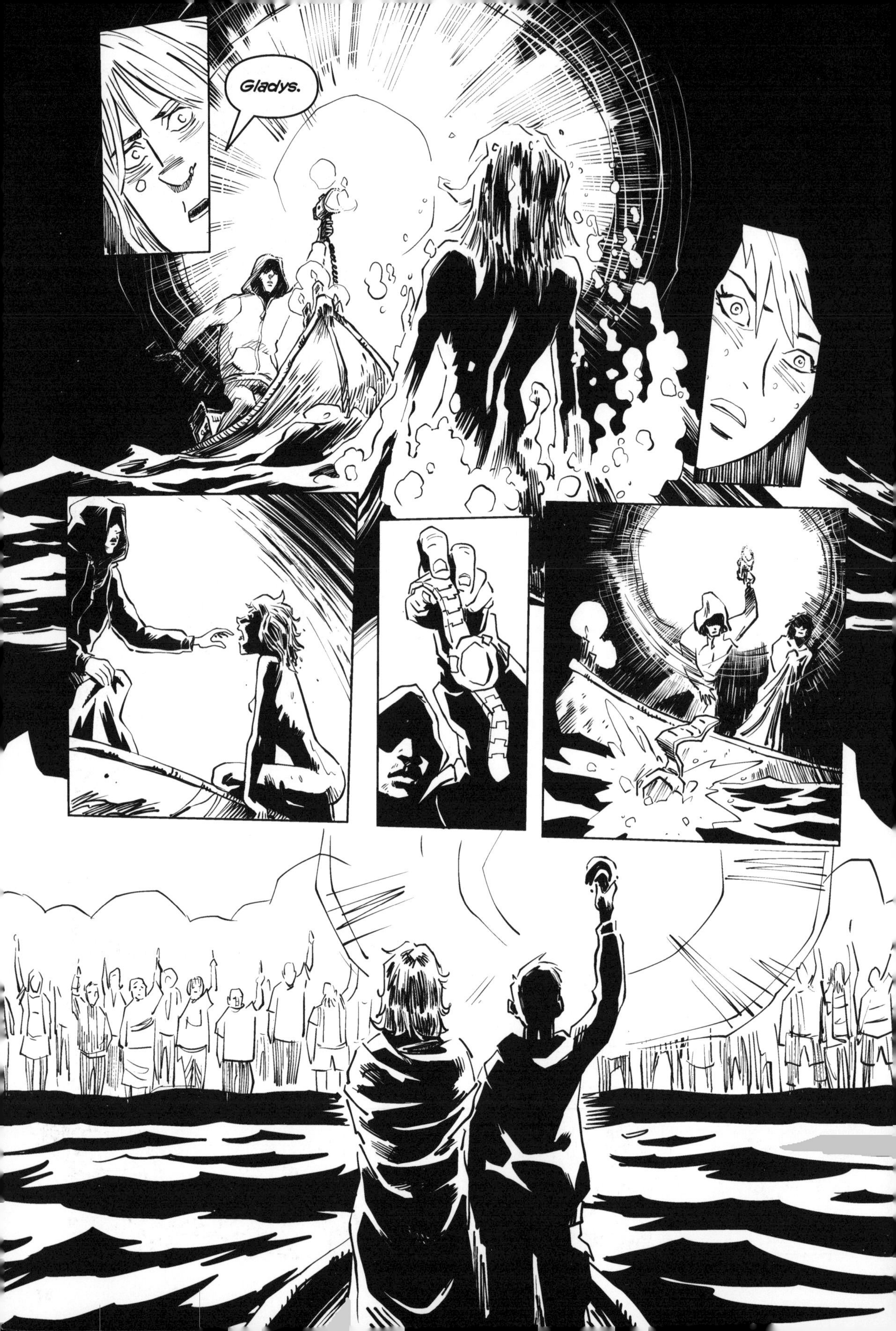
Gladys.

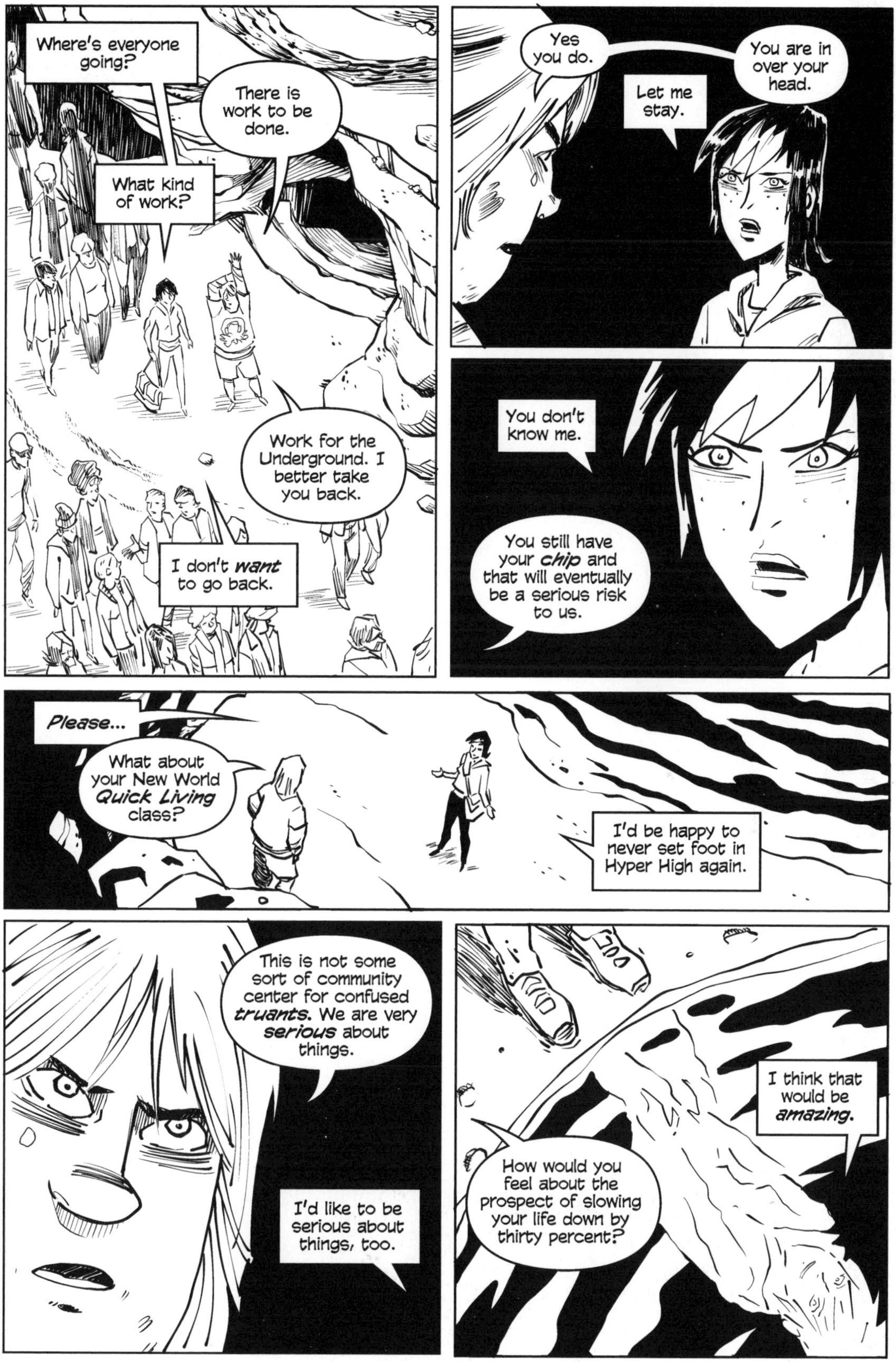
Where's everyone going?
There is work to be done.
What kind of work?
Work for the Underground. I better take you back.
I don't *want* to go back.
Let me stay.
You are in over your head.
Yes you do.
You don't know me.
You still have your *chip* and that will eventually be a serious risk to us.
*Please...*
What about your New World *Quick Living* class?
I'd be happy to never set foot in Hyper High again.
This is not some sort of community center for confused *truants.* We are very *serious* about things.
I'd like to be serious about things, too.
How would you feel about the prospect of slowing your life down by thirty percent?
I think that would be *amazing.*

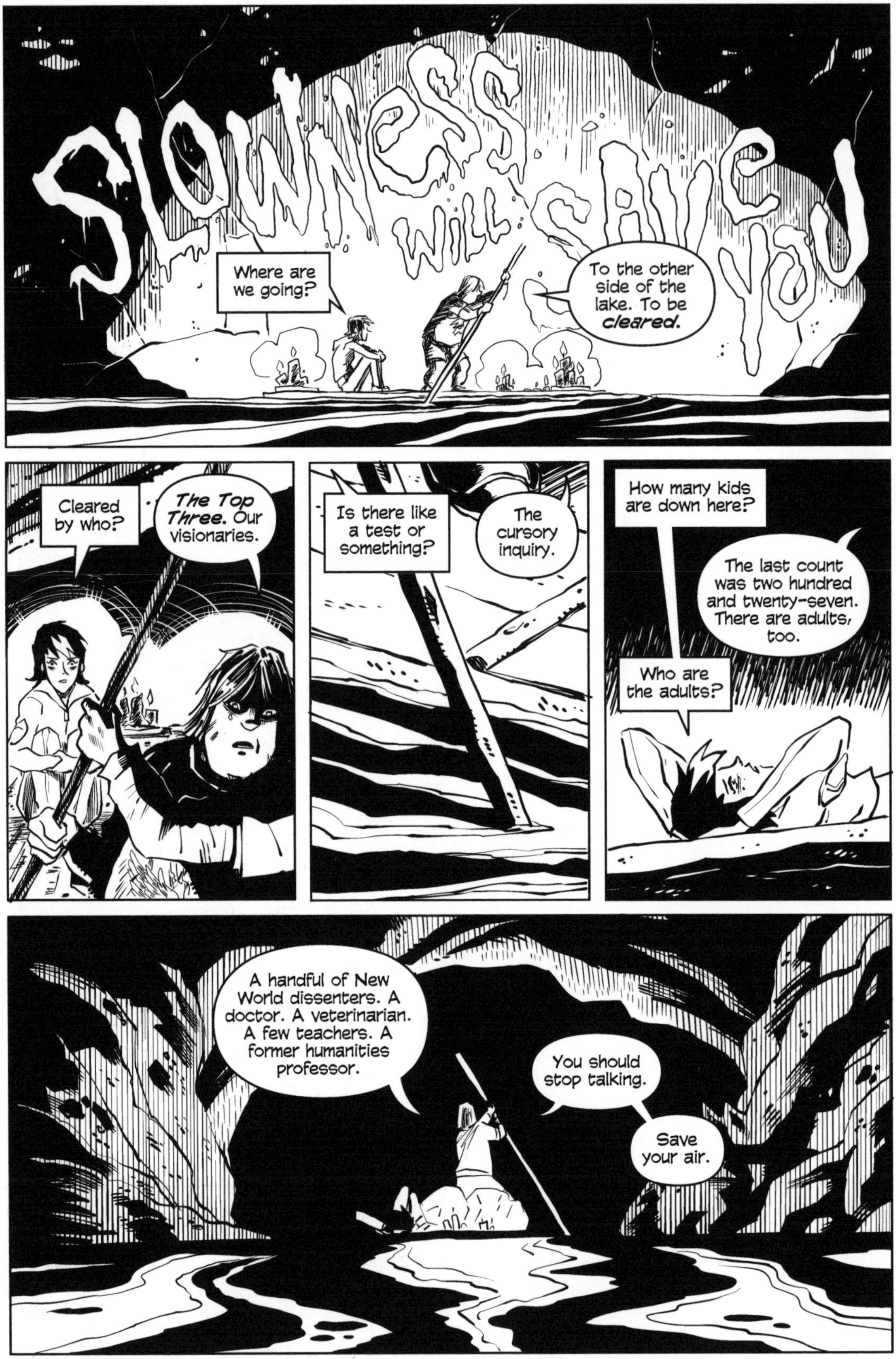
SLOWNESS WILL SAVE YOU
Where are we going?
To the other side of the lake. To be *cleared*.
Cleared by who?
*The Top Three.* Our visionaries.
Is there like a test or something?
The cursory inquiry.
How many kids are down here?
The last count was two hundred and twenty-seven. There are adults, too.
Who are the adults?
A handful of New World dissenters. A doctor. A veterinarian. A few teachers. A former humanities professor.
You should stop talking.
Save your air.

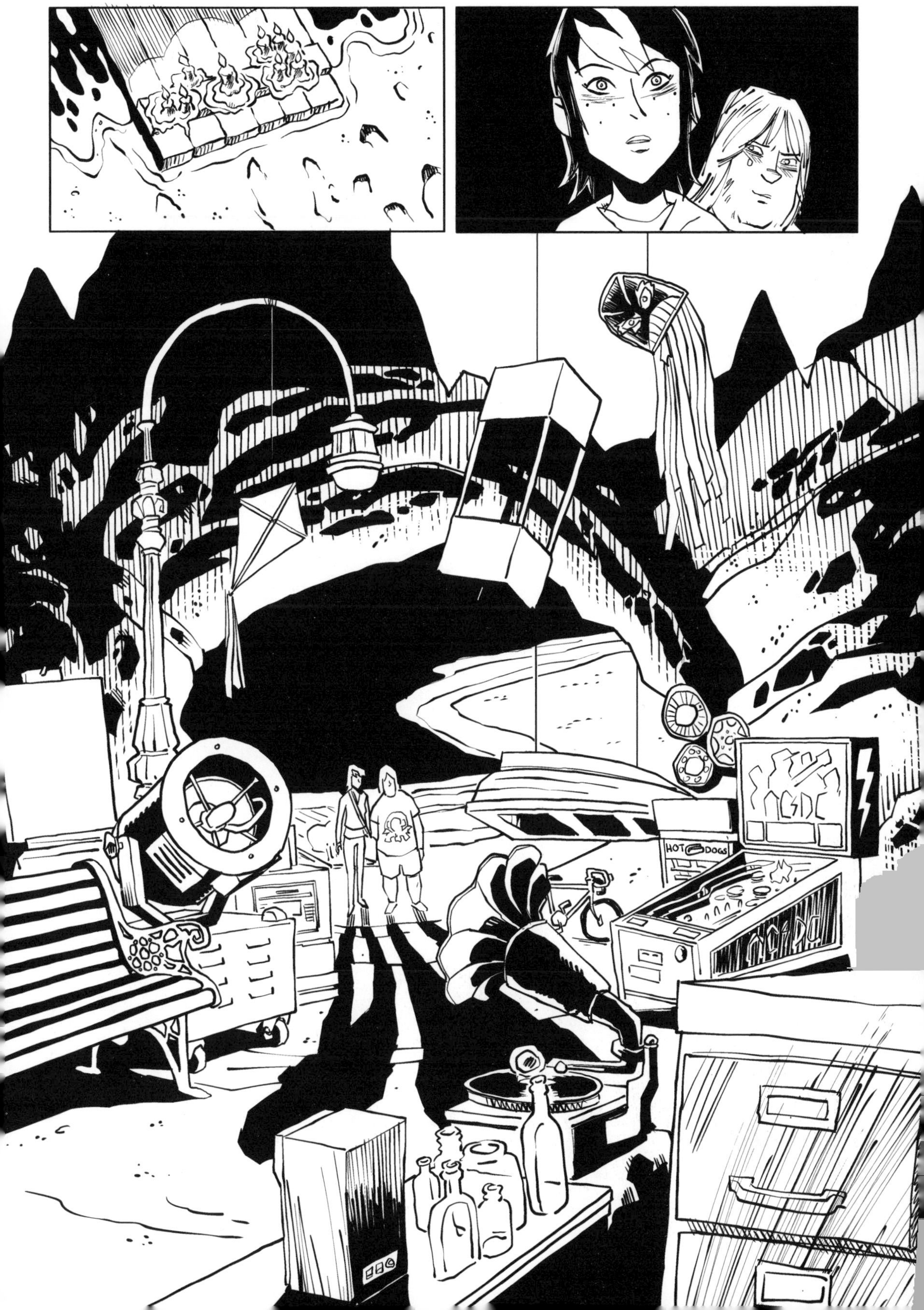
HOT DOGS

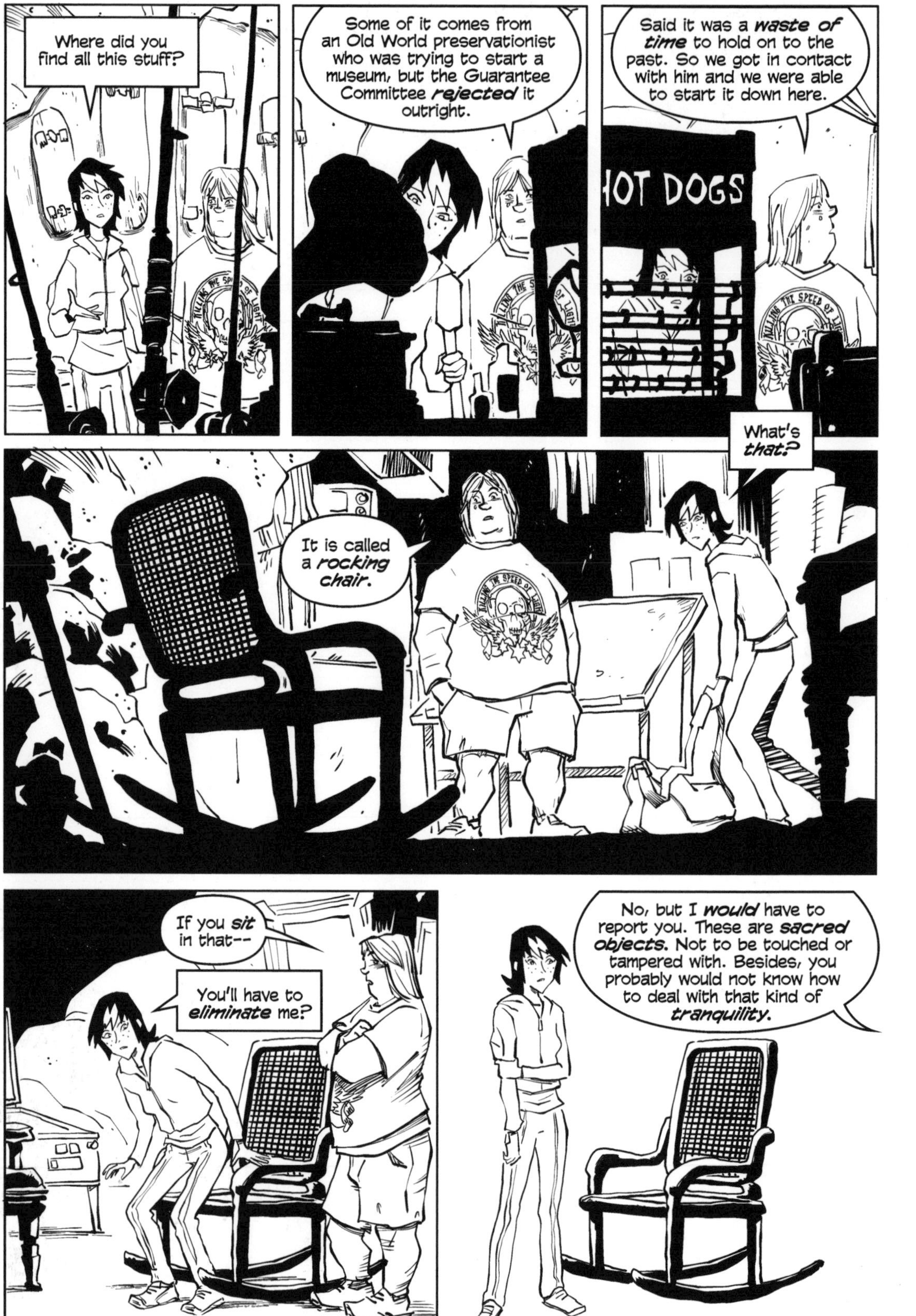
Where did you find all this stuff?
Some of it comes from an Old World preservationist who was trying to start a museum, but the Guarantee Committee *rejected* it outright.
Said it was a *waste of time* to hold on to the past. So we got in contact with him and we were able to start it down here.
HOT DOGS
What's *that?*
It is called a *rocking chair.*
If you *sit* in that--
You'll have to *eliminate* me?
No, but I *would* have to report you. These are *sacred objects.* Not to be touched or tampered with. Besides, you probably would not know how to deal with that kind of *tranquility.*

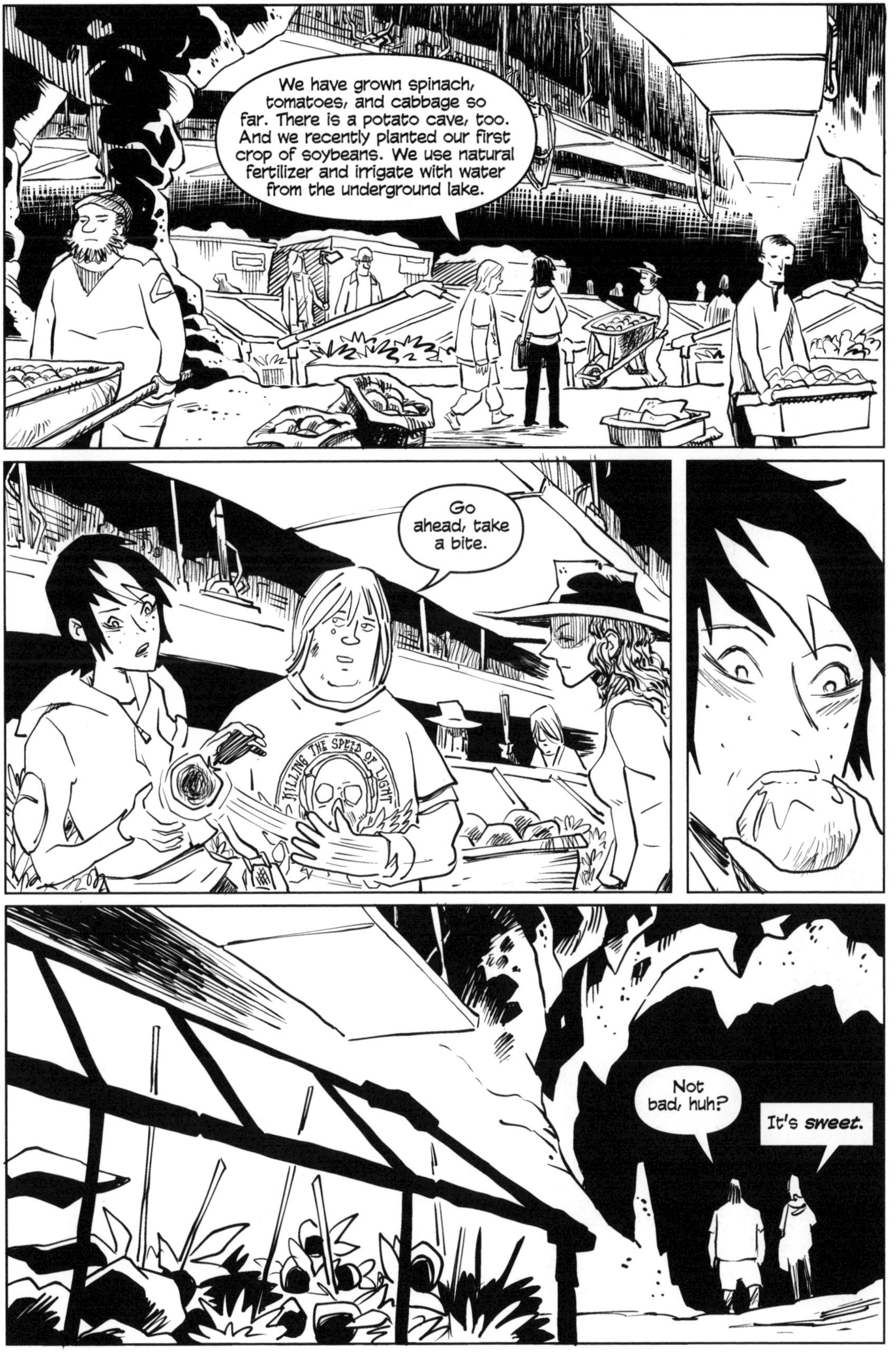
We have grown spinach, tomatoes, and cabbage so far. There is a potato cave, too. And we recently planted our first crop of soybeans. We use natural fertilizer and irrigate with water from the underground lake.
Go ahead, take a bite.
KILLING THE SPEED OF LIGHT
Not bad, huh?
It's sweet.

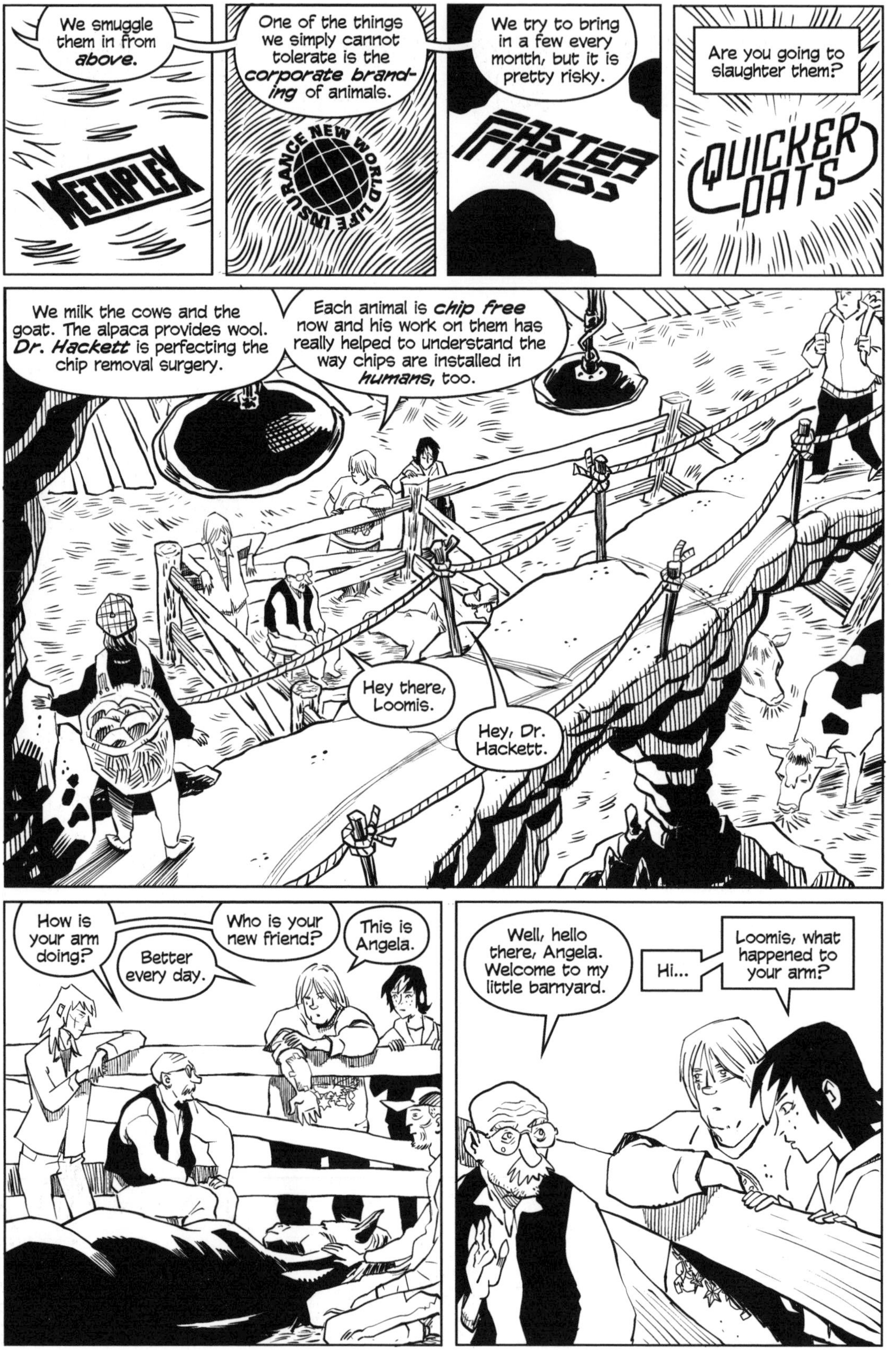
We smuggle them in from above.
METAPLEX
One of the things we simply cannot tolerate is the corporate branding of animals.
NEW WORLD LIFE INSURANCE
We try to bring in a few every month, but it is pretty risky.
FASTER FITNESS
Are you going to slaughter them?
QUICKER OATS
We milk the cows and the goat. The alpaca provides wool. Dr. Hackett is perfecting the chip removal surgery.
Each animal is chip free now and his work on them has really helped to understand the way chips are installed in humans, too.
Hey there, Loomis.
Hey, Dr. Hackett.
How is your arm doing?
Better every day.
Who is your new friend?
This is Angela.
Well, hello there, Angela. Welcome to my little barnyard.
Hi...
Loomis, what happened to your arm?

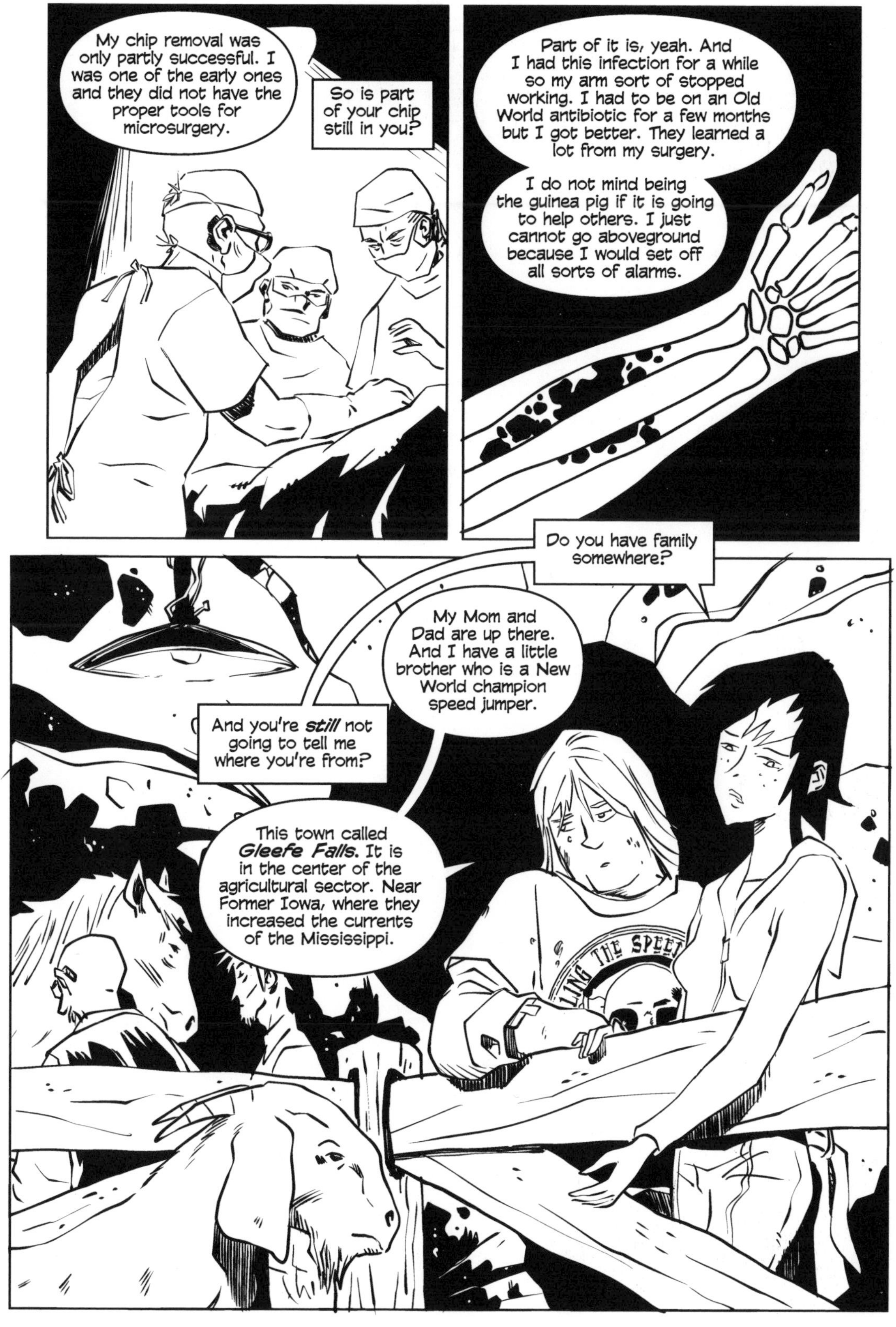

My chip removal was only partly successful. I was one of the early ones and they did not have the proper tools for microsurgery.
So is part of your chip still in you?
Part of it is, yeah. And I had this infection for a while so my arm sort of stopped working. I had to be on an Old World antibiotic for a few months but I got better. They learned a lot from my surgery.
I do not mind being the guinea pig if it is going to help others. I just cannot go aboveground because I would set off all sorts of alarms.
Do you have family somewhere?
My Mom and Dad are up there. And I have a little brother who is a New World champion speed jumper.
And you're *still* not going to tell me where you're from?
This town called *Gleefe Falls*. It is in the center of the agricultural sector. Near Former Iowa, where they increased the currents of the Mississippi.

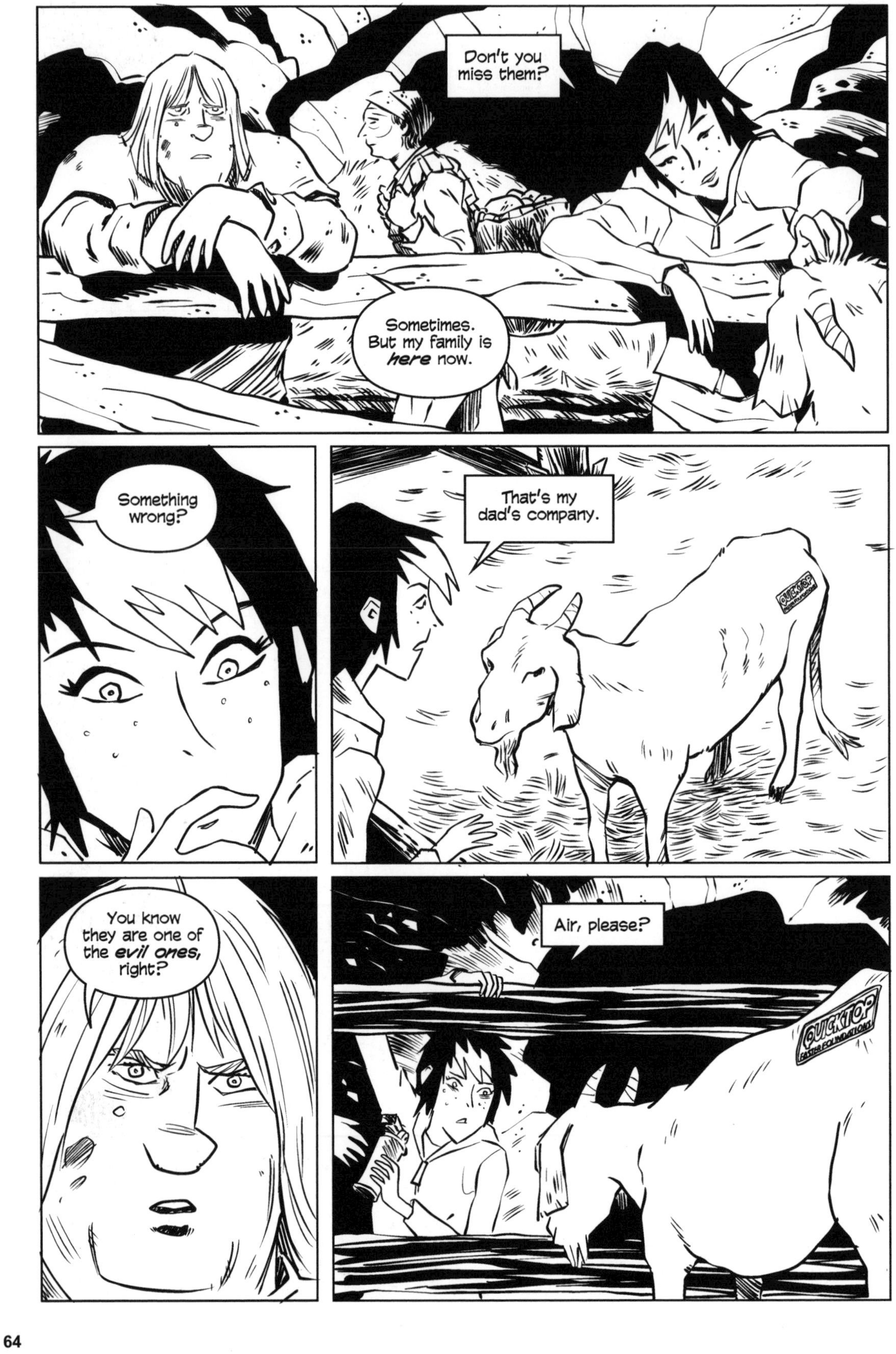
Don't you miss them?
Sometimes. But my family is *here* now.
Something wrong?
That's my dad's company.
You know they are one of the *evil ones*, right?
Air, please?
QUICKTOP
FASTER FOUNDATIONS

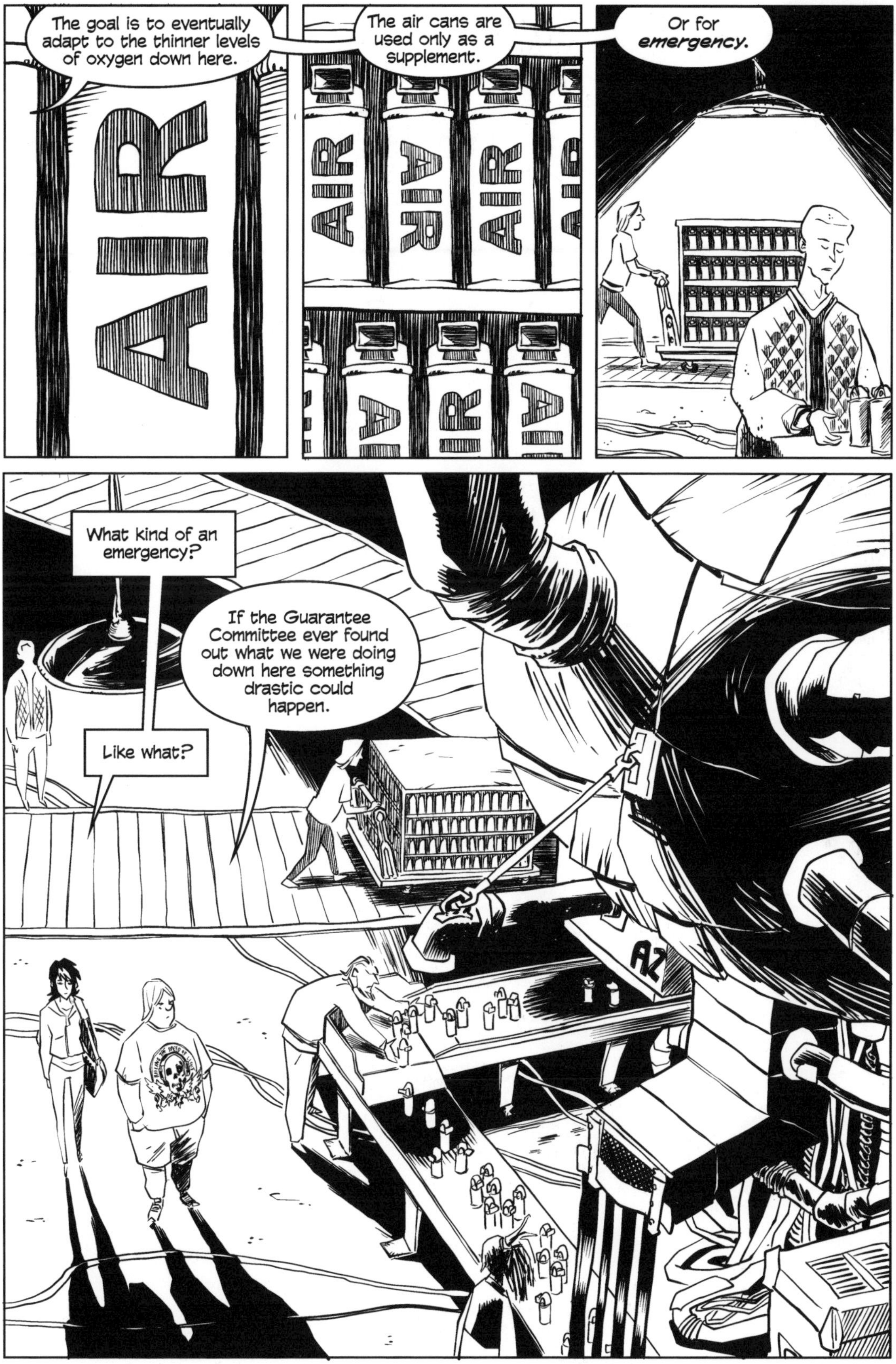
The goal is to eventually adapt to the thinner levels of oxygen down here.
AIR
The air cans are used only as a supplement.
AIR
Or for *emergency.*
What kind of an emergency?
If the Guarantee Committee ever found out what we were doing down here something drastic could happen.
Like what?
AZ

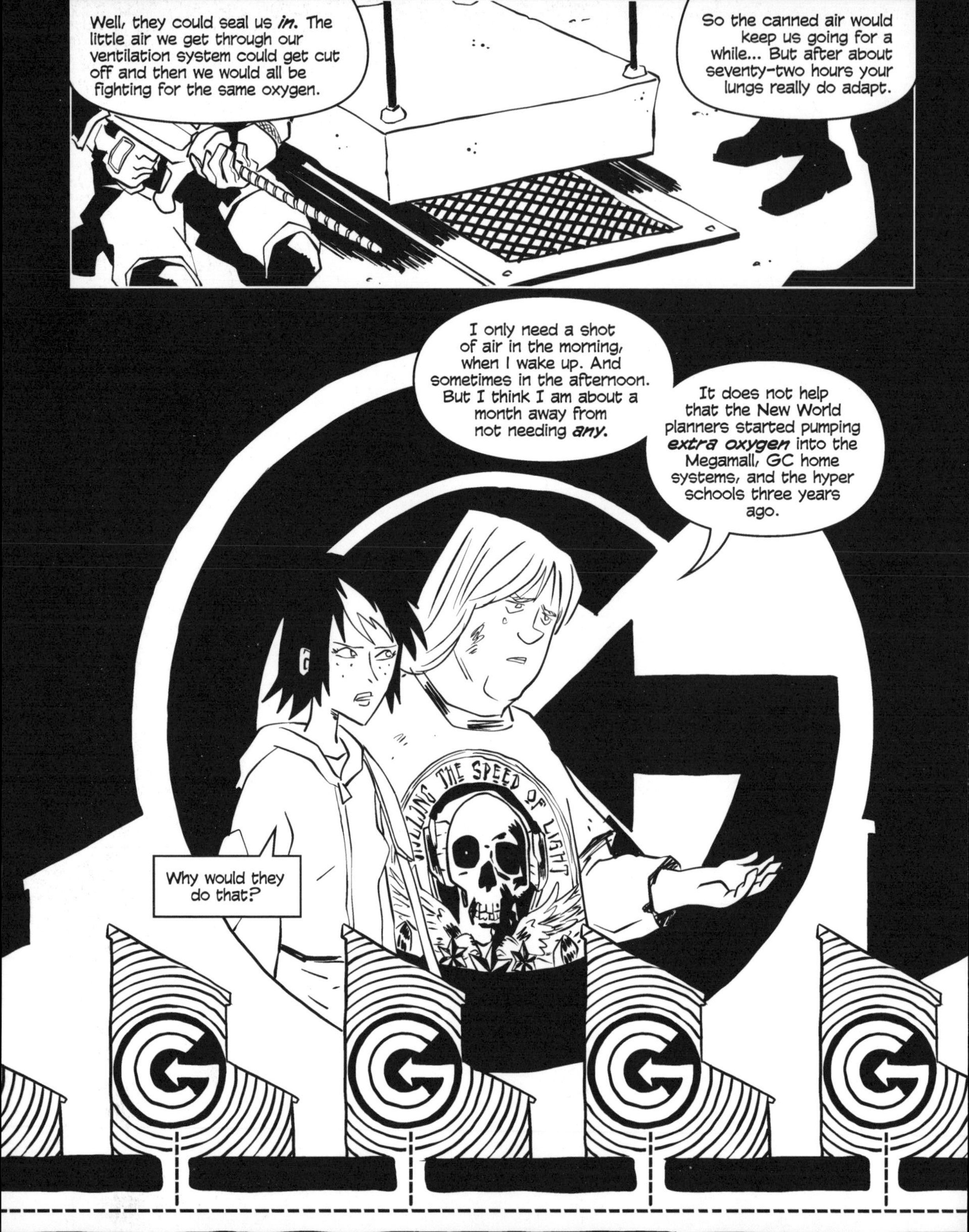
Well, they could seal us *in.* The little air we get through our ventilation system could get cut off and then we would all be fighting for the same oxygen.
So the canned air would keep us going for a while... But after about seventy-two hours your lungs really do adapt.
I only need a shot of air in the morning, when I wake up. And sometimes in the afternoon. But I think I am about a month away from not needing *any.*
It does not help that the New World planners started pumping ***extra oxygen*** into the Megamall, GC home systems, and the hyper schools three years ago.
Why would they do that?
THE SPEED OF LIGHT

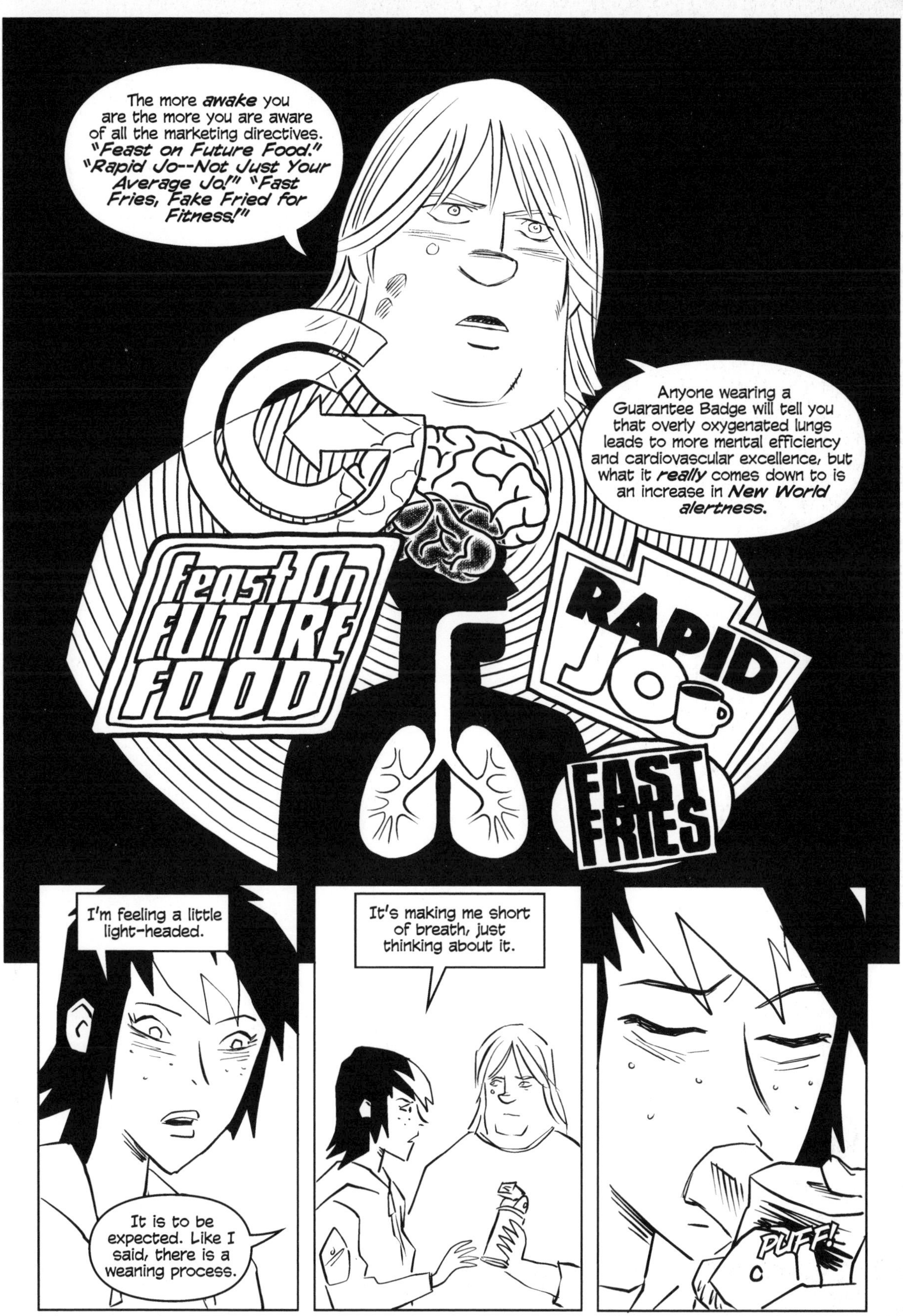

The more *awake* you are the more you are aware of all the marketing directives. *"Feast on Future Food." "Rapid Jo--Not Just Your Average Jo!" "Fast Fries, Fake Fried for Fitness!"*
Anyone wearing a Guarantee Badge will tell you that overly oxygenated lungs leads to more mental efficiency and cardiovascular excellence, but what it *really* comes down to is an increase in *New World alertness.*
Feast On FUTURE FOOD
RAPID JO
FAST FRIES
I'm feeling a little light-headed.
It is to be expected. Like I said, there is a weaning process.
It's making me short of breath, just thinking about it.
PUFF!

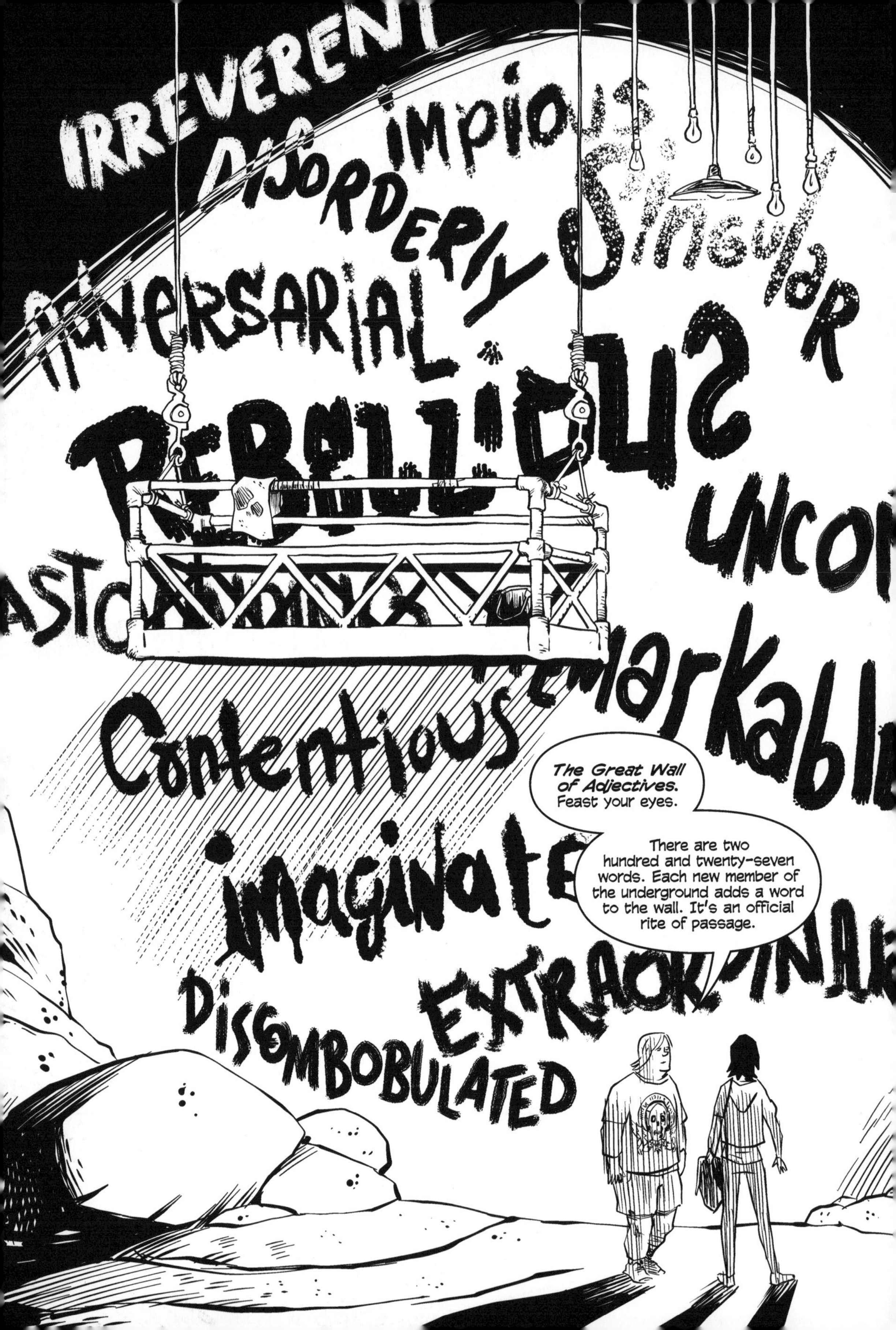

impious
DISORDERLY
ADVERSARIAL
Singular
Contentious
imaginate
DISCOMBOBULATED
*The Great Wall of Adjectives.* Feast your eyes.
There are two hundred and twenty-seven words. Each new member of the underground adds a word to the wall. It's an official rite of passage.

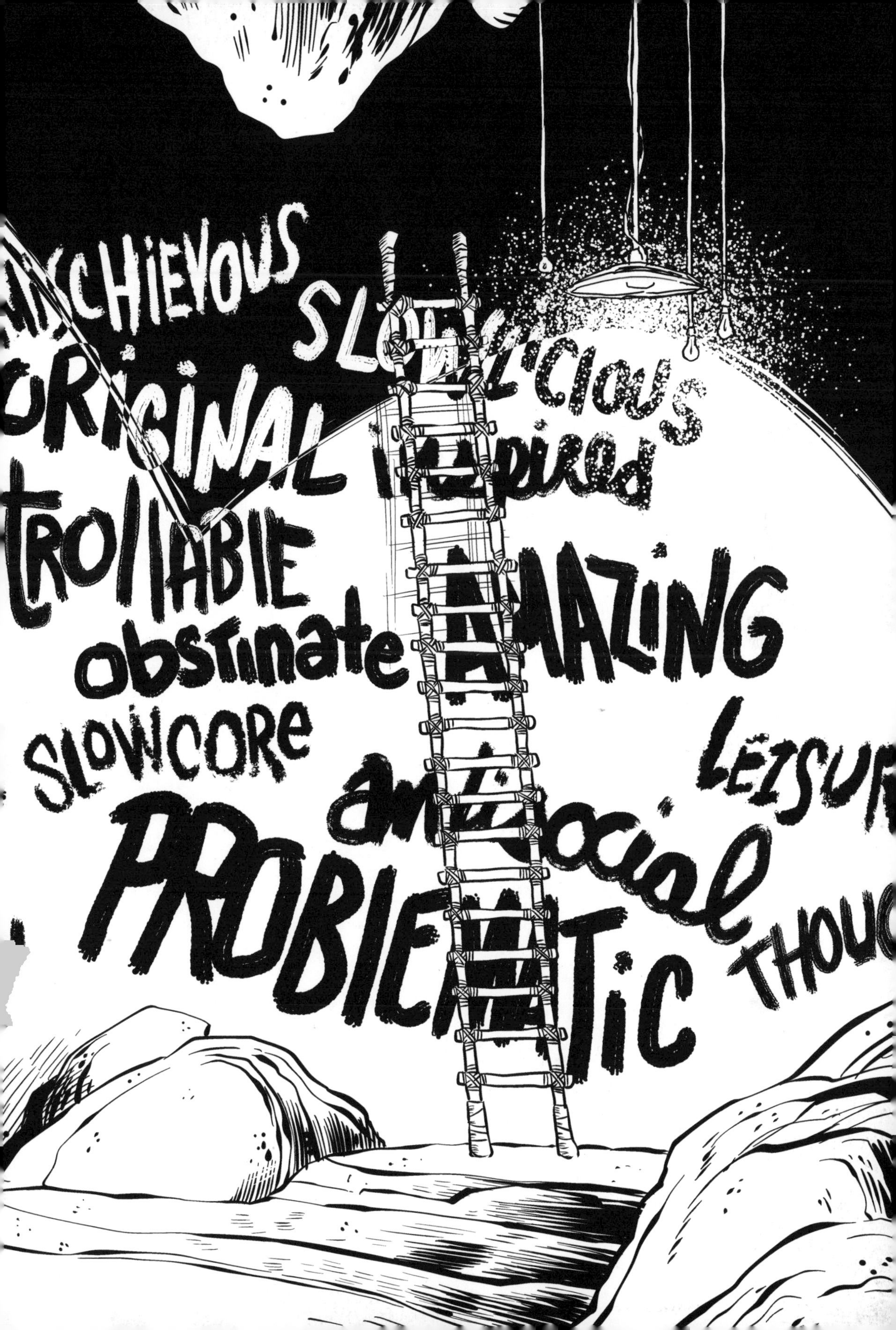
ORIGINAL
obstinate
AMAZING
SLOWCORE
PROBLEMATIC

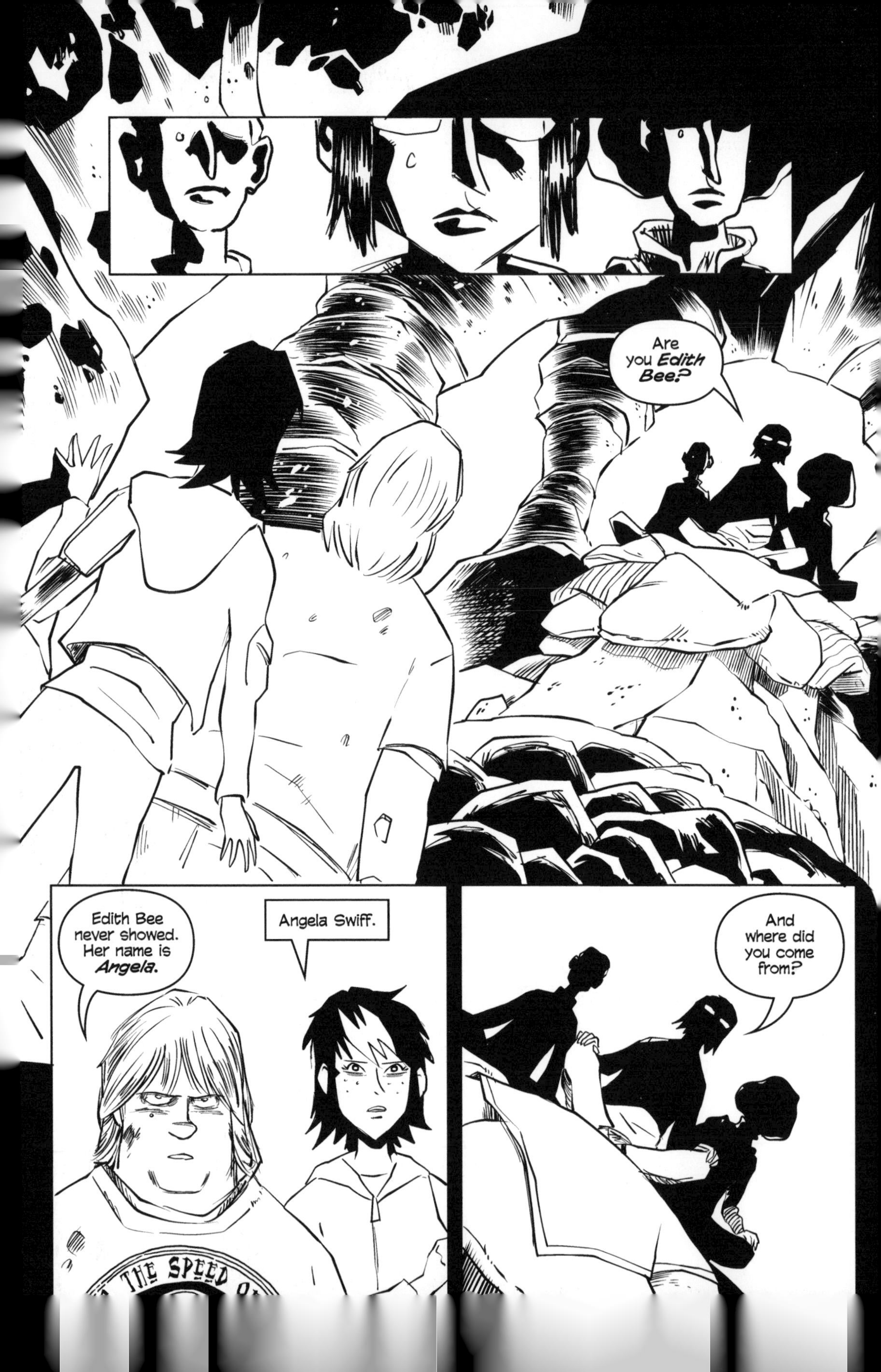
Are you Edith Bee?
Edith Bee never showed. Her name is Angela.
Angela Swiff.
And where did you come from?
THE SPEED O

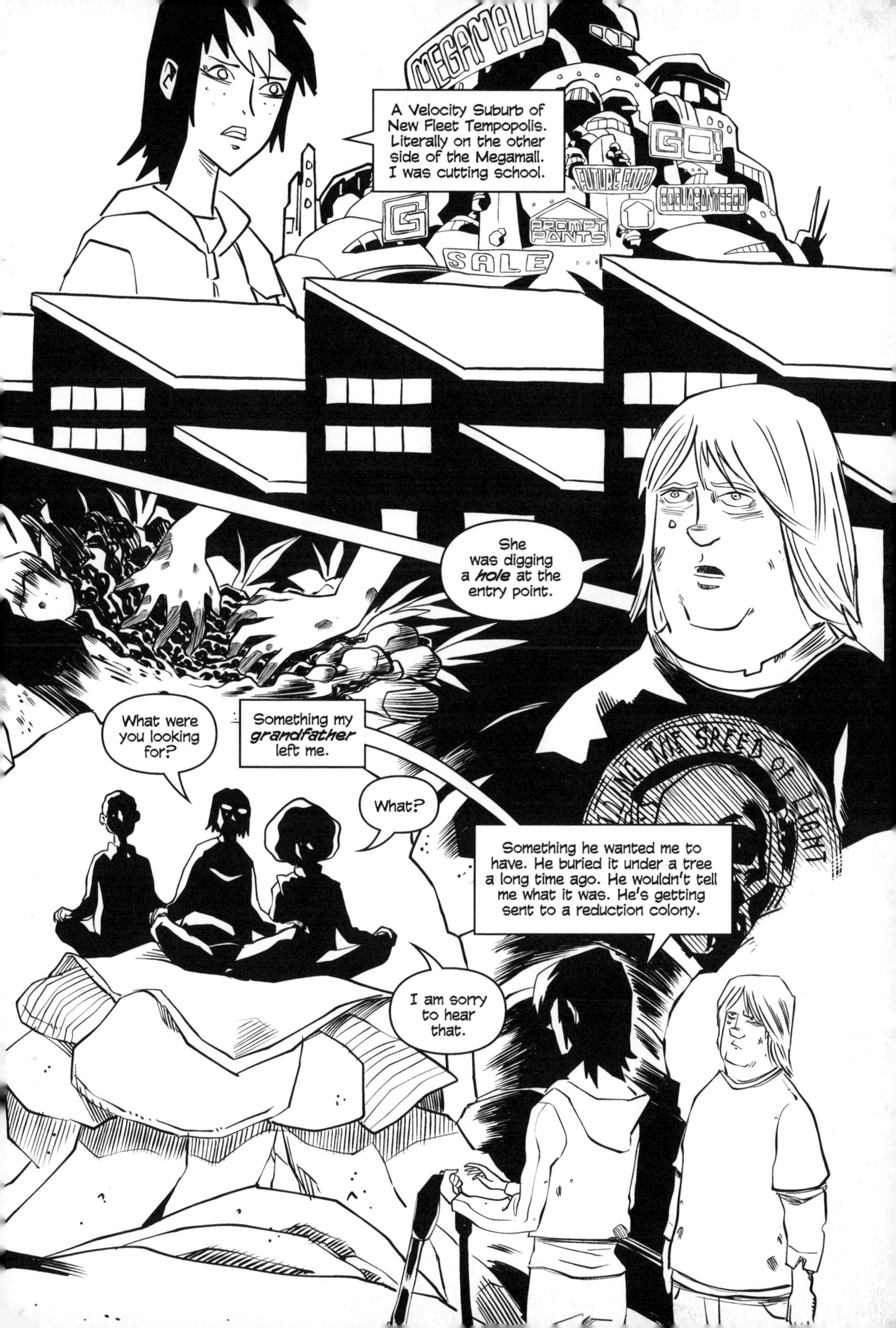
MEGAMALL
A Velocity Suburb of New Fleet Tempopolis. Literally on the other side of the Megamall. I was cutting school.
GO!
FUTURE FOOD
GOGUARANTEEGO
PROMPT PANTS
SALE
She was digging a *hole* at the entry point.
What were you looking for?
Something my *grandfather* left me.
What?
Something he wanted me to have. He buried it under a tree a long time ago. He wouldn't tell me what it was. He's getting sent to a reduction colony.
I am sorry to hear that.

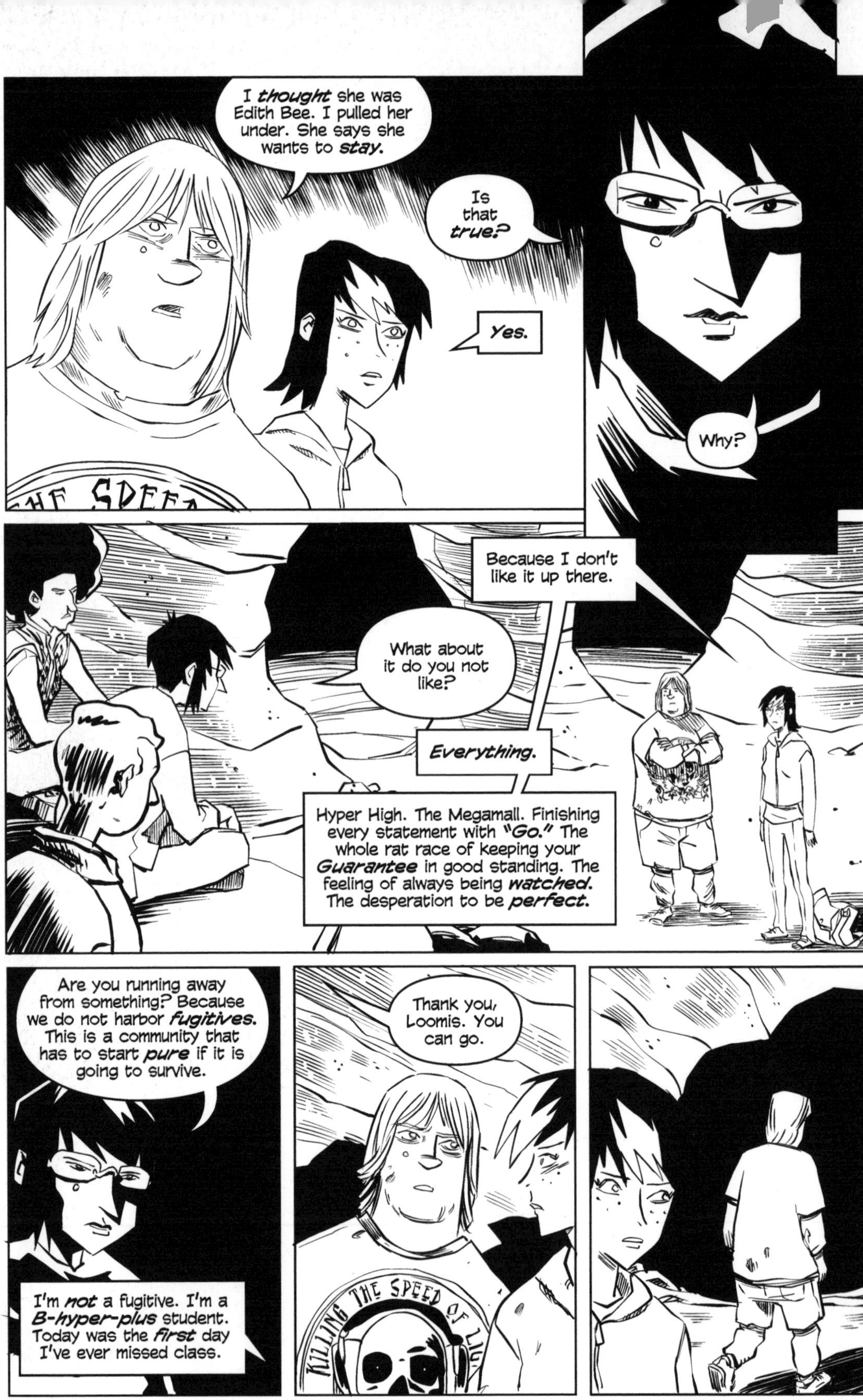
I *thought* she was Edith Bee. I pulled her under. She says she wants to *stay.*
Is that *true?*
*Yes.*
Why?
Because I don't like it up there.
What about it do you not like?
*Everything.*
Hyper High. The Megamall. Finishing every statement with *"Go."* The whole rat race of keeping your *Guarantee* in good standing. The feeling of always being *watched.* The desperation to be *perfect.*
Are you running away from something? Because we do not harbor *fugitives.* This is a community that has to start *pure* if it is going to survive.
I'm *not* a fugitive. I'm a *B-hyper-plus* student. Today was the *first* day I've ever missed class.
Thank you, Loomis. You can go.
KILLING THE SPEED OF LIG

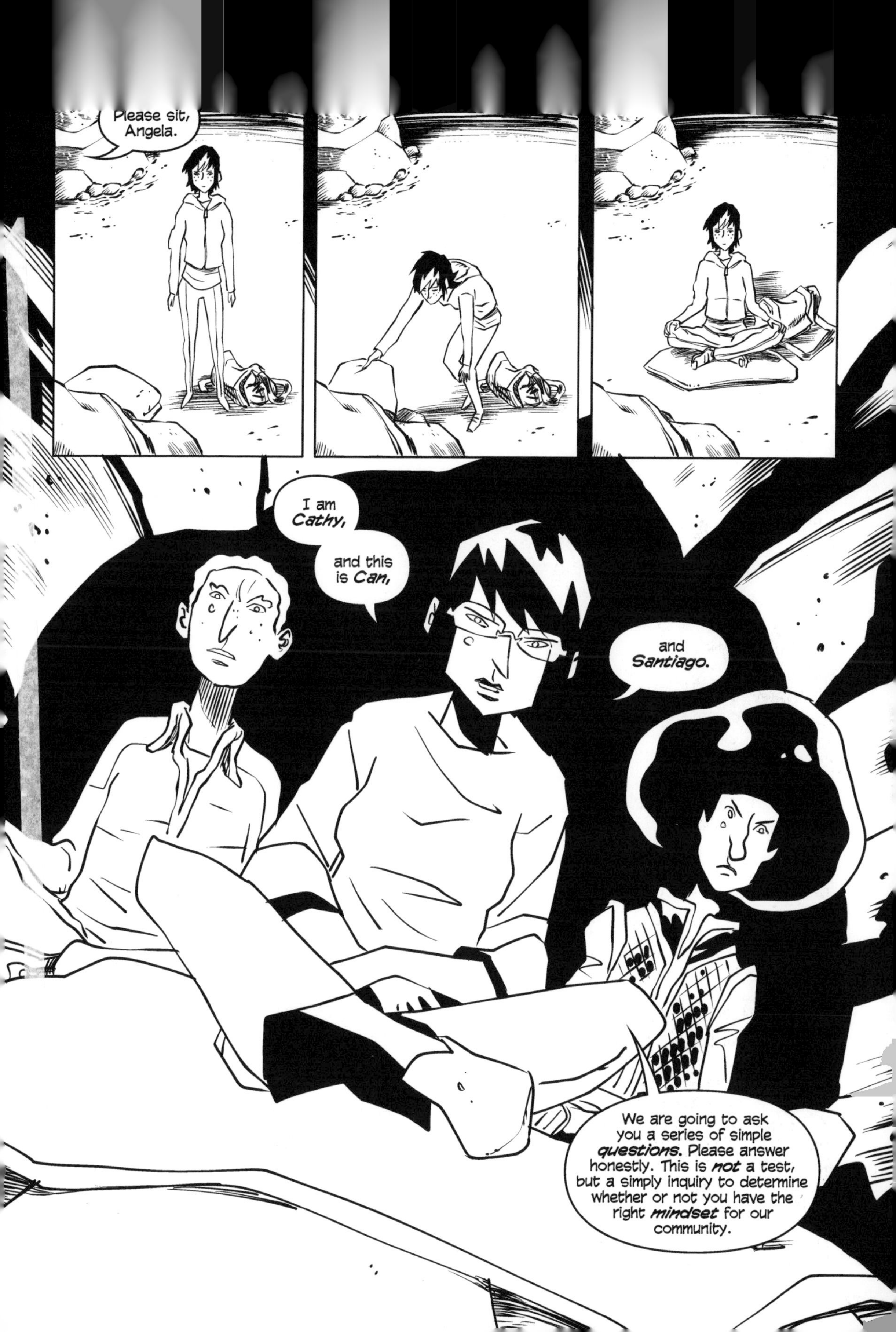
Please sit, Angela.
I am Cathy,
and this is Can,
and Santiago.
We are going to ask you a series of simple questions. Please answer honestly. This is not a test, but a simply inquiry to determine whether or not you have the right mindset for our community.

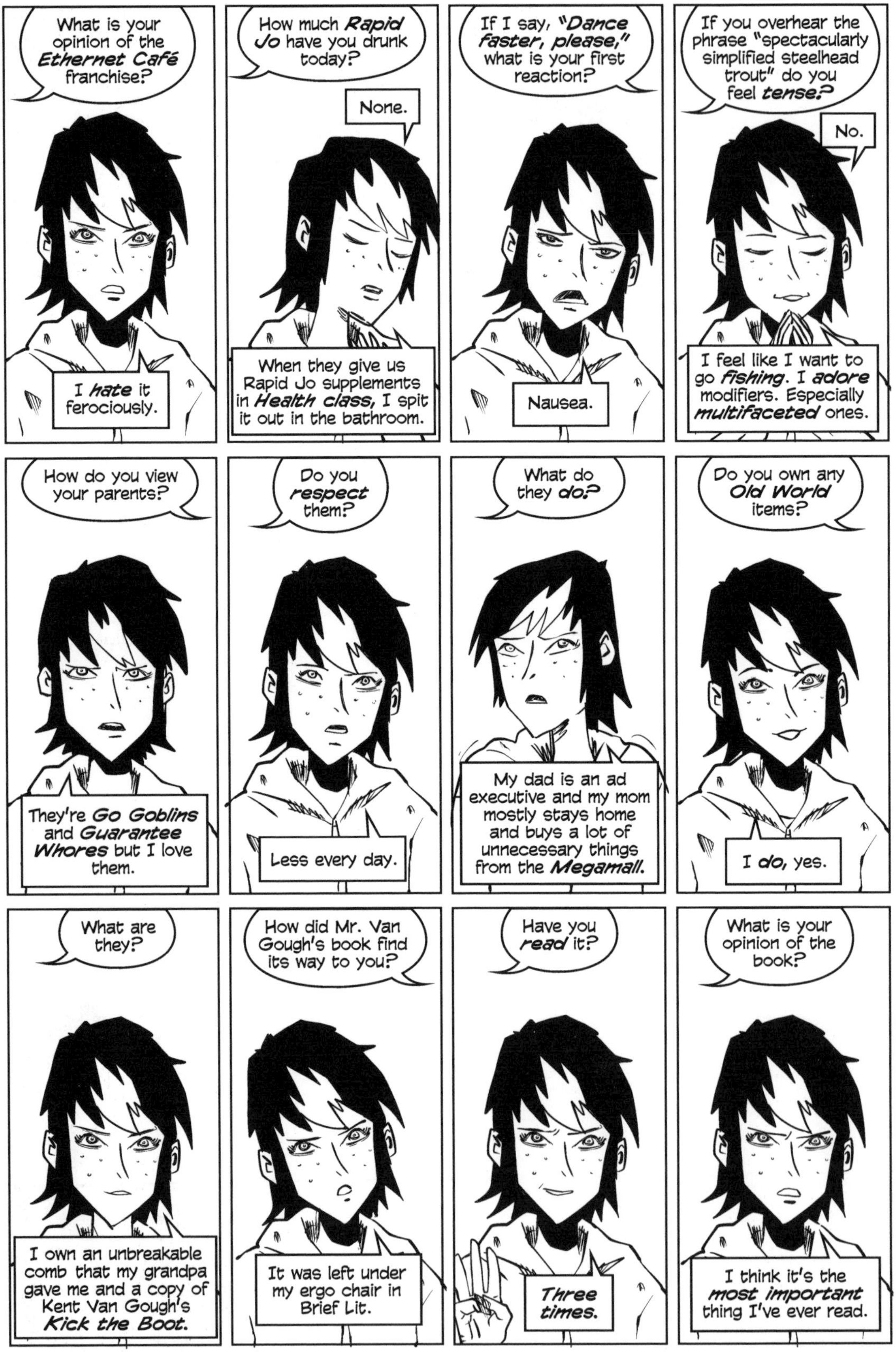

What is your opinion of the Ethernet Café franchise?
I hate it ferociously.
How much Rapid Jo have you drunk today?
None.
When they give us Rapid Jo supplements in Health class, I spit it out in the bathroom.
If I say, "Dance faster, please," what is your first reaction?
Nausea.
If you overhear the phrase "spectacularly simplified steelhead trout" do you feel tense?
No.
I feel like I want to go fishing. I adore modifiers. Especially multifaceted ones.
How do you view your parents?
They're Go Goblins and Guarantee Whores but I love them.
Do you respect them?
Less every day.
What do they do?
My dad is an ad executive and my mom mostly stays home and buys a lot of unnecessary things from the Megamall.
Do you own any Old World items?
I do, yes.
What are they?
I own an unbreakable comb that my grandpa gave me and a copy of Kent Van Gough's Kick the Boot.
How did Mr. Van Gough's book find its way to you?
It was left under my ergo chair in Brief Lit.
Have you read it?
Three times.
What is your opinion of the book?
I think it's the most important thing I've ever read.

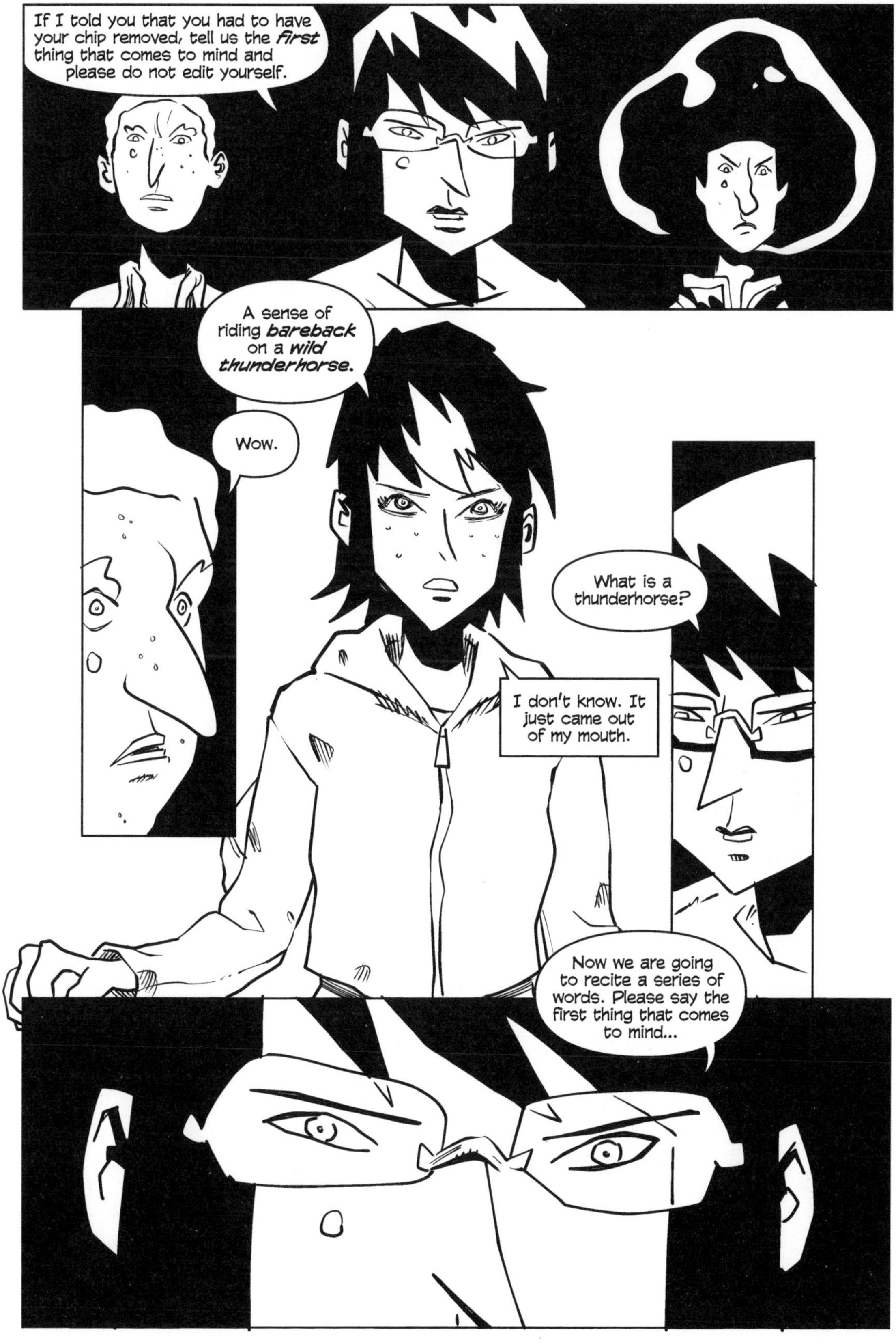
If I told you that you had to have your chip removed, tell us the *first* thing that comes to mind and please do not edit yourself.
A sense of riding *bareback* on a *wild thunderhorse.*
Wow.
What is a thunderhorse?
I don't know. It just came out of my mouth.
Now we are going to recite a series of words. Please say the first thing that comes to mind...

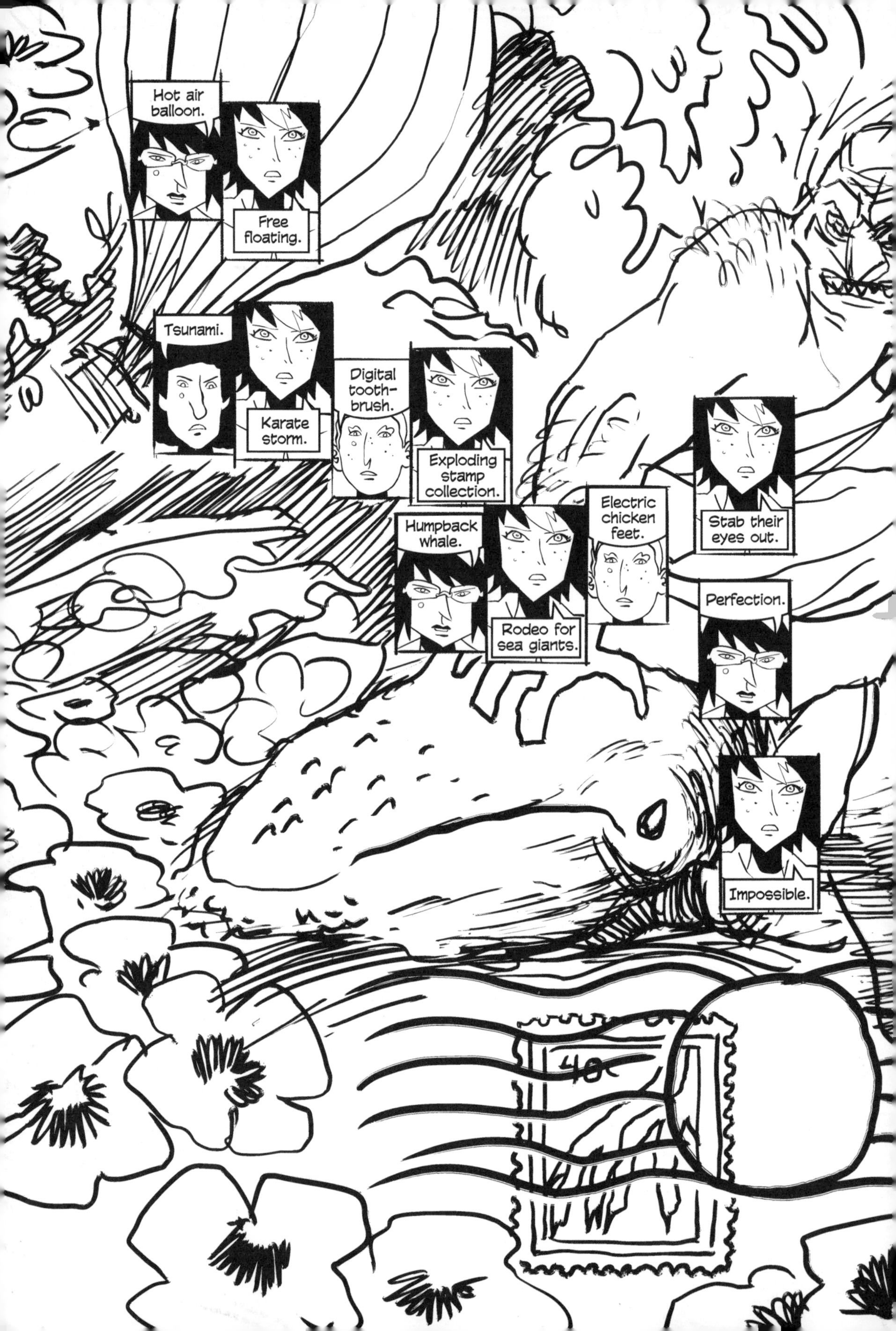
Hot air balloon.
Free floating.
Tsunami.
Karate storm.
Digital tooth-brush.
Exploding stamp collection.
Humpback whale.
Rodeo for sea giants.
Electric chicken feet.
Stab their eyes out.
Perfection.
Impossible.
40

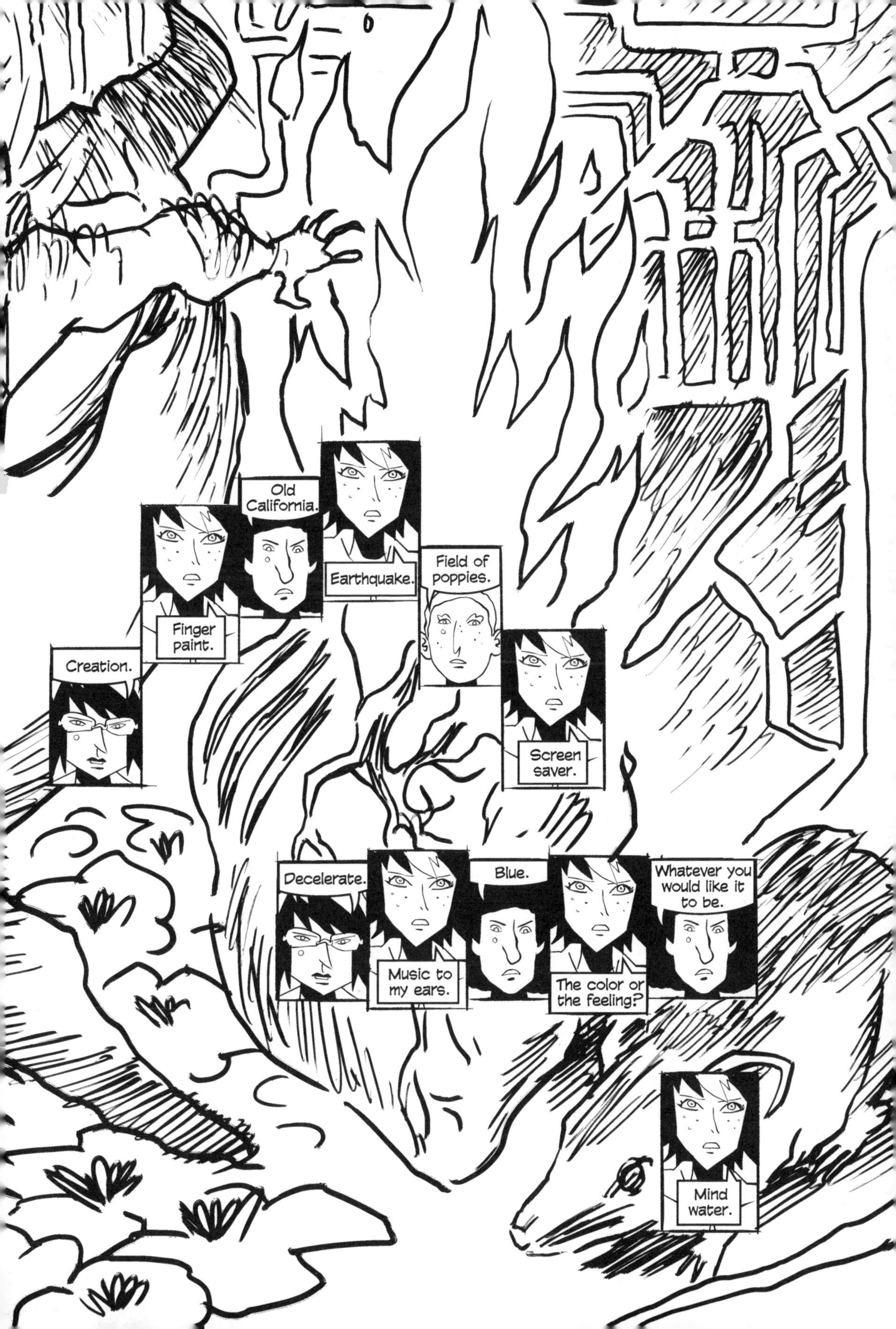
Creation.
Finger paint.
Old California.
Earthquake.
Field of poppies.
Screen saver.
Decelerate.
Music to my ears.
Blue.
The color or the feeling?
Whatever you would like it to be.
Mind water.

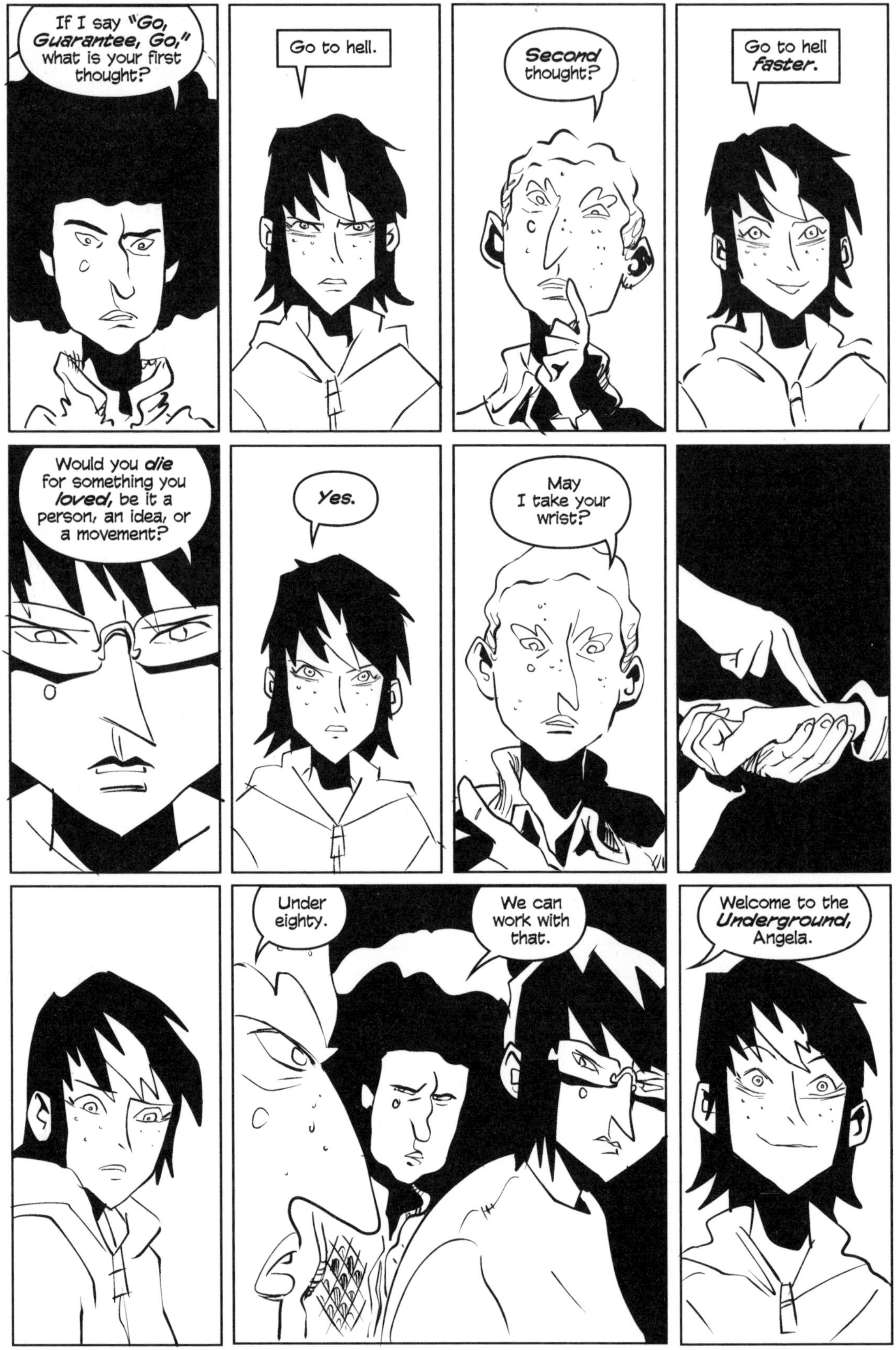
If I say "*Go, Guarantee, Go,*" what is your first thought?
Go to hell.
*Second* thought?
Go to hell *faster*.
Would you *die* for something you *loved,* be it a person, an idea, or a movement?
*Yes.*
May I take your wrist?
Under eighty.
We can work with that.
Welcome to the *Underground,* Angela.

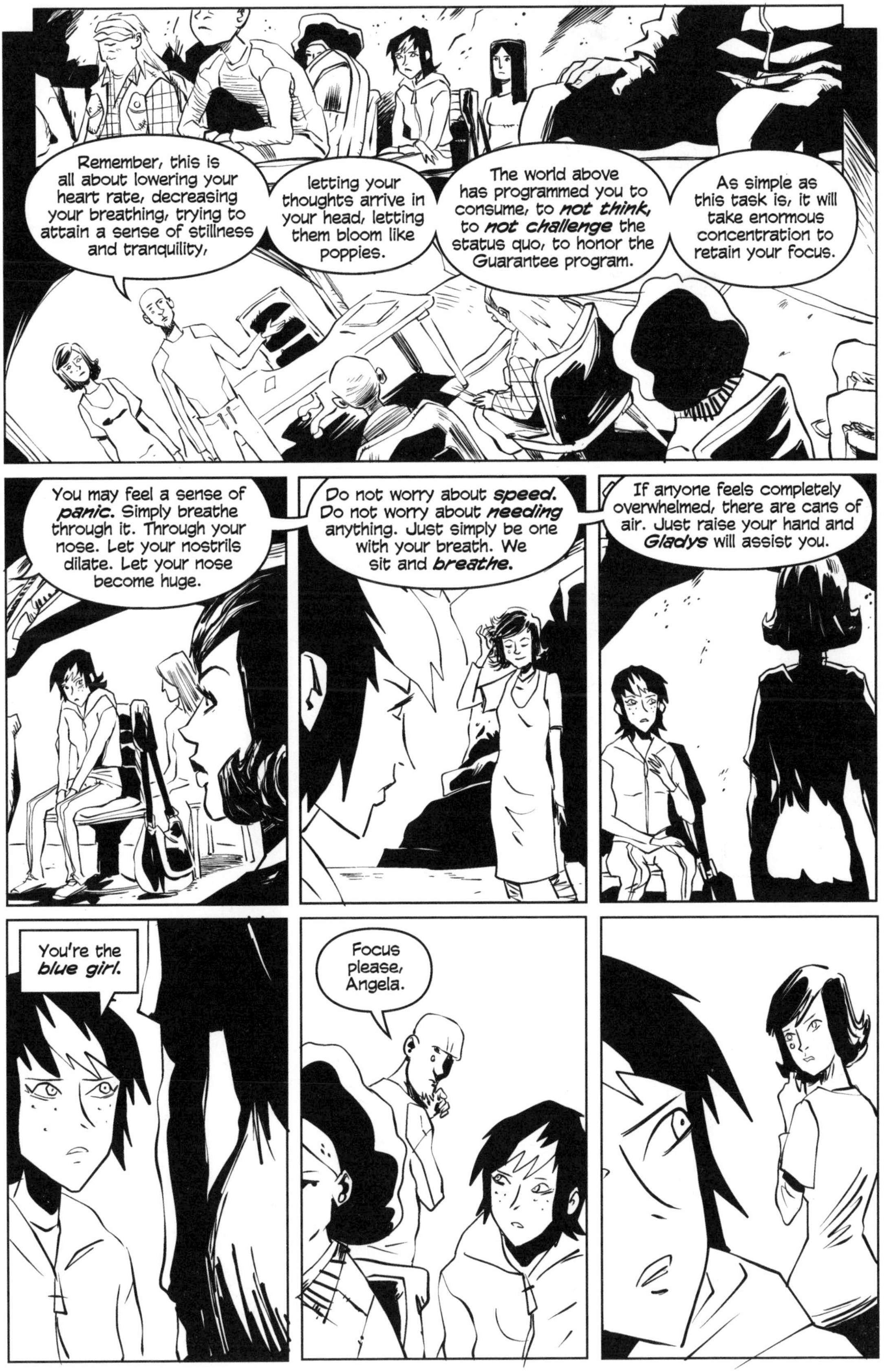
Remember, this is all about lowering your heart rate, decreasing your breathing, trying to attain a sense of stillness and tranquility,
letting your thoughts arrive in your head, letting them bloom like poppies.
The world above has programmed you to consume, to *not think,* to *not challenge* the status quo, to honor the Guarantee program.
As simple as this task is, it will take enormous concentration to retain your focus.
You may feel a sense of *panic.* Simply breathe through it. Through your nose. Let your nostrils dilate. Let your nose become huge.
Do not worry about *speed.* Do not worry about *needing* anything. Just simply be one with your breath. We sit and *breathe.*
If anyone feels completely overwhelmed, there are cans of air. Just raise your hand and *Gladys* will assist you.
You're the *blue girl.*
Focus please, Angela.

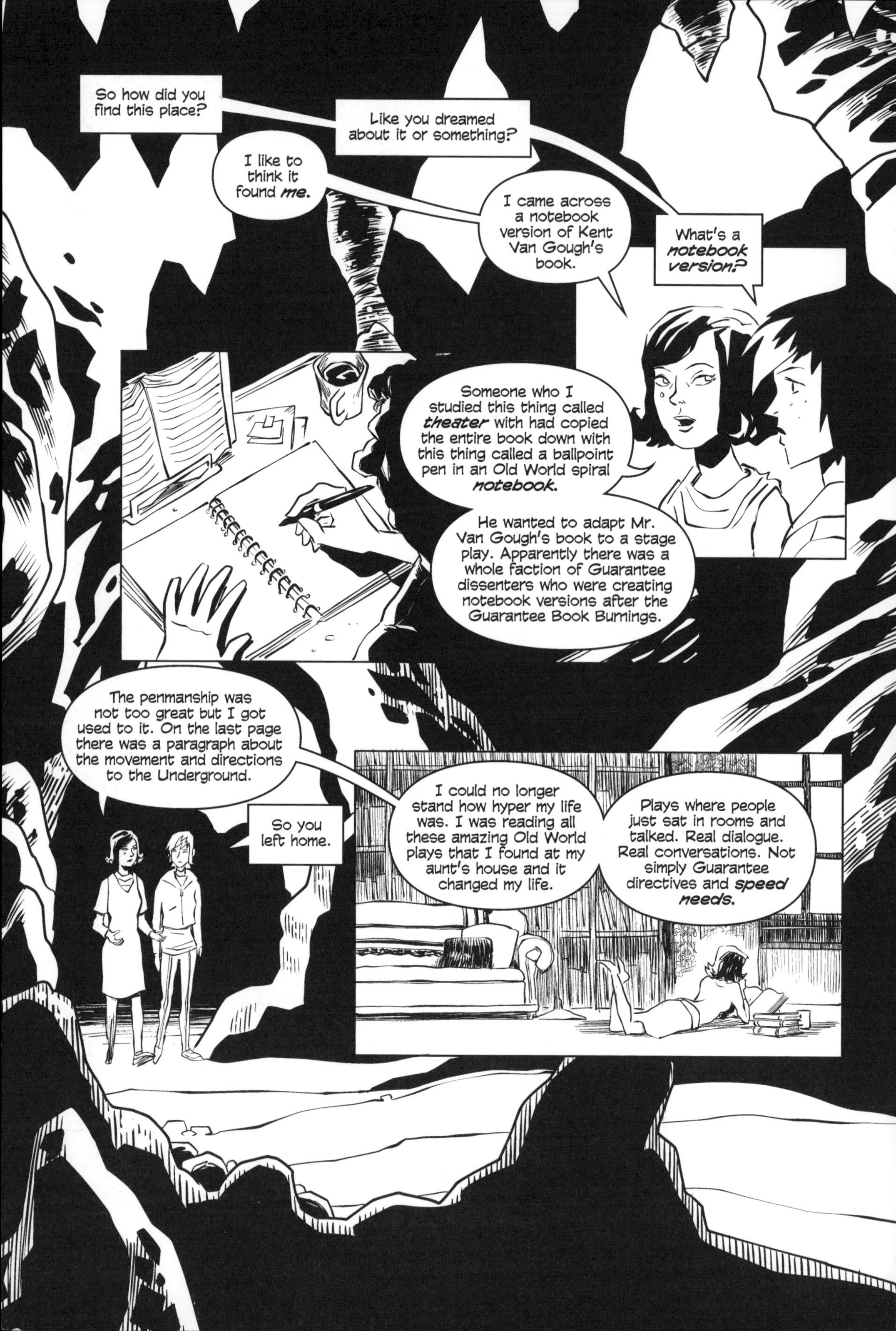

So how did you find this place?
Like you dreamed about it or something?
I like to think it found *me.*
I came across a notebook version of Kent Van Gough's book.
What's a *notebook version?*
Someone who I studied this thing called *theater* with had copied the entire book down with this thing called a ballpoint pen in an Old World spiral *notebook.*
He wanted to adapt Mr. Van Gough's book to a stage play. Apparently there was a whole faction of Guarantee dissenters who were creating notebook versions after the Guarantee Book Burnings.
The penmanship was not too great but I got used to it. On the last page there was a paragraph about the movement and directions to the Underground.
So you left home.
I could no longer stand how hyper my life was. I was reading all these amazing Old World plays that I found at my aunt's house and it changed my life.
Plays where people just sat in rooms and talked. Real dialogue. Real conversations. Not simply Guarantee directives and *speed needs.*

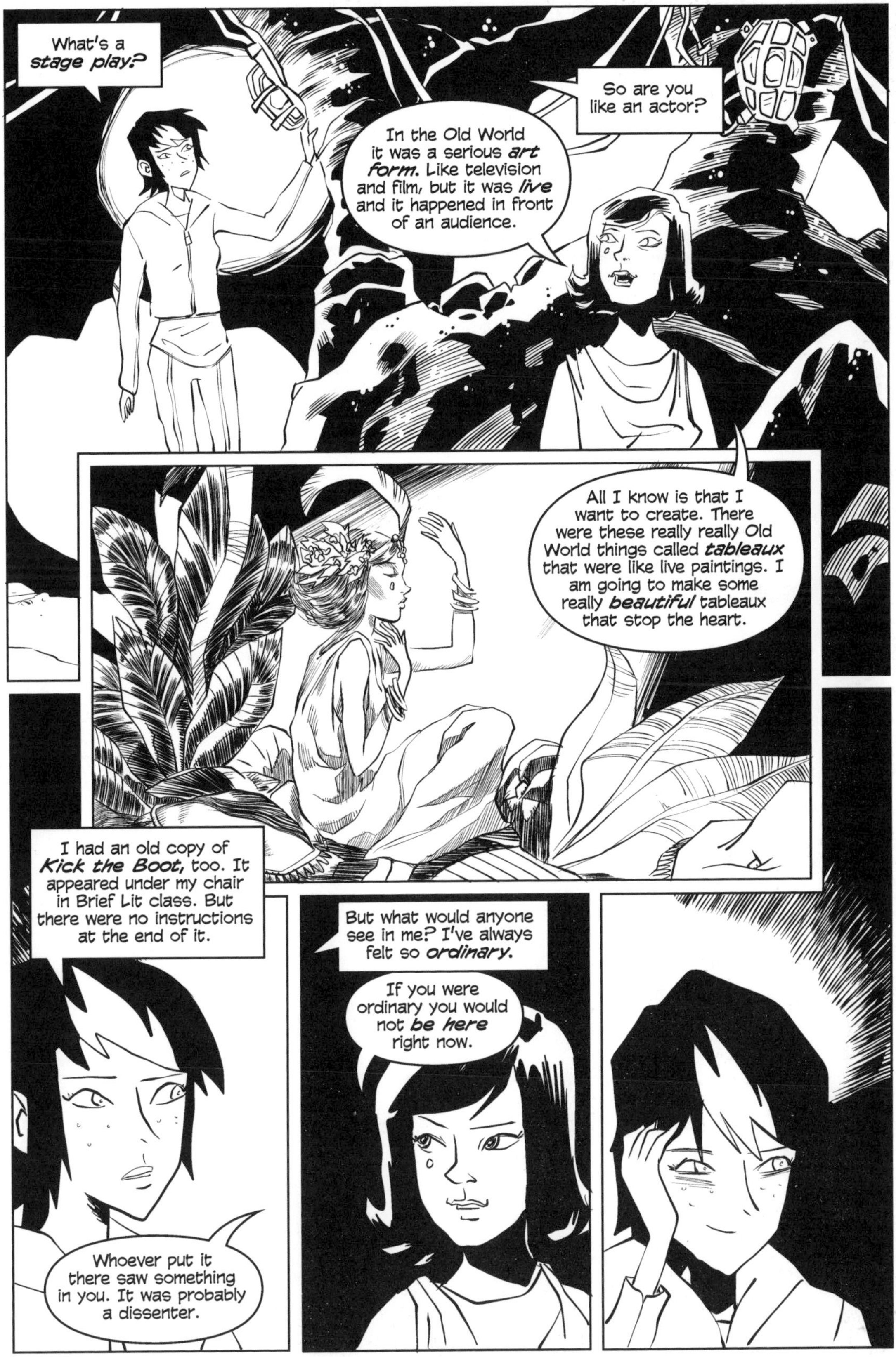
What's a *stage play?*
In the Old World it was a serious *art form.* Like television and film, but it was *live* and it happened in front of an audience.
So are you like an actor?
All I know is that I want to create. There were these really really Old World things called *tableaux* that were like live paintings. I am going to make some really *beautiful* tableaux that stop the heart.
I had an old copy of *Kick the Boot,* too. It appeared under my chair in Brief Lit class. But there were no instructions at the end of it.
Whoever put it there saw something in you. It was probably a dissenter.
But what would anyone see in me? I've always felt so *ordinary.*
If you were ordinary you would not *be here* right now.

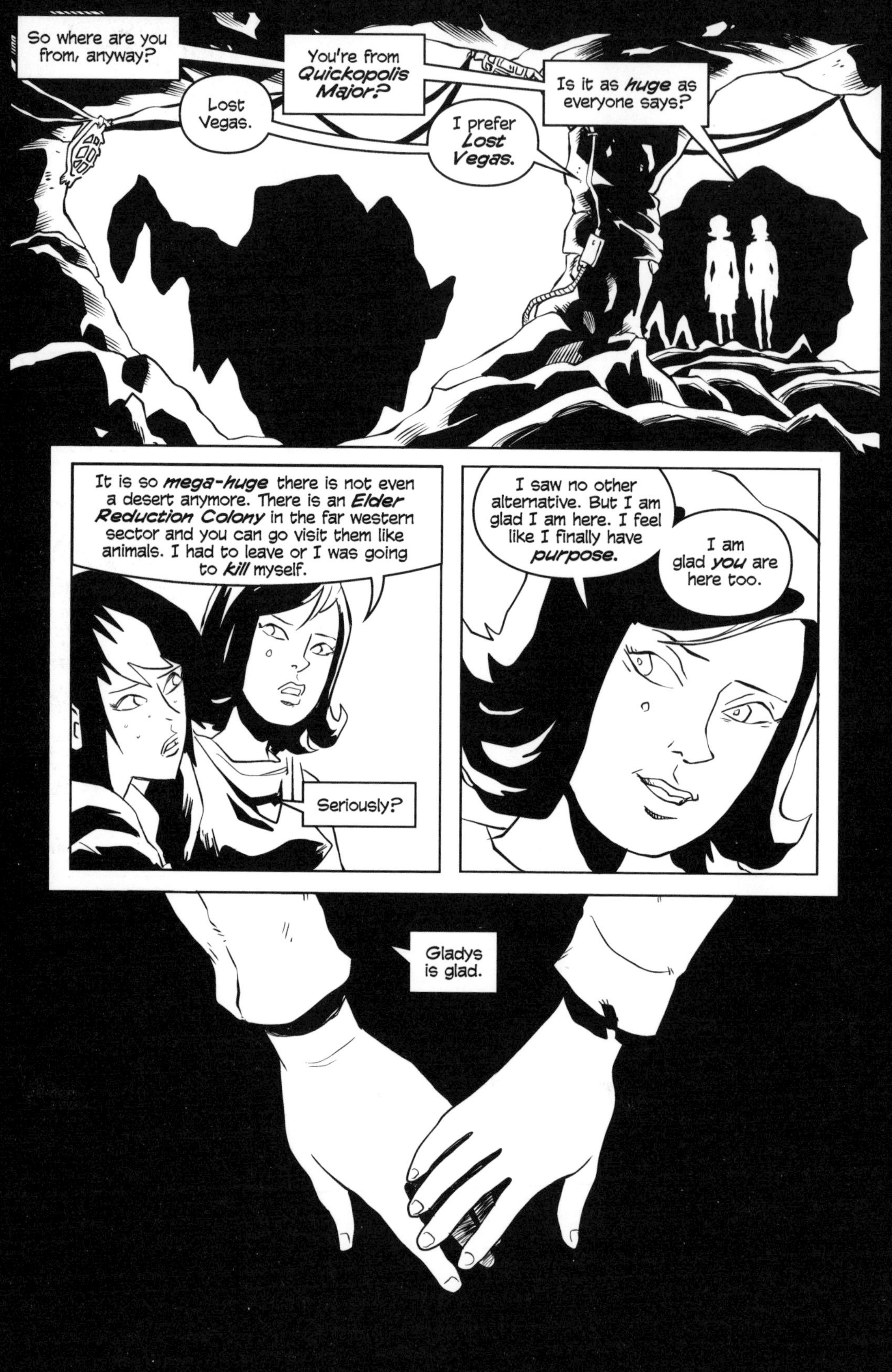

So where are you from, anyway?
Lost Vegas.
You're from Quickopolis Major?
I prefer Lost Vegas.
Is it as huge as everyone says?
It is so mega-huge there is not even a desert anymore. There is an Elder Reduction Colony in the far western sector and you can go visit them like animals. I had to leave or I was going to kill myself.
Seriously?
I saw no other alternative. But I am glad I am here. I feel like I finally have purpose.
I am glad you are here too.
Gladys is glad.

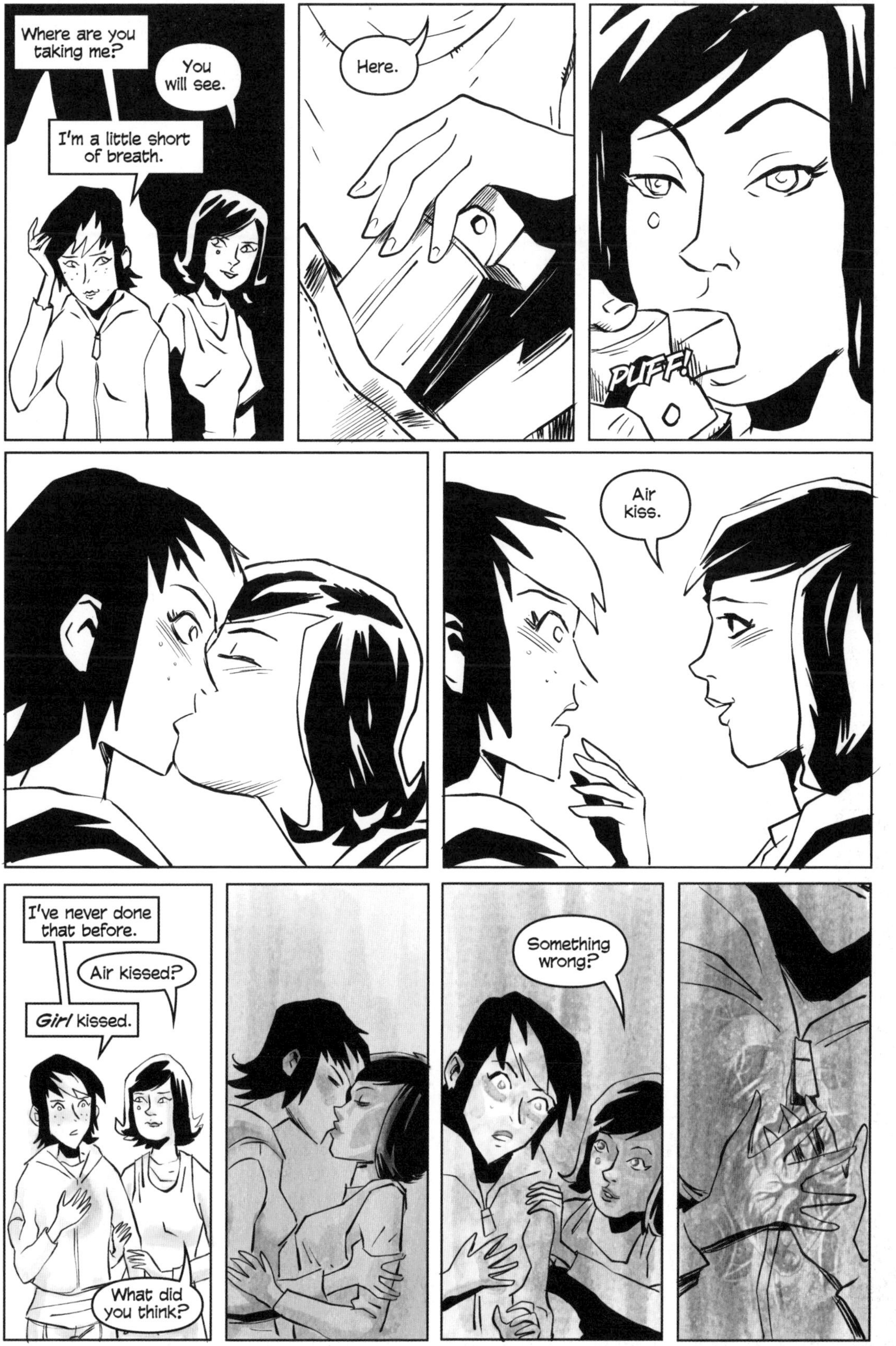
Where are you taking me?
You will see.
I'm a little short of breath.
Here.
PUFF!
Air kiss.
I've never done that before.
Air kissed?
*Girl* kissed.
What did you think?
Something wrong?

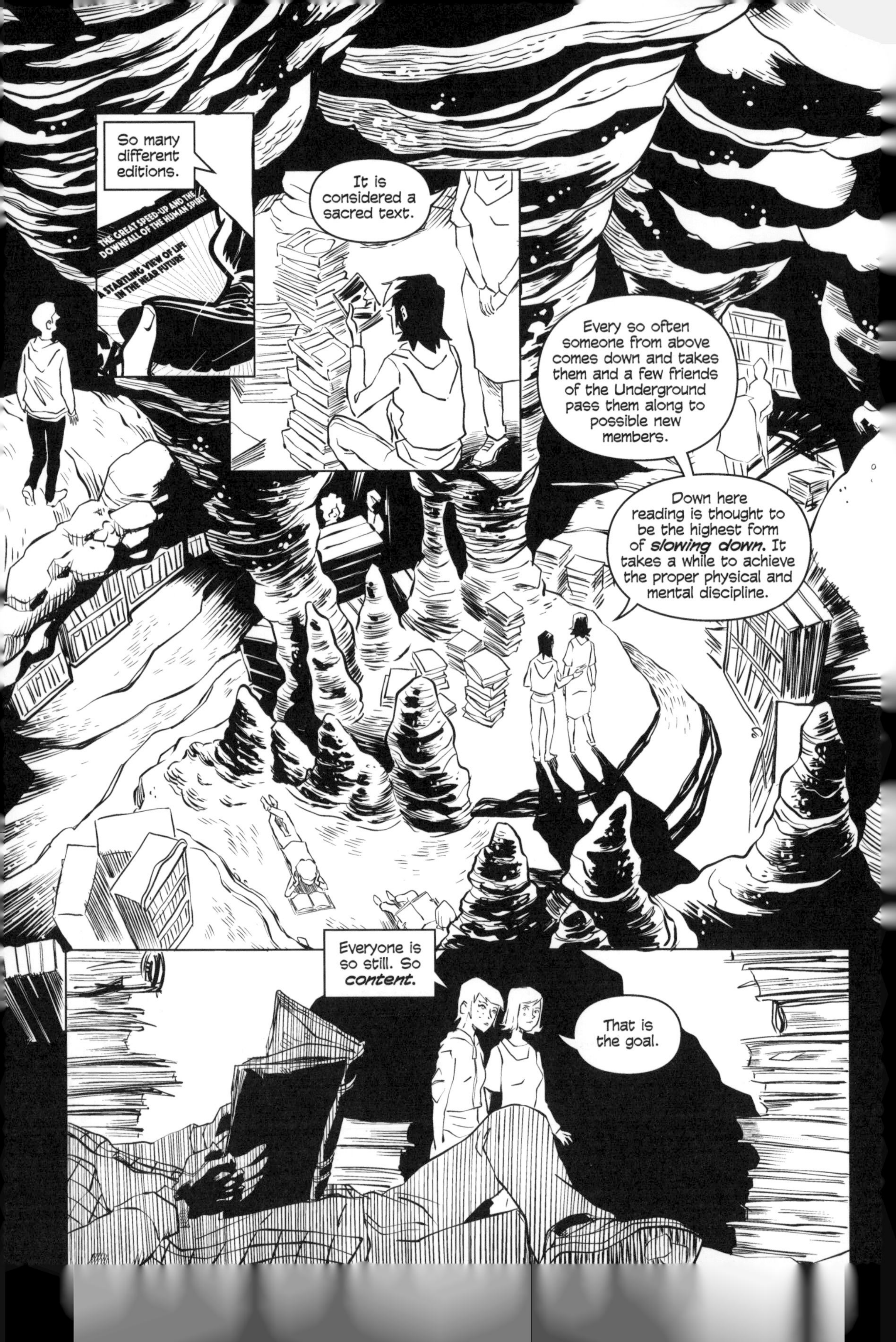

So many different editions.
THE GREAT SPEED-UP AND THE DOWNFALL OF THE HUMAN SPIRIT
A STARTLING VIEW OF LIFE IN THE NEAR FUTURE
It is considered a sacred text.
Every so often someone from above comes down and takes them and a few friends of the Underground pass them along to possible new members.
Down here reading is thought to be the highest form of *slowing down*. It takes a while to achieve the proper physical and mental discipline.
Everyone is so still. So *content*.
That is the goal.

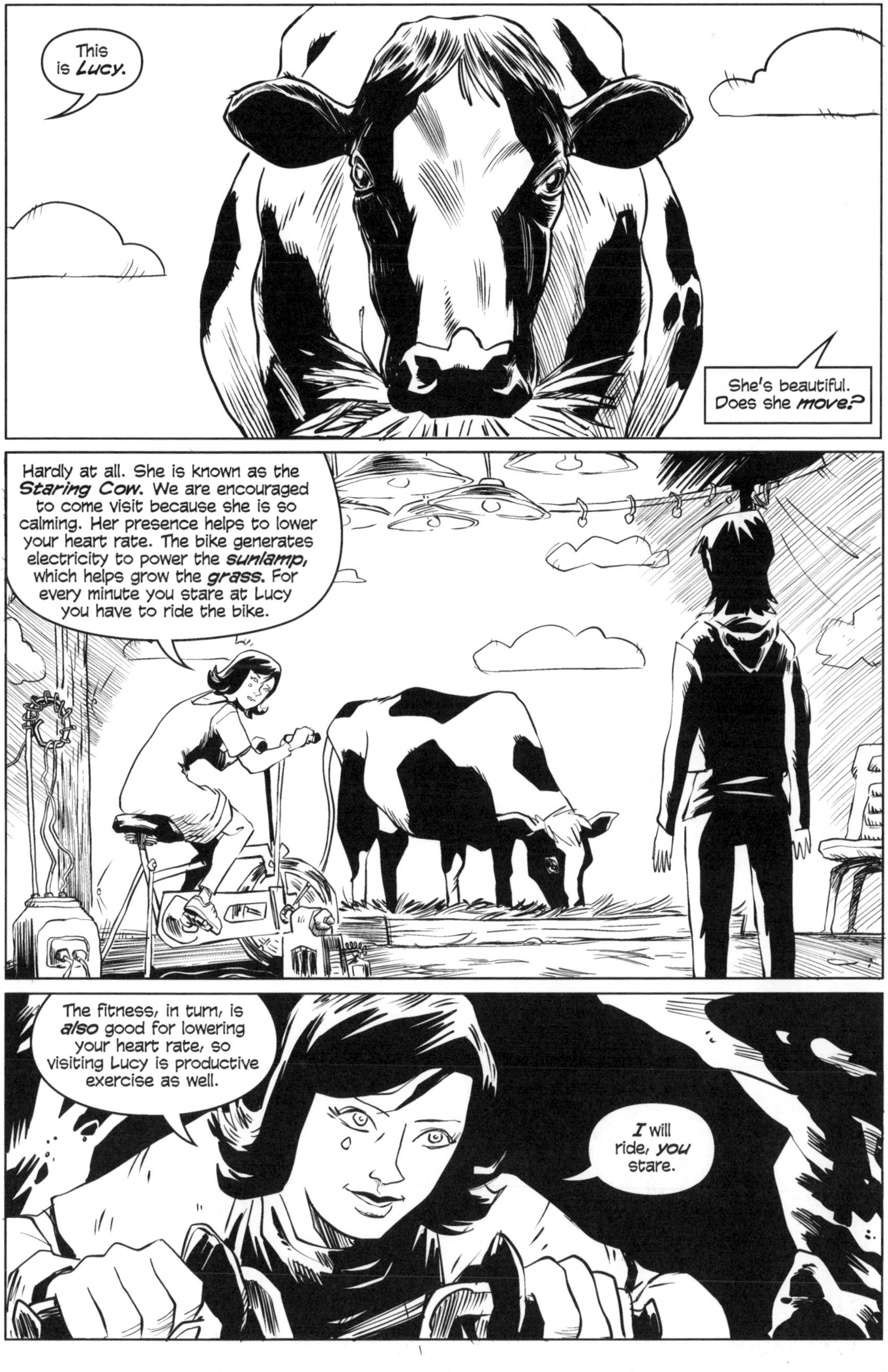
This is *Lucy.*
She's beautiful. Does she *move?*
Hardly at all. She is known as the *Staring Cow.* We are encouraged to come visit because she is so calming. Her presence helps to lower your heart rate. The bike generates electricity to power the *sunlamp,* which helps grow the *grass.* For every minute you stare at Lucy you have to ride the bike.
The fitness, in turn, is *also* good for lowering your heart rate, so visiting Lucy is productive exercise as well.
*I* will ride, *you* stare.

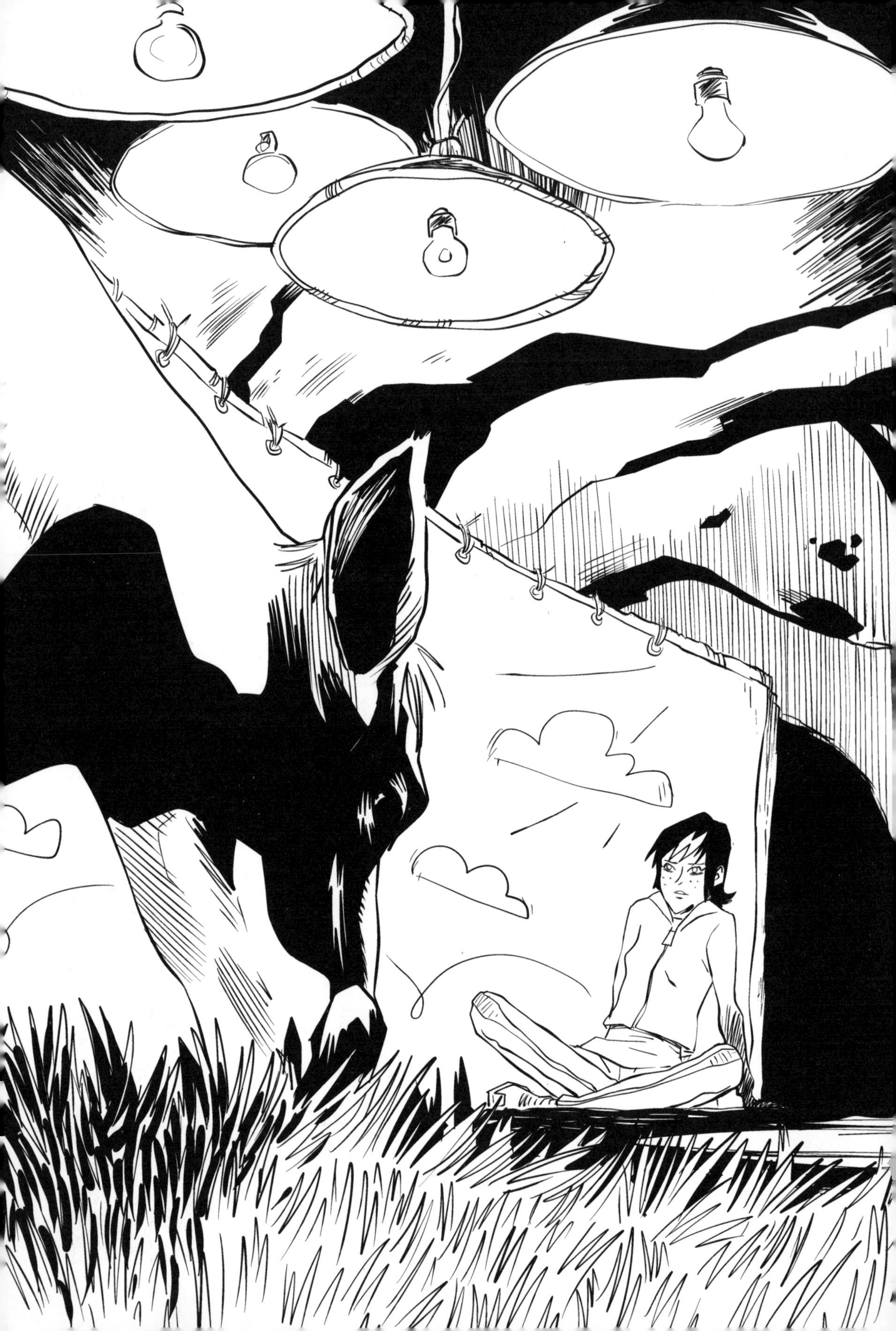

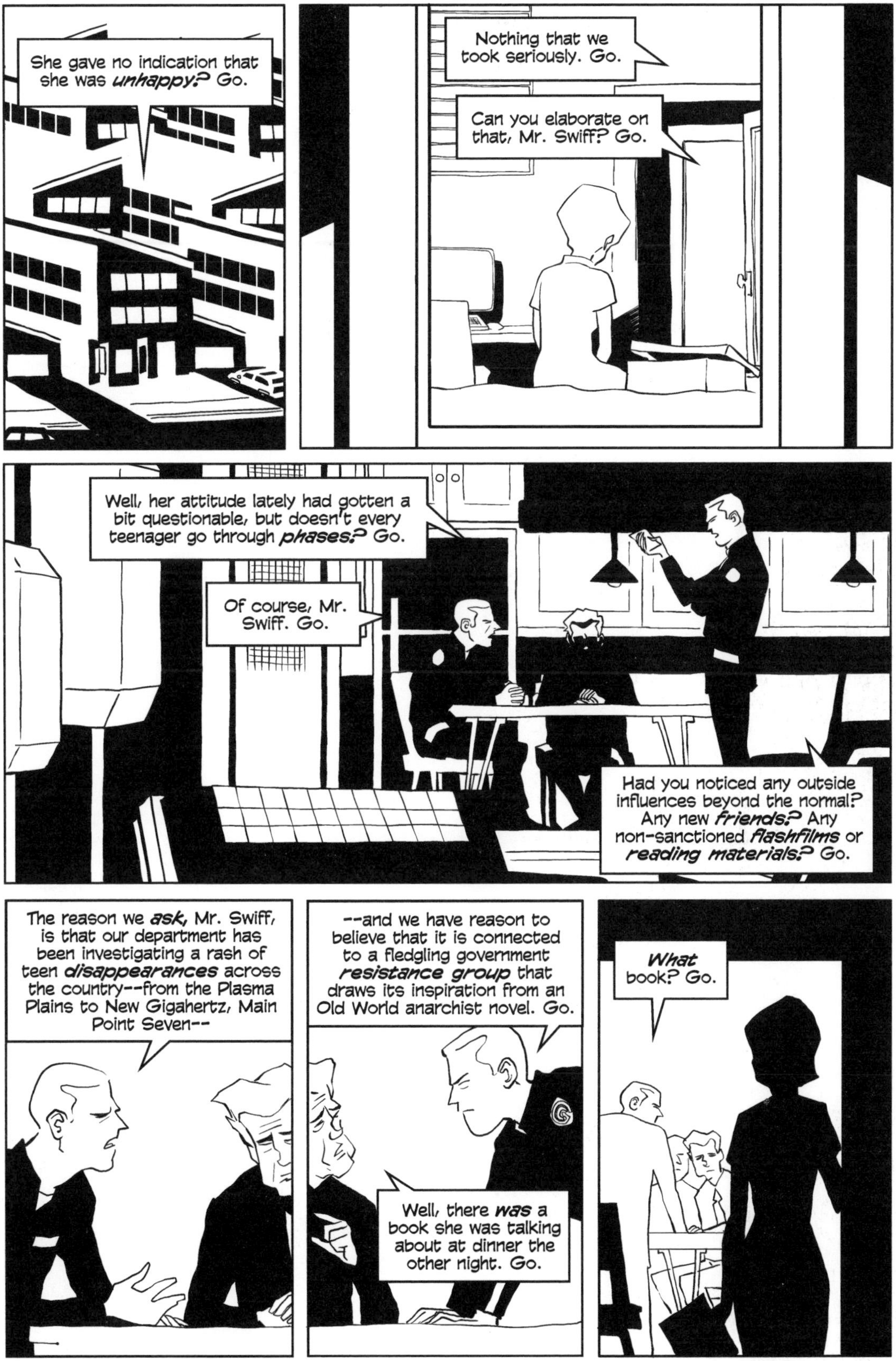
She gave no indication that she was *unhappy?* Go.
Nothing that we took seriously. Go.
Can you elaborate on that, Mr. Swiff? Go.
Well, her attitude lately had gotten a bit questionable, but doesn't every teenager go through *phases?* Go.
Of course, Mr. Swiff. Go.
Had you noticed any outside influences beyond the normal? Any new *friends?* Any non-sanctioned *flashfilms* or *reading materials?* Go.
The reason we *ask,* Mr. Swiff, is that our department has been investigating a rash of teen *disappearances* across the country--from the Plasma Plains to New Gigahertz, Main Point Seven--
--and we have reason to believe that it is connected to a fledgling government *resistance group* that draws its inspiration from an Old World anarchist novel. Go.
Well, there *was* a book she was talking about at dinner the other night. Go.
*What* book? Go.

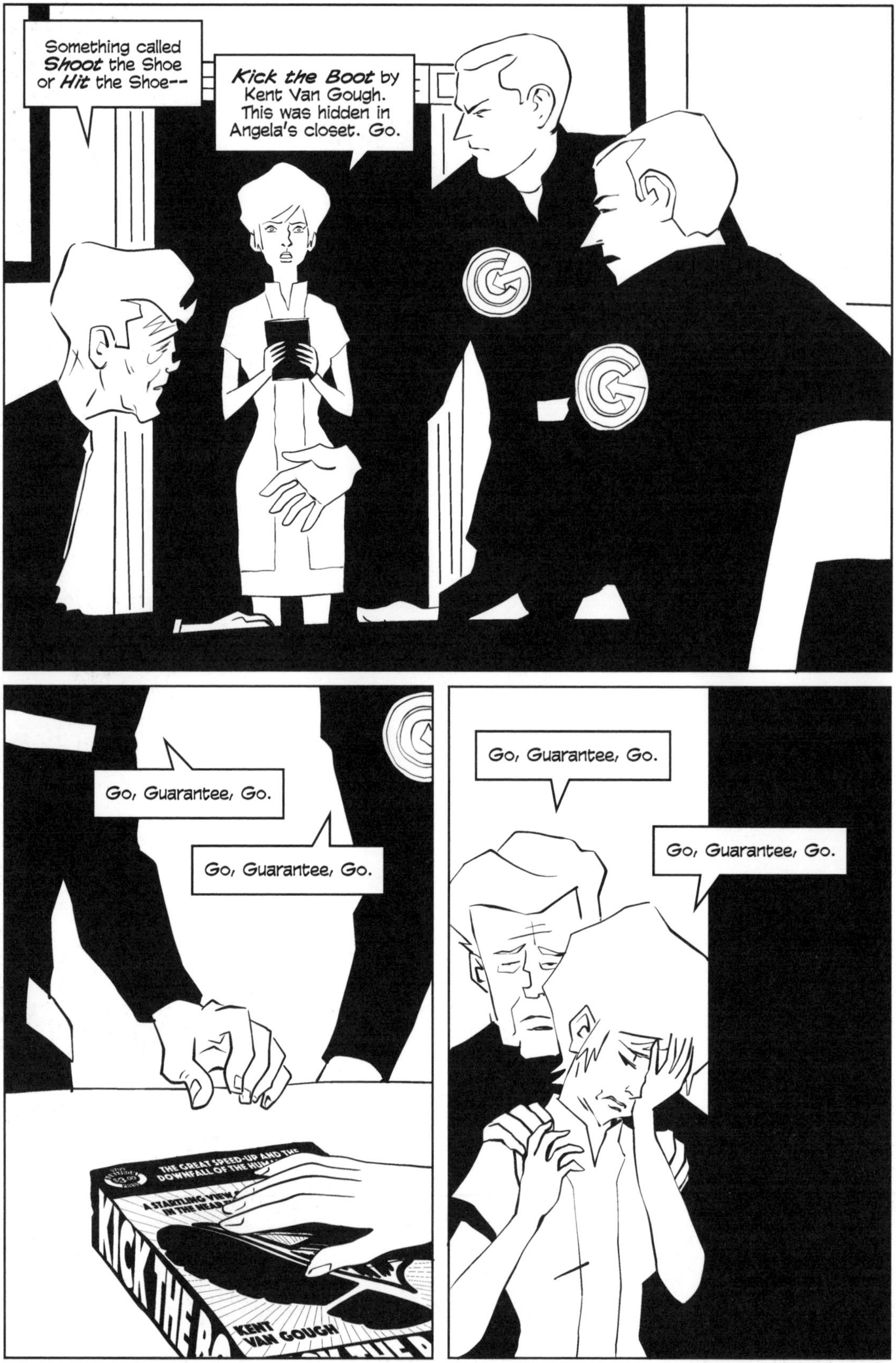
Something called *Shoot* the Shoe or *Hit* the Shoe--
*Kick the Boot* by Kent Van Gough. This was hidden in Angela's closet. Go.
Go, Guarantee, Go.
Go, Guarantee, Go.
THE GREAT SPEED-UP AND THE
KENT VAN GOUGH
Go, Guarantee, Go.
Go, Guarantee, Go.

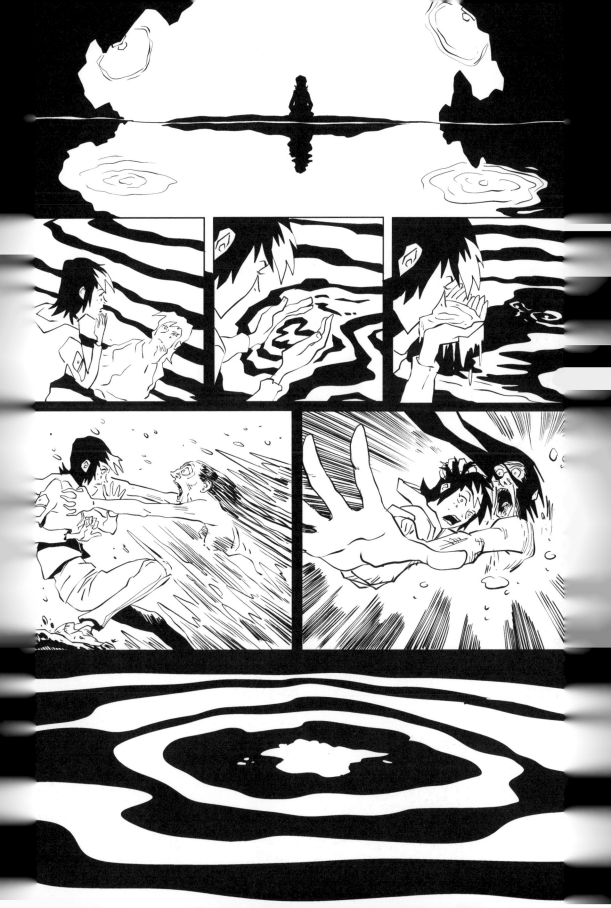

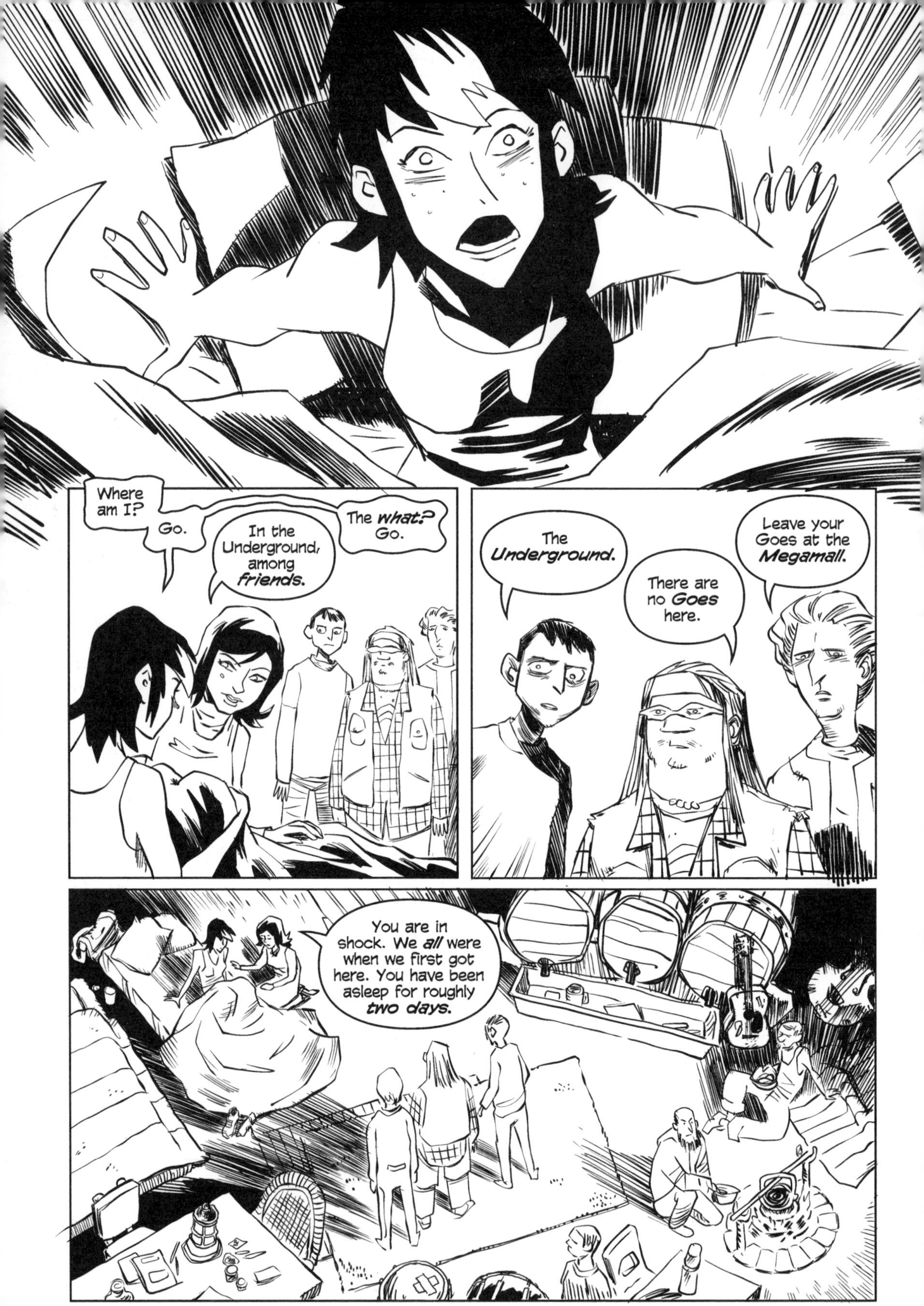

Where am I?
Go.
In the Underground, among *friends*.
The *what?* Go.
The *Underground.*
There are no *Goes* here.
Leave your Goes at the *Megamall.*
You are in shock. We *all* were when we first got here. You have been asleep for roughly *two days.*

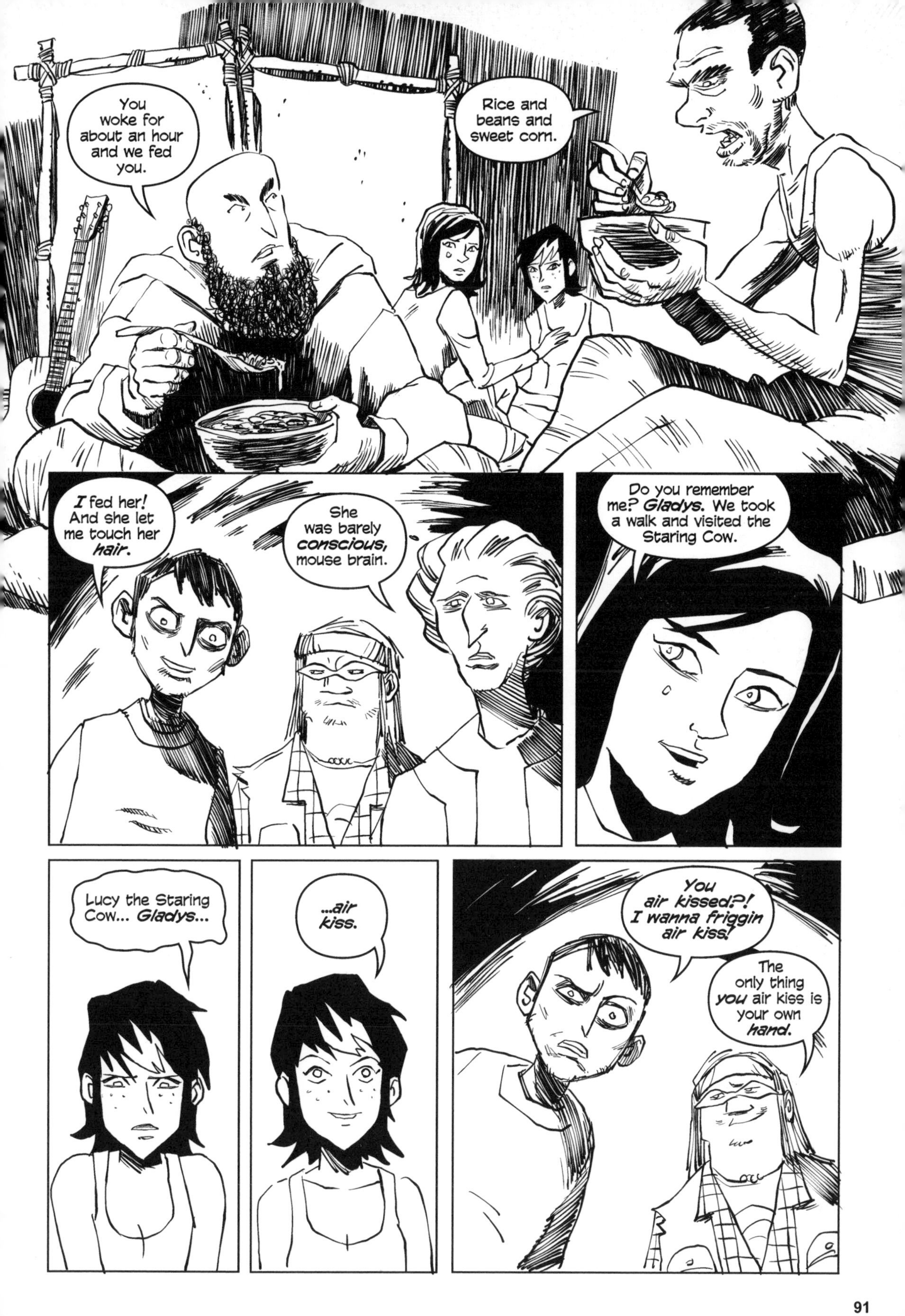
You woke for about an hour and we fed you.
Rice and beans and sweet corn.
*I* fed her! And she let me touch her *hair*.
She was barely *conscious*, mouse brain.
Do you remember me? *Gladys.* We took a walk and visited the Staring Cow.
Lucy the Staring Cow... *Gladys...*
...*air kiss.*
*You air kissed?! I wanna friggin air kiss!*
The only thing *you* air kiss is your own *hand.*

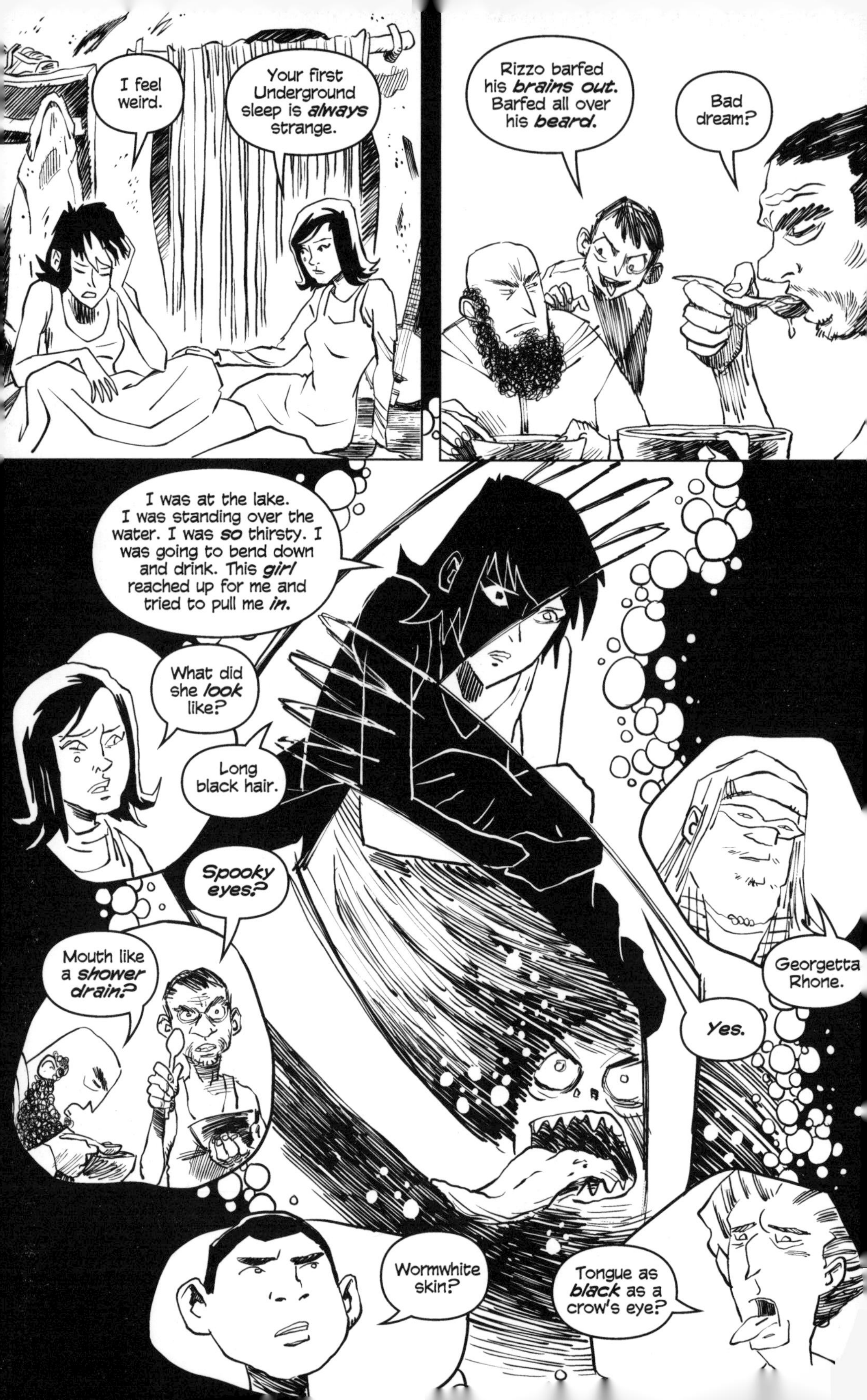
I feel weird.
Your first Underground sleep is *always* strange.
Rizzo barfed his *brains out.* Barfed all over his *beard.*
Bad dream?
I was at the lake. I was standing over the water. I was *so* thirsty. I was going to bend down and drink. This *girl* reached up for me and tried to pull me *in.*
What did she *look* like?
Long black hair.
*Spooky eyes?*
Mouth like a *shower drain?*
Georgetta Rhone.
*Yes.*
Wormwhite skin?
Tongue as *black* as a crow's eye?

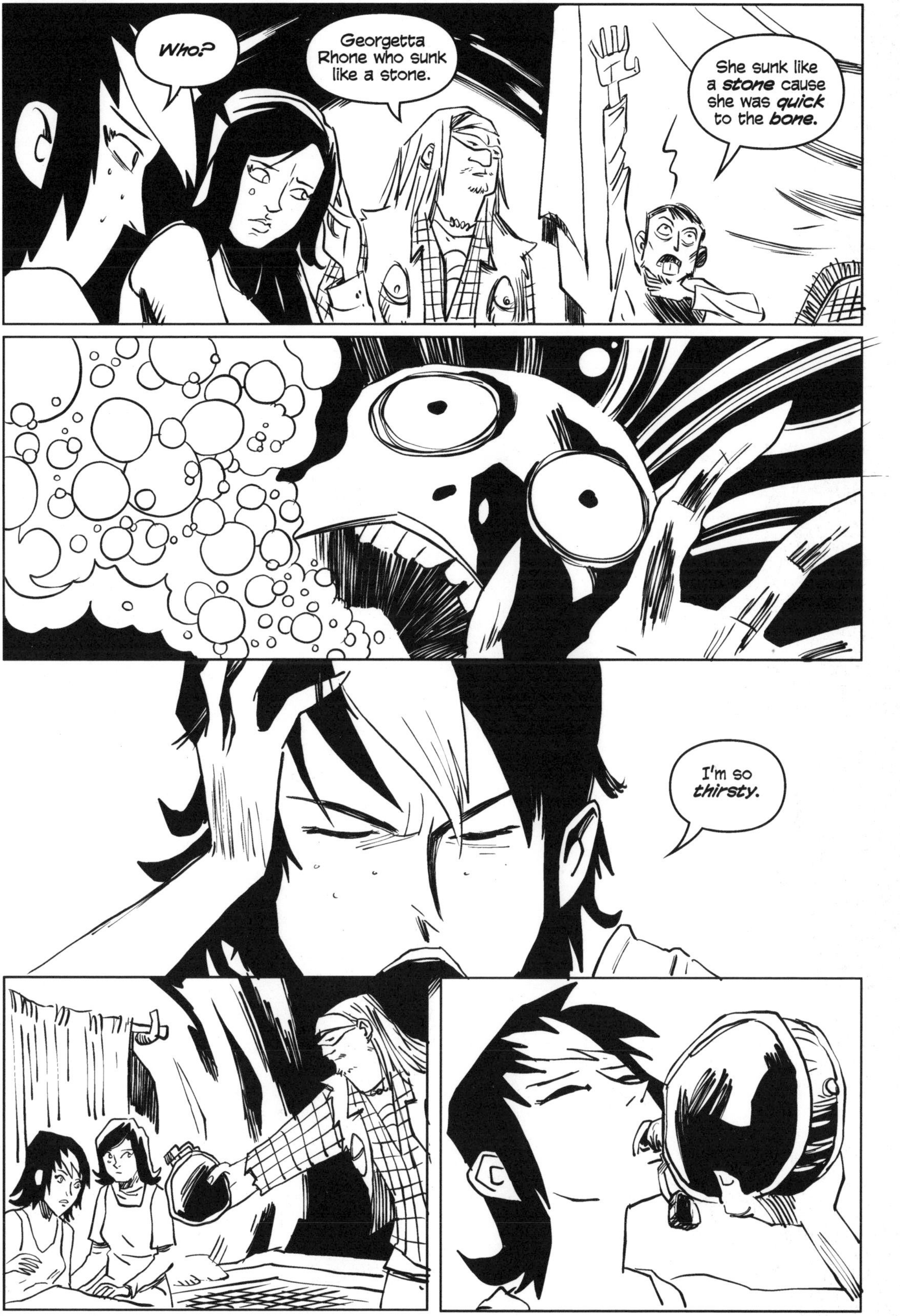
Who?
Georgetta Rhone who sunk like a stone.
She sunk like a stone cause she was quick to the bone.
I'm so thirsty.

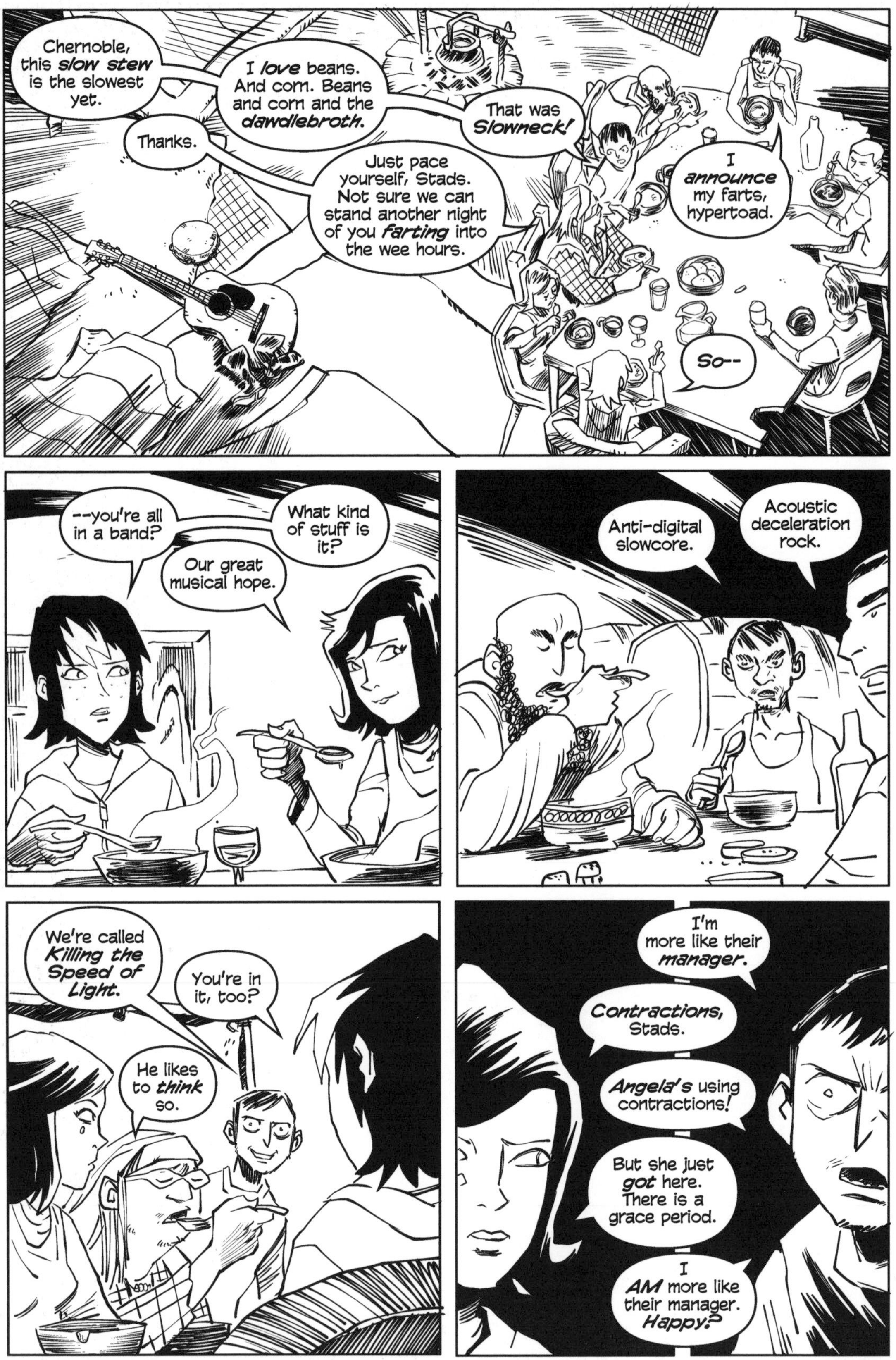
Chernoble, this slow stew is the slowest yet.
Thanks.
I love beans. And corn. Beans and corn and the dawdlebroth.
Just pace yourself, Stads. Not sure we can stand another night of you farting into the wee hours.
That was Slowneck!
I announce my farts, hypertoad.
So--
--you're all in a band?
What kind of stuff is it?
Our great musical hope.
Anti-digital slowcore.
Acoustic deceleration rock.
We're called Killing the Speed of Light.
You're in it, too?
He likes to think so.
I'm more like their manager.
Contractions, Stads.
Angela's using contractions!
But she just got here. There is a grace period.
I AM more like their manager. Happy?

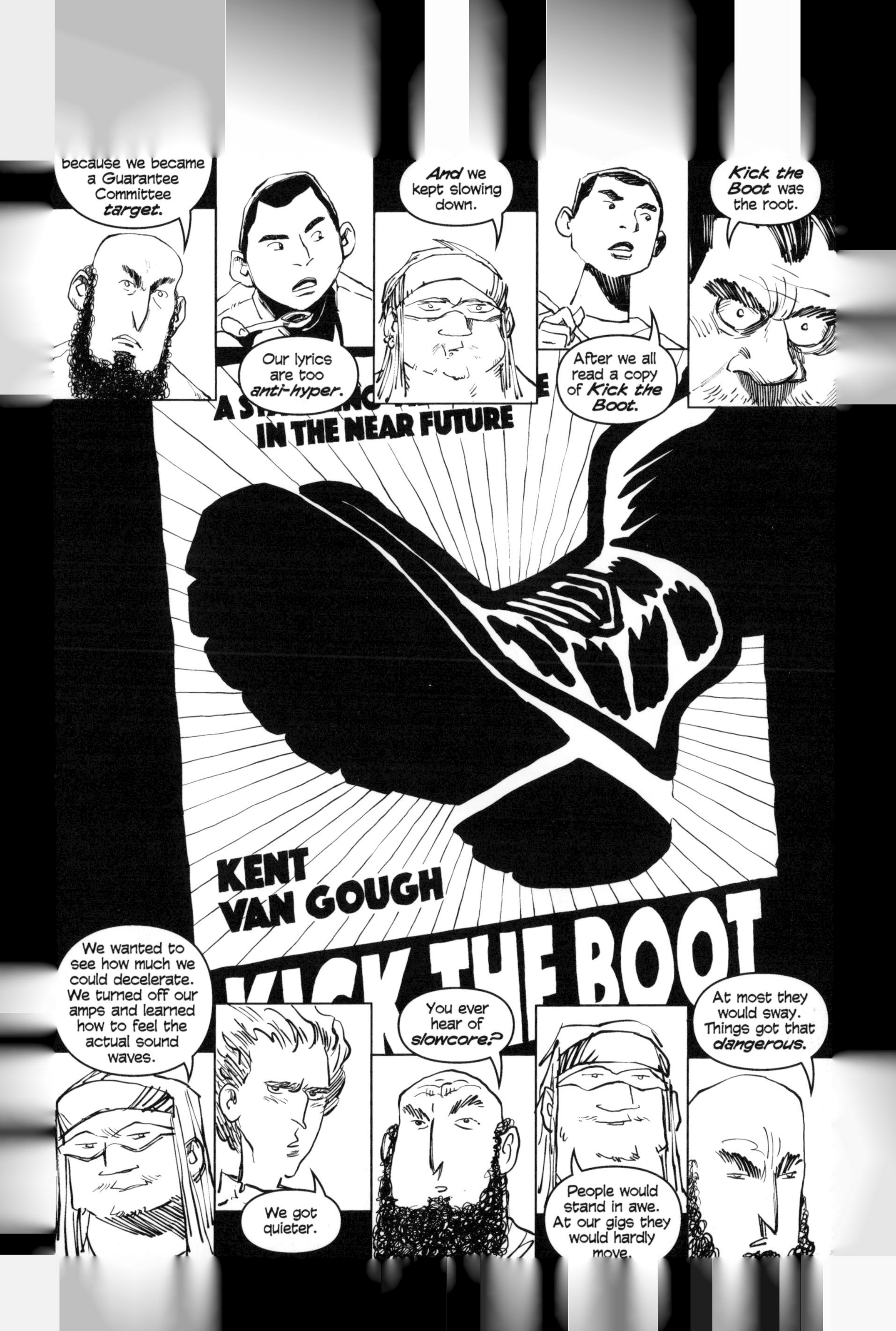

because we became a Guarantee Committee *target*.
Our lyrics are too *anti-hyper*.
*And* we kept slowing down.
After we all read a copy of *Kick the Boot*.
*Kick the Boot* was the root.
IN THE NEAR FUTURE
KENT VAN GOUGH
We wanted to see how much we could decelerate. We turned off our amps and learned how to feel the actual sound waves.
We got quieter.
You ever hear of *slowcore?*
People would stand in awe. At our gigs they would hardly move.
At most they would sway. Things got that *dangerous*.

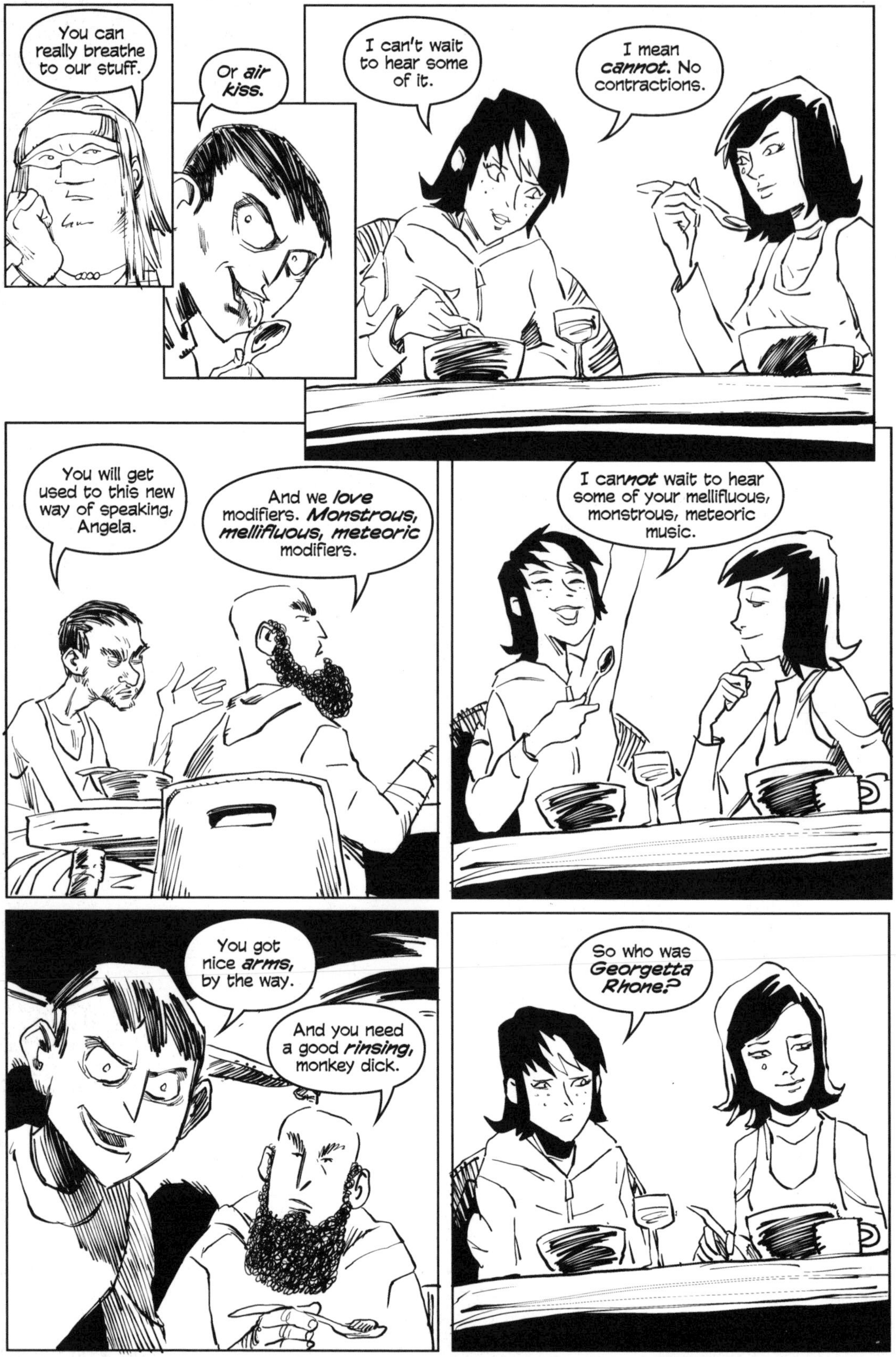
You can really breathe to our stuff.
Or *air kiss.*
I can't wait to hear some of it.
I mean *cannot.* No contractions.
You will get used to this new way of speaking, Angela.
And we *love* modifiers. *Monstrous, mellifluous, meteoric* modifiers.
I can*not* wait to hear some of your mellifluous, monstrous, meteoric music.
You got nice *arms,* by the way.
And you need a good *rinsing,* monkey dick.
So who was *Georgetta Rhone?*

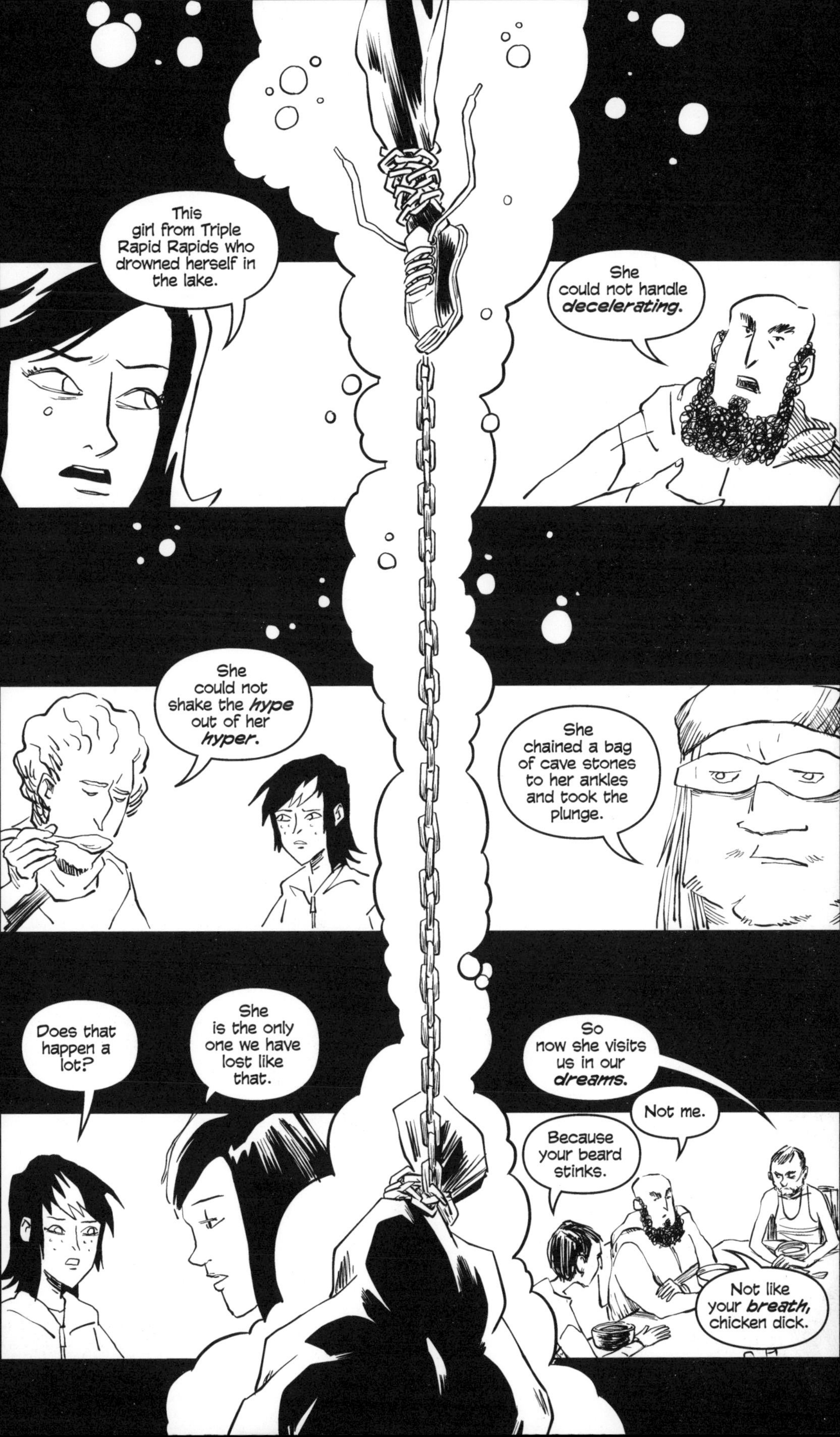

This girl from Triple Rapid Rapids who drowned herself in the lake.
She could not handle *decelerating*.
She could not shake the *hype* out of her *hyper*.
She chained a bag of cave stones to her ankles and took the plunge.
Does that happen a lot?
She is the only one we have lost like that.
So now she visits us in our *dreams*.
Not me.
Because your beard stinks.
Not like your *breath*, chicken dick.

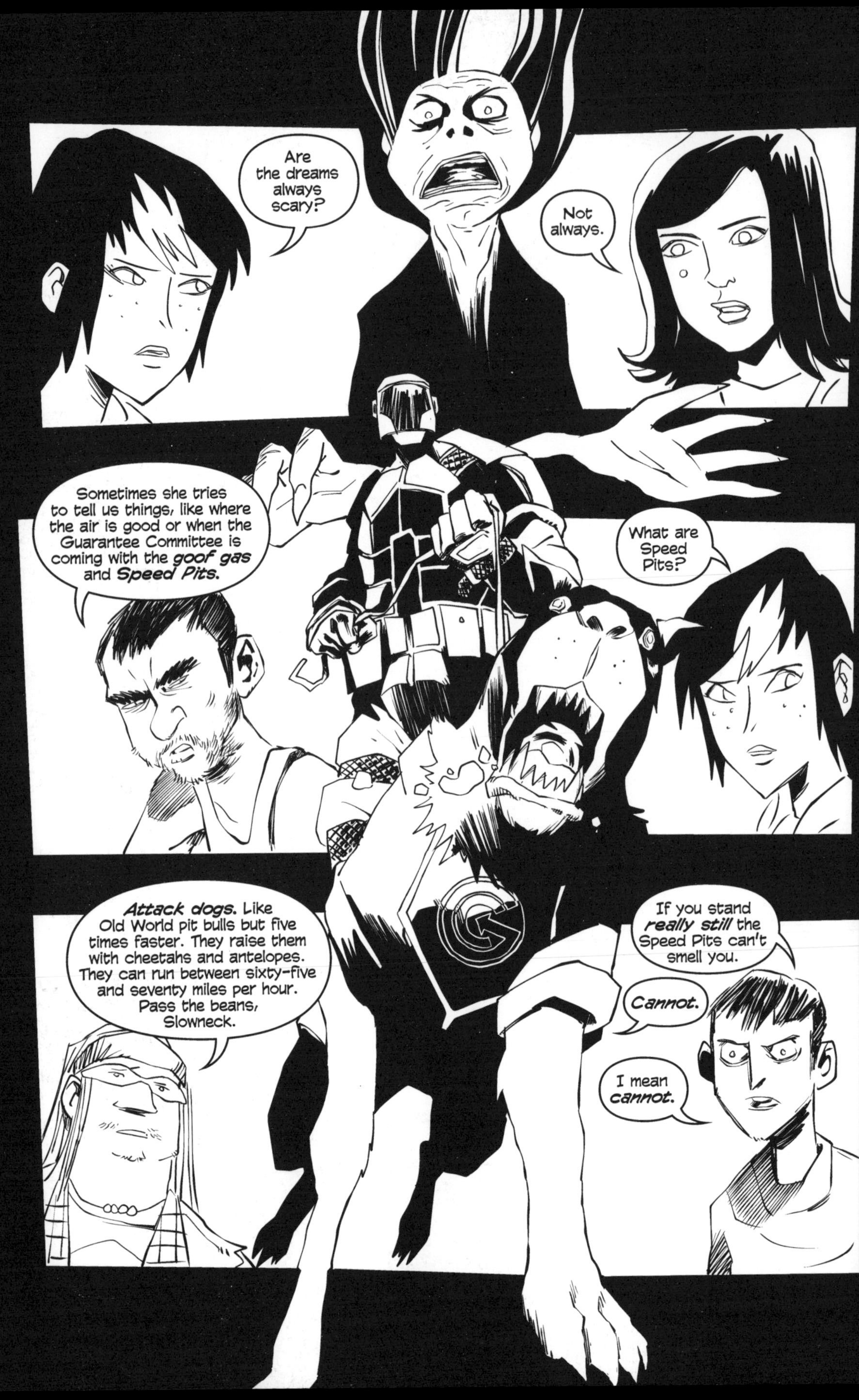

Are the dreams always scary?
Not always.
Sometimes she tries to tell us things, like where the air is good or when the Guarantee Committee is coming with the goof gas and Speed Pits.
What are Speed Pits?
Attack dogs. Like Old World pit bulls but five times faster. They raise them with cheetahs and antelopes. They can run between sixty-five and seventy miles per hour. Pass the beans, Slowneck.
If you stand really still the Speed Pits can't smell you.
Cannot.
I mean cannot.

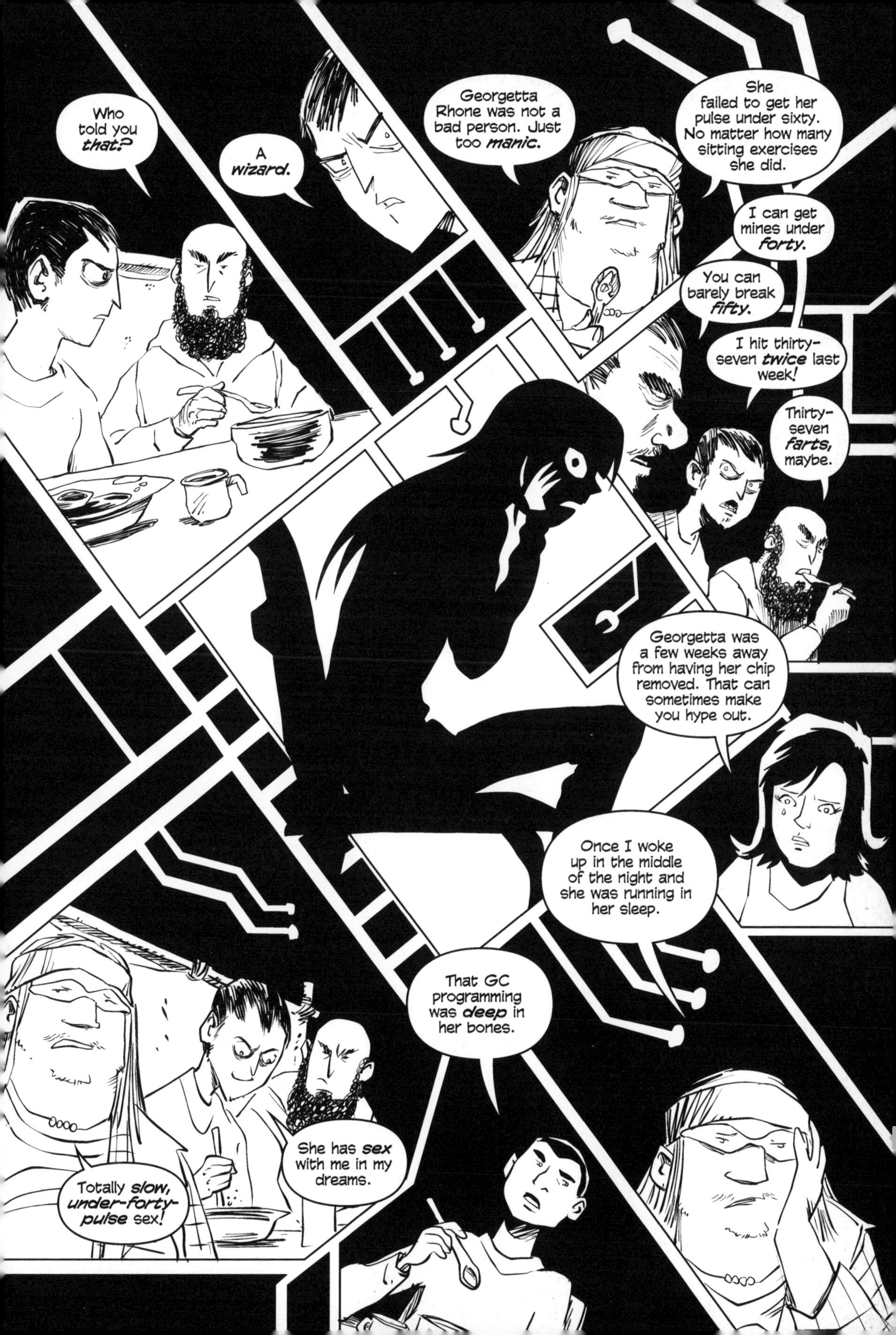

Who told you *that?*
A *wizard.*
Georgetta Rhone was not a bad person. Just too *manic.*
She failed to get her pulse under sixty. No matter how many sitting exercises she did.
I can get mines under *forty.*
You can barely break *fifty.*
I hit thirty-seven *twice* last week!
Thirty-seven *farts,* maybe.
Georgetta was a few weeks away from having her chip removed. That can sometimes make you hype out.
Once I woke up in the middle of the night and she was running in her sleep.
That GC programming was *deep* in her bones.
She has *sex* with me in my dreams.
Totally *slow, under-forty-pulse* sex!

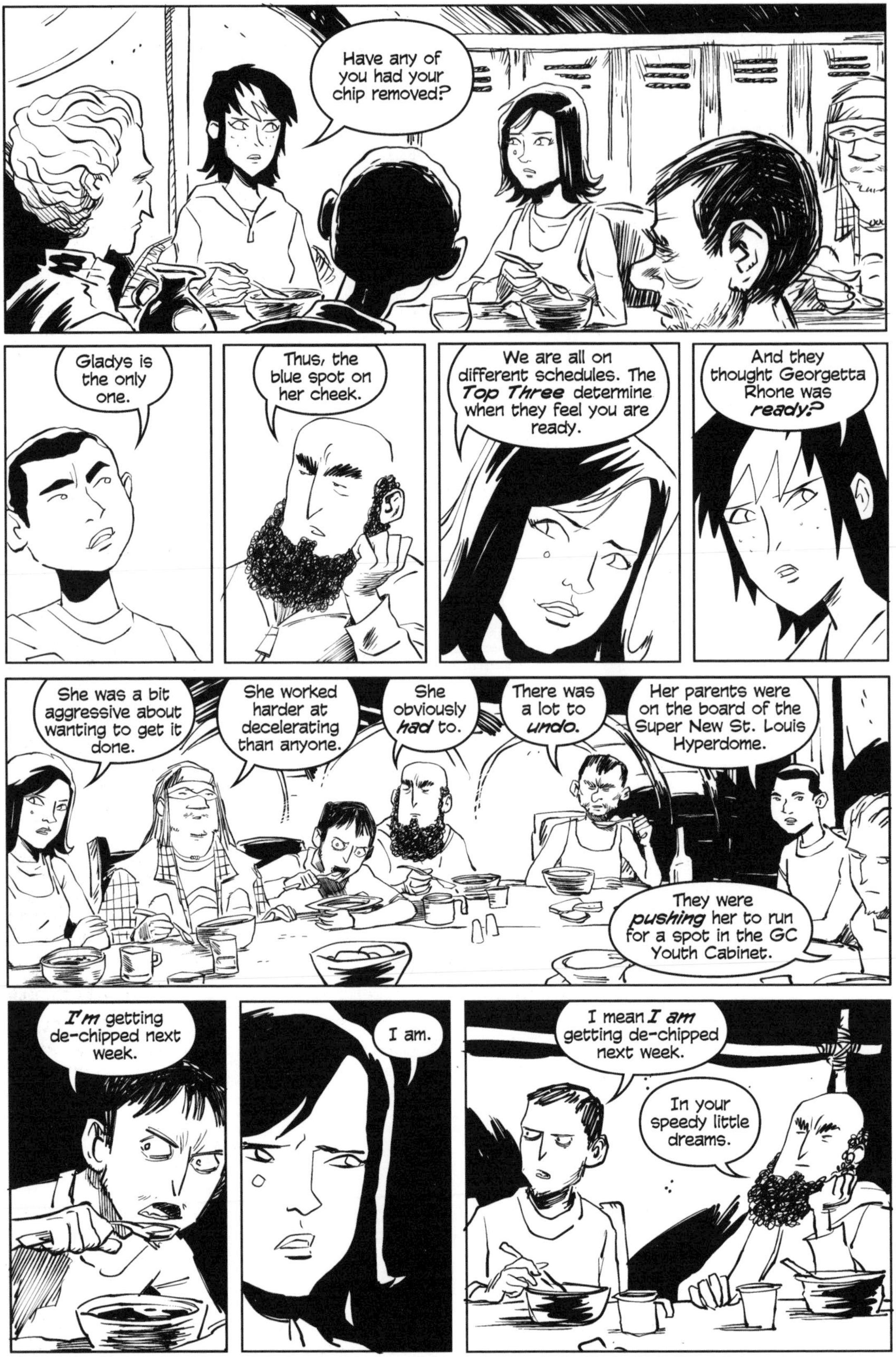
Have any of you had your chip removed?
Gladys is the only one.
Thus, the blue spot on her cheek.
We are all on different schedules. The *Top Three* determine when they feel you are ready.
And they thought Georgetta Rhone was *ready?*
She was a bit aggressive about wanting to get it done.
She worked harder at decelerating than anyone.
She obviously *had* to.
There was a lot to *undo.*
Her parents were on the board of the Super New St. Louis Hyperdome.
They were *pushing* her to run for a spot in the GC Youth Cabinet.
*I'm* getting de-chipped next week.
I am.
I mean *I am* getting de-chipped next week.
In your speedy little dreams.

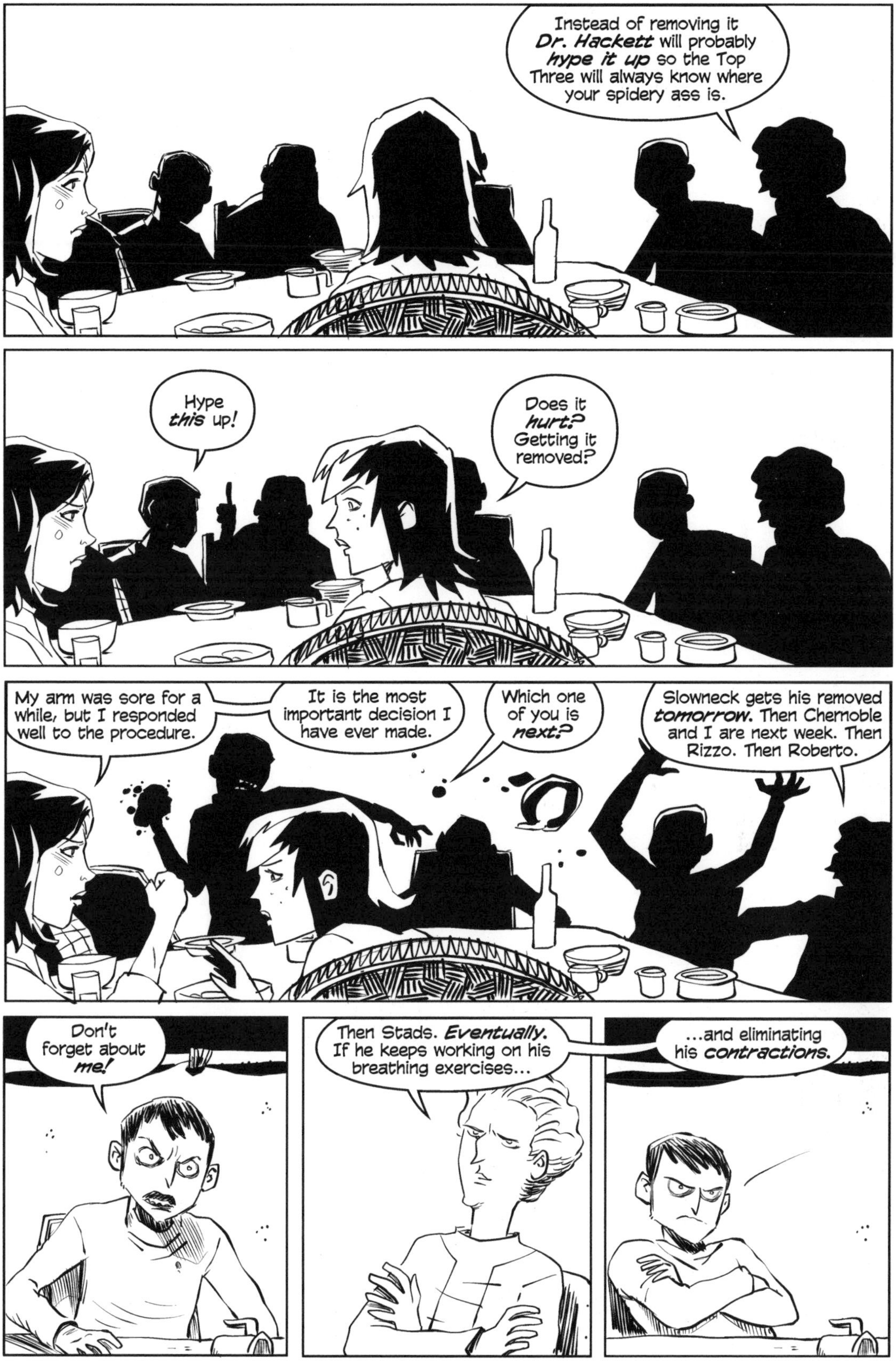
Instead of removing it Dr. Hackett will probably hype it up so the Top Three will always know where your spidery ass is.
Hype this up!
Does it hurt? Getting it removed?
My arm was sore for a while, but I responded well to the procedure.
It is the most important decision I have ever made.
Which one of you is next?
Slowneck gets his removed tomorrow. Then Chernoble and I are next week. Then Rizzo. Then Roberto.
Don't forget about me!
Then Stads. Eventually. If he keeps working on his breathing exercises...
...and eliminating his contractions.

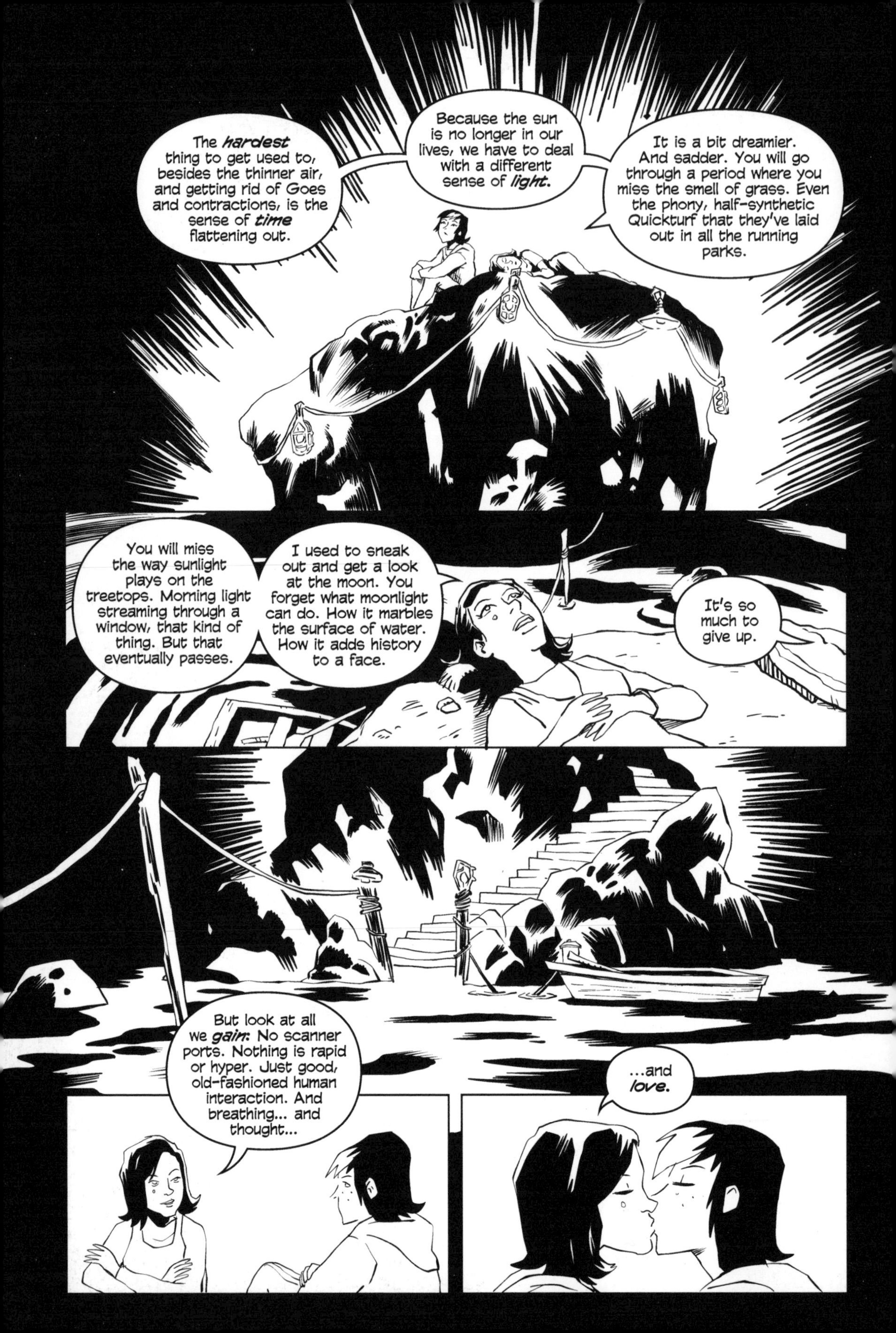
The *hardest* thing to get used to, besides the thinner air, and getting rid of Goes and contractions, is the sense of *time* flattening out.
Because the sun is no longer in our lives, we have to deal with a different sense of *light*.
It is a bit dreamier. And sadder. You will go through a period where you miss the smell of grass. Even the phony, half-synthetic Quickturf that they've laid out in all the running parks.
You will miss the way sunlight plays on the treetops. Morning light streaming through a window, that kind of thing. But that eventually passes.
I used to sneak out and get a look at the moon. You forget what moonlight can do. How it marbles the surface of water. How it adds history to a face.
It's so much to give up.
But look at all we *gain*: No scanner ports. Nothing is rapid or hyper. Just good, old-fashioned human interaction. And breathing... and thought...
...and *love*.

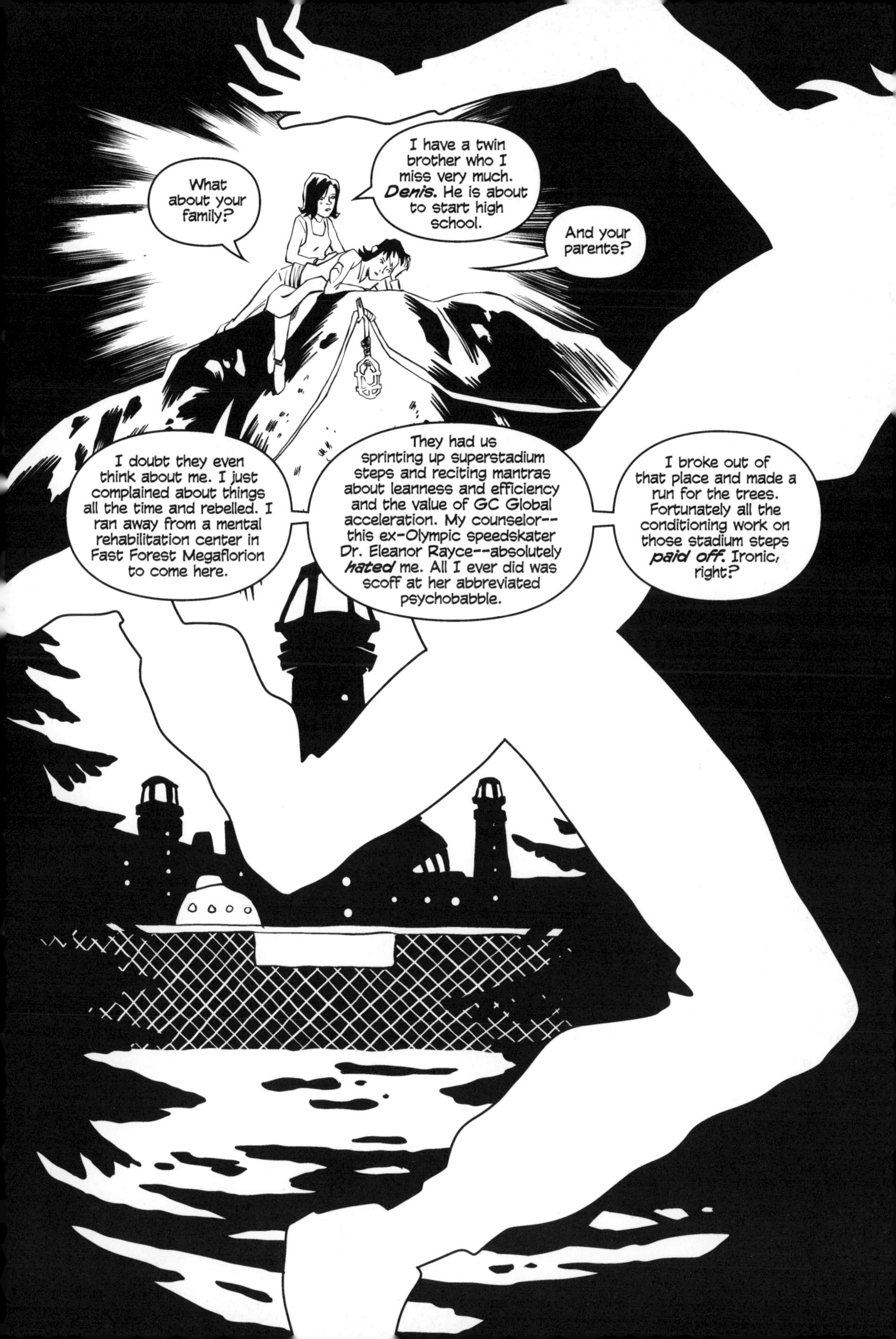
What about your family?
I have a twin brother who I miss very much. *Denis.* He is about to start high school.
And your parents?
I doubt they even think about me. I just complained about things all the time and rebelled. I ran away from a mental rehabilitation center in Fast Forest Megaflorion to come here.
They had us sprinting up superstadium steps and reciting mantras about leanness and efficiency and the value of GC Global acceleration. My counselor--this ex-Olympic speedskater Dr. Eleanor Rayce--absolutely *hated* me. All I ever did was scoff at her abbreviated psychobabble.
I broke out of that place and made a run for the trees. Fortunately all the conditioning work on those stadium steps *paid off*. Ironic, right?

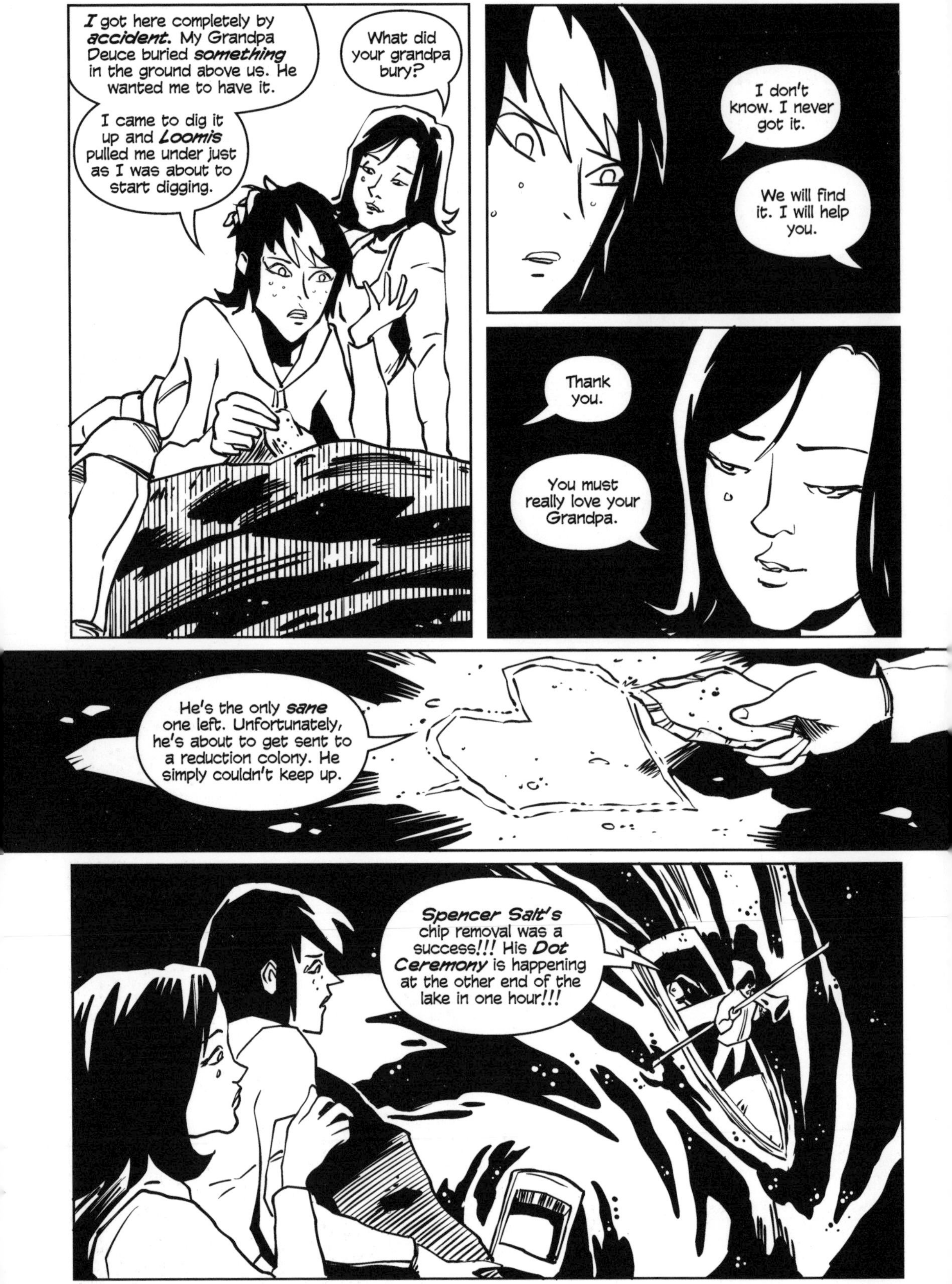
I got here completely by accident. My Grandpa Deuce buried something in the ground above us. He wanted me to have it.
What did your grandpa bury?
I came to dig it up and Loomis pulled me under just as I was about to start digging.
I don't know. I never got it.
We will find it. I will help you.
Thank you.
You must really love your Grandpa.
He's the only sane one left. Unfortunately, he's about to get sent to a reduction colony. He simply couldn't keep up.
Spencer Salt's chip removal was a success!!! His Dot Ceremony is happening at the other end of the lake in one hour!!!

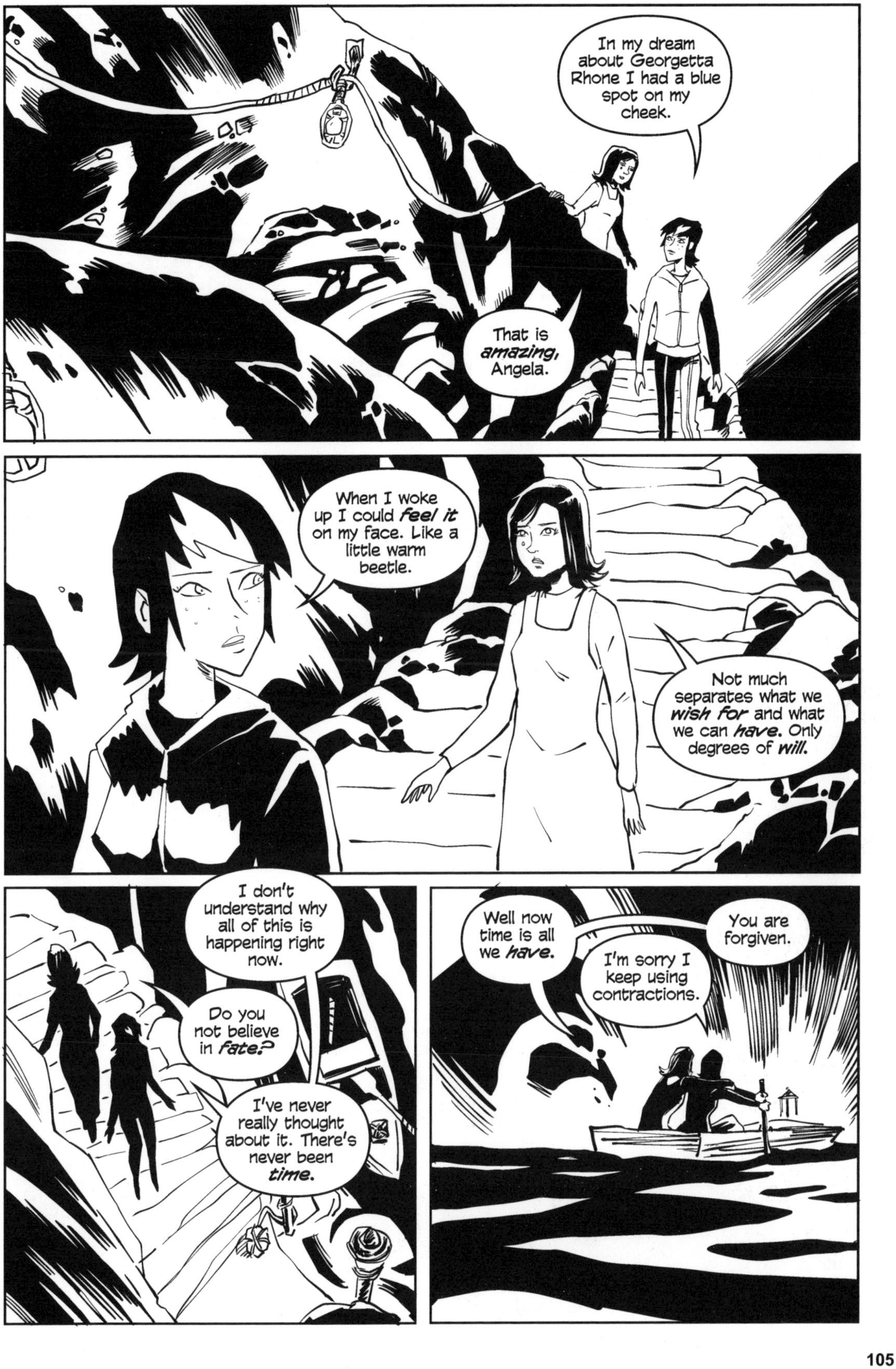

In my dream about Georgetta Rhone I had a blue spot on my cheek.
That is amazing, Angela.
When I woke up I could feel it on my face. Like a little warm beetle.
Not much separates what we wish for and what we can have. Only degrees of will.
I don't understand why all of this is happening right now.
Do you not believe in fate?
I've never really thought about it. There's never been time.
Well now time is all we have.
You are forgiven.
I'm sorry I keep using contractions.

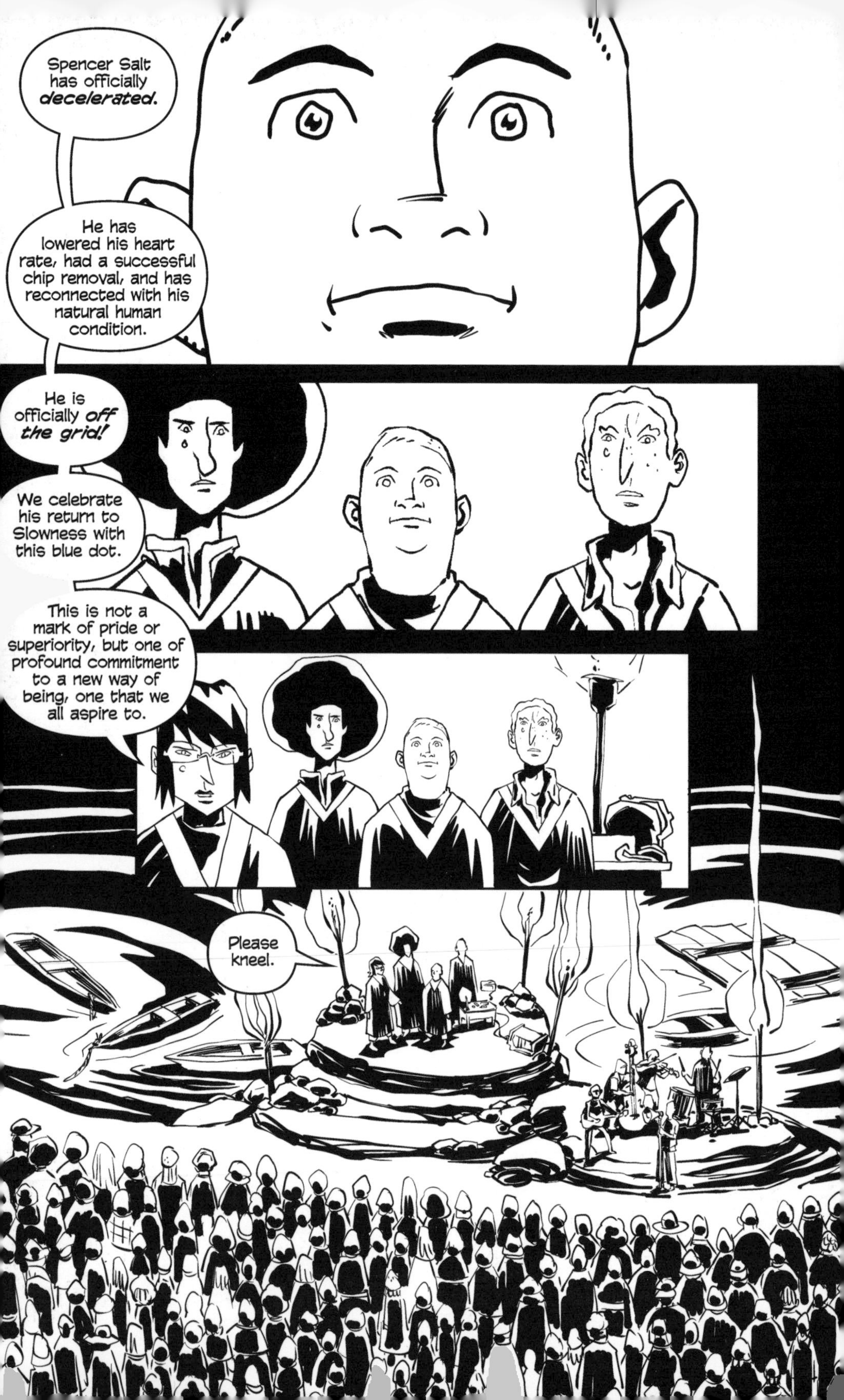
Spencer Salt has officially *decelerated*.
He has lowered his heart rate, had a successful chip removal, and has reconnected with his natural human condition.
He is officially *off the grid!*
We celebrate his return to Slowness with this blue dot.
This is not a mark of pride or superiority, but one of profound commitment to a new way of being, one that we all aspire to.
Please kneel.

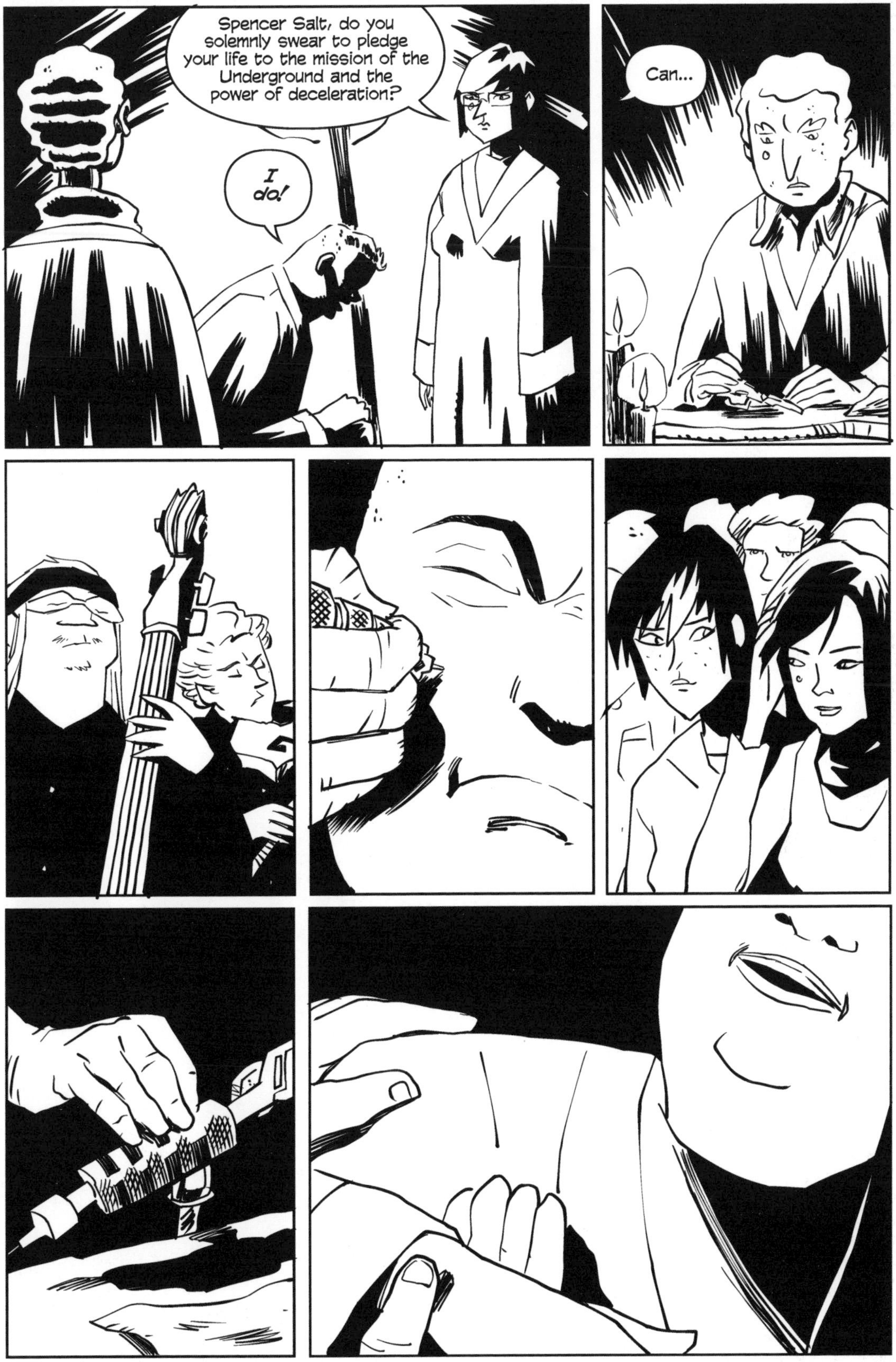
Spencer Salt, do you solemnly swear to pledge your life to the mission of the Underground and the power of deceleration?
I do!
Can...

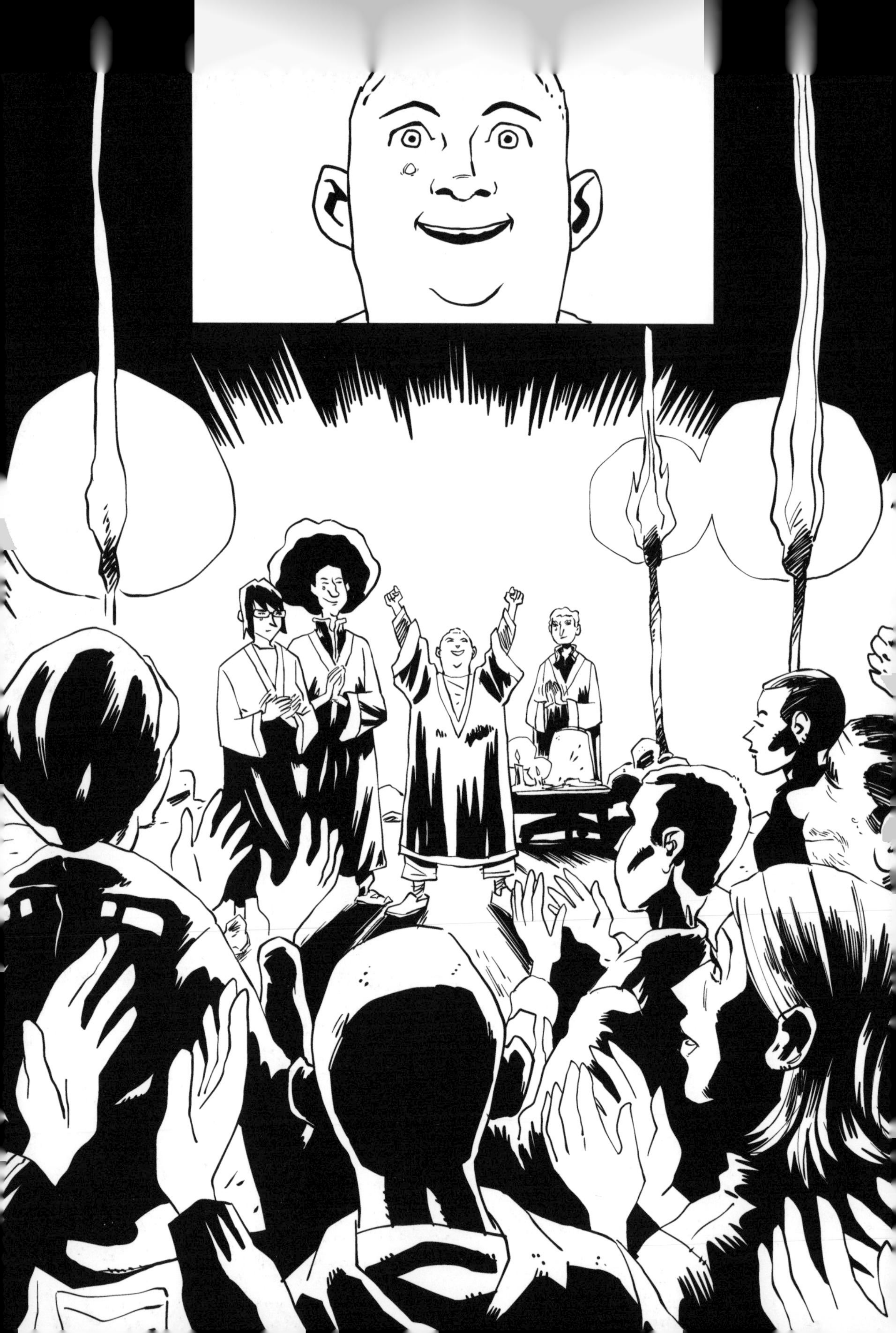

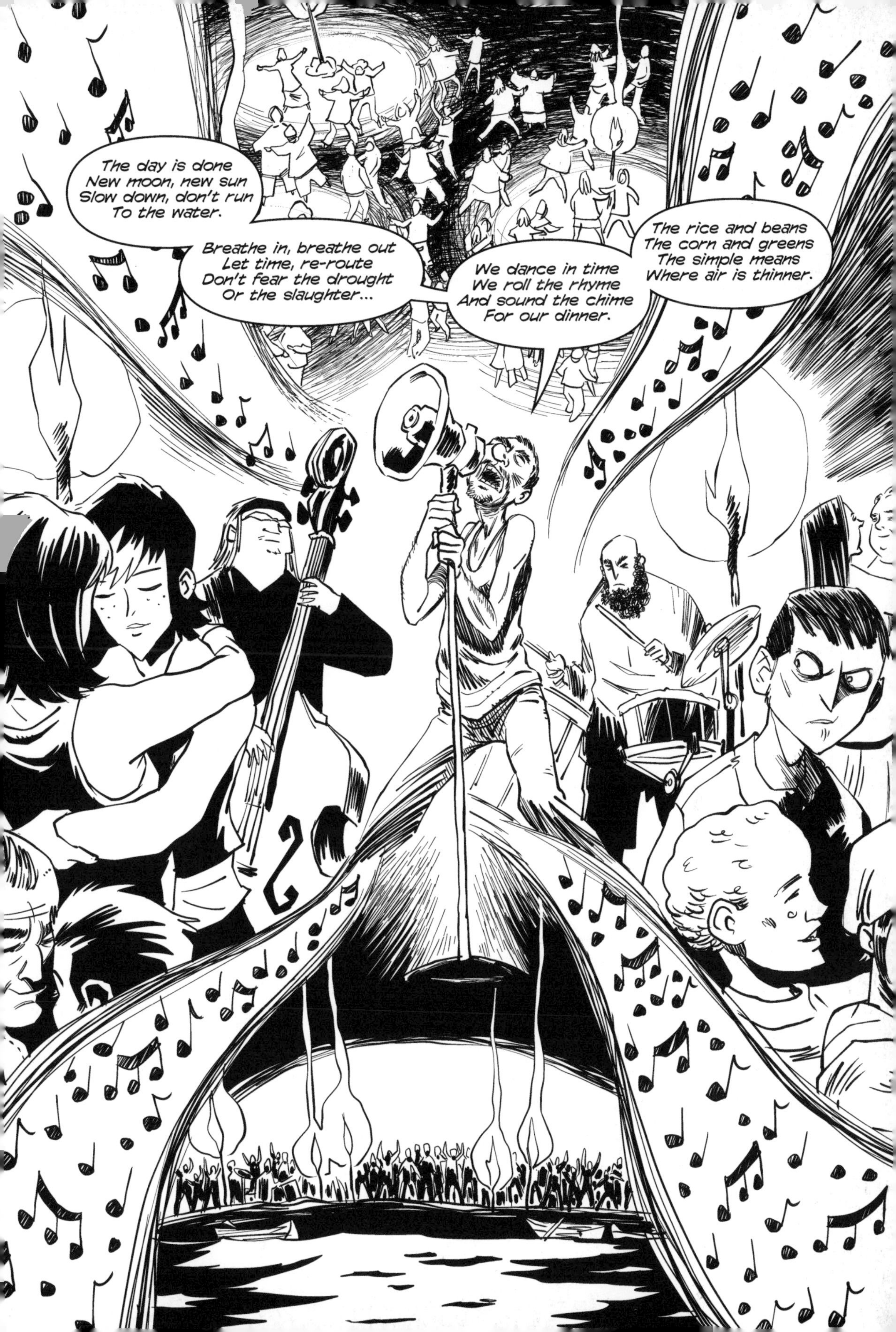
The day is done
New moon, new sun
Slow down, don't run
To the water.
Breathe in, breathe out
Let time, re-route
Don't fear the drought
Or the slaughter...
We dance in time
We roll the rhyme
And sound the chime
For our dinner.
The rice and beans
The corn and greens
The simple means
Where air is thinner.

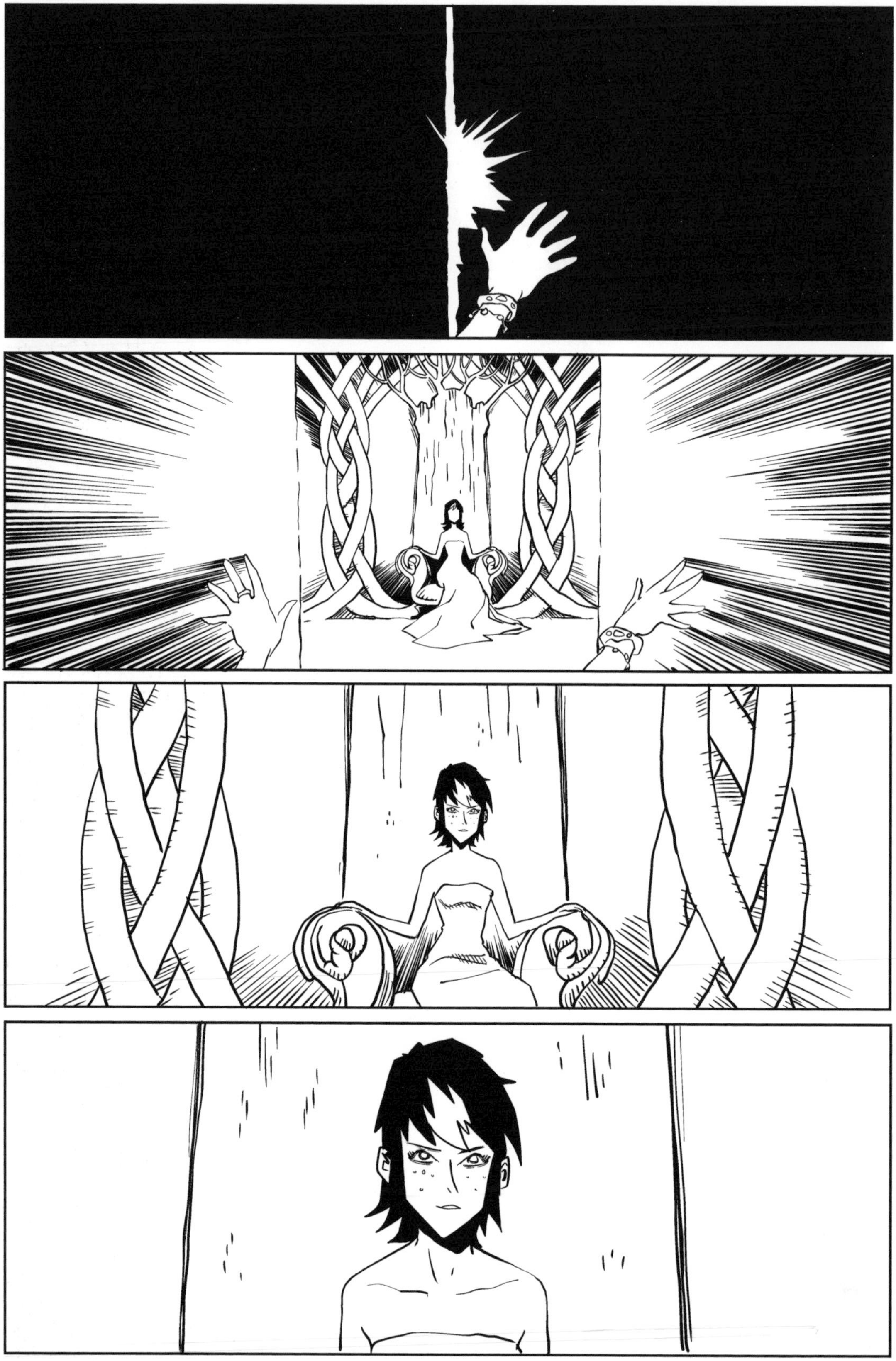

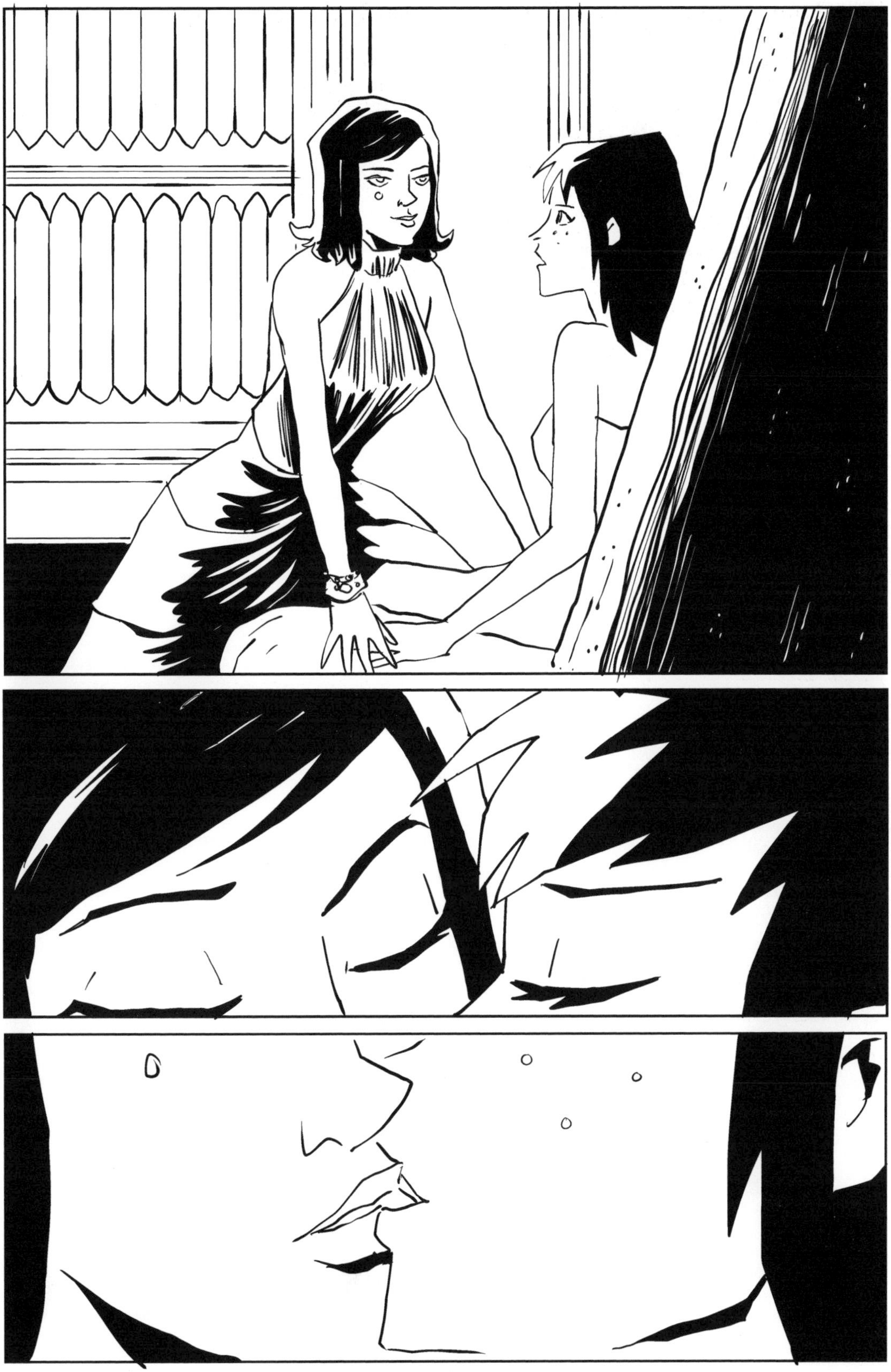

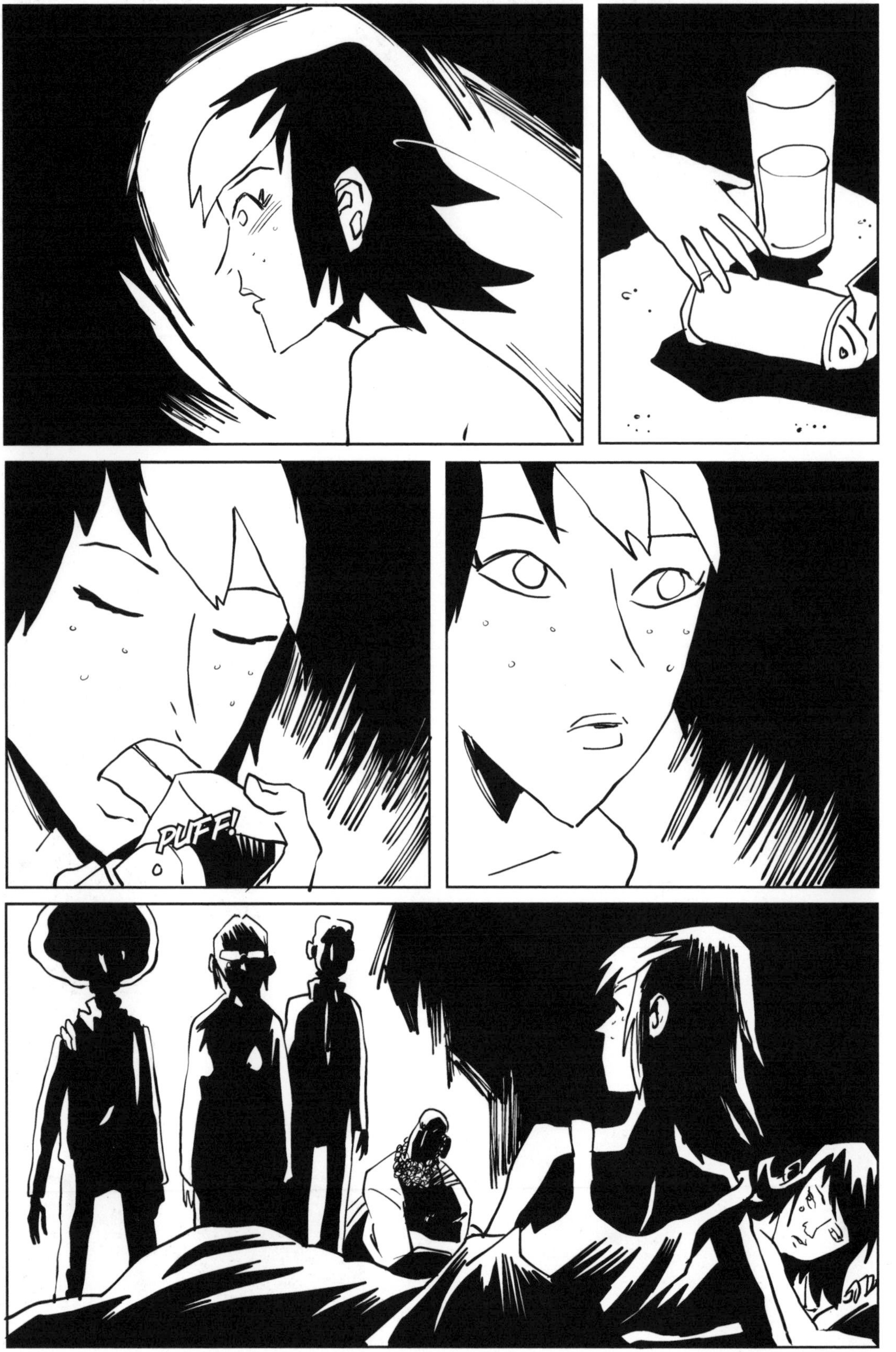
PUFF!

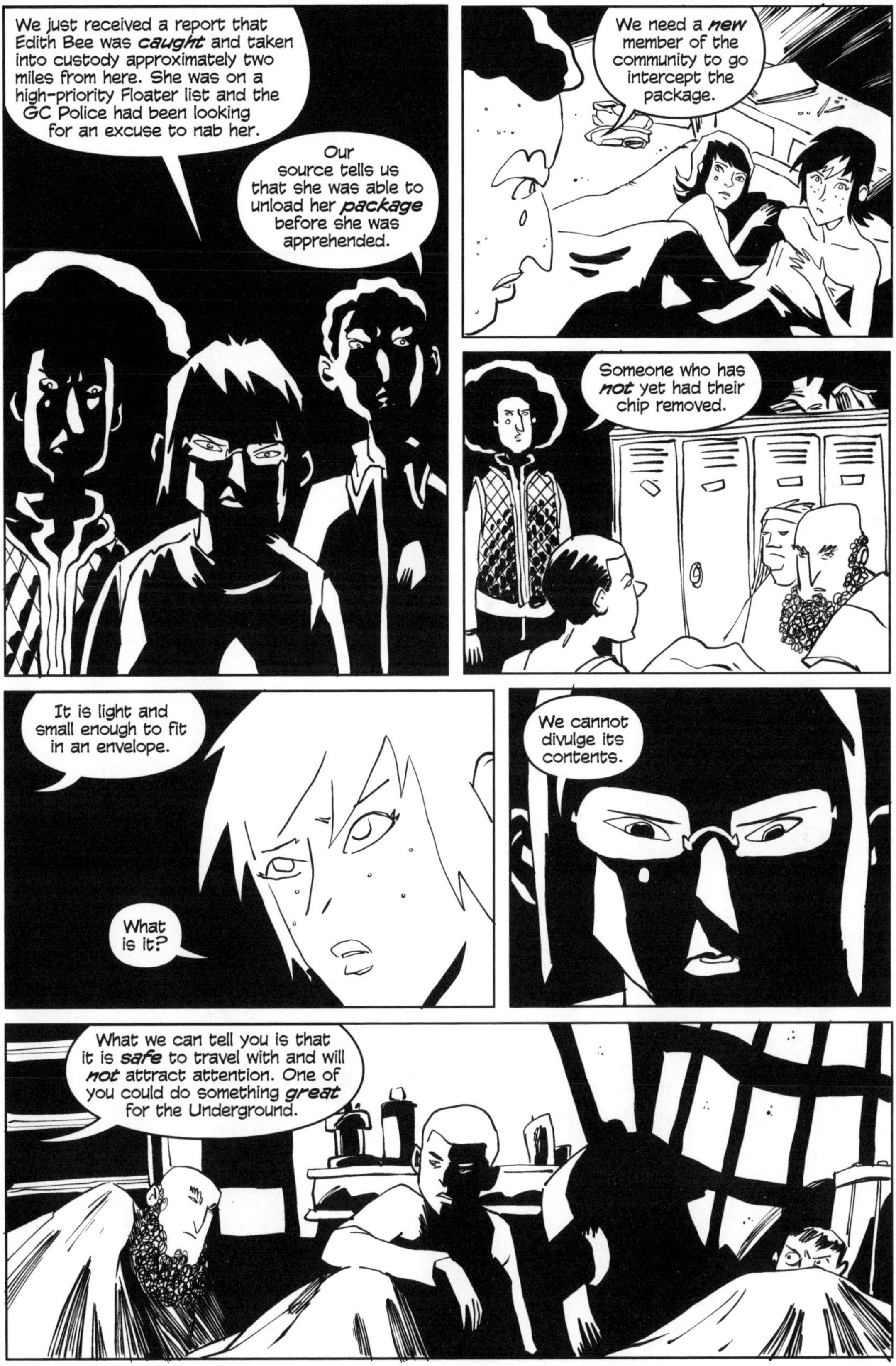
We just received a report that Edith Bee was *caught* and taken into custody approximately two miles from here. She was on a high-priority Floater list and the GC Police had been looking for an excuse to nab her.
Our source tells us that she was able to unload her *package* before she was apprehended.
We need a *new* member of the community to go intercept the package.
Someone who has *not* yet had their chip removed.
It is light and small enough to fit in an envelope.
What is it?
We cannot divulge its contents.
What we can tell you is that it is *safe* to travel with and will *not* attract attention. One of you could do something *great* for the Underground.

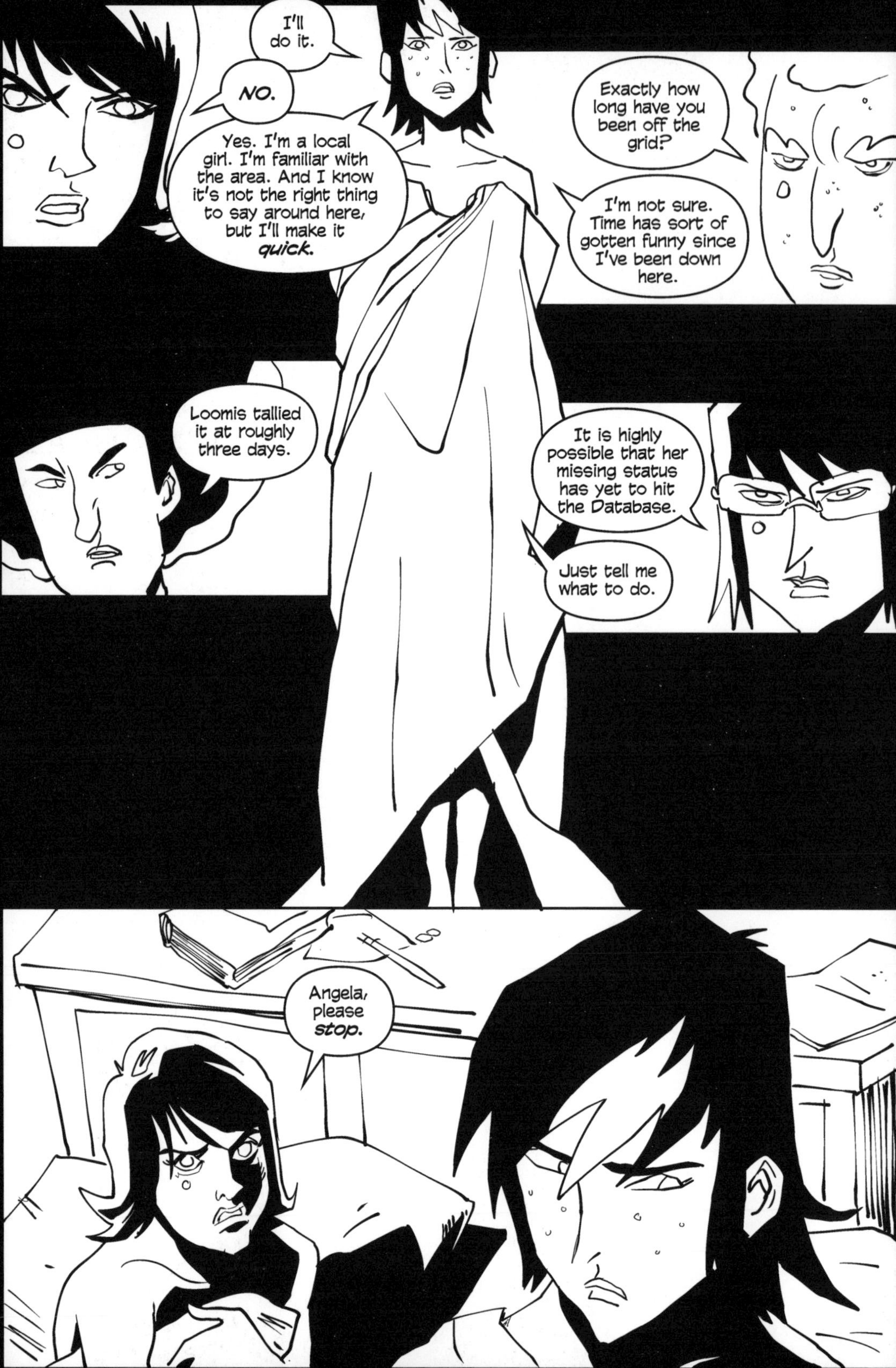
I'll do it.
*NO.*
Yes. I'm a local girl. I'm familiar with the area. And I know it's not the right thing to say around here, but I'll make it *quick.*
Exactly how long have you been off the grid?
I'm not sure. Time has sort of gotten funny since I've been down here.
Loomis tallied it at roughly three days.
It is highly possible that her missing status has yet to hit the Database.
Just tell me what to do.
Angela, please *stop.*

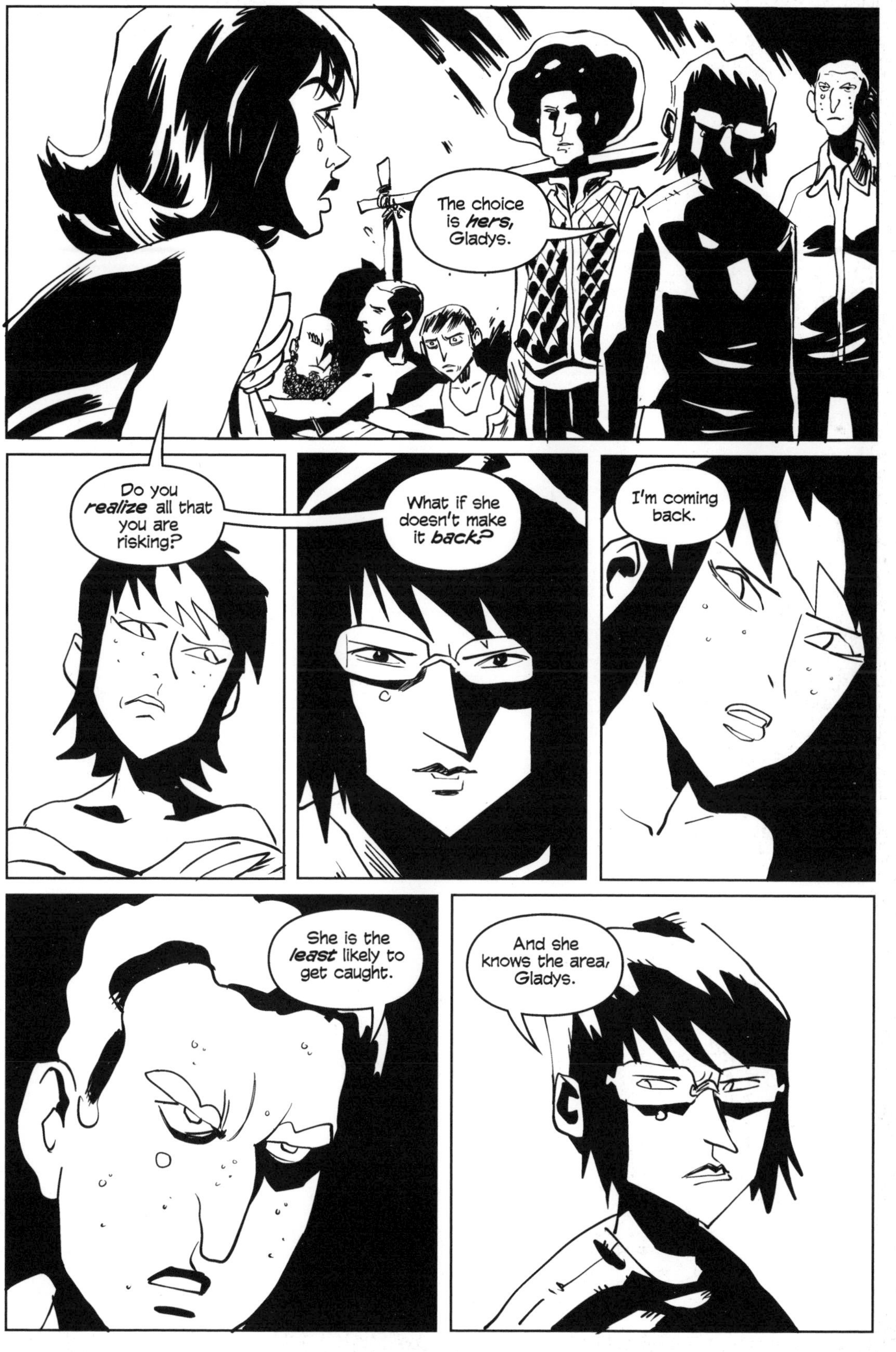

The choice is *hers*, Gladys.
Do you *realize* all that you are risking?
What if she doesn't make it *back*?
I'm coming back.
She is the *least* likely to get caught.
And she knows the area, Gladys.

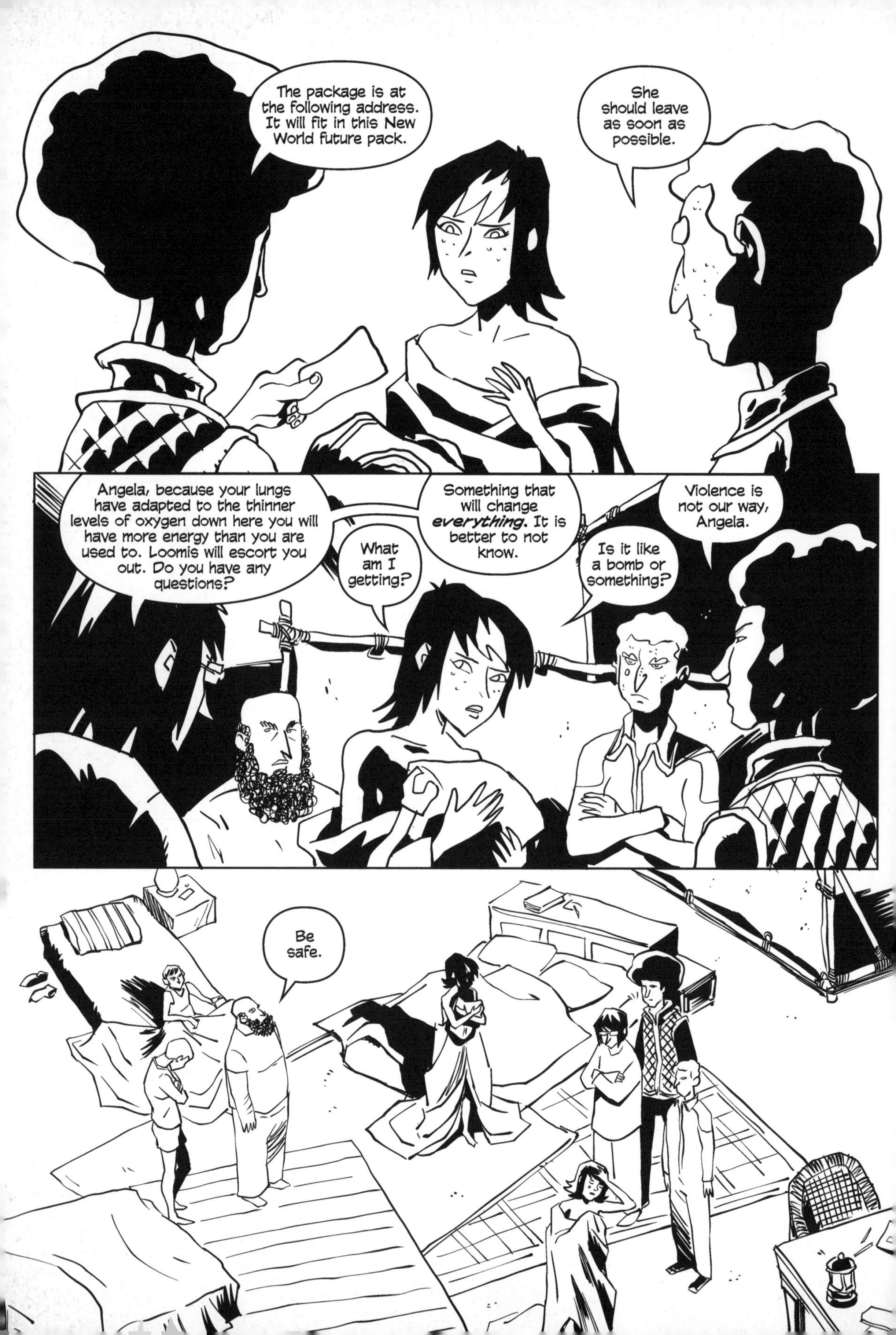

The package is at the following address. It will fit in this New World future pack.
She should leave as soon as possible.
Angela, because your lungs have adapted to the thinner levels of oxygen down here you will have more energy than you are used to. Loomis will escort you out. Do you have any questions?
What am I getting?
Something that will change ***everything***. It is better to not know.
Is it like a bomb or something?
Violence is not our way, Angela.
Be safe.

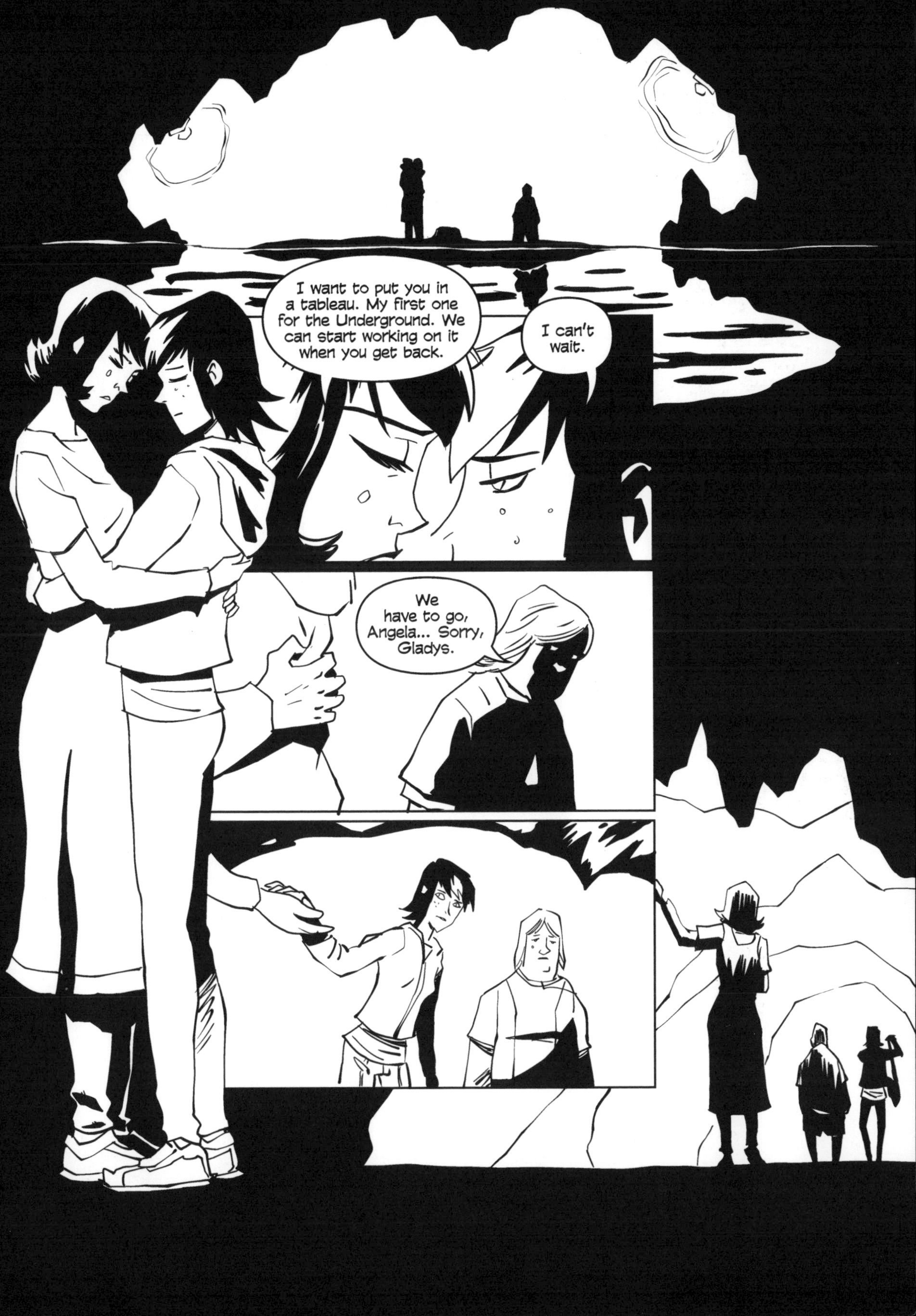
I want to put you in a tableau. My first one for the Underground. We can start working on it when you get back.
I can't wait.
We have to go, Angela... Sorry, Gladys.

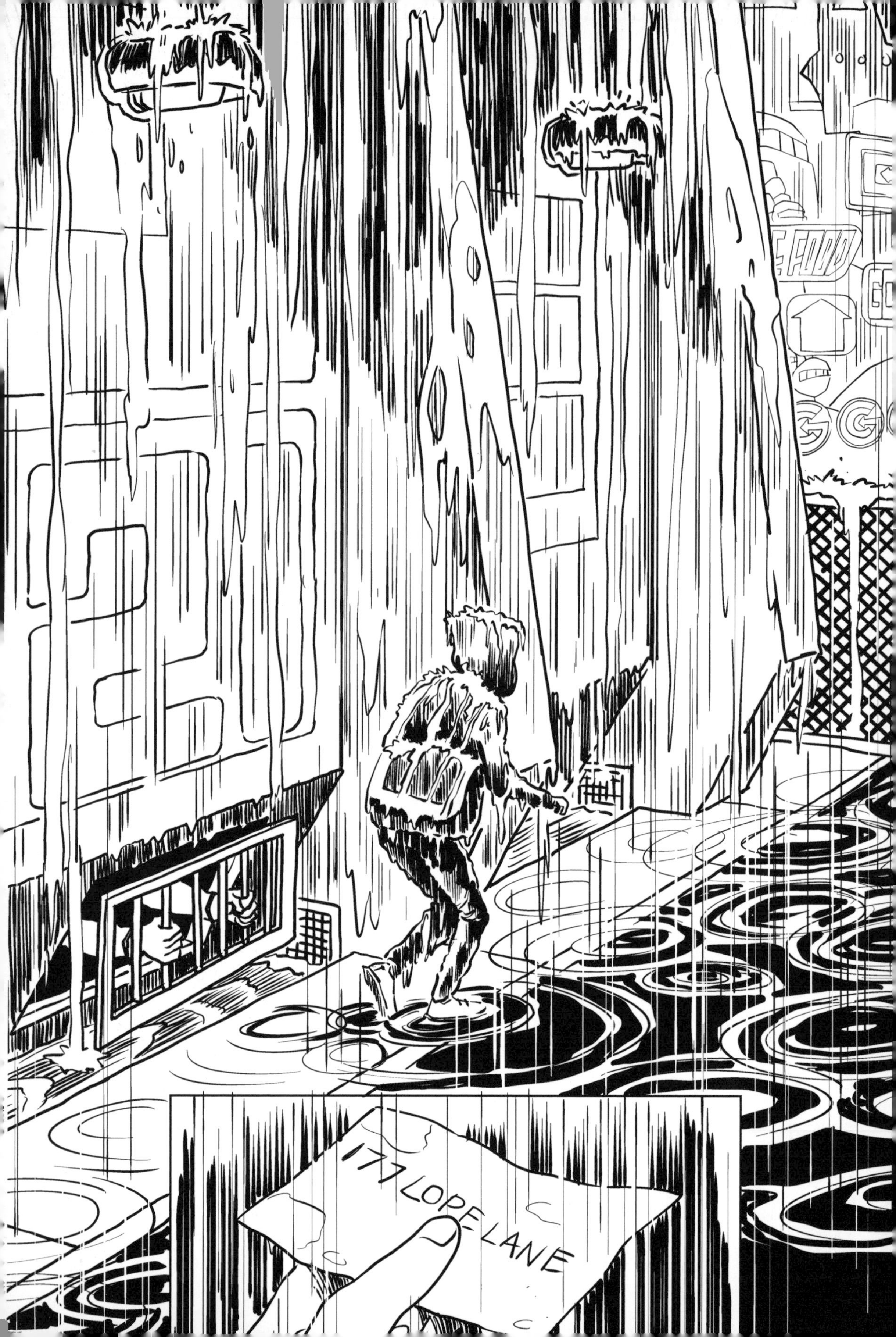
177 LOPE LANE

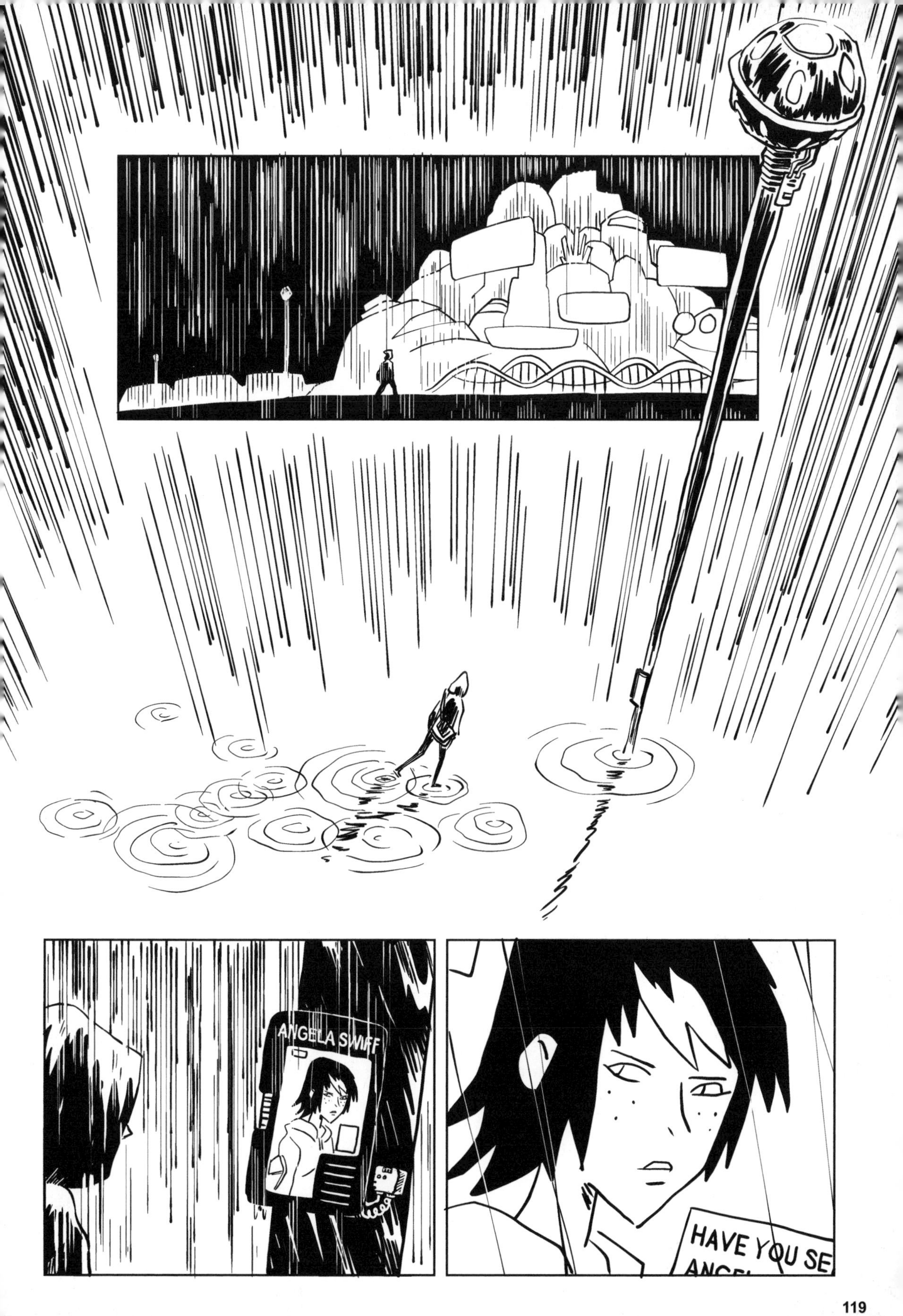
ANGELA SWIFF
HAVE YOU SE

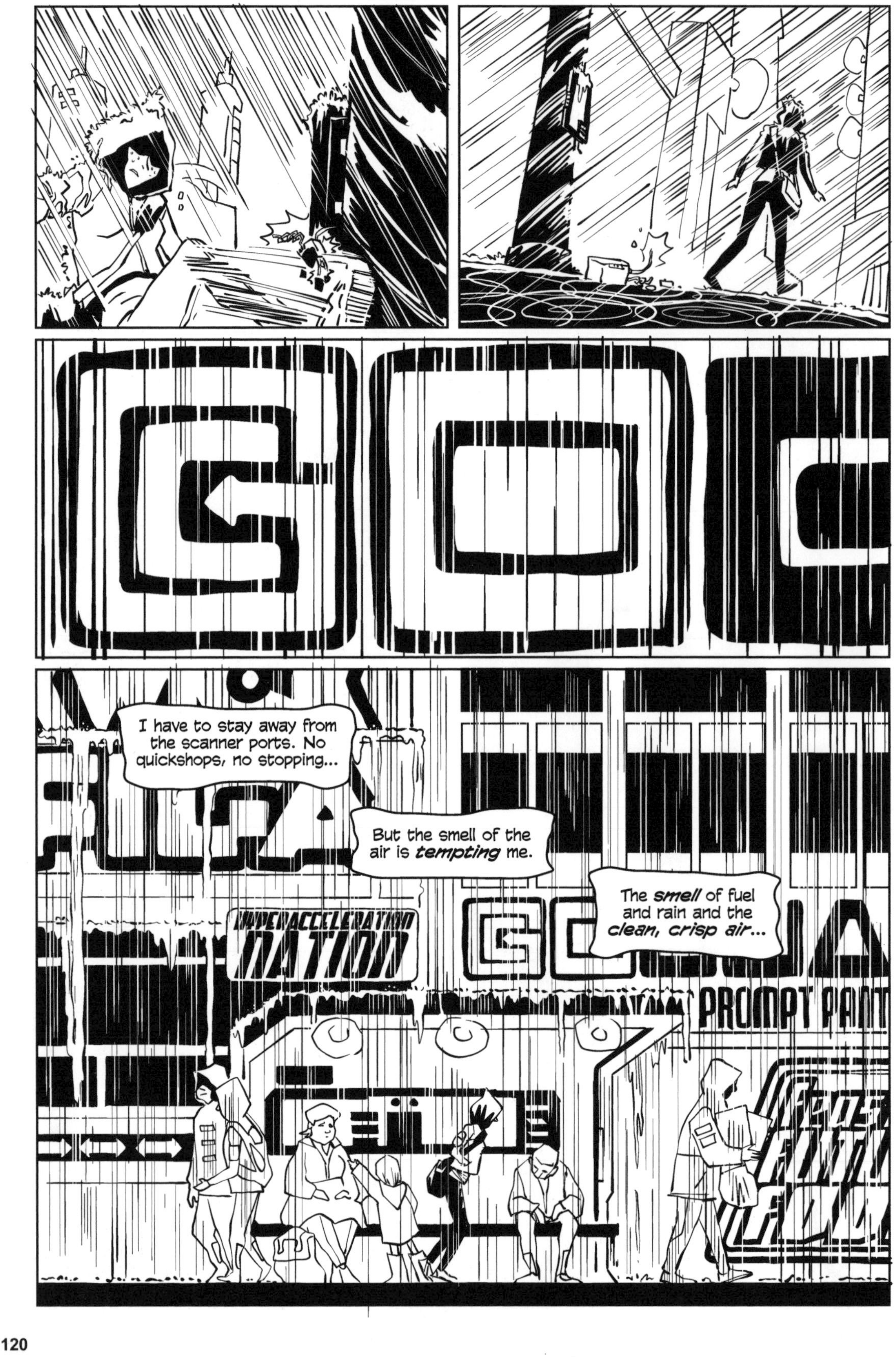
I have to stay away from the scanner ports. No quickshops, no stopping...
But the smell of the air is *tempting* me.
The *smell* of fuel and rain and the *clean, crisp air*...

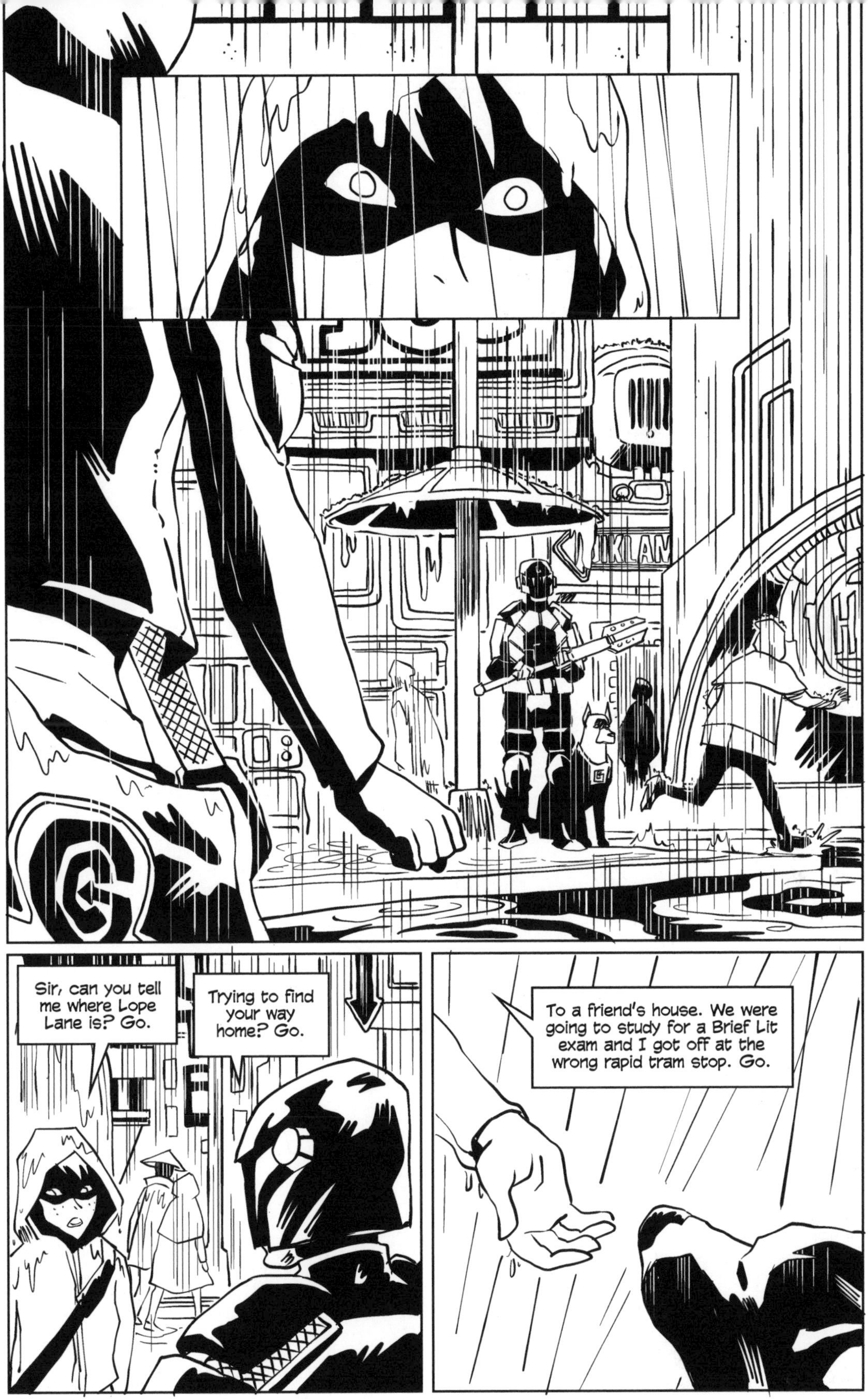
Sir, can you tell me where Lope Lane is? Go.
Trying to find your way home? Go.
To a friend's house. We were going to study for a Brief Lit exam and I got off at the wrong rapid tram stop. Go.

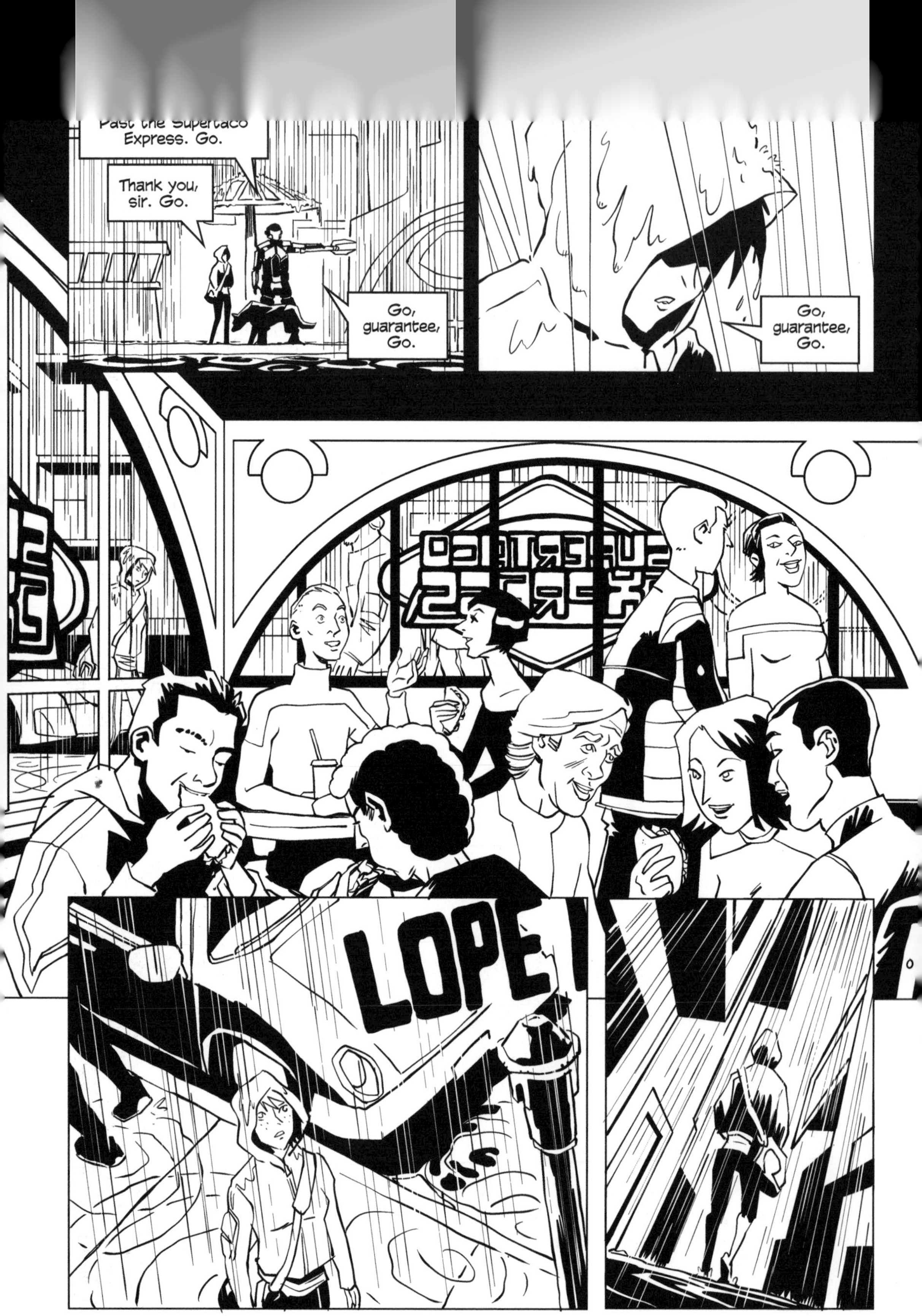
Past the Supertaco Express. Go.
Thank you, sir. Go.
Go, guarantee, Go.
Go, guarantee, Go.
LOPE

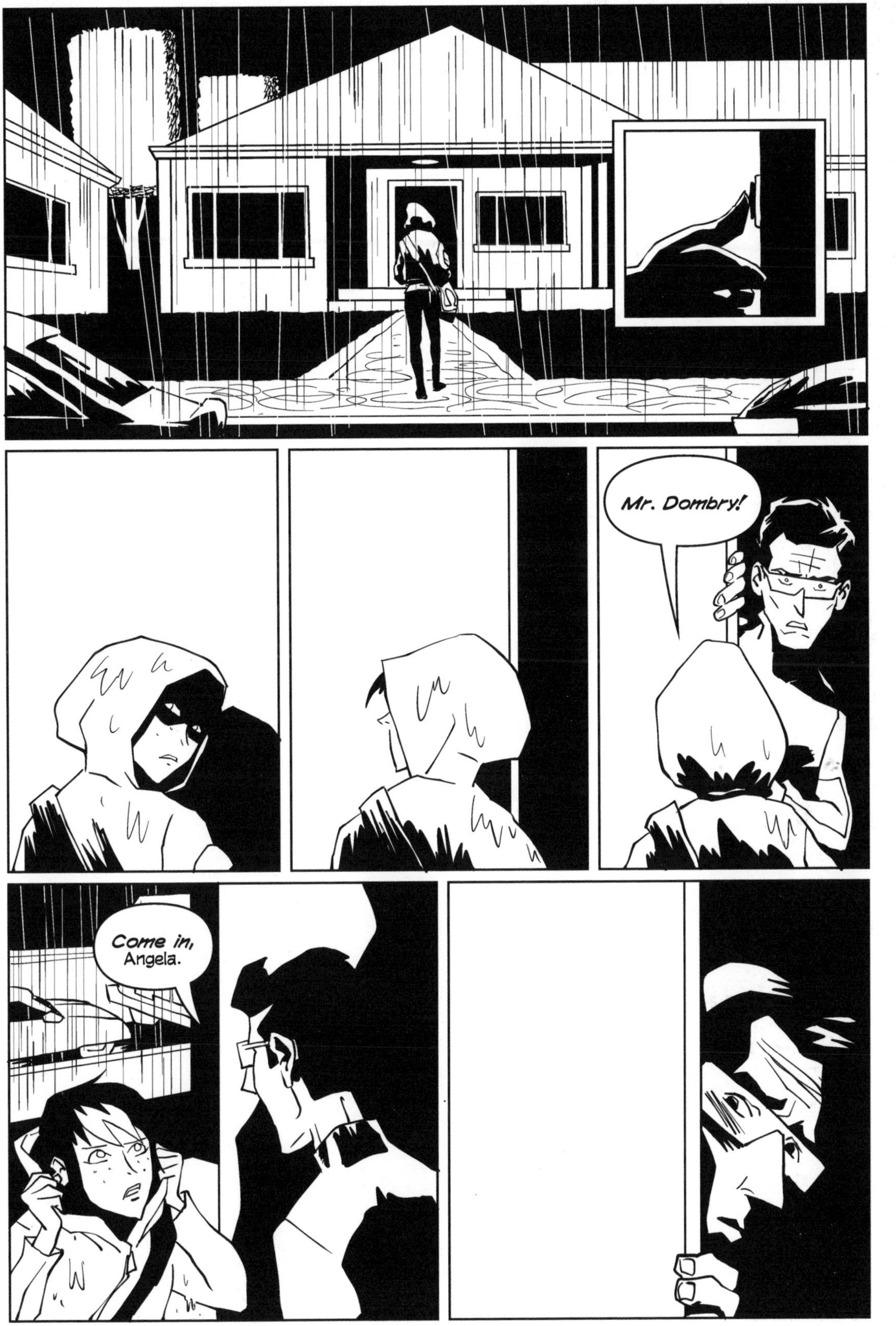
Mr. Dombry!
Come in, Angela.

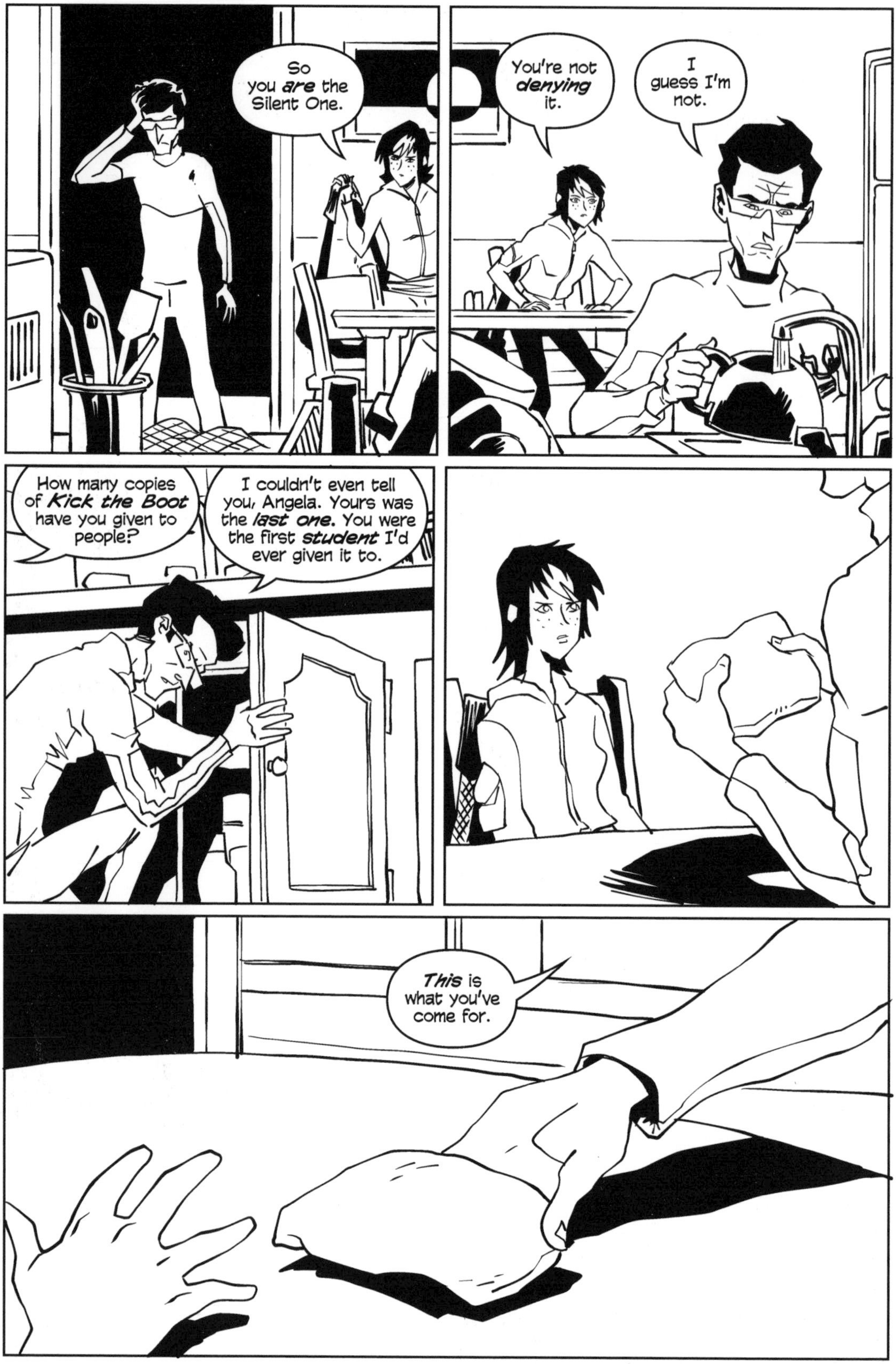
So you *are* the Silent One.
You're not *denying* it.
I guess I'm not.
How many copies of *Kick the Boot* have you given to people?
I couldn't even tell you, Angela. Yours was the *last one.* You were the first *student* I'd ever given it to.
*This* is what you've come for.

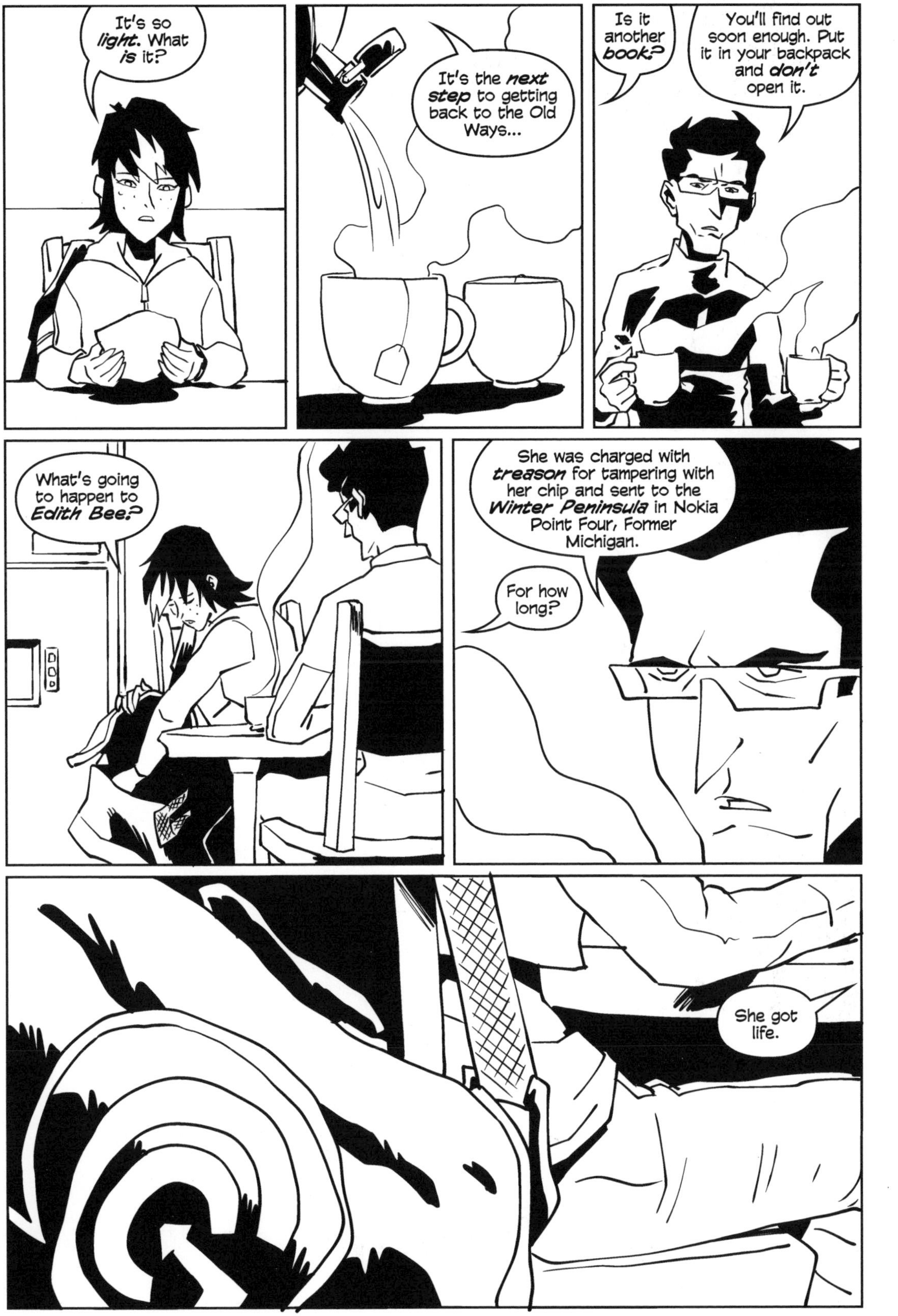

It's so *light*. What *is* it?
It's the *next step* to getting back to the Old Ways...
Is it another *book?*
You'll find out soon enough. Put it in your backpack and *don't* open it.
What's going to happen to *Edith Bee?*
She was charged with *treason* for tampering with her chip and sent to the *Winter Peninsula* in Nokia Point Four, Former Michigan.
For how long?
She got life.

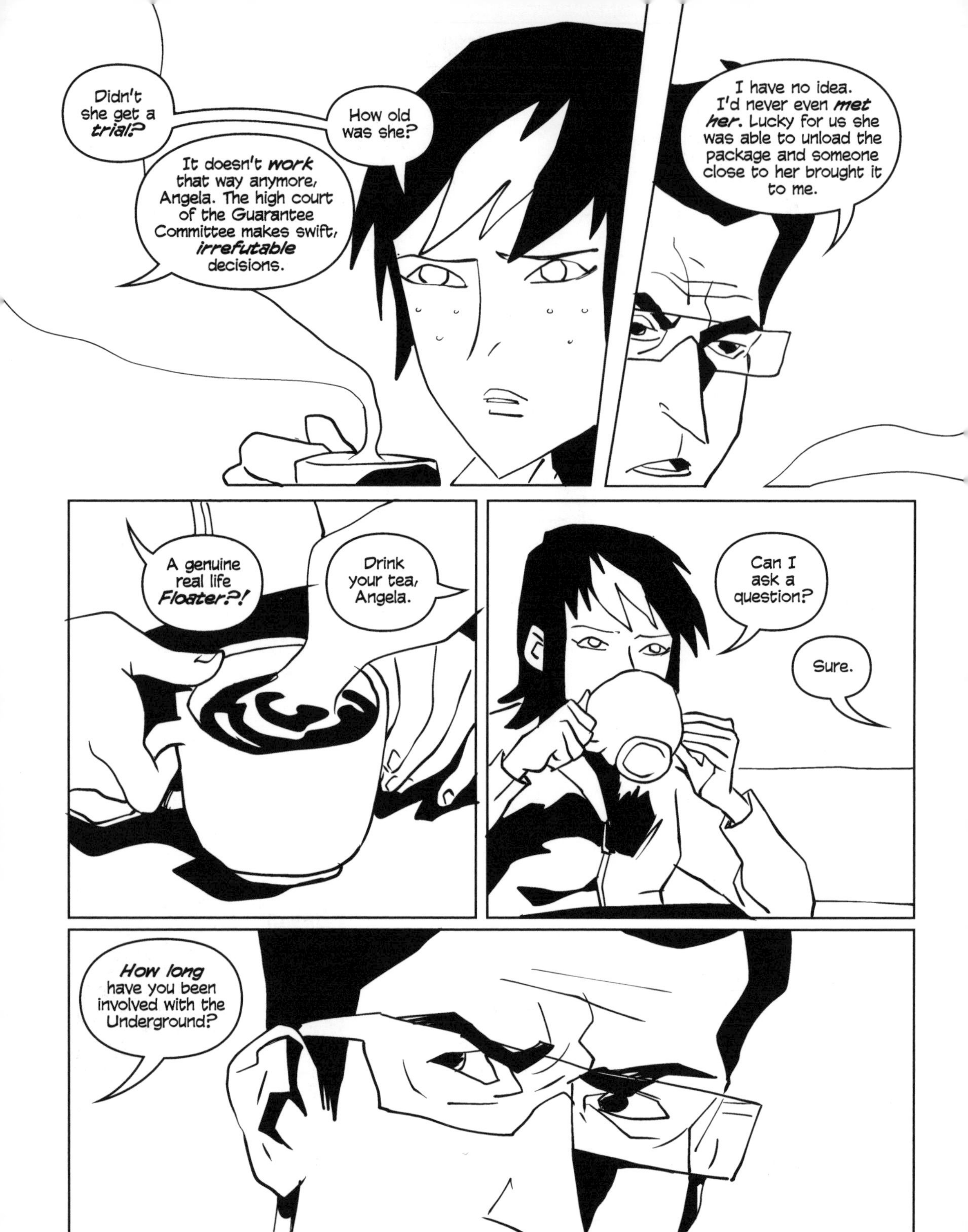
Didn't she get a *trial?*
How old was she?
It doesn't *work* that way anymore, Angela. The high court of the Guarantee Committee makes swift, *irrefutable* decisions.
I have no idea. I'd never even *met her*. Lucky for us she was able to unload the package and someone close to her brought it to me.
A genuine real life *Floater?!*
Drink your tea, Angela.
Can I ask a question?
Sure.
*How long* have you been involved with the Underground?

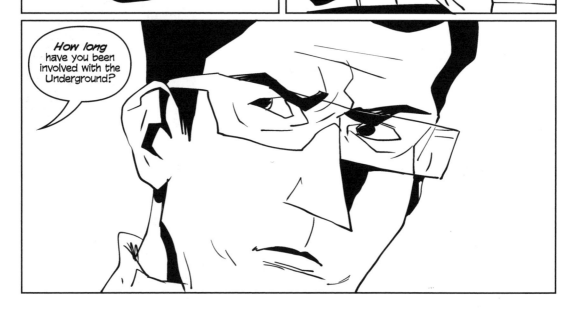

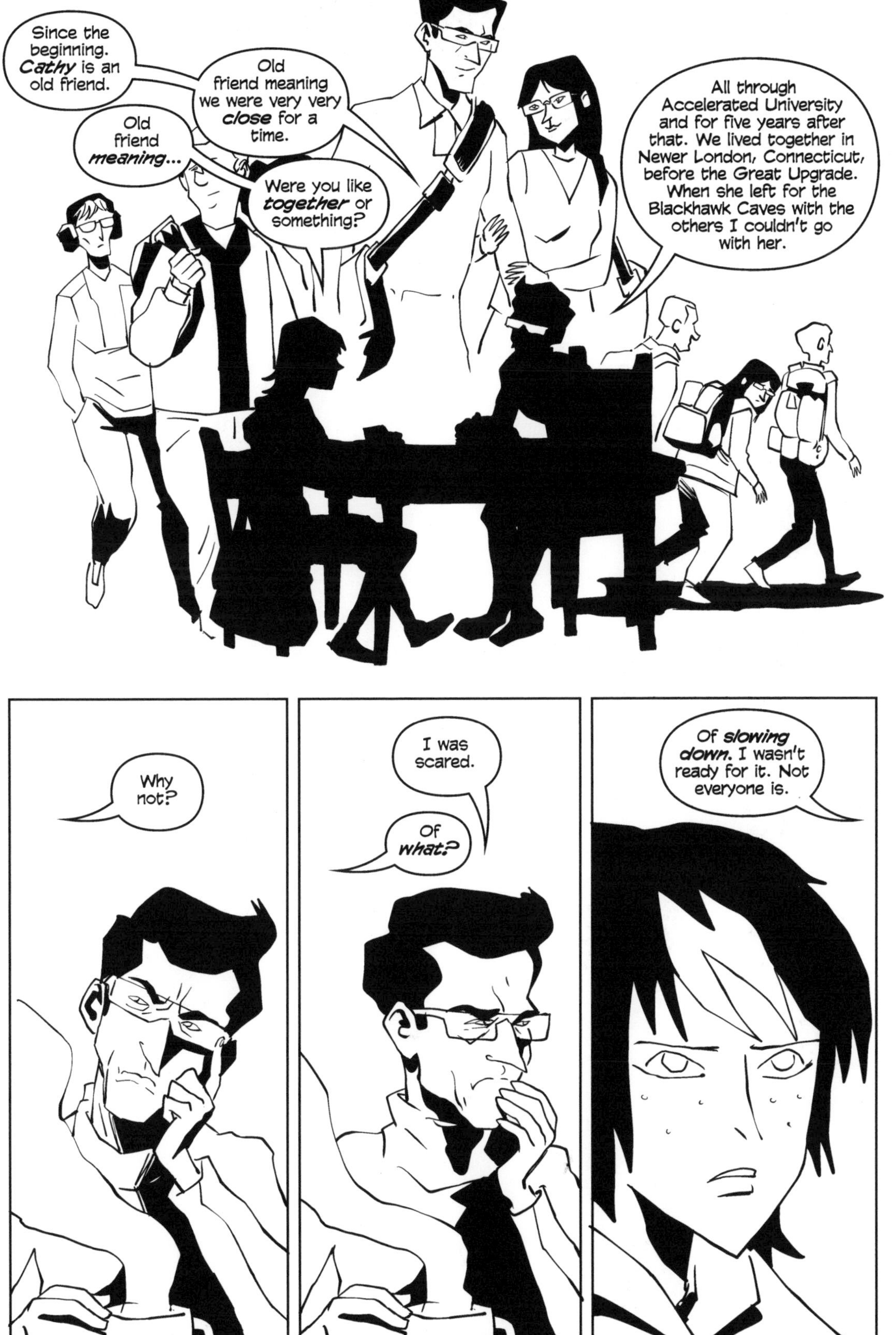
Since the beginning. Cathy is an old friend.
Old friend meaning...
Old friend meaning we were very very close for a time.
Were you like together or something?
All through Accelerated University and for five years after that. We lived together in Newer London, Connecticut, before the Great Upgrade. When she left for the Blackhawk Caves with the others I couldn't go with her.
Why not?
I was scared.
Of what?
Of slowing down. I wasn't ready for it. Not everyone is.

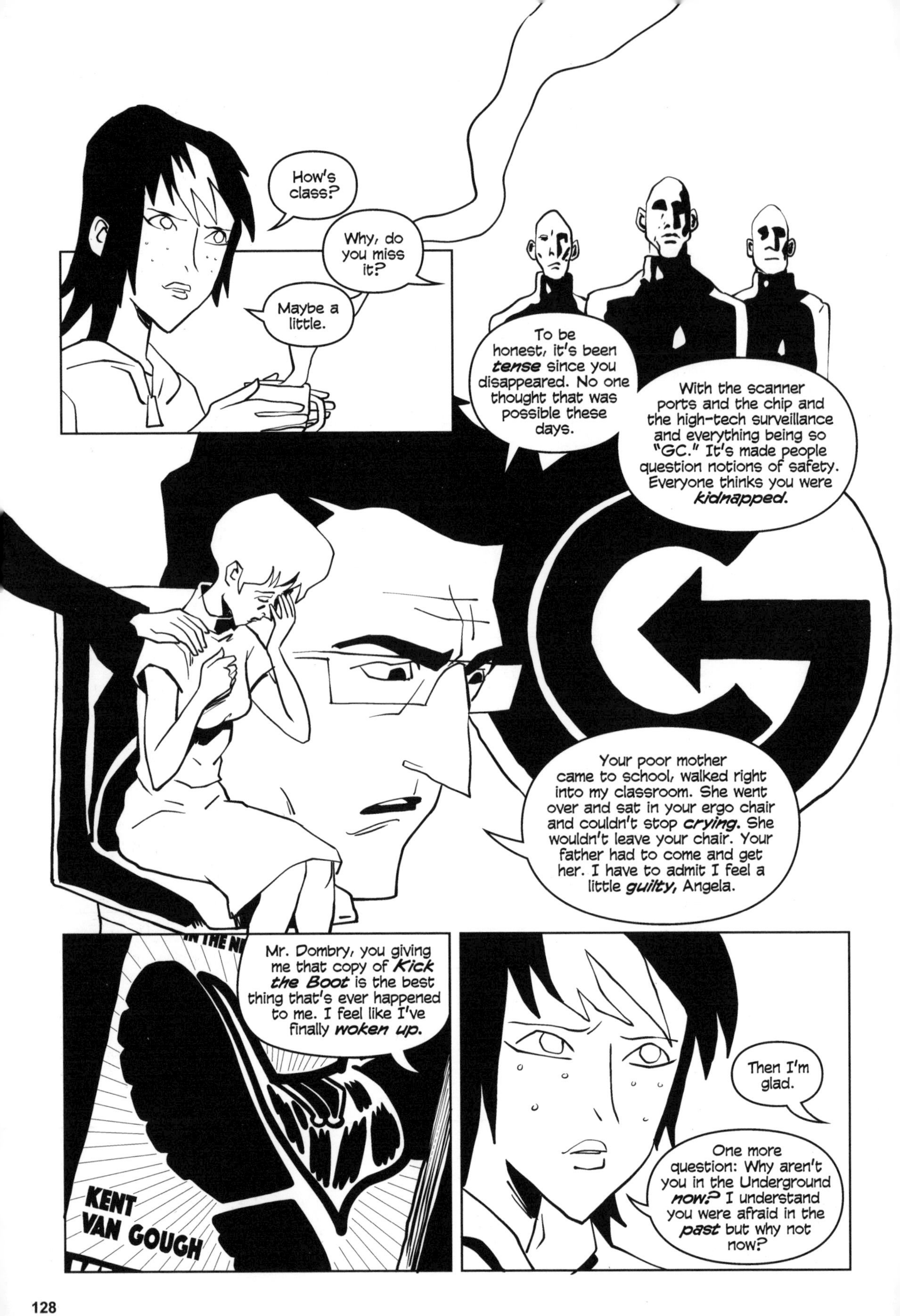
How's class?
Why, do you miss it?
Maybe a little.
To be honest, it's been *tense* since you disappeared. No one thought that was possible these days.
With the scanner ports and the chip and the high-tech surveillance and everything being so "GC." It's made people question notions of safety. Everyone thinks you were *kidnapped.*
Your poor mother came to school, walked right into my classroom. She went over and sat in your ergo chair and couldn't stop *crying.* She wouldn't leave your chair. Your father had to come and get her. I have to admit I feel a little *guilty,* Angela.
Mr. Dombry, you giving me that copy of *Kick the Boot* is the best thing that's ever happened to me. I feel like I've finally *woken up.*
KENT VAN GOUGH
Then I'm glad.
One more question: Why aren't you in the Underground *now?* I understand you were afraid in the *past* but why not now?

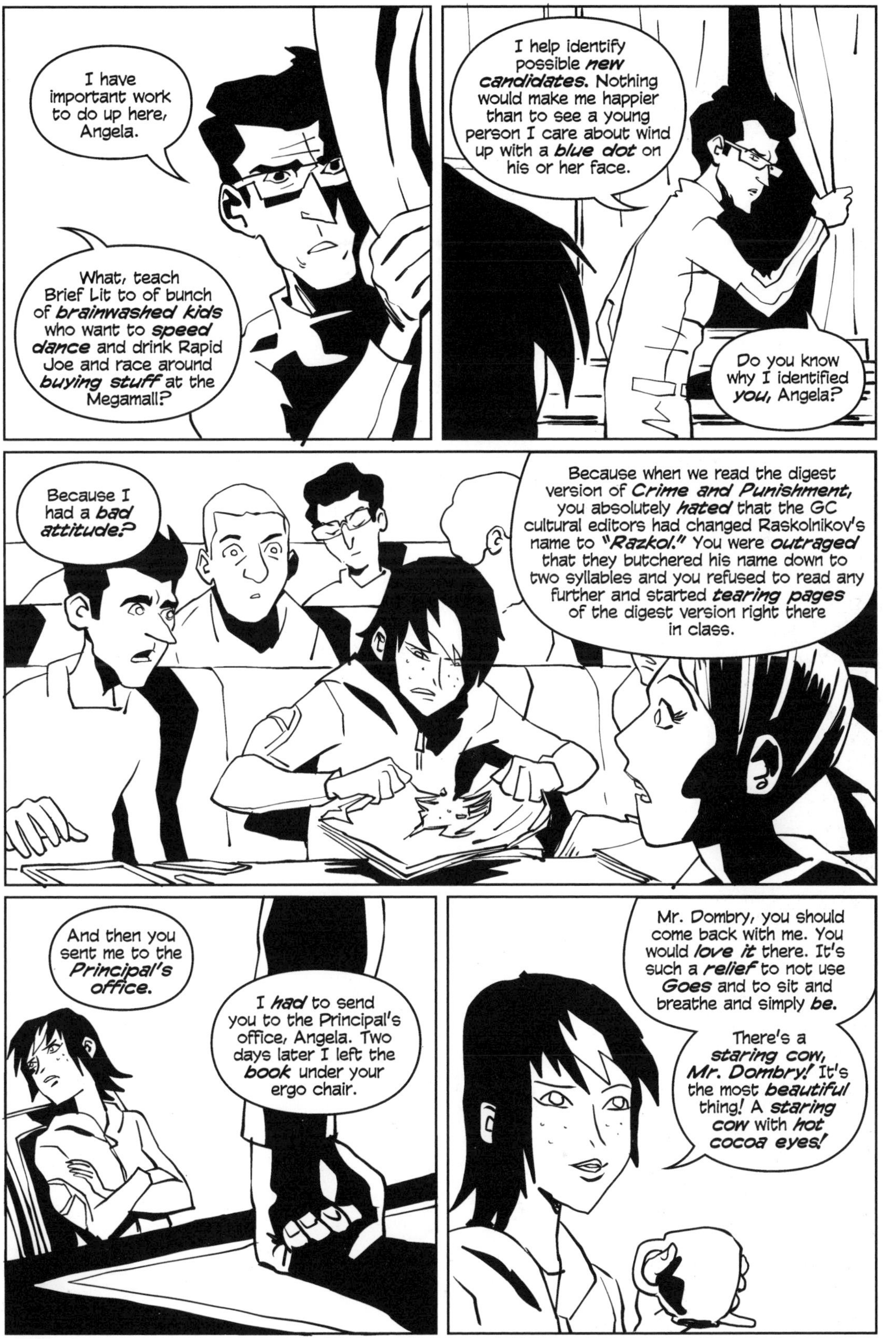

I have important work to do up here, Angela.
What, teach Brief Lit to of bunch of *brainwashed kids* who want to *speed dance* and drink Rapid Joe and race around *buying stuff* at the Megamall?
I help identify possible *new candidates.* Nothing would make me happier than to see a young person I care about wind up with a *blue dot* on his or her face.
Do you know why I identified *you,* Angela?
Because I had a *bad attitude?*
Because when we read the digest version of *Crime and Punishment,* you absolutely *hated* that the GC cultural editors had changed Raskolnikov's name to *"Razkol."* You were *outraged* that they butchered his name down to two syllables and you refused to read any further and started *tearing pages* of the digest version right there in class.
And then you sent me to the *Principal's office.*
I *had* to send you to the Principal's office, Angela. Two days later I left the *book* under your ergo chair.
Mr. Dombry, you should come back with me. You would *love it* there. It's such a *relief* to not use *Goes* and to sit and breathe and simply *be.*
There's a *staring cow, Mr. Dombry!* It's the most *beautiful* thing! A *staring cow* with *hot cocoa eyes!*

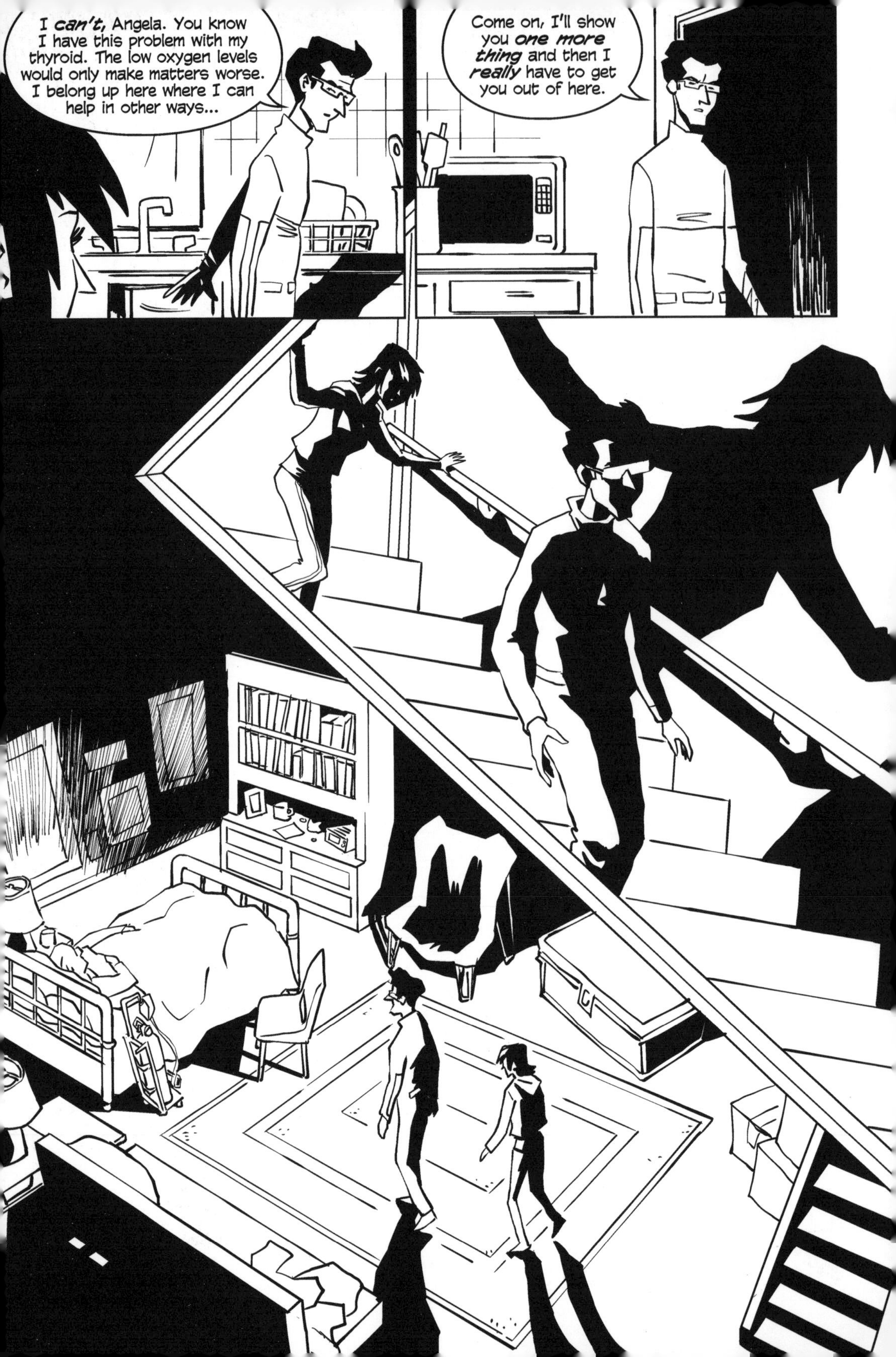

I *can't,* Angela. You know I have this problem with my thyroid. The low oxygen levels would only make matters worse. I belong up here where I can help in other ways...
Come on, I'll show you *one more thing* and then I *really* have to get you out of here.

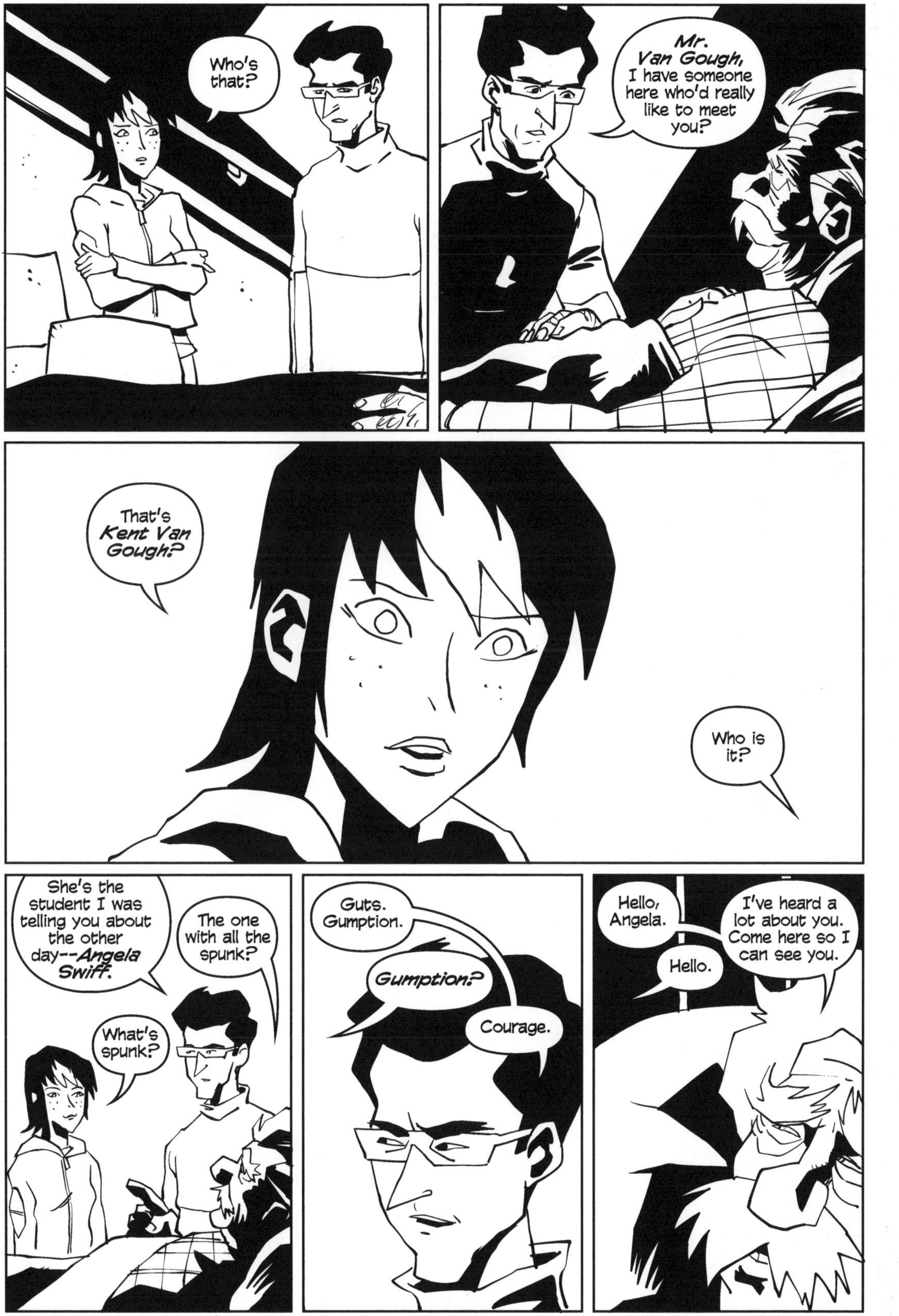
Who's that?
Mr. Van Gough, I have someone here who'd really like to meet you?
That's Kent Van Gough?
Who is it?
She's the student I was telling you about the other day--Angela Swift.
The one with all the spunk?
What's spunk?
Guts. Gumption.
Gumption?
Courage.
Hello, Angela.
Hello.
I've heard a lot about you. Come here so I can see you.

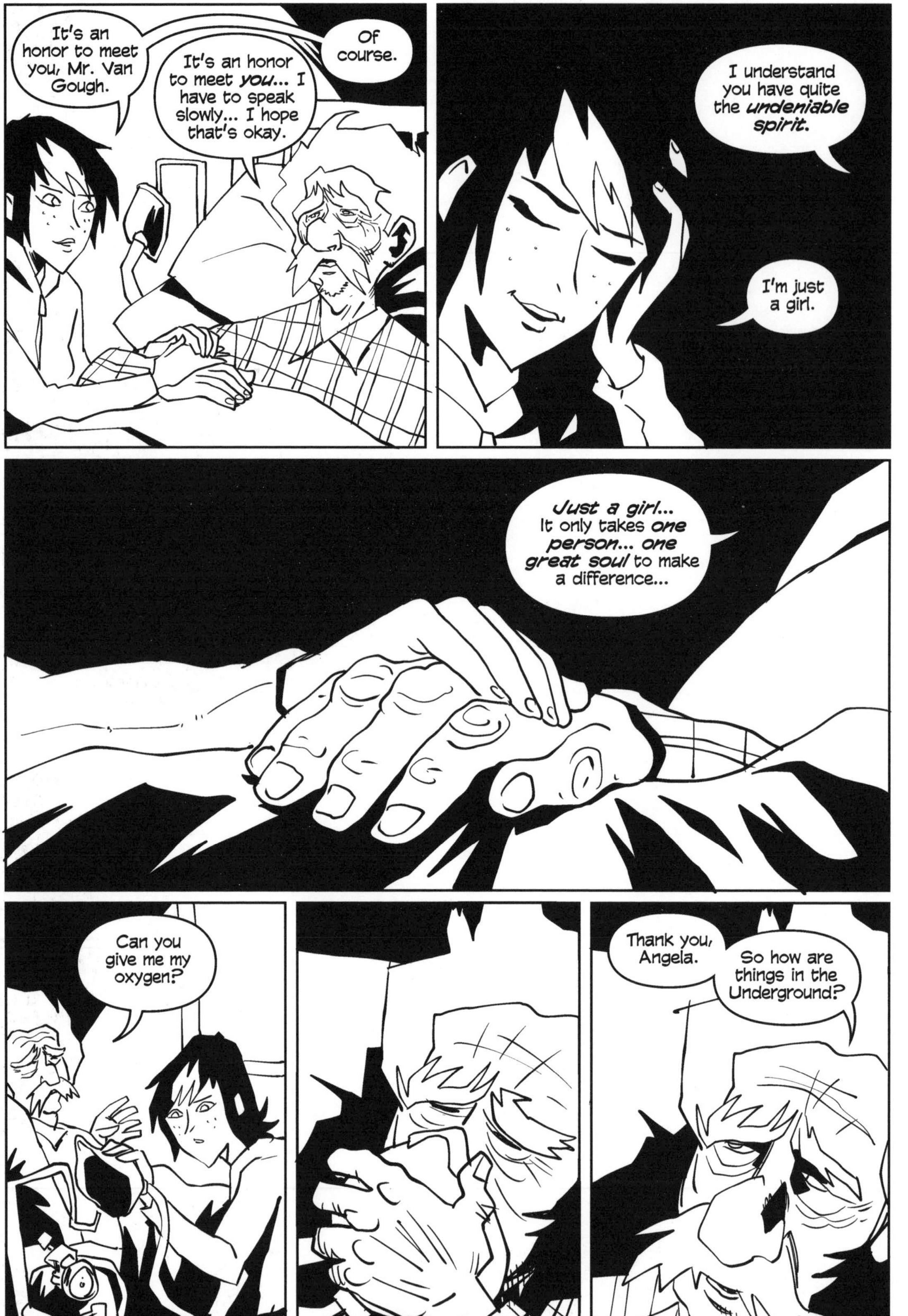

It's an honor to meet you, Mr. Van Gough.
It's an honor to meet *you*... I have to speak slowly... I hope that's okay.
Of course.
I understand you have quite the *undeniable spirit*.
I'm just a girl.
*Just a girl*... It only takes *one person... one great soul* to make a difference...
Can you give me my oxygen?
Thank you, Angela.
So how are things in the Underground?

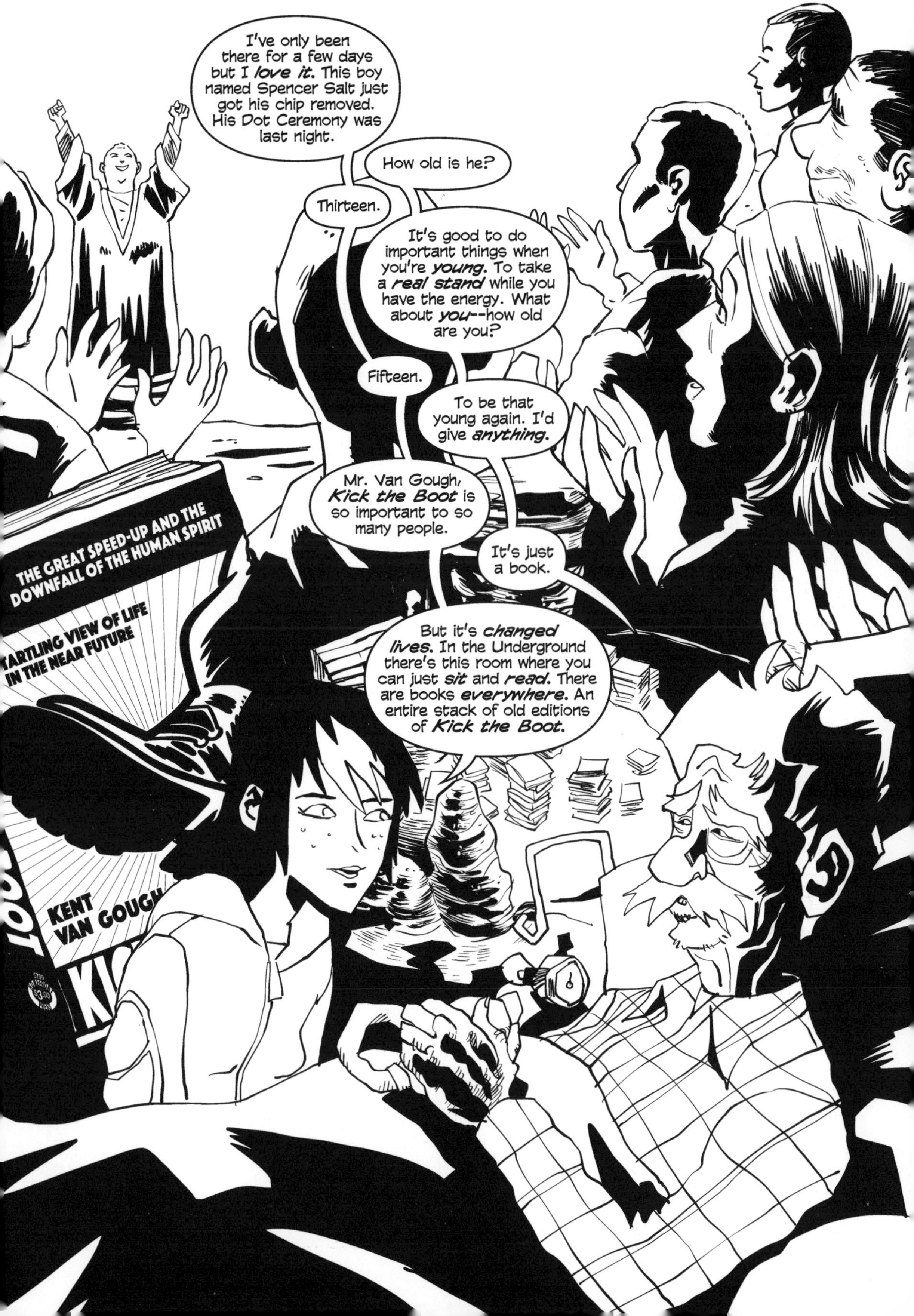

I've only been there for a few days but I love it. This boy named Spencer Salt just got his chip removed. His Dot Ceremony was last night.
How old is he?
Thirteen.
It's good to do important things when you're young. To take a real stand while you have the energy. What about you--how old are you?
Fifteen.
To be that young again. I'd give anything.
Mr. Van Gough, Kick the Boot is so important to so many people.
It's just a book.
But it's changed lives. In the Underground there's this room where you can just sit and read. There are books everywhere. An entire stack of old editions of Kick the Boot.
THE GREAT SPEED-UP AND THE DOWNFALL OF THE HUMAN SPIRIT
TARTLING VIEW OF LIFE IN THE NEAR FUTURE
KENT VAN GOUGH

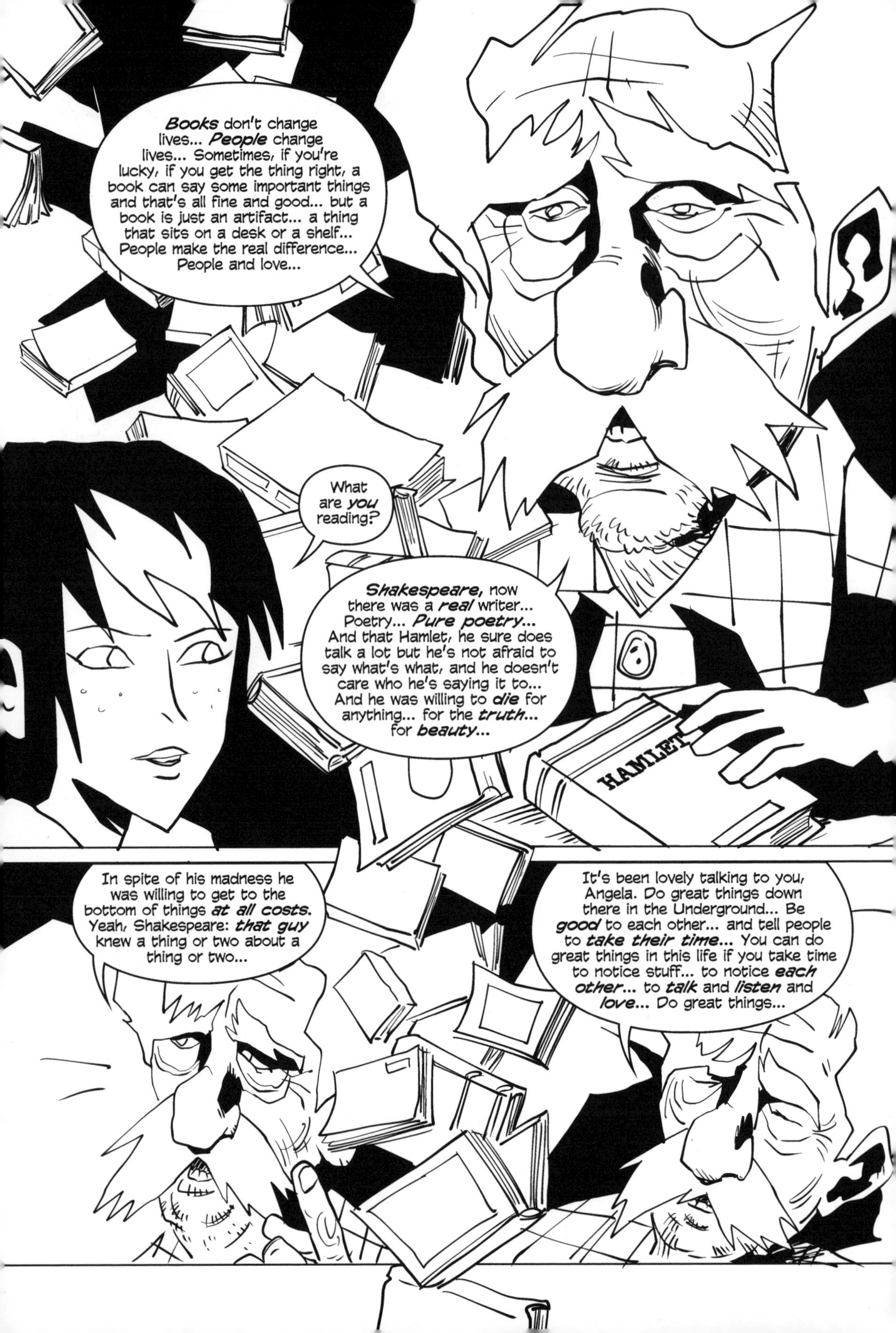
Books don't change lives... People change lives... Sometimes, if you're lucky, if you get the thing right, a book can say some important things and that's all fine and good... but a book is just an artifact... a thing that sits on a desk or a shelf... People make the real difference... People and love...
What are you reading?
Shakespeare, now there was a real writer... Poetry... Pure poetry... And that Hamlet, he sure does talk a lot but he's not afraid to say what's what, and he doesn't care who he's saying it to... And he was willing to die for anything... for the truth... for beauty...
HAMLET
In spite of his madness he was willing to get to the bottom of things at all costs. Yeah, Shakespeare: that guy knew a thing or two about a thing or two...
It's been lovely talking to you, Angela. Do great things down there in the Underground... Be good to each other... and tell people to take their time... You can do great things in this life if you take time to notice stuff... to notice each other... to talk and listen and love... Do great things...

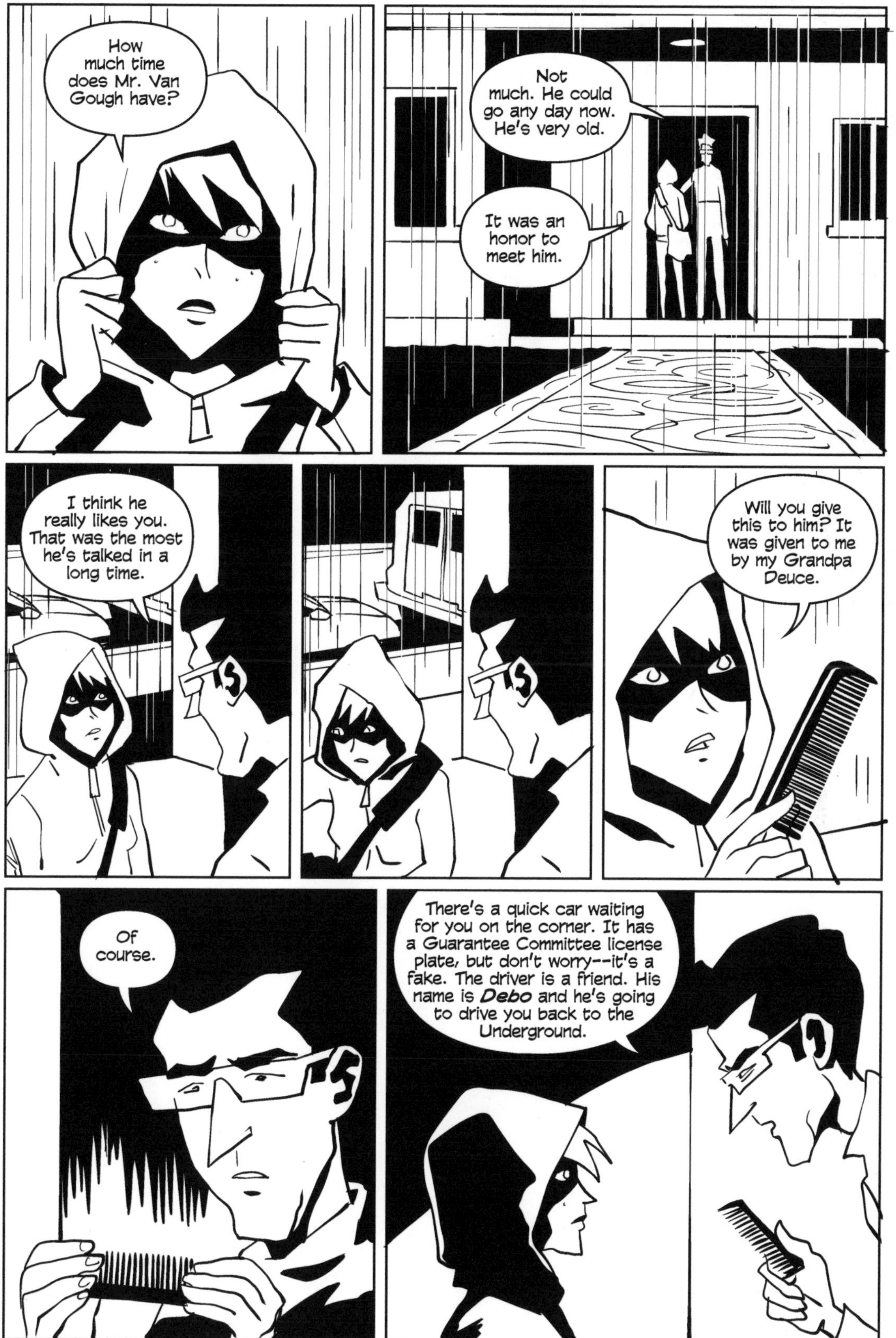
How much time does Mr. Van Gough have?
Not much. He could go any day now. He's very old.
It was an honor to meet him.
I think he really likes you. That was the most he's talked in a long time.
Will you give this to him? It was given to me by my Grandpa Deuce.
Of course.
There's a quick car waiting for you on the corner. It has a Guarantee Committee license plate, but don't worry--it's a fake. The driver is a friend. His name is *Debo* and he's going to drive you back to the Underground.

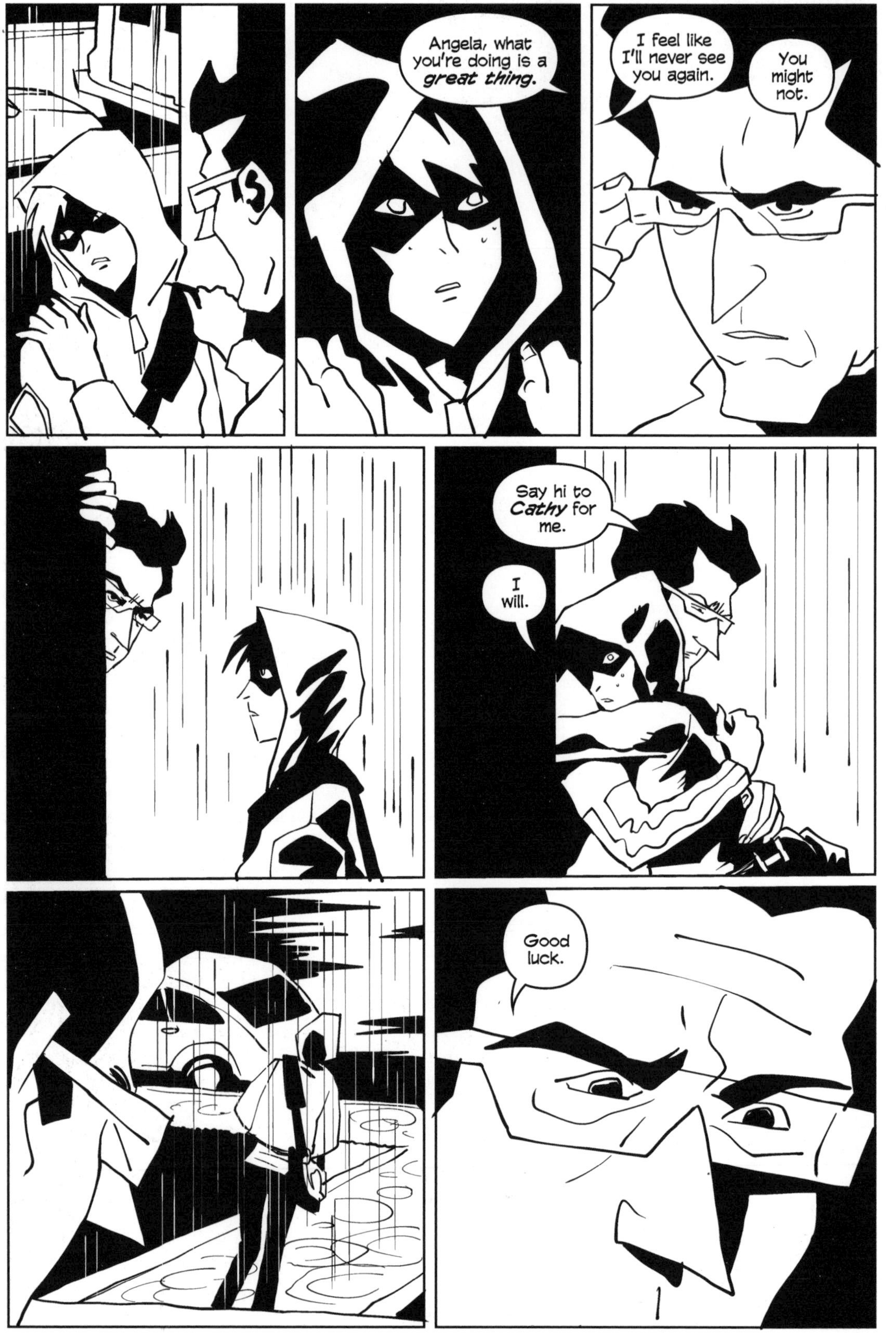

Angela, what you're doing is a *great thing*.
I feel like I'll never see you again.
You might not.
Say hi to *Cathy* for me.
I will.
Good luck.

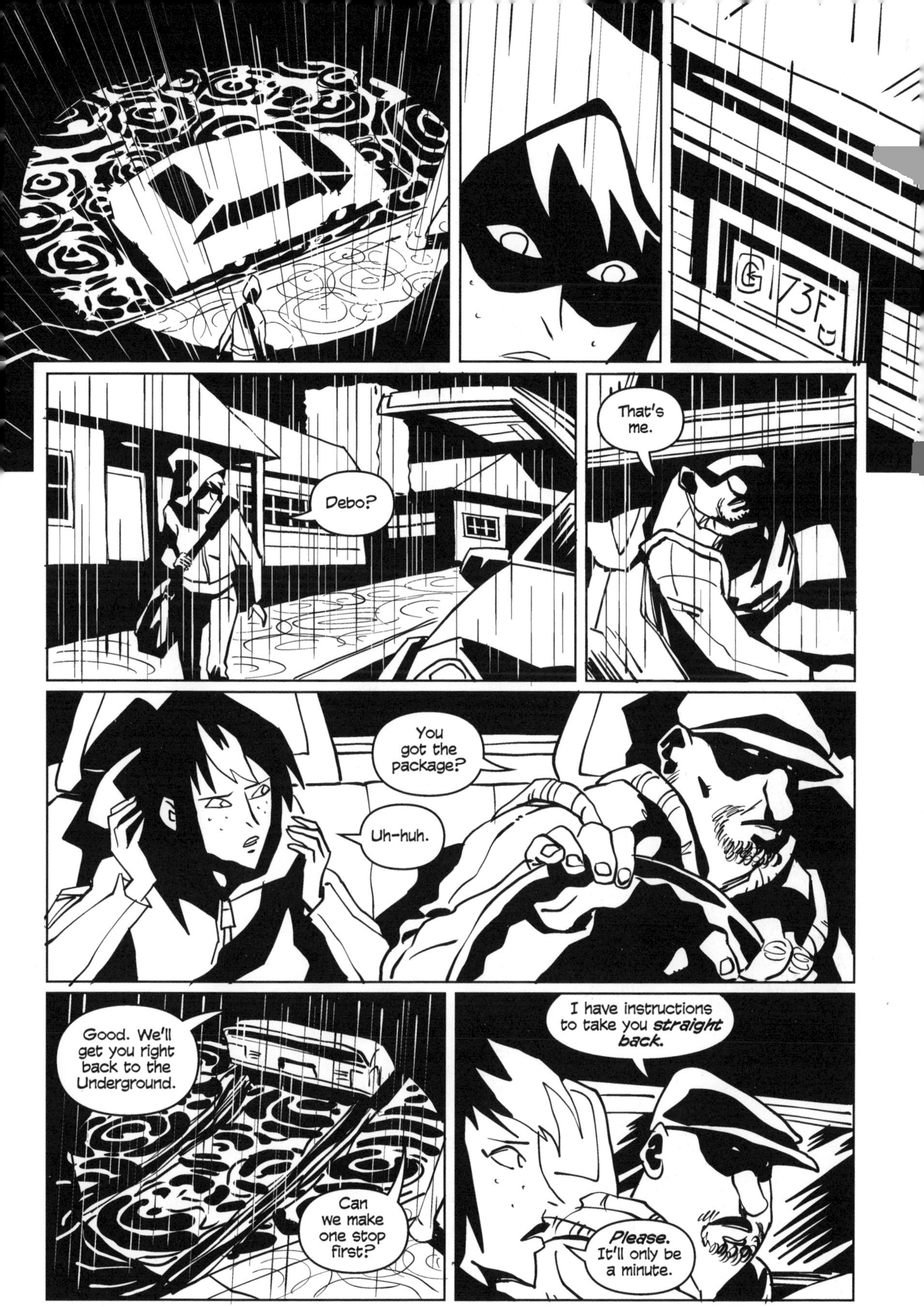
G 73F
Debo?
That's me.
You got the package?
Uh-huh.
Good. We'll get you right back to the Underground.
Can we make one stop first?
I have instructions to take you *straight back.*
*Please.* It'll only be a minute.

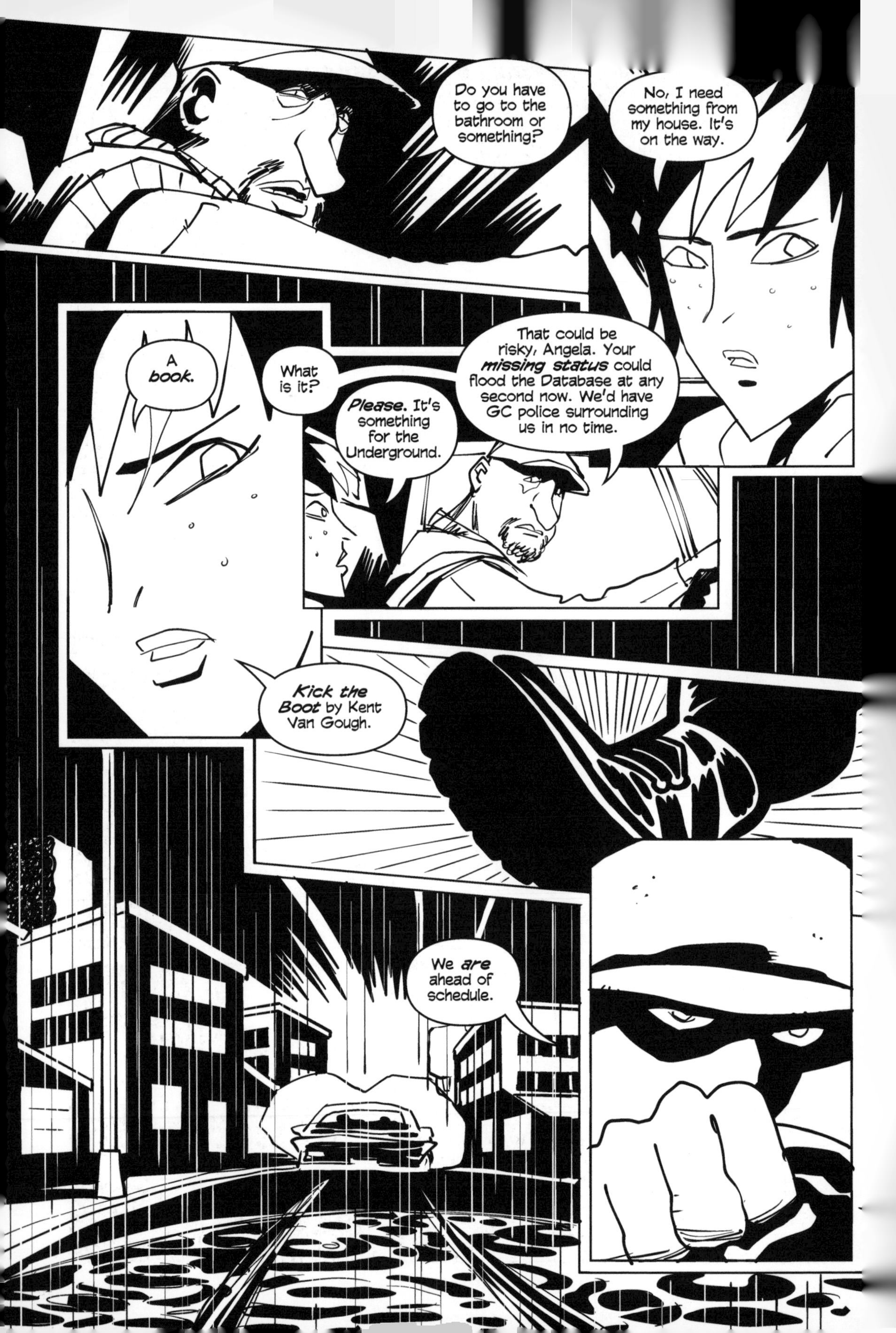
Do you have to go to the bathroom or something?
No, I need something from my house. It's on the way.
What is it?
A book.
That could be risky, Angela. Your missing status could flood the Database at any second now. We'd have GC police surrounding us in no time.
Please. It's something for the Underground.
Kick the Boot by Kent Van Gough.
We are ahead of schedule.

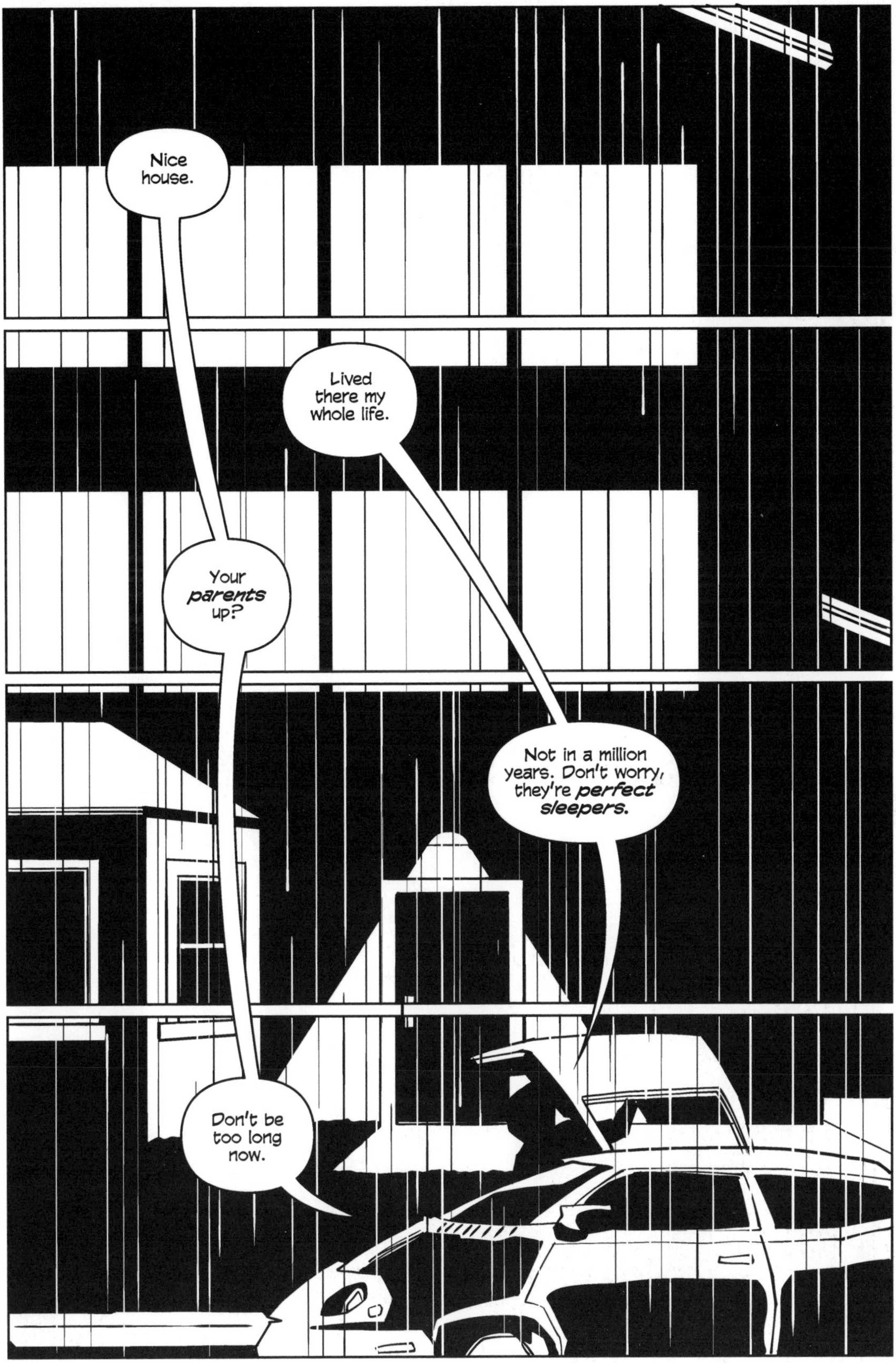
Nice house.
Lived there my whole life.
Your parents up?
Not in a million years. Don't worry, they're perfect sleepers.
Don't be too long now.

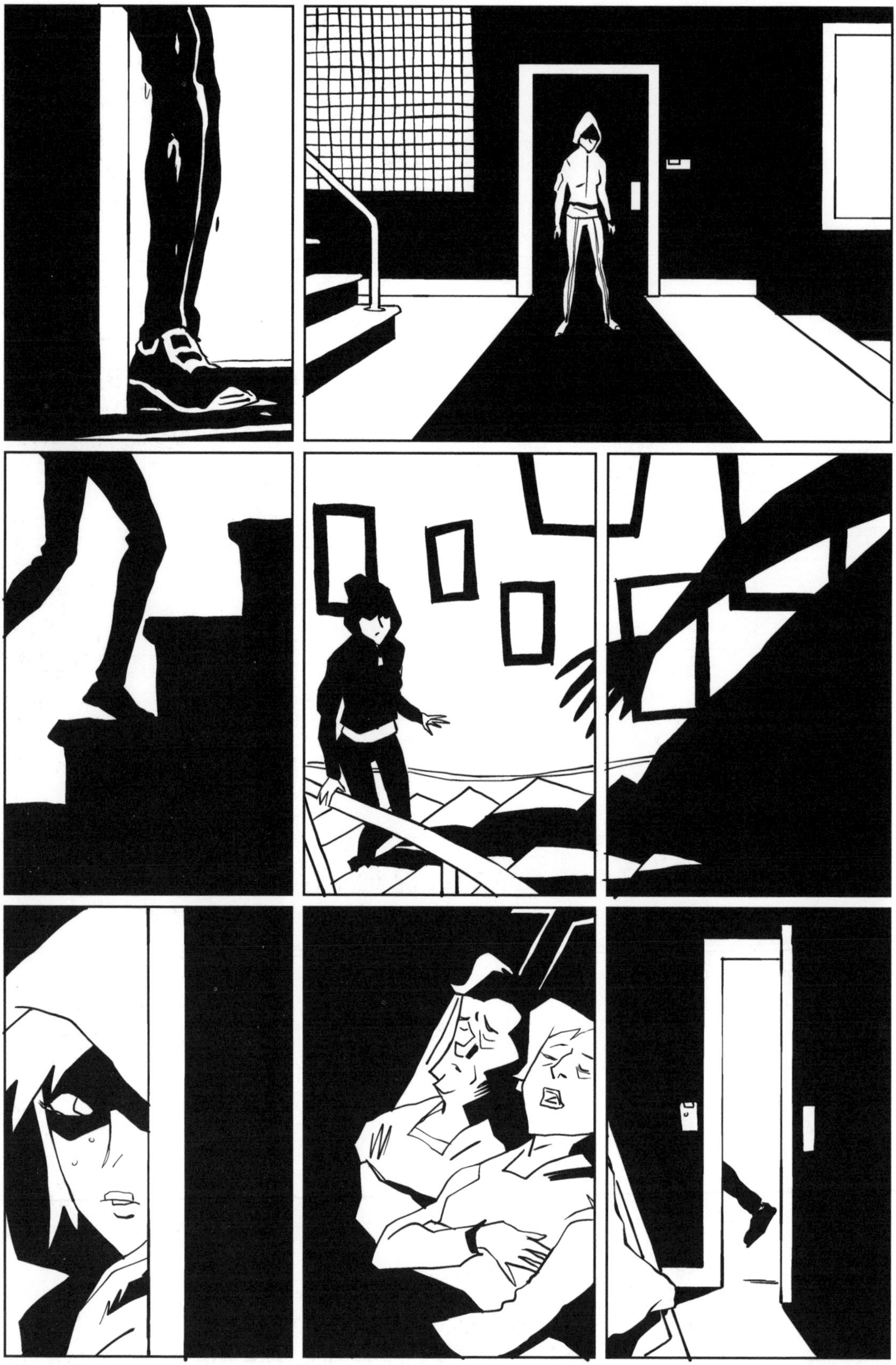

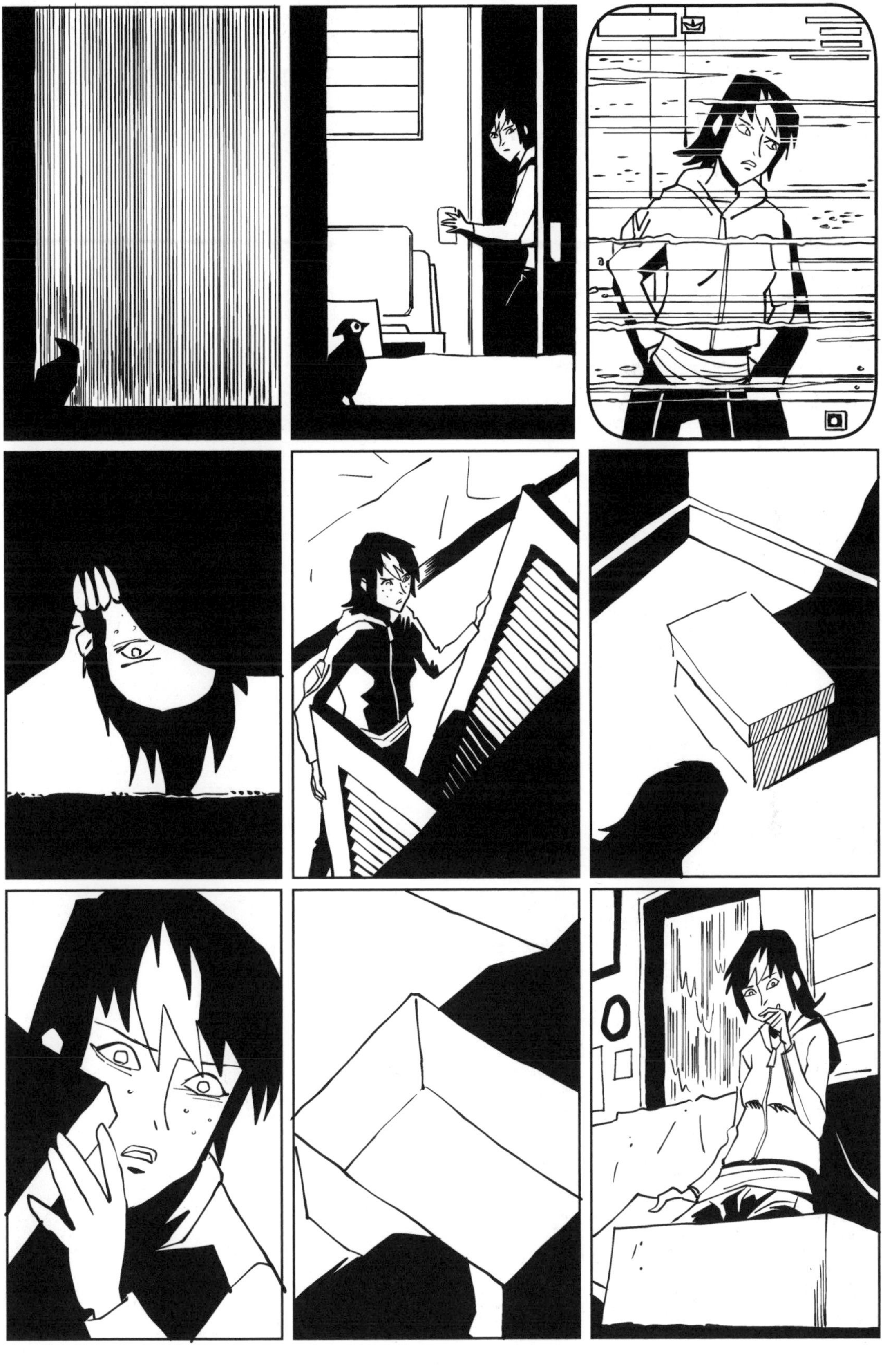

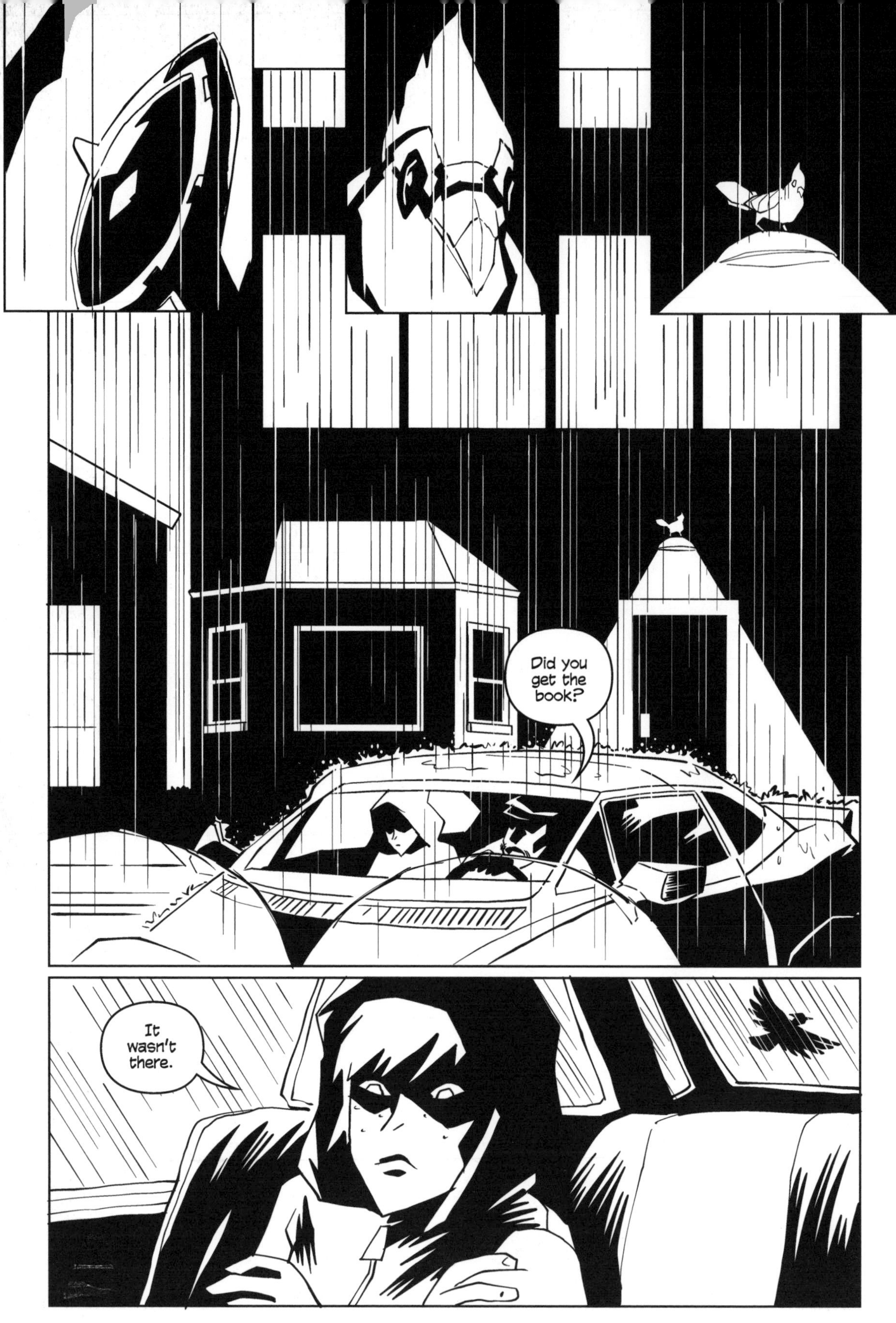
Did you get the book?
It wasn't there.

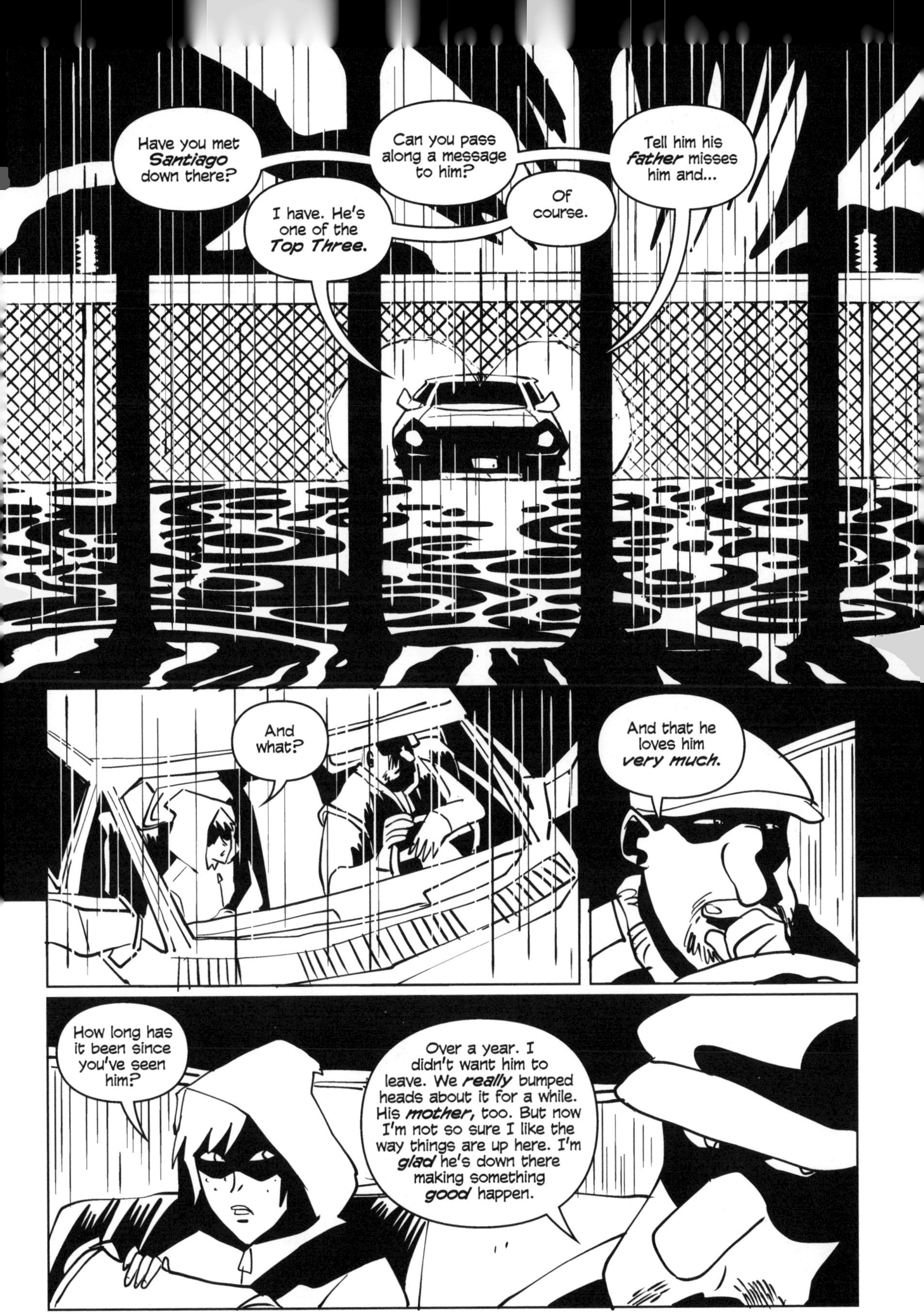
Have you met *Santiago* down there?
I have. He's one of the *Top Three.*
Can you pass along a message to him?
Of course.
Tell him his *father* misses him and...
And what?
And that he loves him *very much.*
How long has it been since you've seen him?
Over a year. I didn't want him to leave. We *really* bumped heads about it for a while. His *mother,* too. But now I'm not so sure I like the way things are up here. I'm *glad* he's down there making something *good* happen.

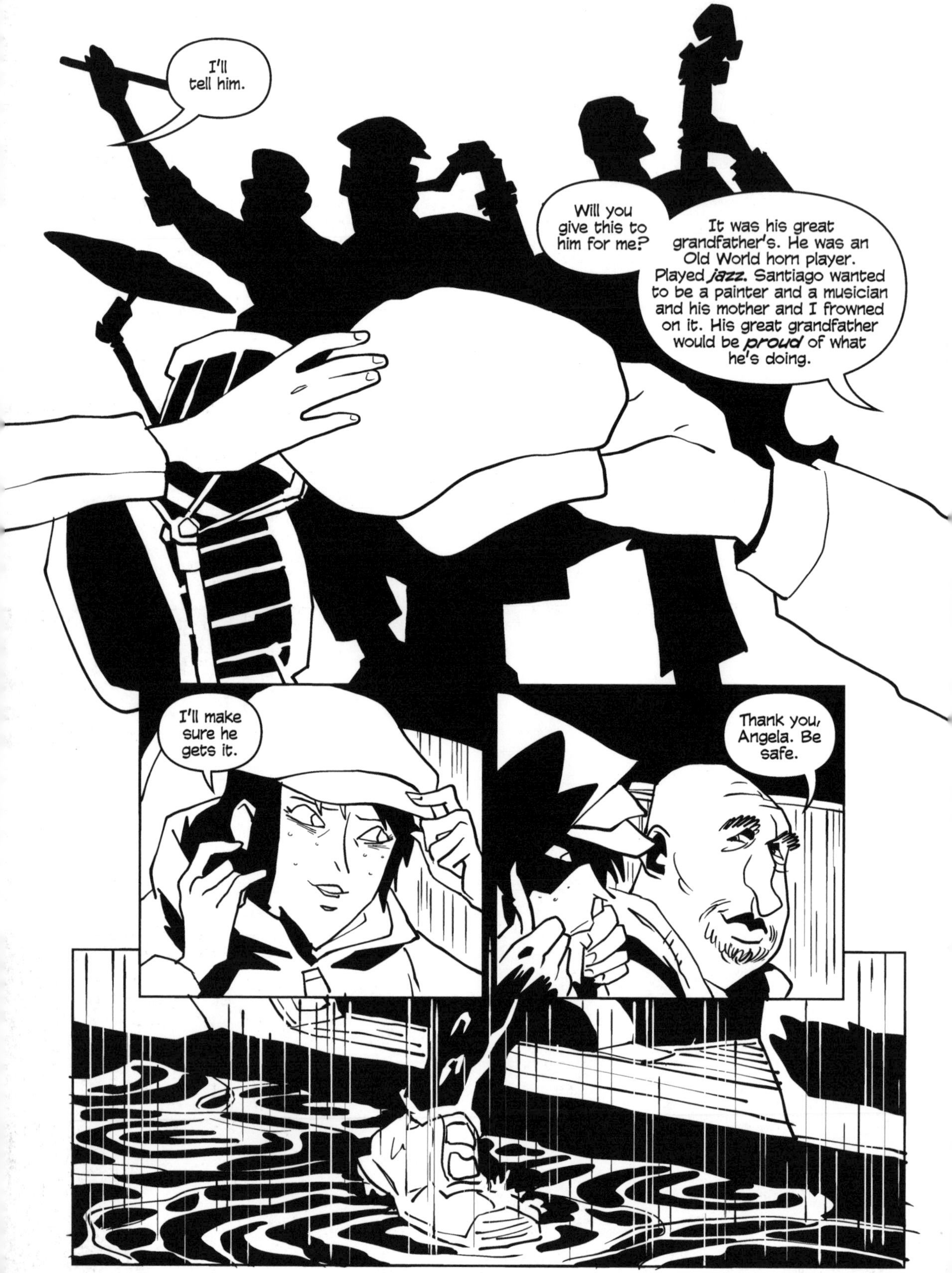
I'll tell him.
Will you give this to him for me?
It was his great grandfather's. He was an Old World horn player. Played *jazz*. Santiago wanted to be a painter and a musician and his mother and I frowned on it. His great grandfather would be *proud* of what he's doing.
I'll make sure he gets it.
Thank you, Angela. Be safe.

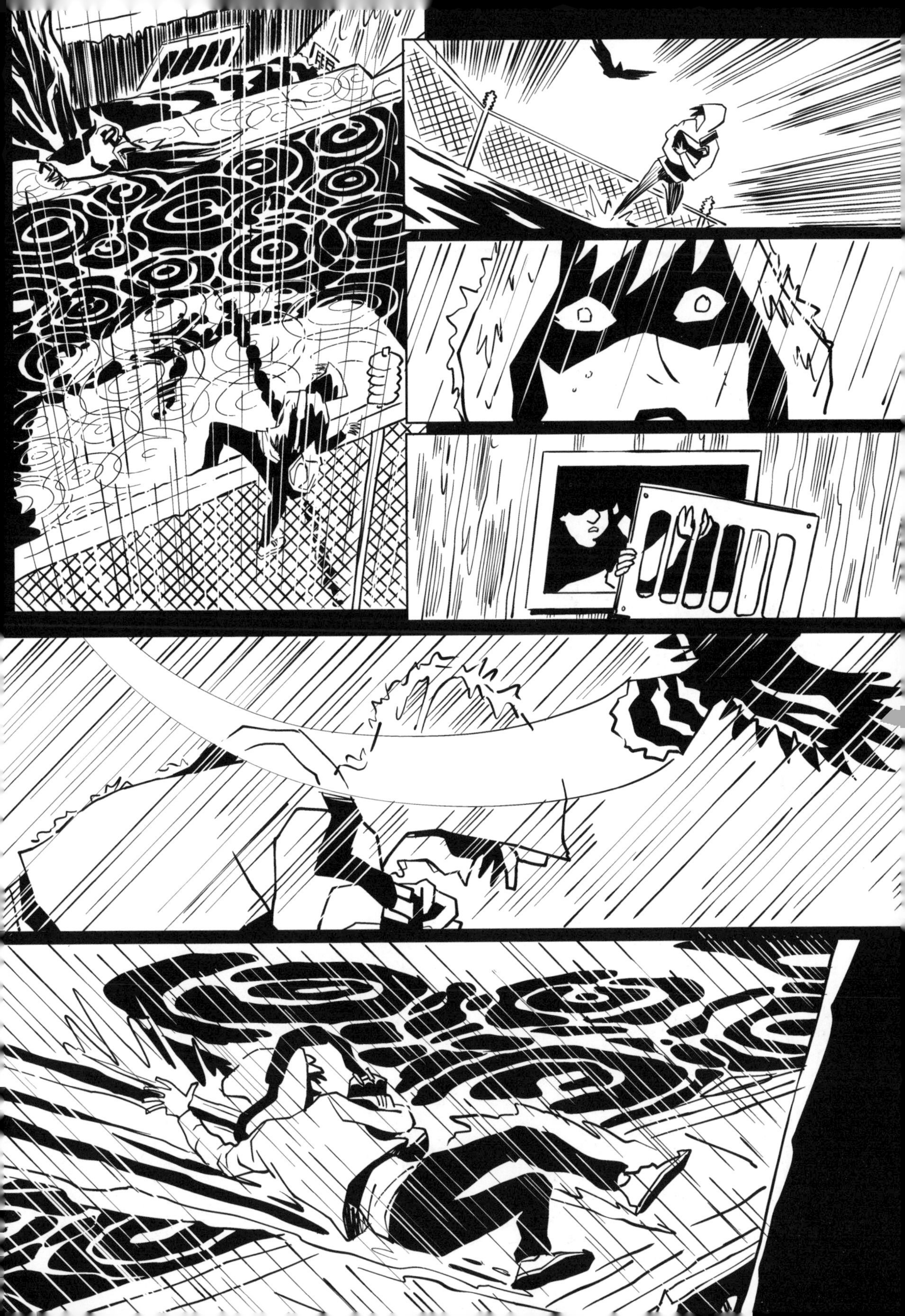

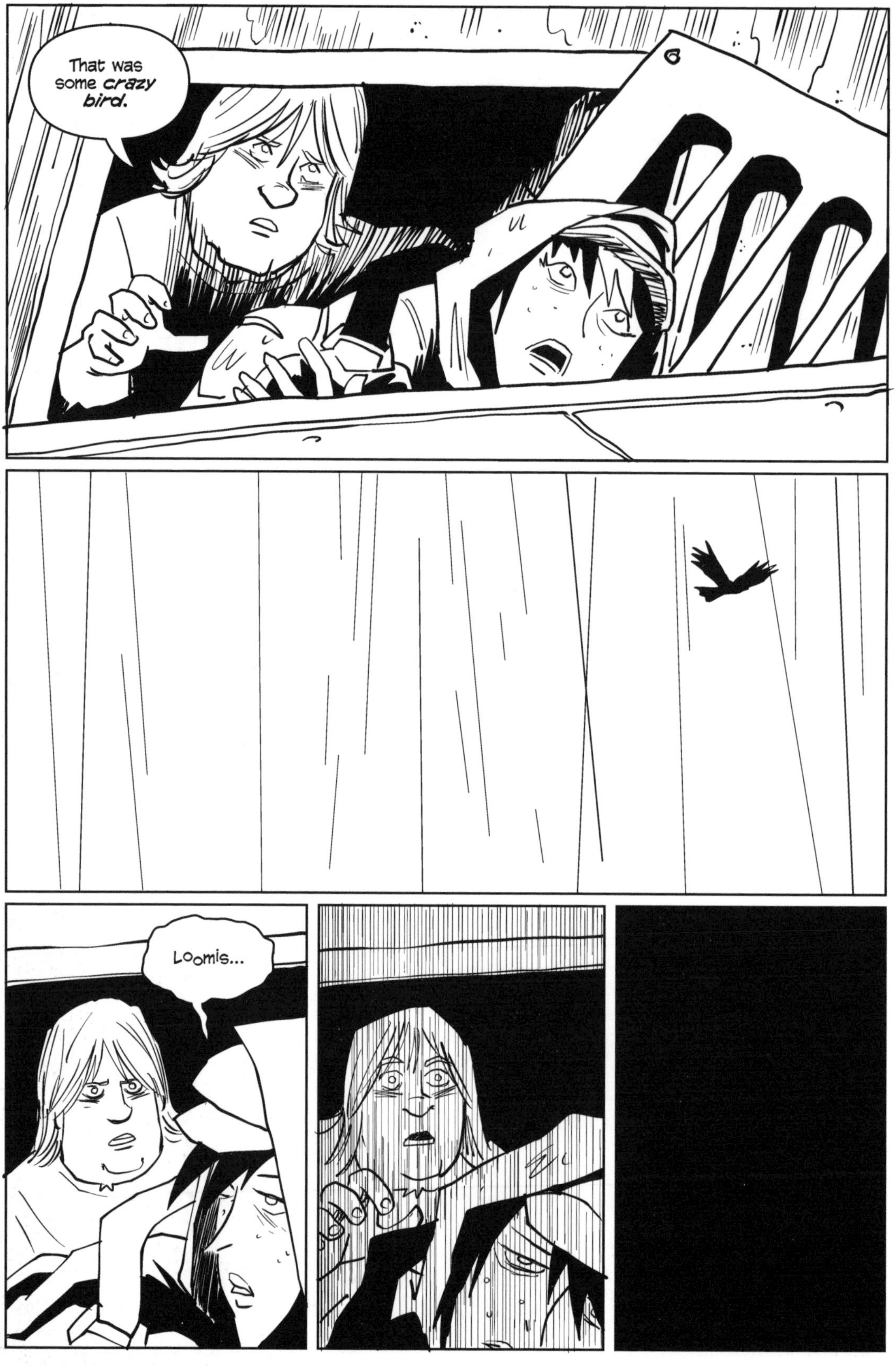
That was some *crazy* *bird*.
Loomis...

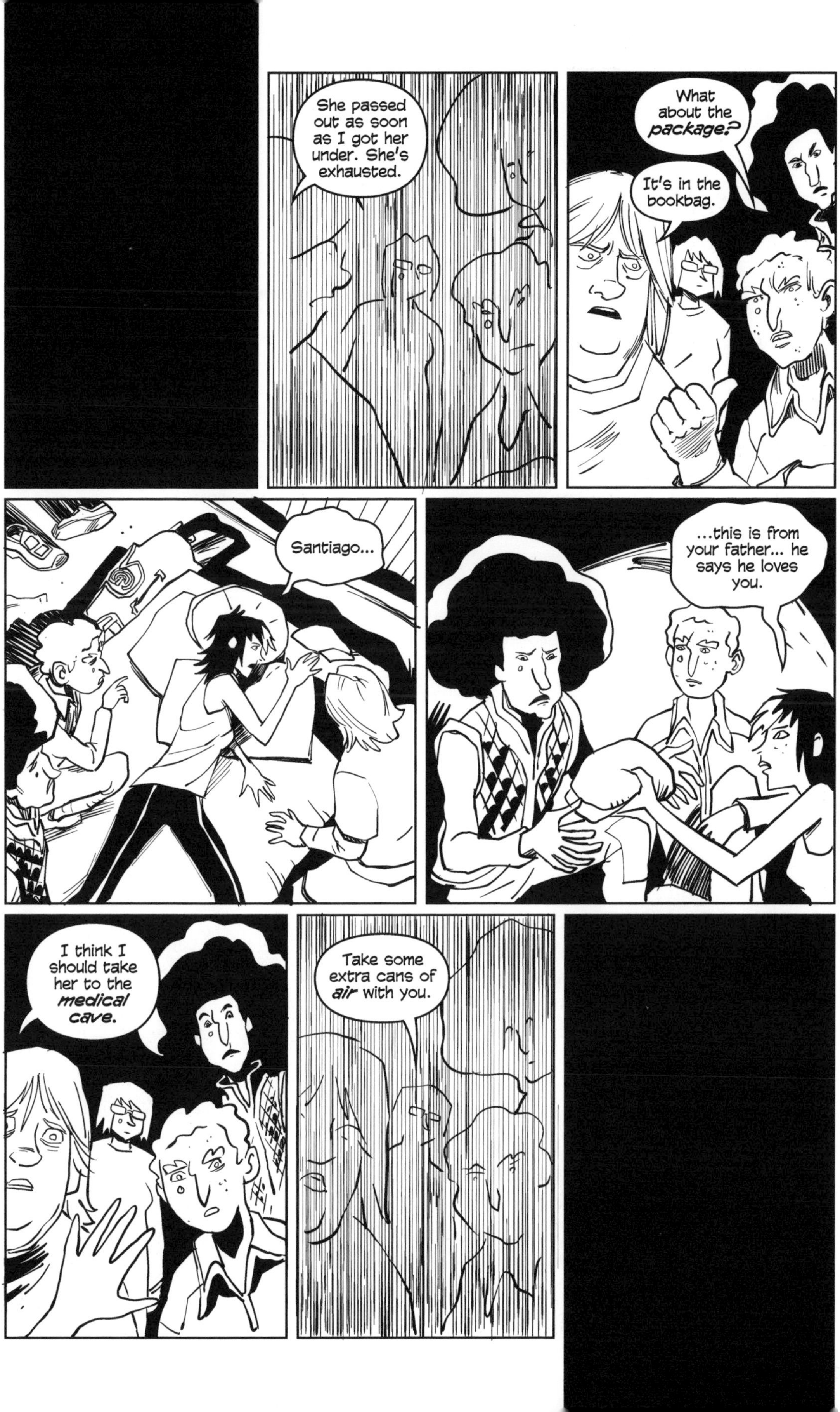
She passed out as soon as I got her under. She's exhausted.
What about the *package?*
It's in the bookbag.
Santiago...
...this is from your father... he says he loves you.
I think I should take her to the *medical cave.*
Take some extra cans of *air* with you.

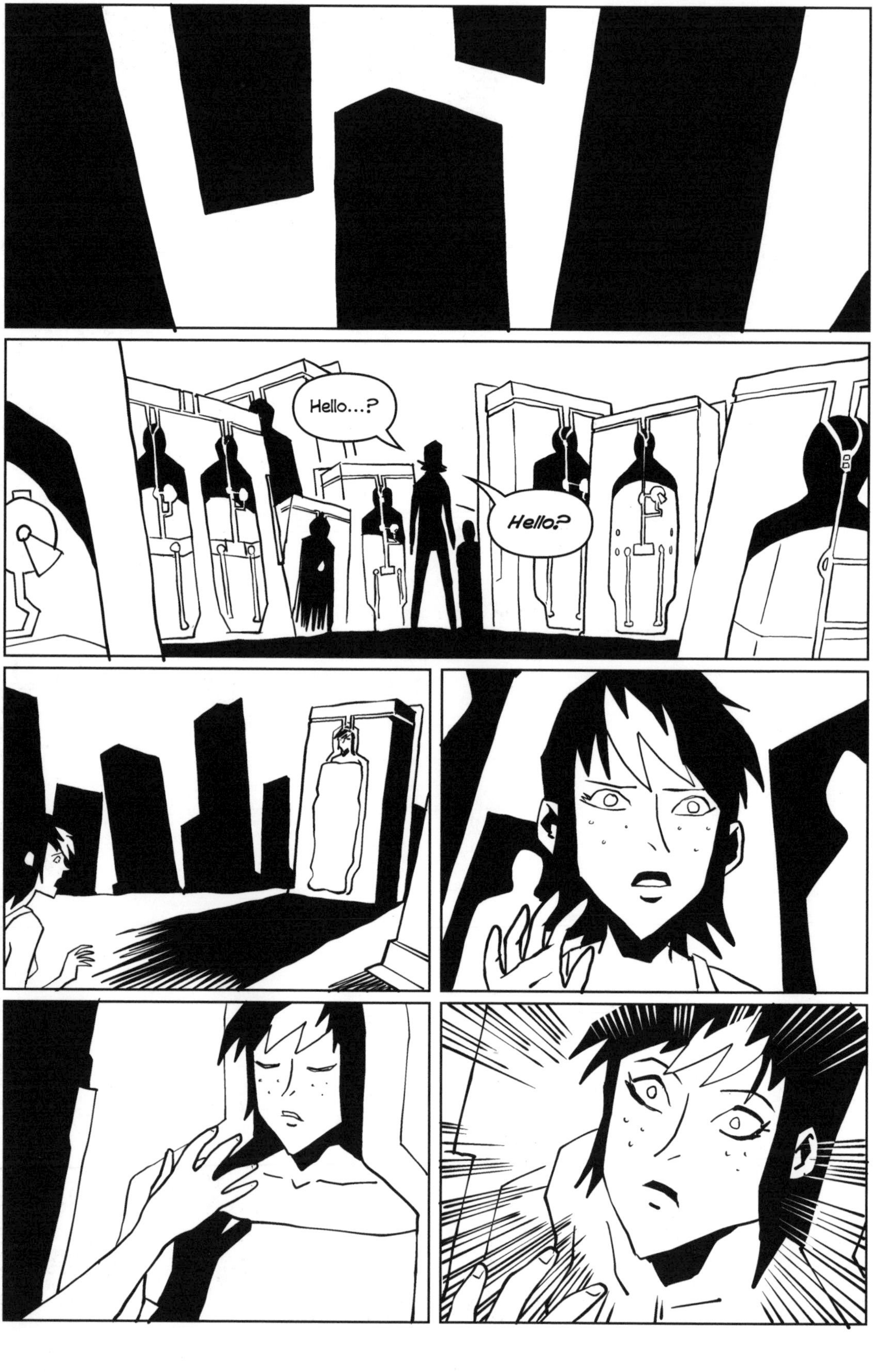
Hello...?
Hello?

**GO!**

Hey.

Hey.

How does it feel to be a *hero?*

Where am I?

*PUFF!*

You are in the medical cave. You have been asleep for half the day. Dr. Hackett says you were severely dehydrated and exhausted. You had a pretty high fever, too, but it broke about three hours ago.

I feel like I got hit in the head with a *rapidhammer.* Have you been here the whole time?

Yes. You are a *lovely* sleeper...

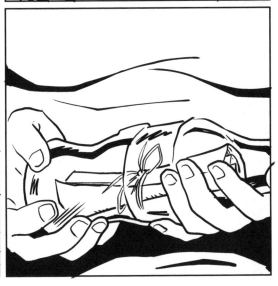

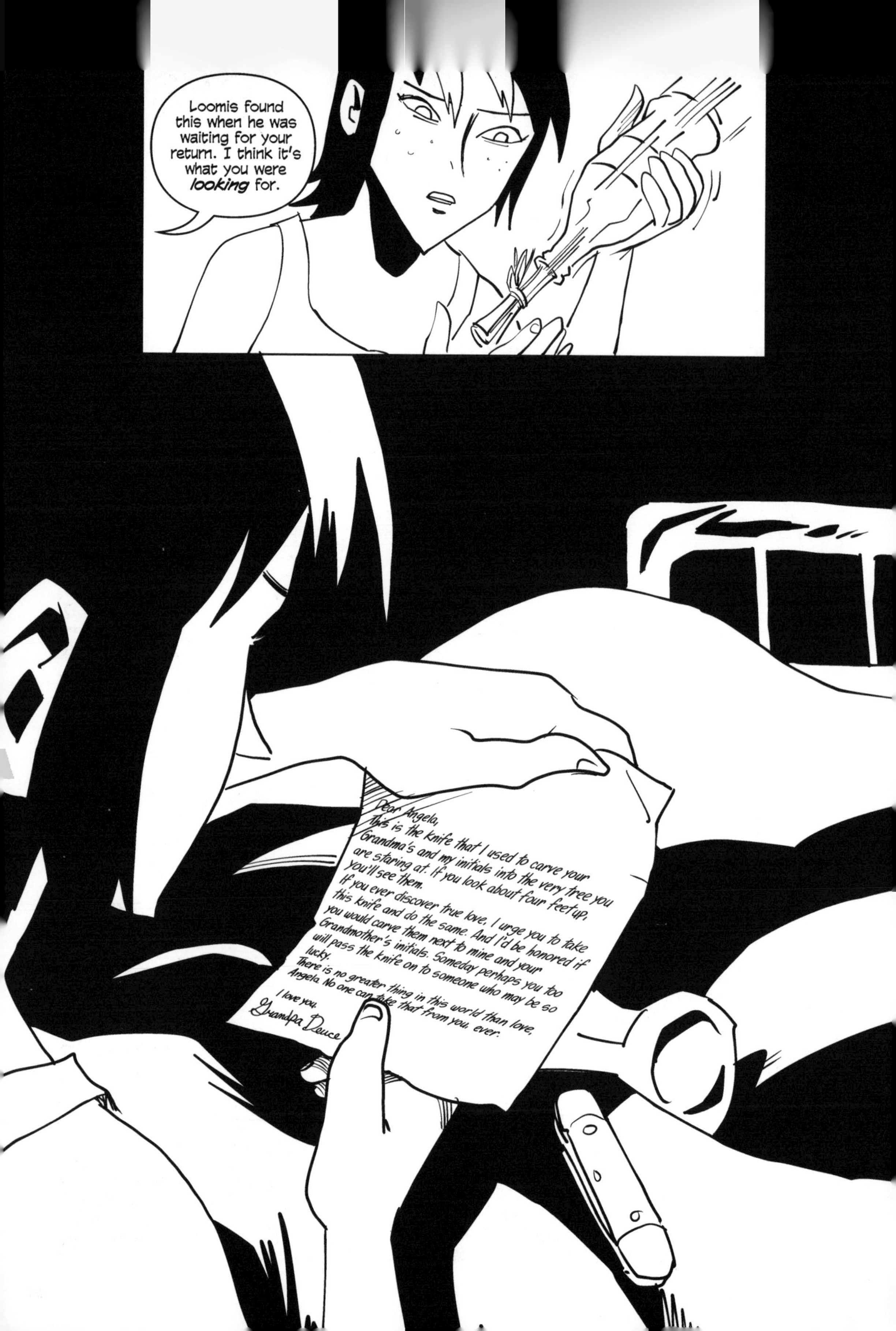
Loomis found this when he was waiting for your return. I think it's what you were *looking* for.
Dear Angela,
This is the knife that I used to carve your Grandma's and my initials into the very tree you are staring at. If you look about four feet up, you'll see them.
If you ever discover true love, I urge you to take this knife and do the same. And I'd be honored if you would carve them next to mine and your Grandmother's initials. Someday perhaps you too will pass the knife on to someone who may be so lucky.
There is no greater thing in this world than love, Angela. No one can take that from you, ever.
I love you.
Grandpa Deuce

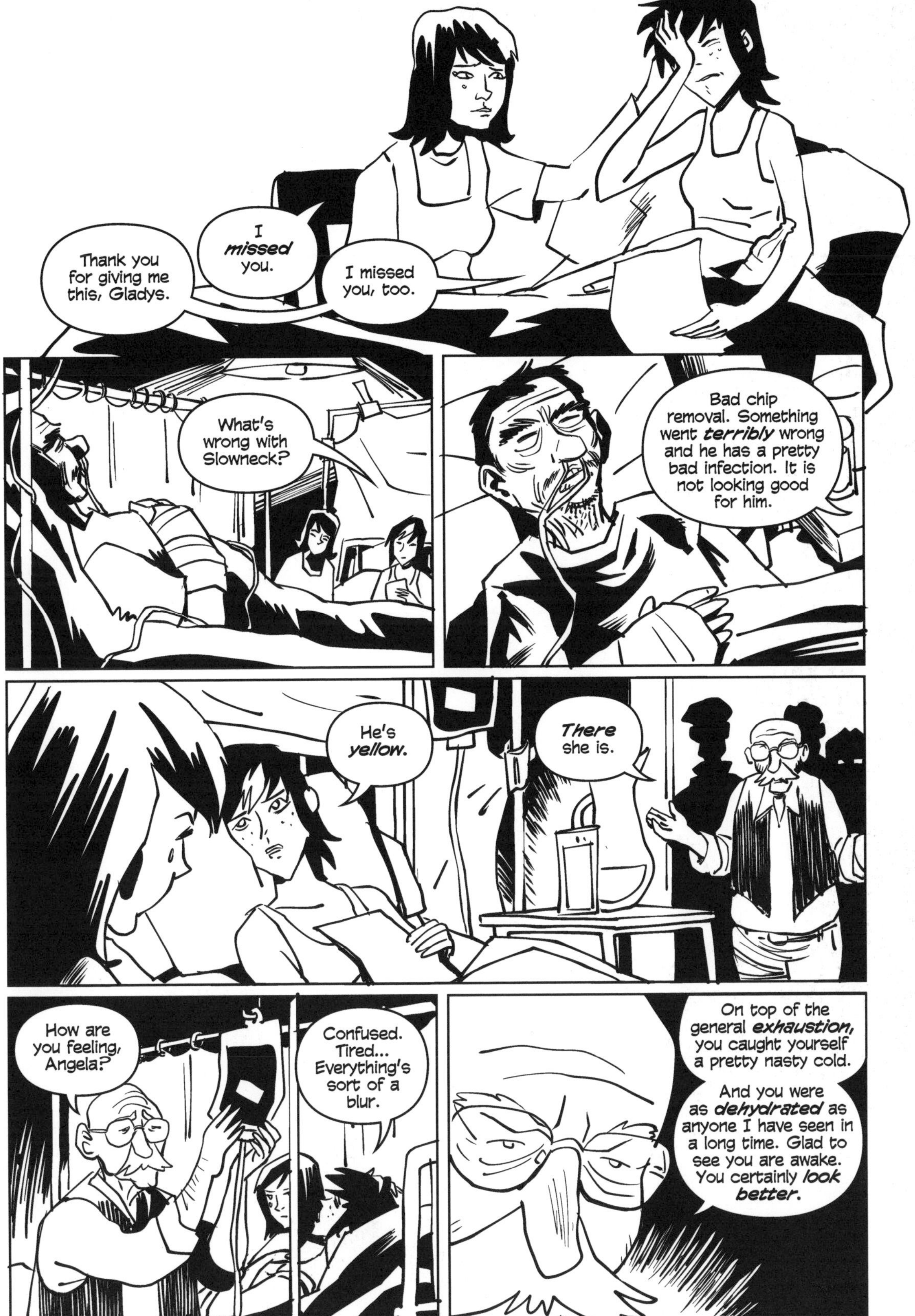
Thank you for giving me this, Gladys.
I *missed* you.
I missed you, too.
What's wrong with Slowneck?
Bad chip removal. Something went *terribly* wrong and he has a pretty bad infection. It is not looking good for him.
He's *yellow.*
*There* she is.
How are you feeling, Angela?
Confused. Tired... Everything's sort of a blur.
On top of the general *exhaustion,* you caught yourself a pretty nasty cold.
And you were as *dehydrated* as anyone I have seen in a long time. Glad to see you are awake. You certainly *look better*.

Angela, on behalf of the *Underground* I want to thank you for intercepting that package.

*Thank you, Angela.*

Thank you, Angela. And thank you for the *hat.*

Now that it's *here,* will someone please tell me what was *in* the package?

Micropills.

*Micropills?*

Highly engineered medical tablets. About the size of a grain of salt.

We're talking about *drugs?*

We are talking about the *next step* toward *full deceleration.*


152

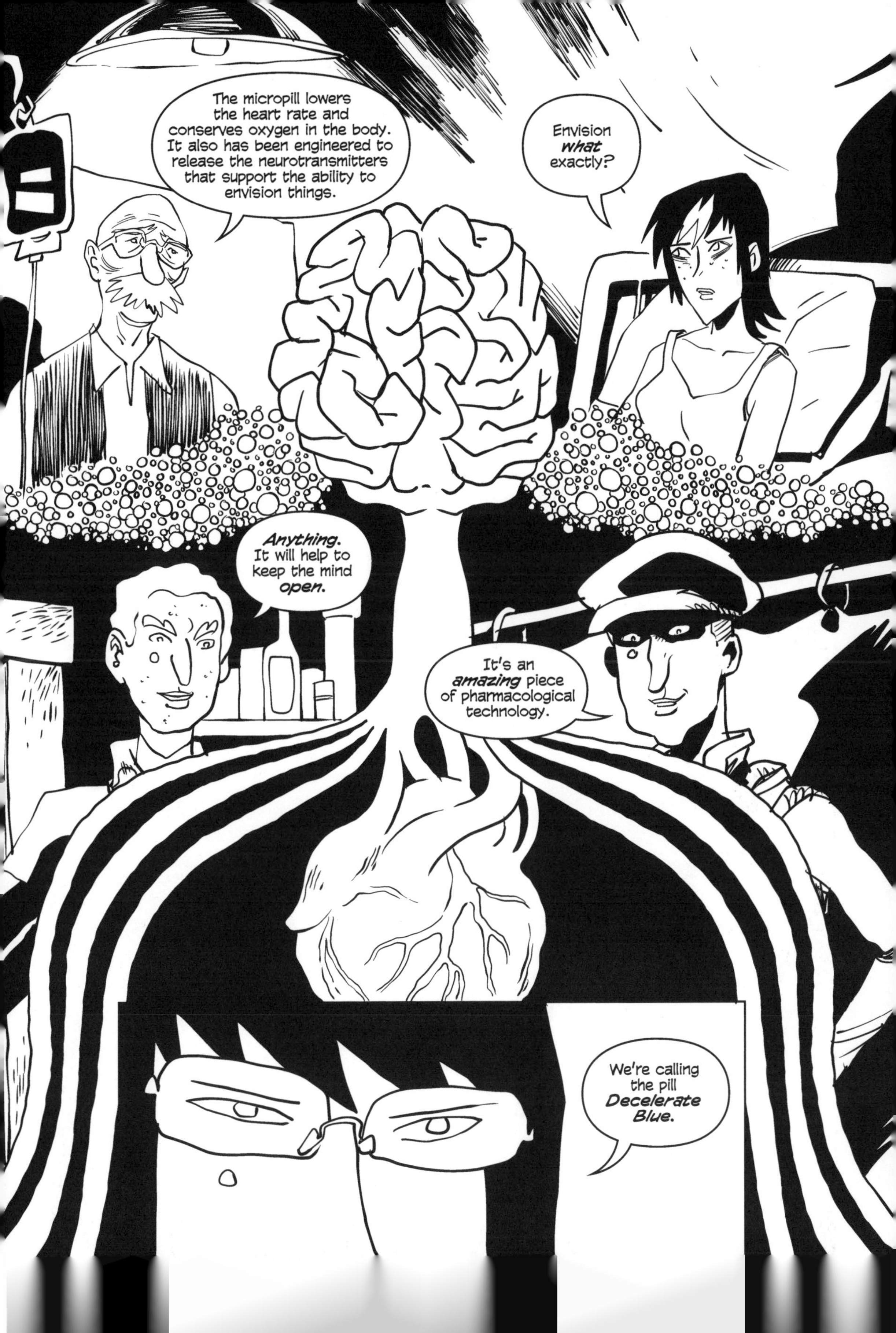
The micropill lowers the heart rate and conserves oxygen in the body. It also has been engineered to release the neurotransmitters that support the ability to envision things.
Envision *what* exactly?
*Anything*. It will help to keep the mind *open*.
It's an *amazing* piece of pharmacological technology.
We're calling the pill *Decelerate Blue*.

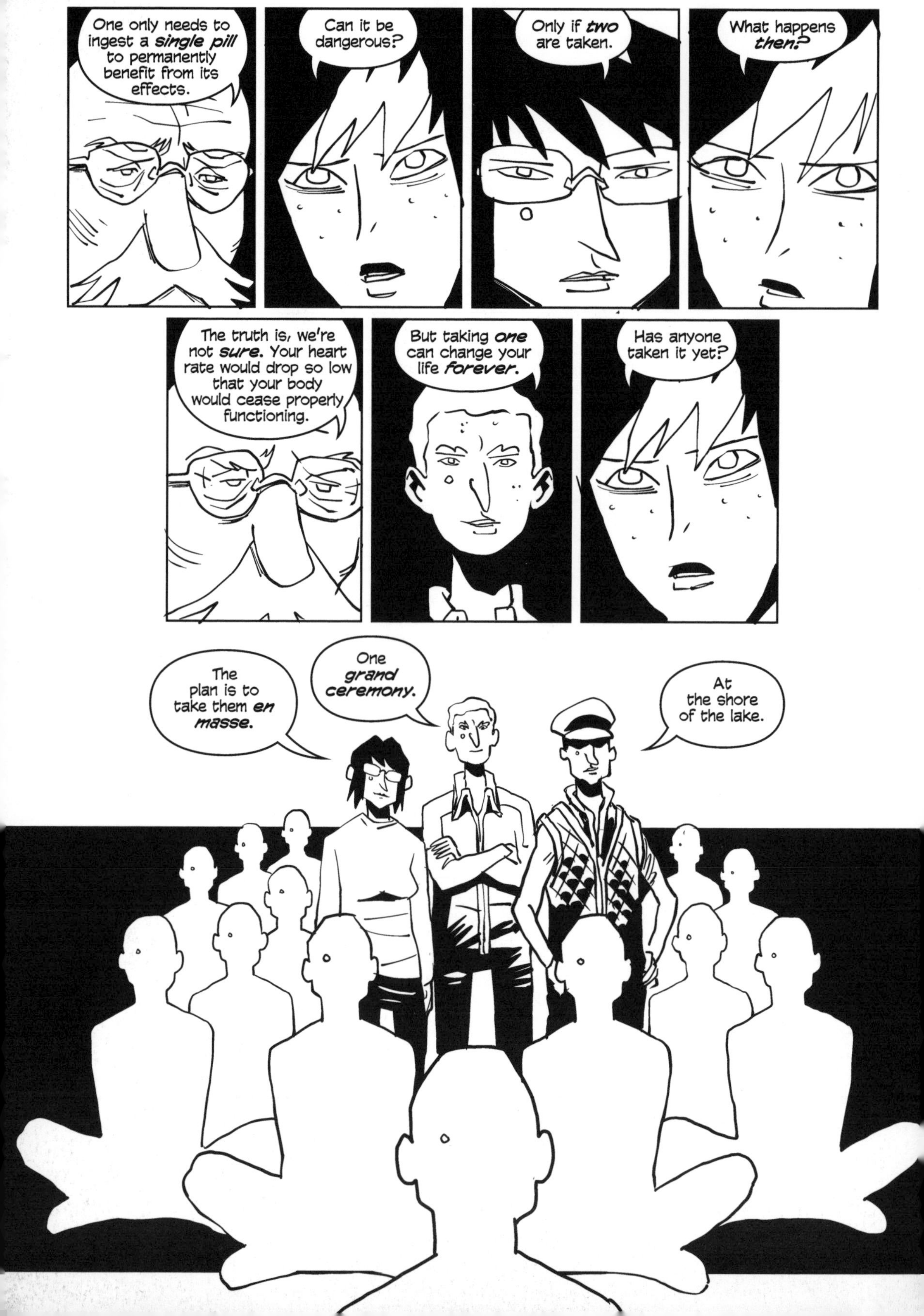

One only needs to ingest a *single pill* to permanently benefit from its effects.
Can it be dangerous?
Only if *two* are taken.
What happens *then?*
The truth is, we're not *sure.* Your heart rate would drop so low that your body would cease properly functioning.
But taking *one* can change your life *forever.*
Has anyone taken it yet?
The plan is to take them *en masse.*
One *grand ceremony.*
At the shore of the lake.

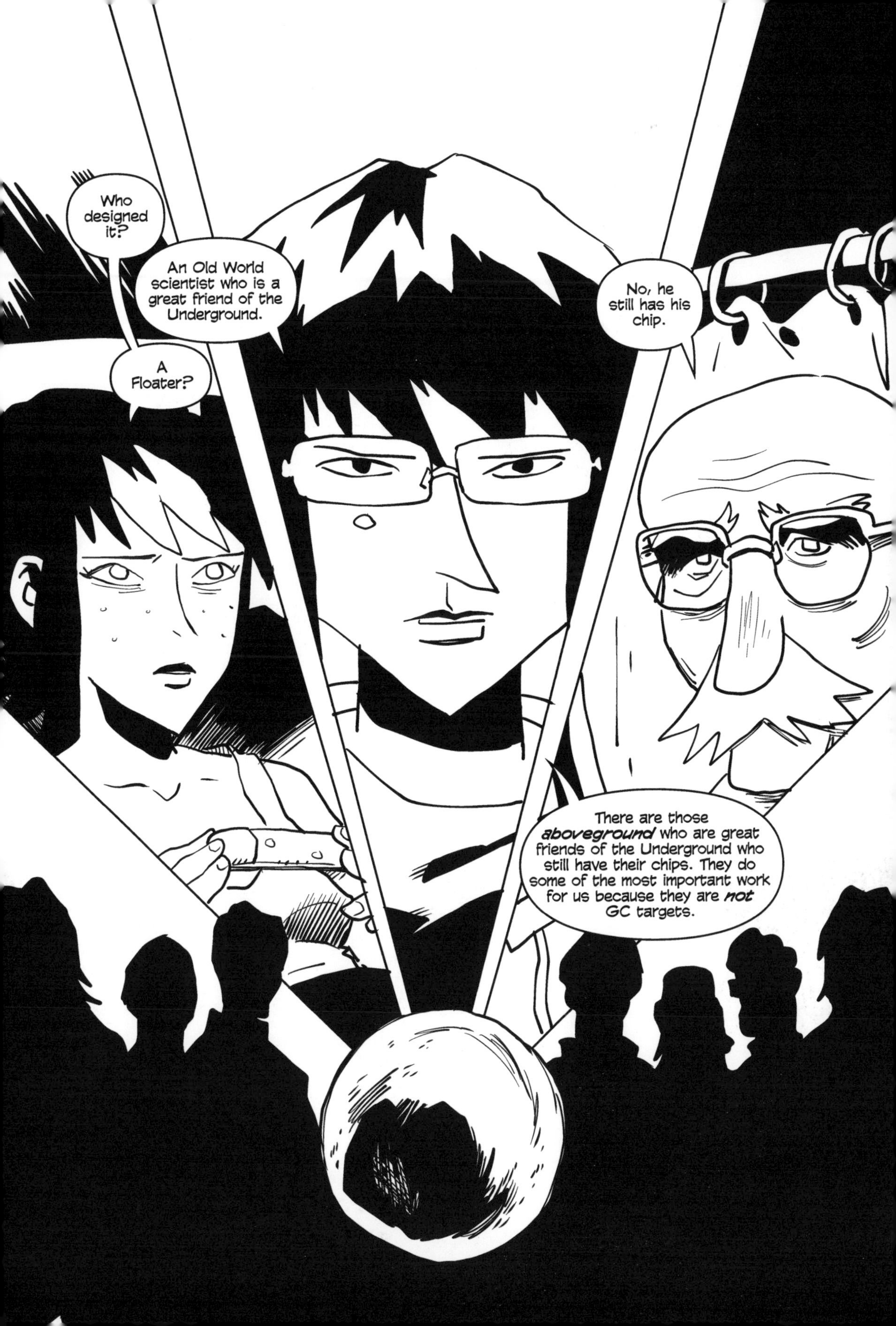
Who designed it?
An Old World scientist who is a great friend of the Underground.
A Floater?
No, he still has his chip.
There are those ***aboveground*** who are great friends of the Underground who still have their chips. They do some of the most important work for us because they are ***not*** GC targets.

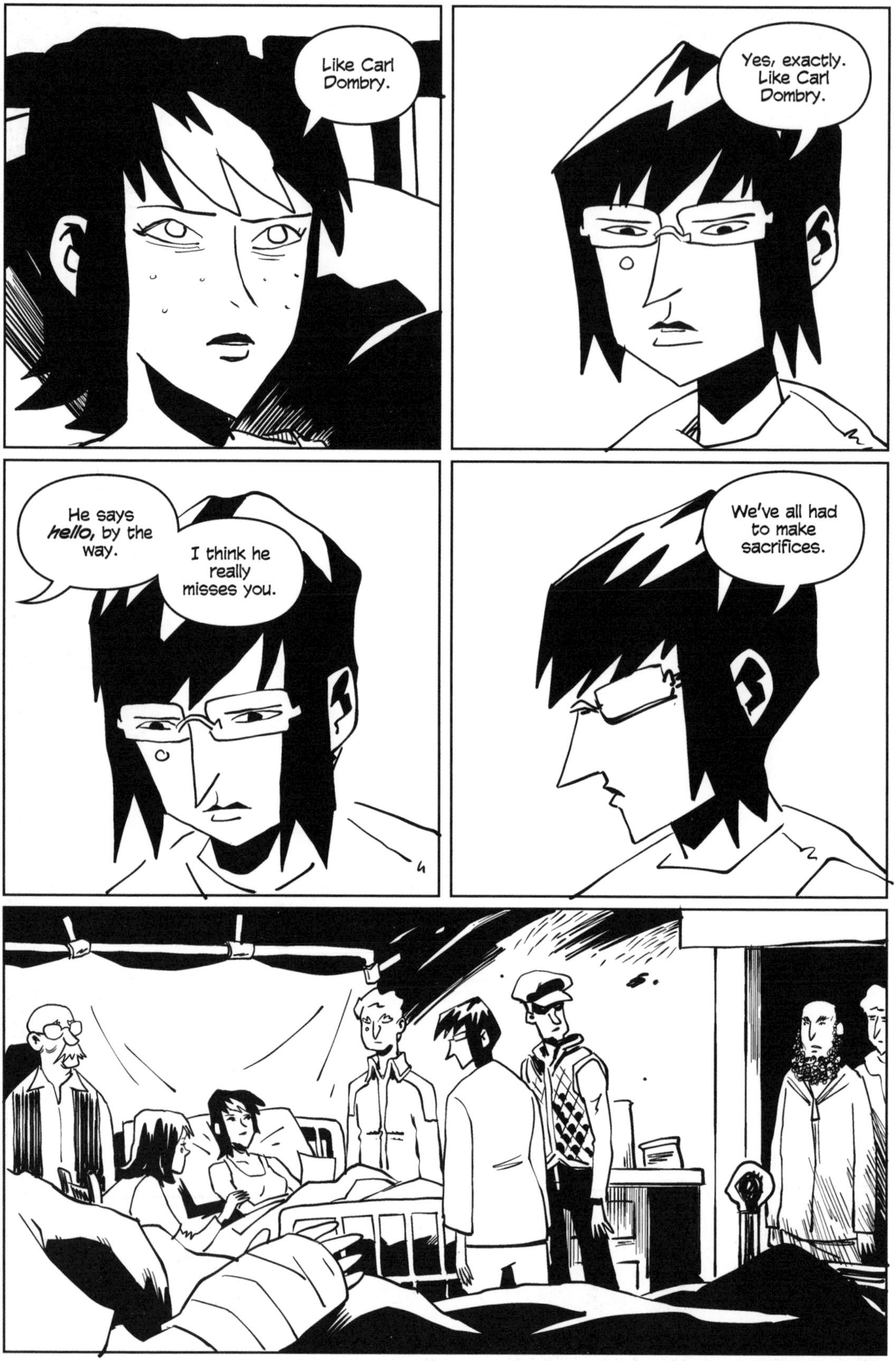
Like Carl Dombry.
Yes, exactly. Like Carl Dombry.
He says *hello,* by the way.
I think he really misses you.
We've all had to make sacrifices.

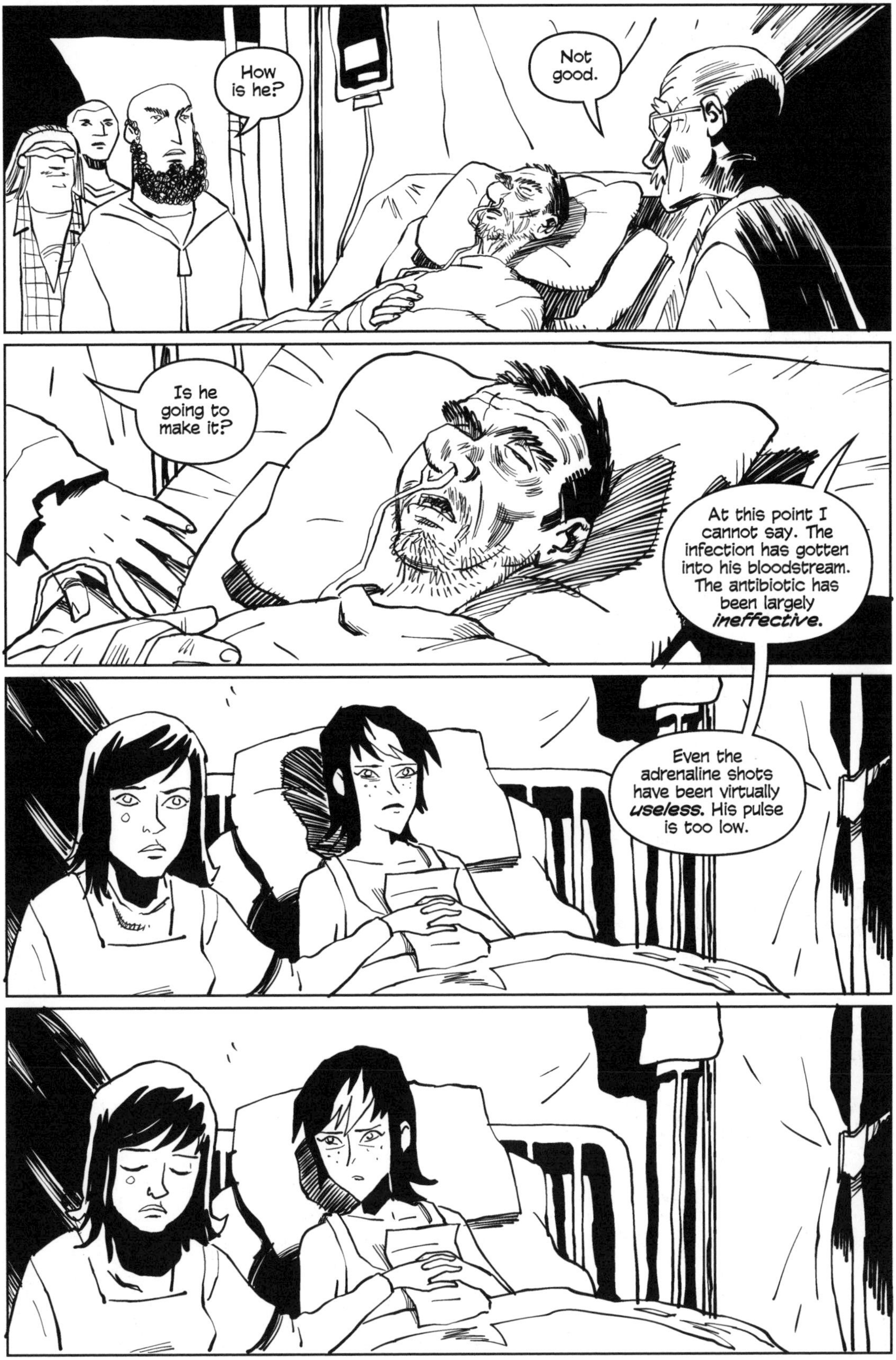
How is he?
Not good.
Is he going to make it?
At this point I cannot say. The infection has gotten into his bloodstream. The antibiotic has been largely *ineffective*.
Even the adrenaline shots have been virtually *useless*. His pulse is too low.

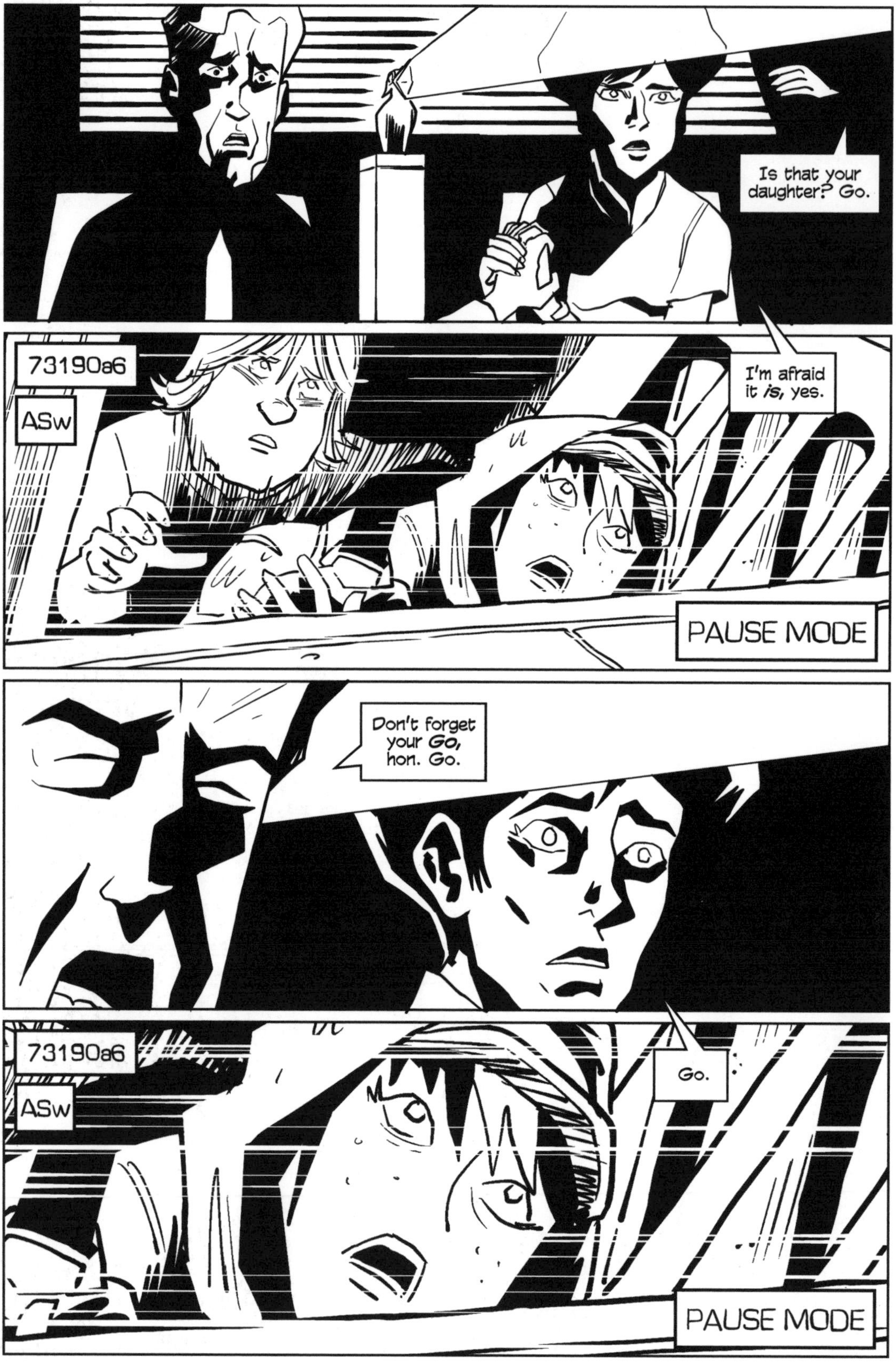
Is that your daughter? Go.
73190a6
ASw
I'm afraid it *is*, yes.
PAUSE MODE
Don't forget your *Go,* hon. Go.
73190a6
ASw
Go.
PAUSE MODE

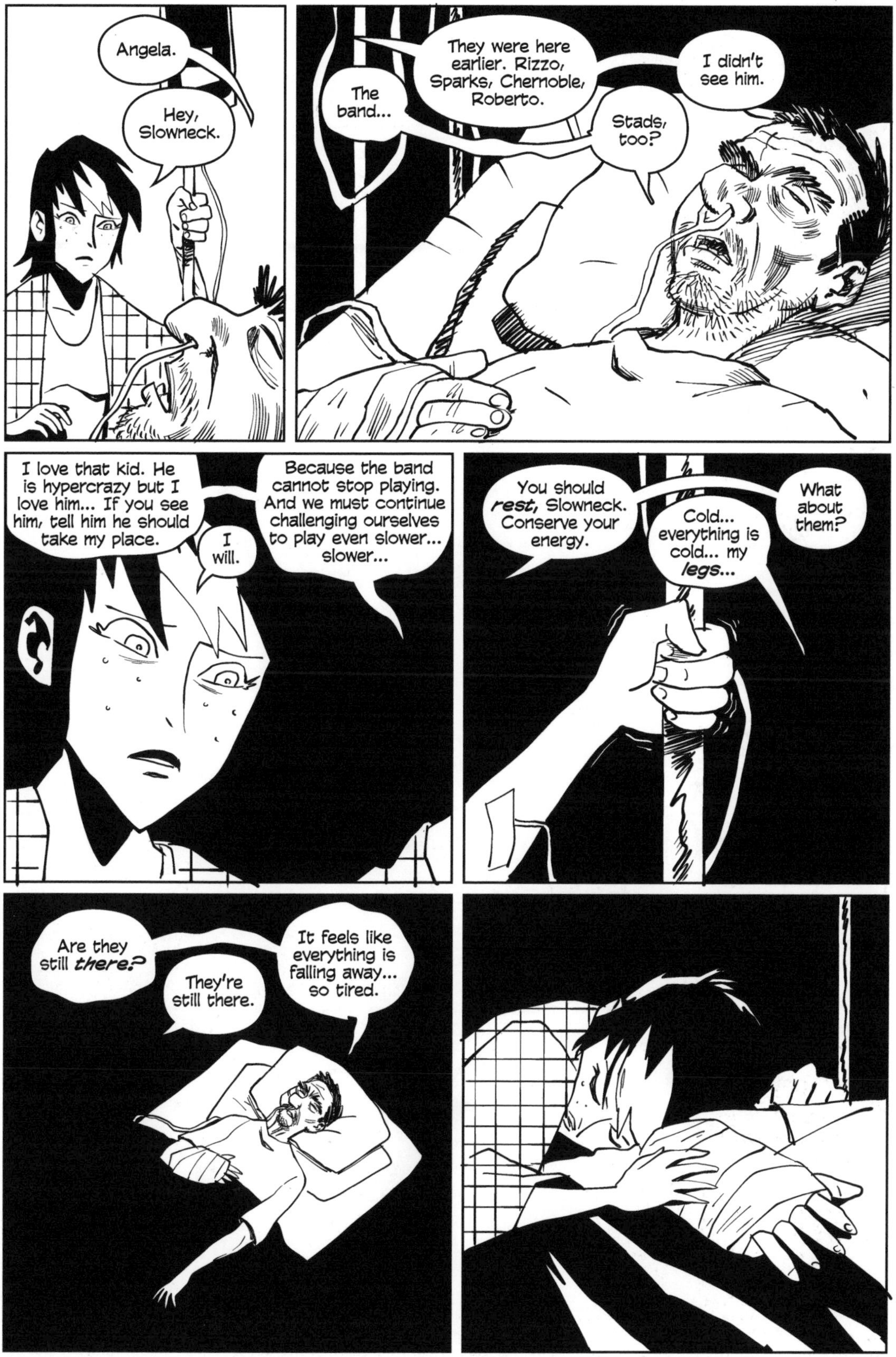
Angela.
Hey, Slowneck.
The band...
They were here earlier. Rizzo, Sparks, Chernoble, Roberto.
Stads, too?
I didn't see him.
I love that kid. He is hypercrazy but I love him... If you see him, tell him he should take my place.
I will.
Because the band cannot stop playing. And we must continue challenging ourselves to play even slower... slower...
You should *rest,* Slowneck. Conserve your energy.
What about them?
Cold... everything is cold... my *legs...*
Are they still *there?*
They're still there.
It feels like everything is falling away... so tired.

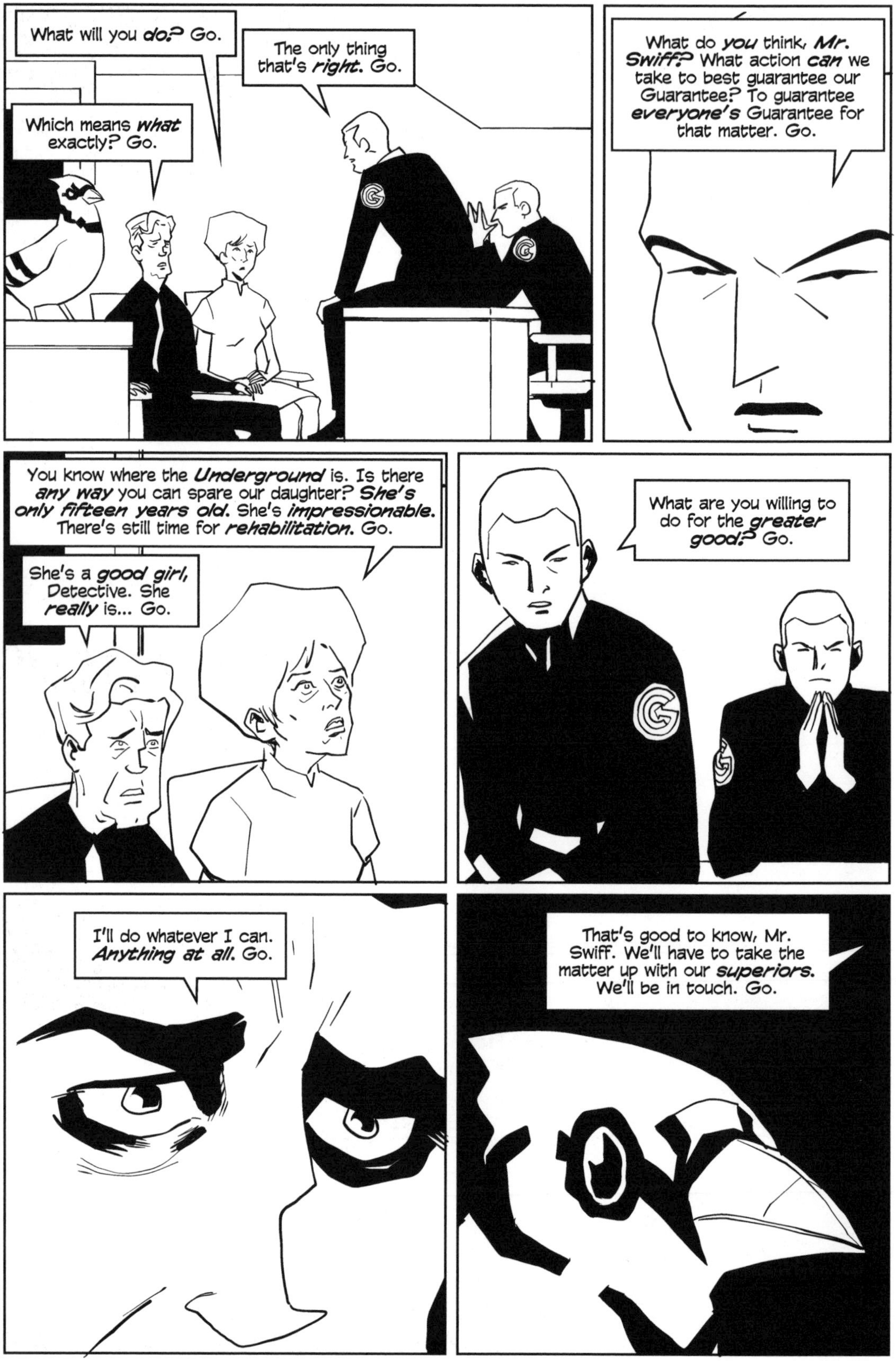
What will you *do?* Go.
The only thing that's *right.* Go.
Which means *what* exactly? Go.
What do *you* think, *Mr. Swiff?* What action *can* we take to best guarantee our Guarantee? To guarantee *everyone's* Guarantee for that matter. Go.
You know where the *Underground* is. Is there *any way* you can spare our daughter? *She's only fifteen years old.* She's *impressionable.* There's still time for *rehabilitation.* Go.
She's a *good girl,* Detective. She *really* is... Go.
What are you willing to do for the *greater good?* Go.
I'll do whatever I can. *Anything at all.* Go.
That's good to know, Mr. Swiff. We'll have to take the matter up with our *superiors.* We'll be in touch. Go.

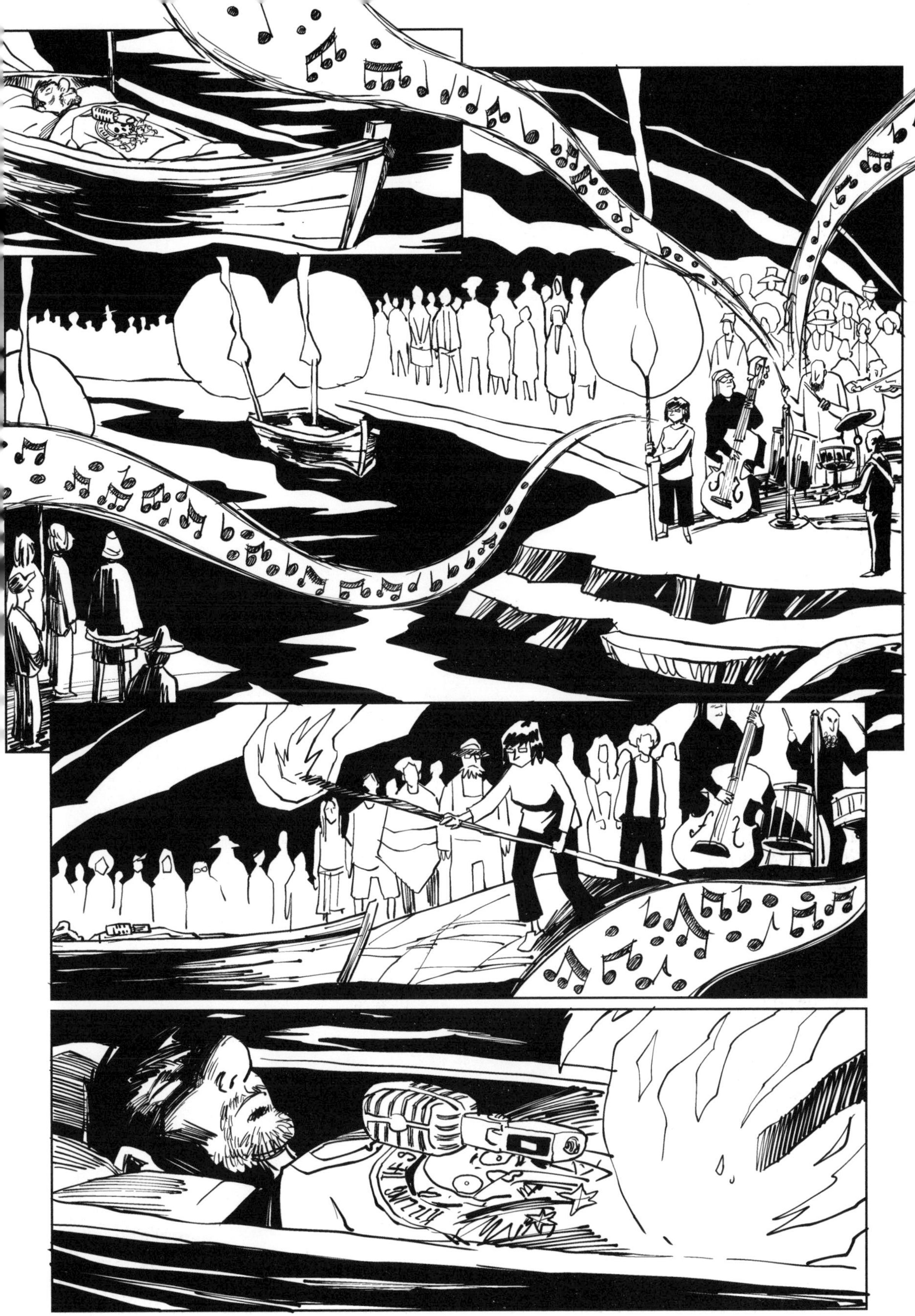

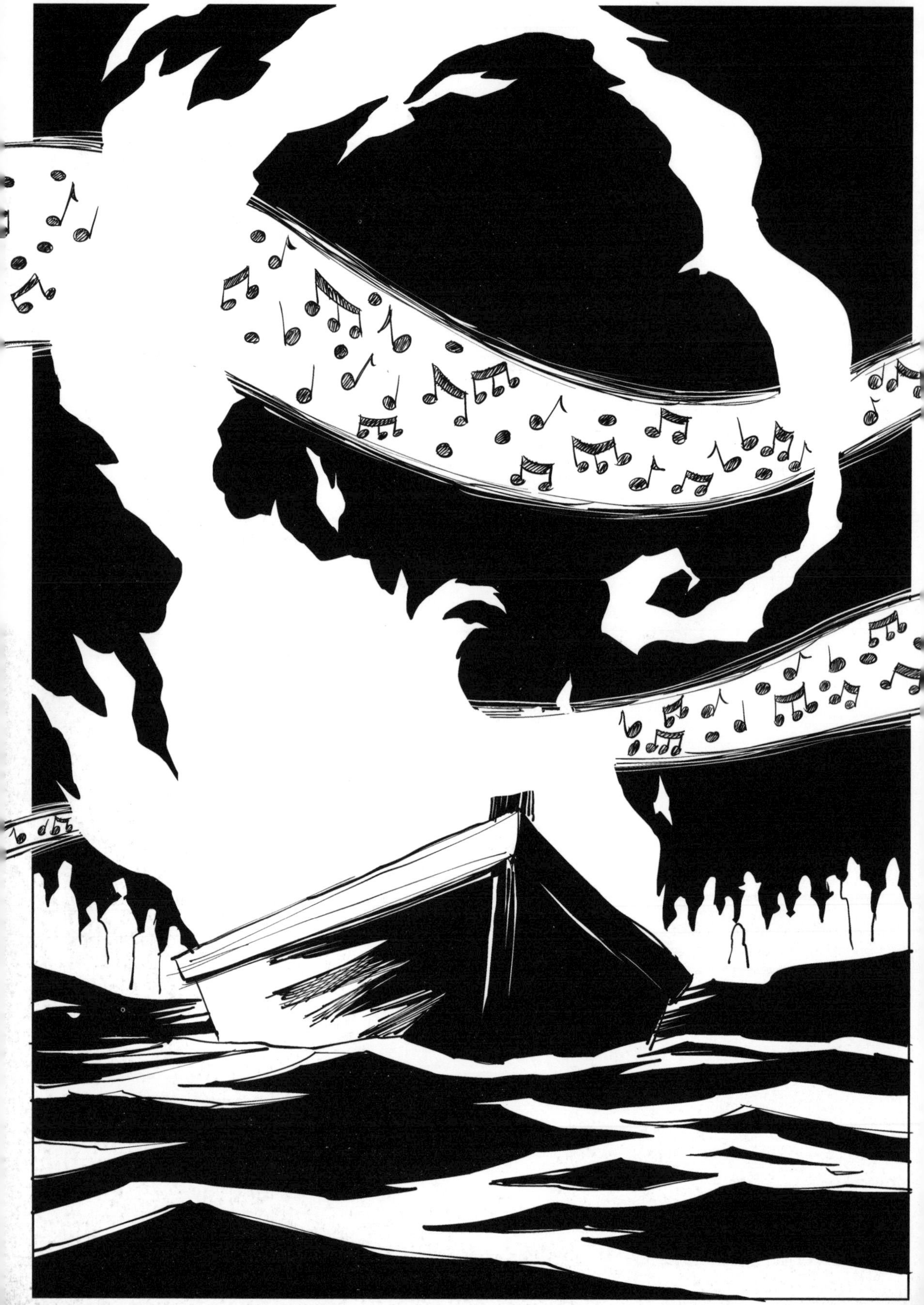

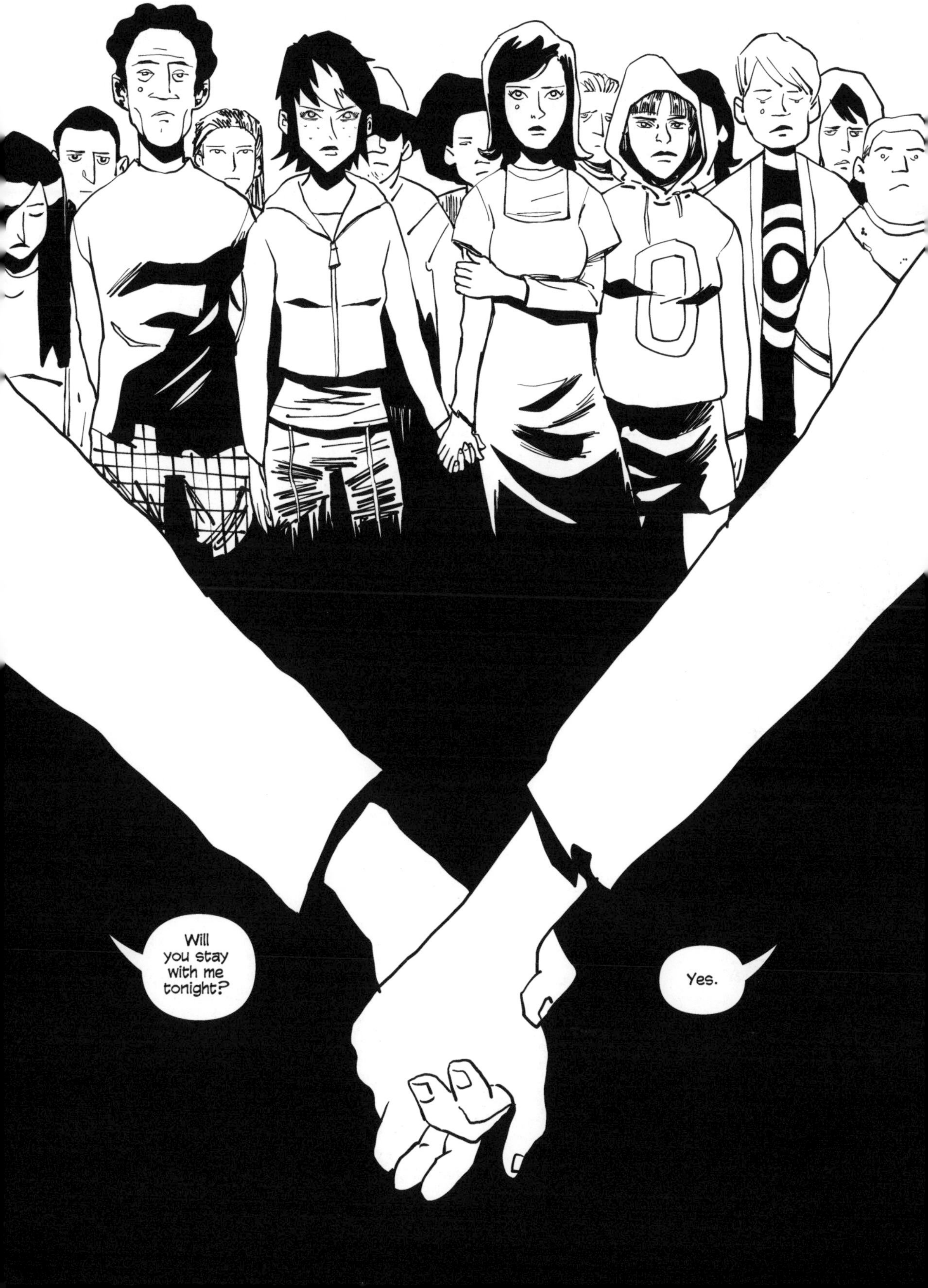
Will you stay with me tonight?
Yes.

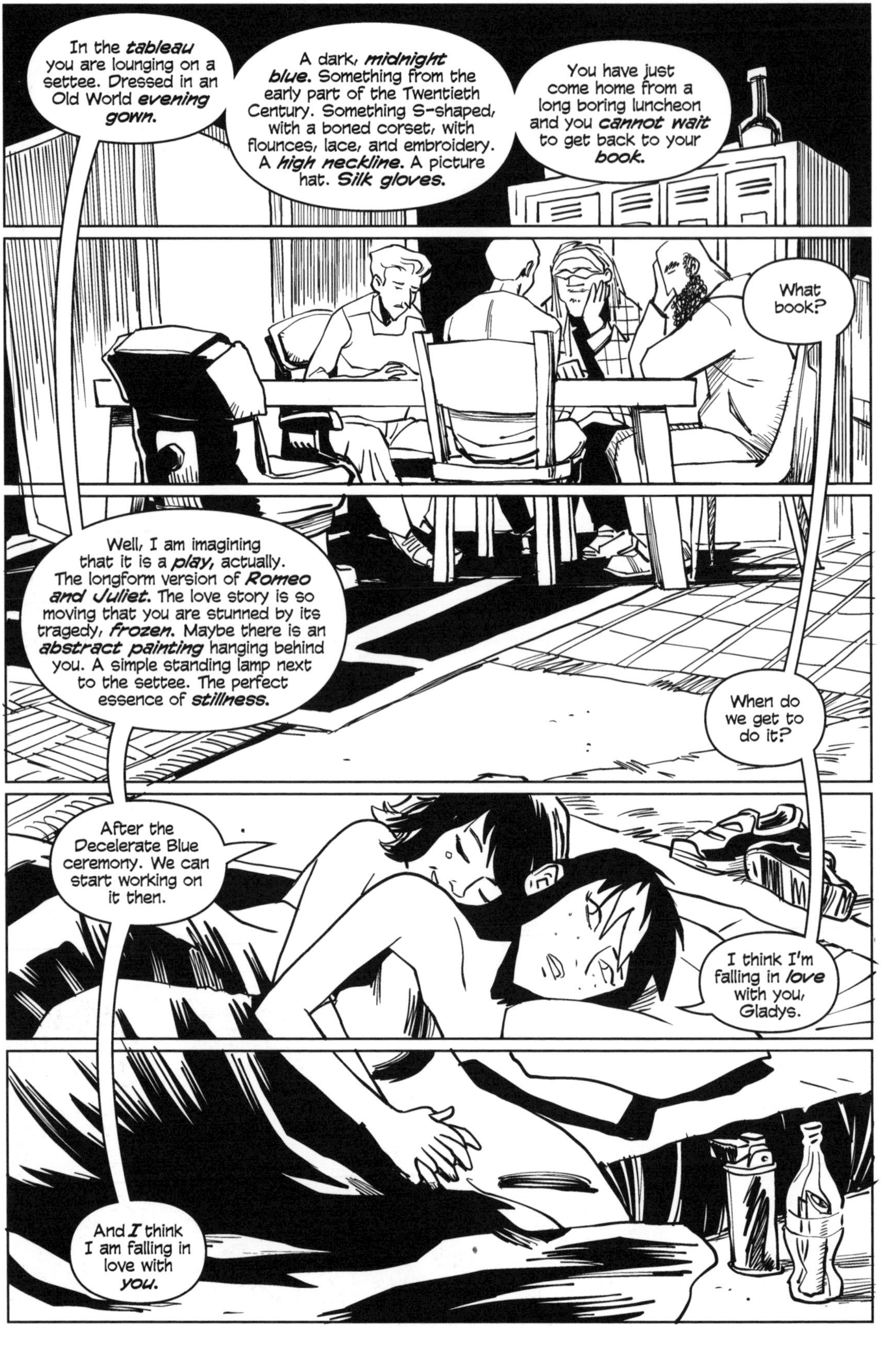
In the tableau you are lounging on a settee. Dressed in an Old World evening gown.
A dark, midnight blue. Something from the early part of the Twentieth Century. Something S-shaped, with a boned corset, with flounces, lace, and embroidery. A high neckline. A picture hat. Silk gloves.
You have just come home from a long boring luncheon and you cannot wait to get back to your book.
What book?
Well, I am imagining that it is a play, actually. The longform version of Romeo and Juliet. The love story is so moving that you are stunned by its tragedy, frozen. Maybe there is an abstract painting hanging behind you. A simple standing lamp next to the settee. The perfect essence of stillness.
When do we get to do it?
After the Decelerate Blue ceremony. We can start working on it then.
I think I'm falling in love with you, Gladys.
And I think I am falling in love with you.

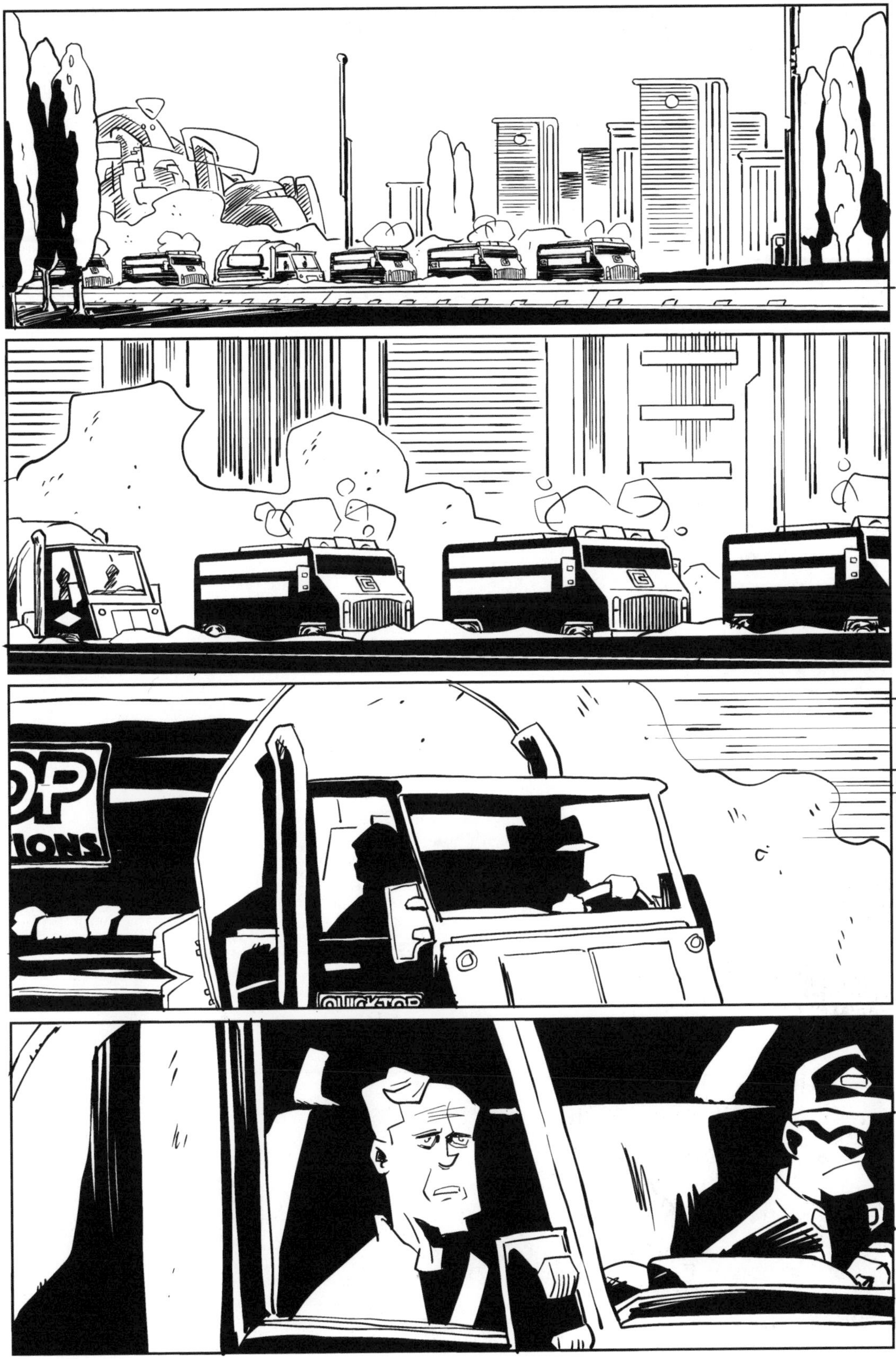

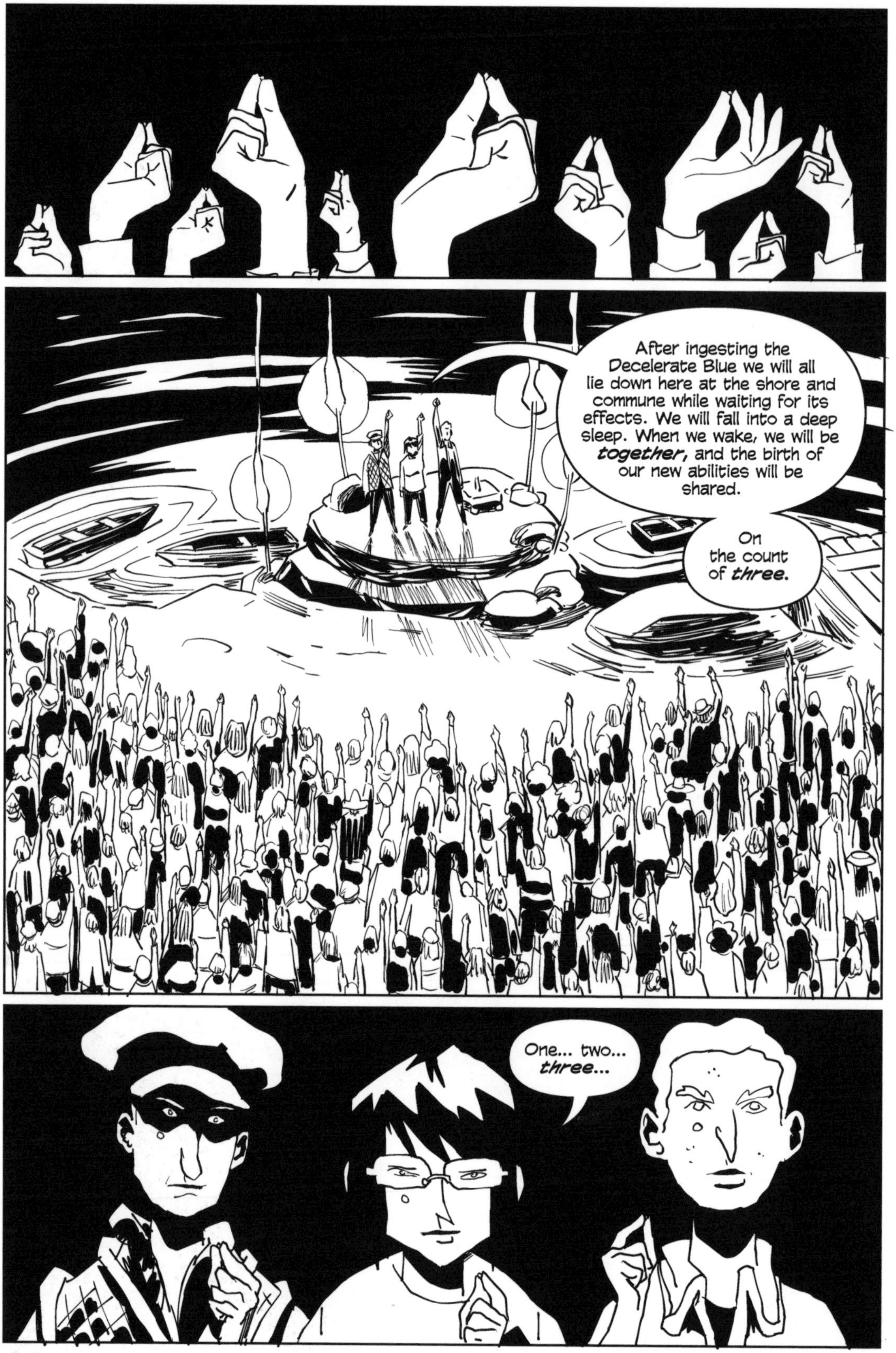
After ingesting the Decelerate Blue we will all lie down here at the shore and commune while waiting for its effects. We will fall into a deep sleep. When we wake, we will be *together*, and the birth of our new abilities will be shared.
On the count of *three*.
One... two... *three*...

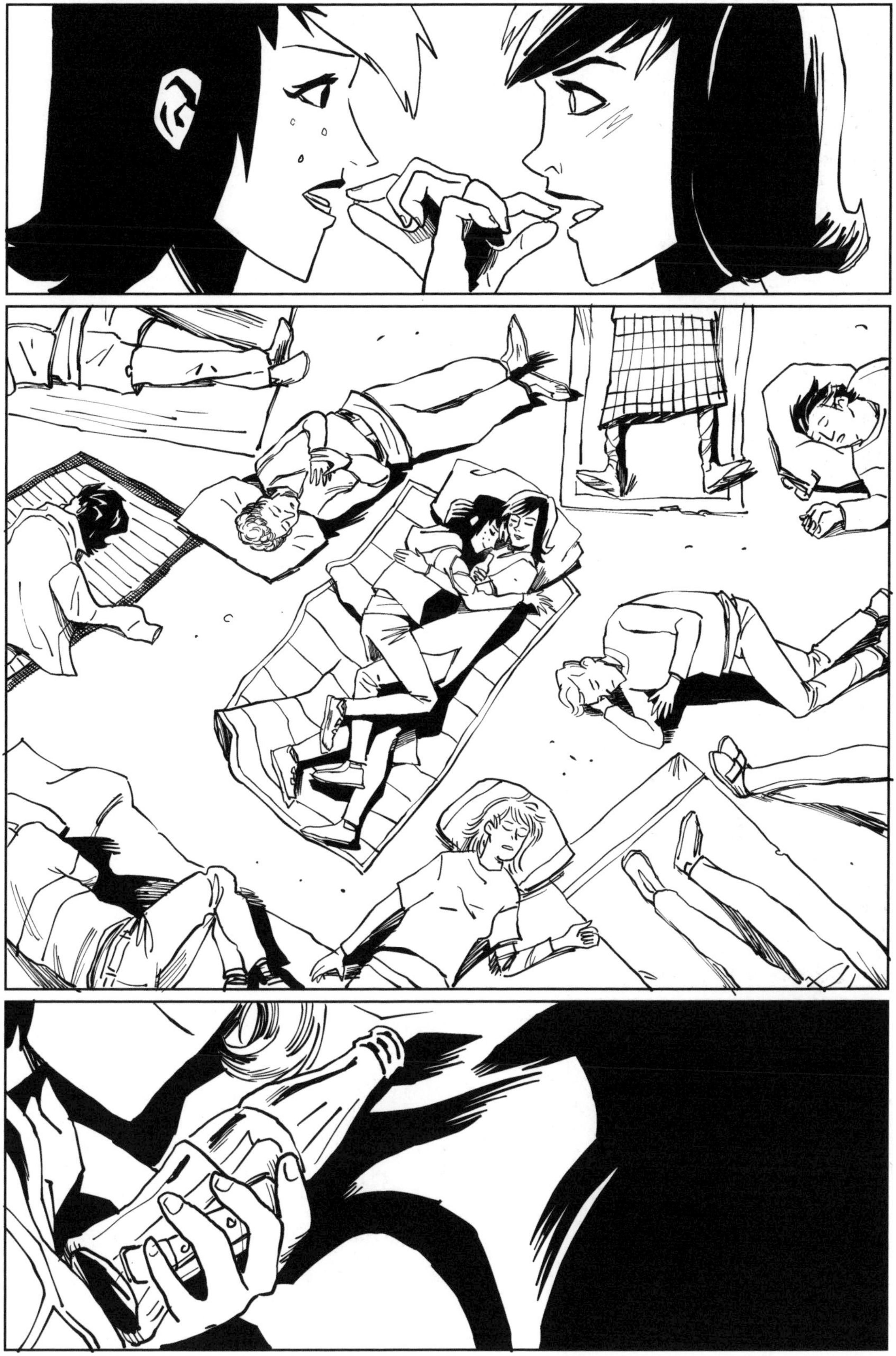

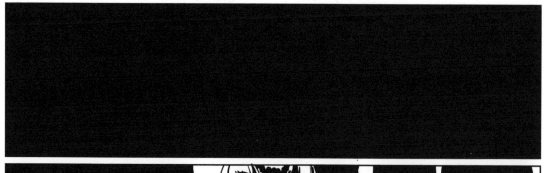

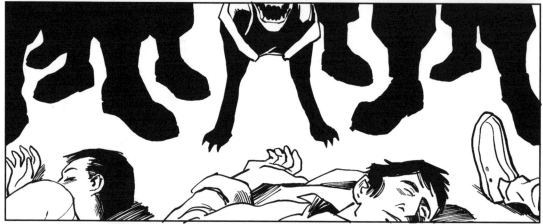

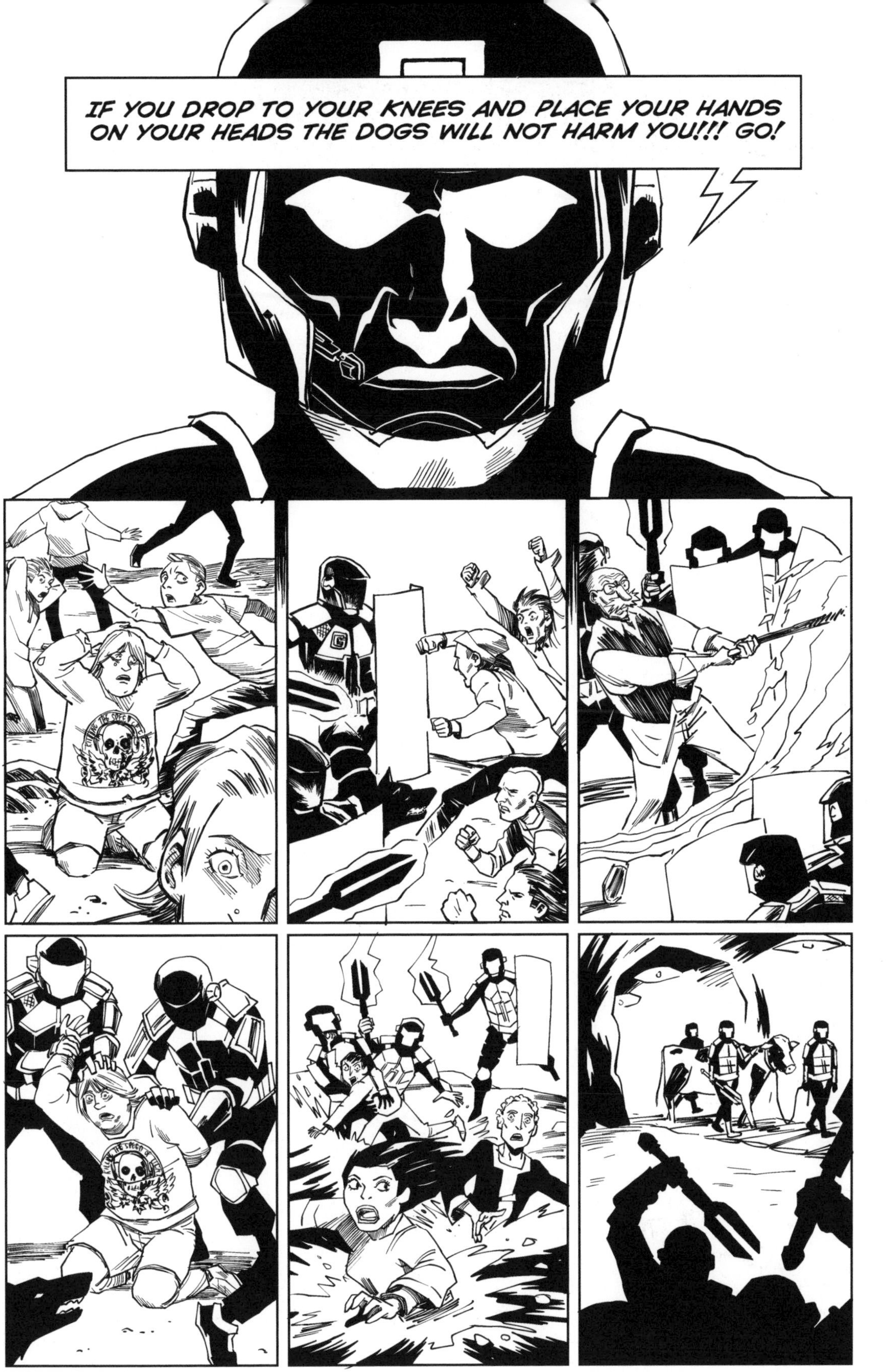
IF YOU DROP TO YOUR KNEES AND PLACE YOUR HANDS ON YOUR HEADS THE DOGS WILL NOT HARM YOU!!! GO!

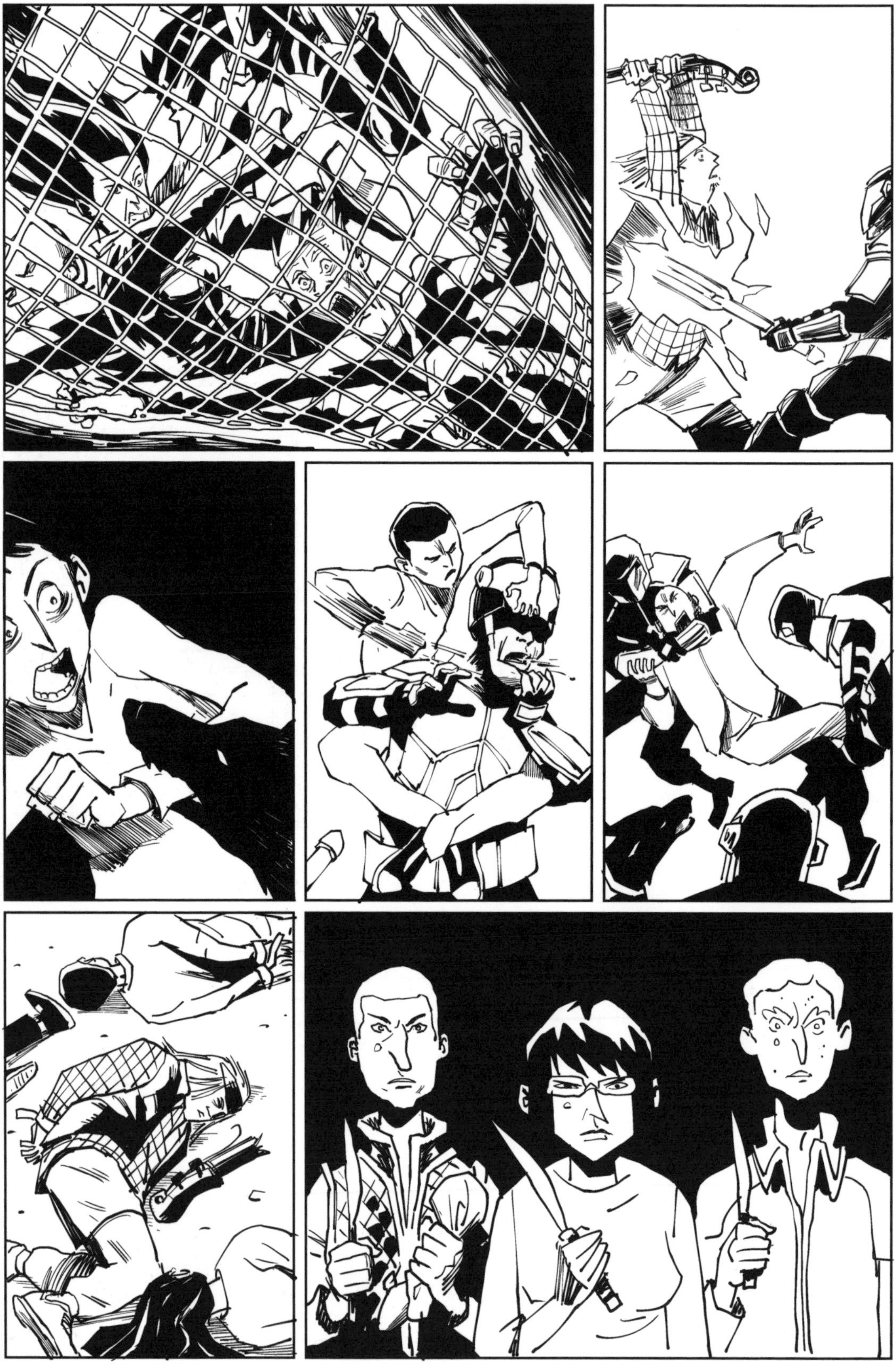

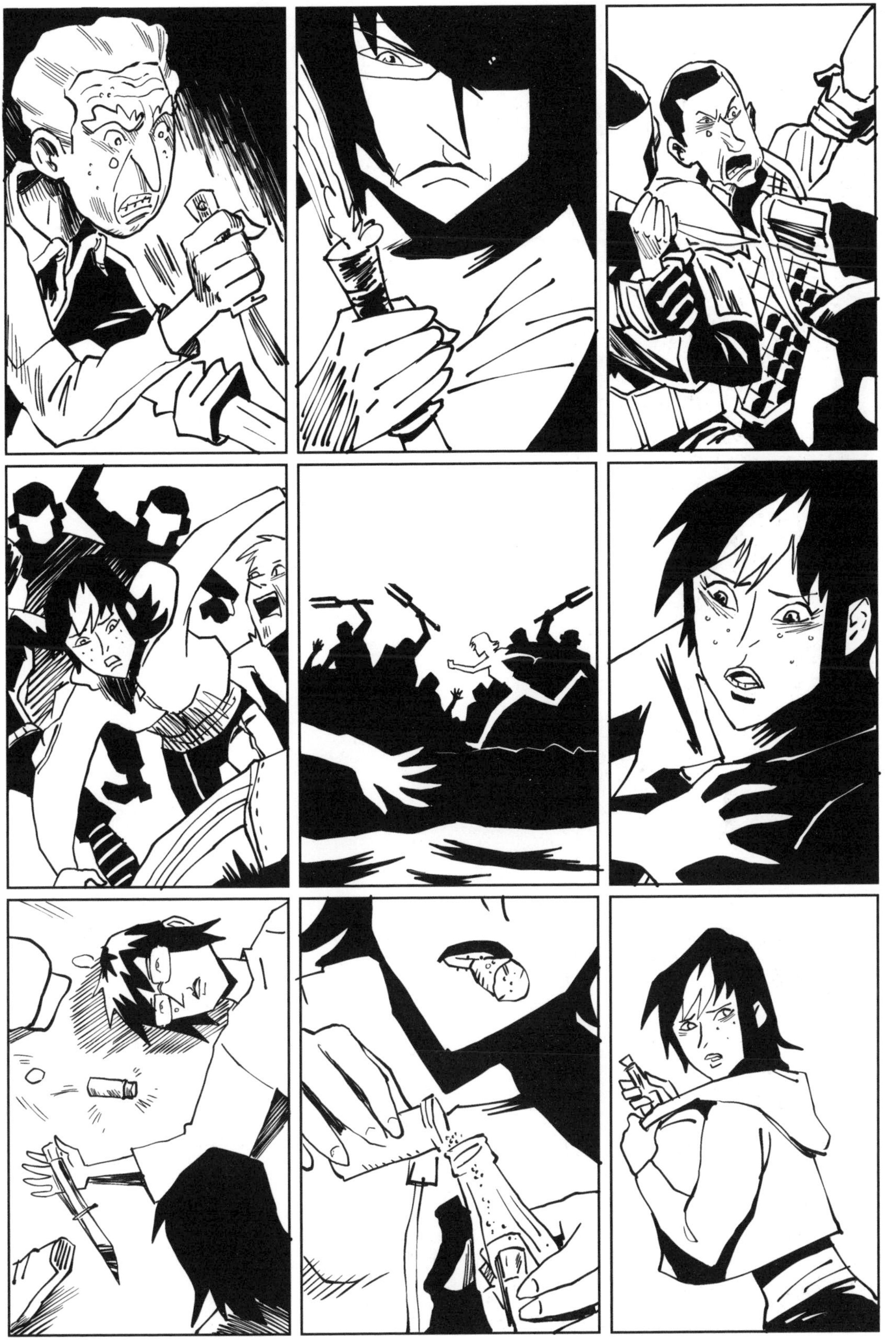

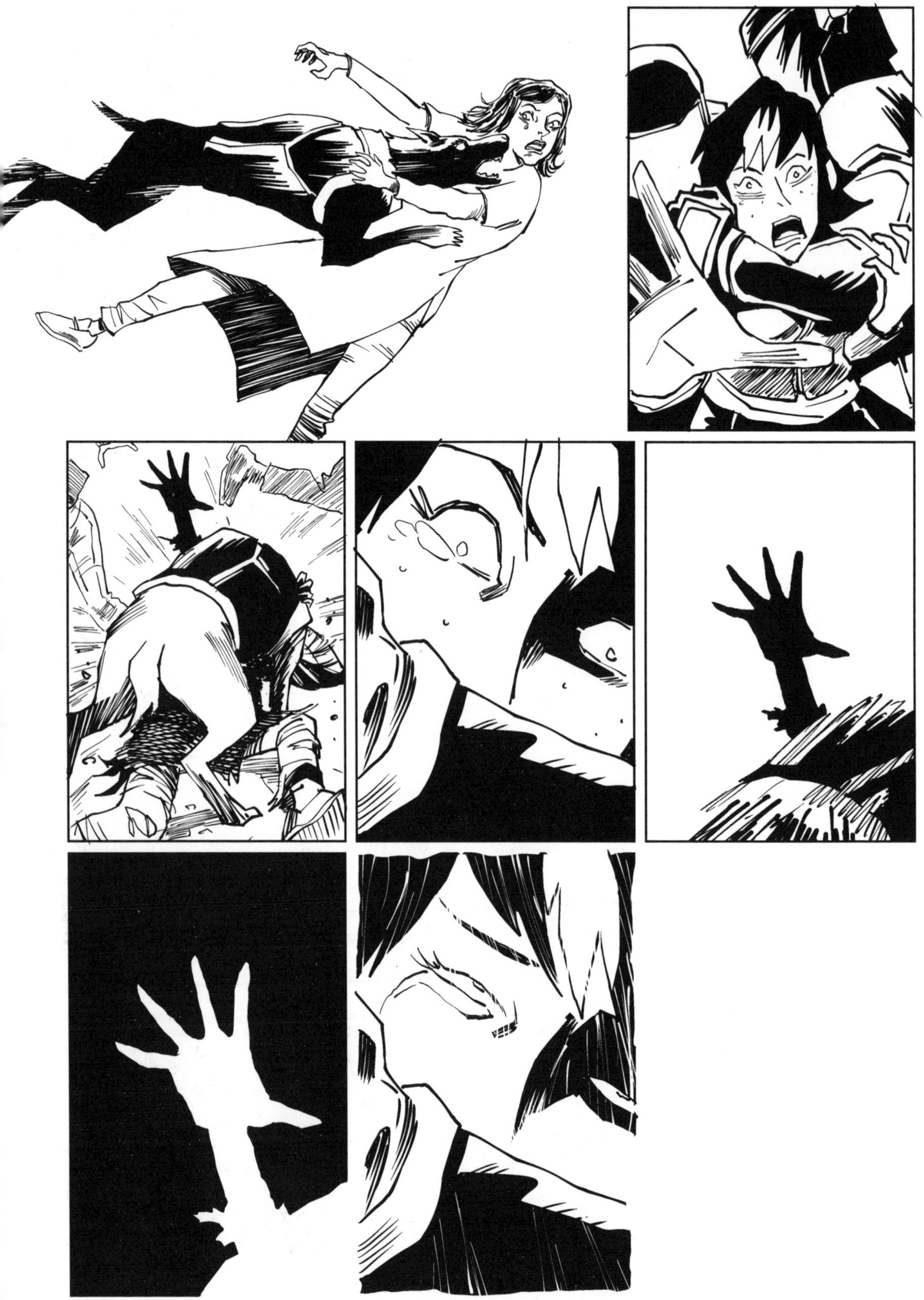

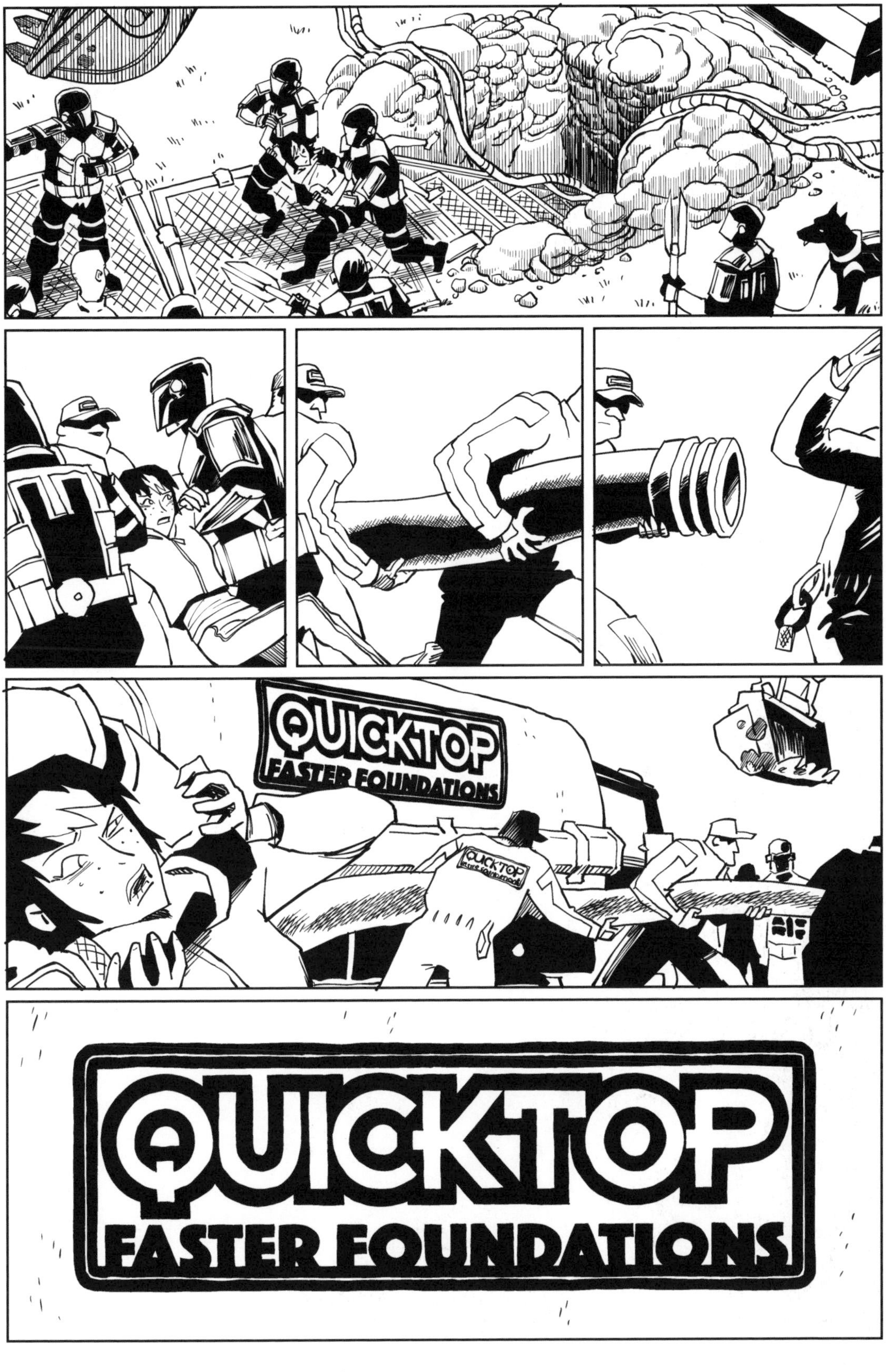
QUICKTOP
FASTER FOUNDATIONS
QUICKTOP
QUICKTOP
FASTER FOUNDATIONS

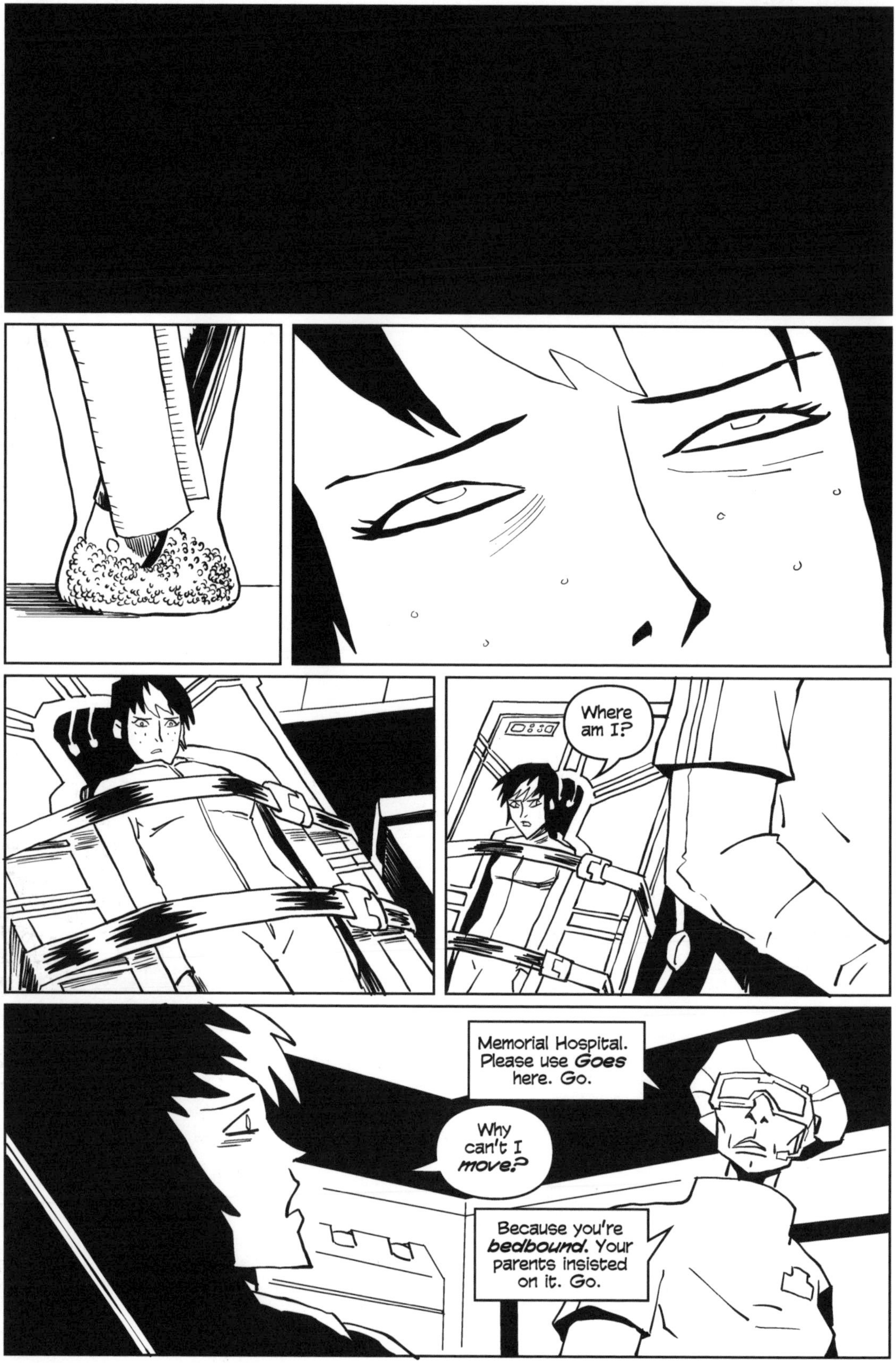
Where am I?
Memorial Hospital. Please use *Goes* here. Go.
Why can't I *move?*
Because you're ***bedbound.*** Your parents insisted on it. Go.

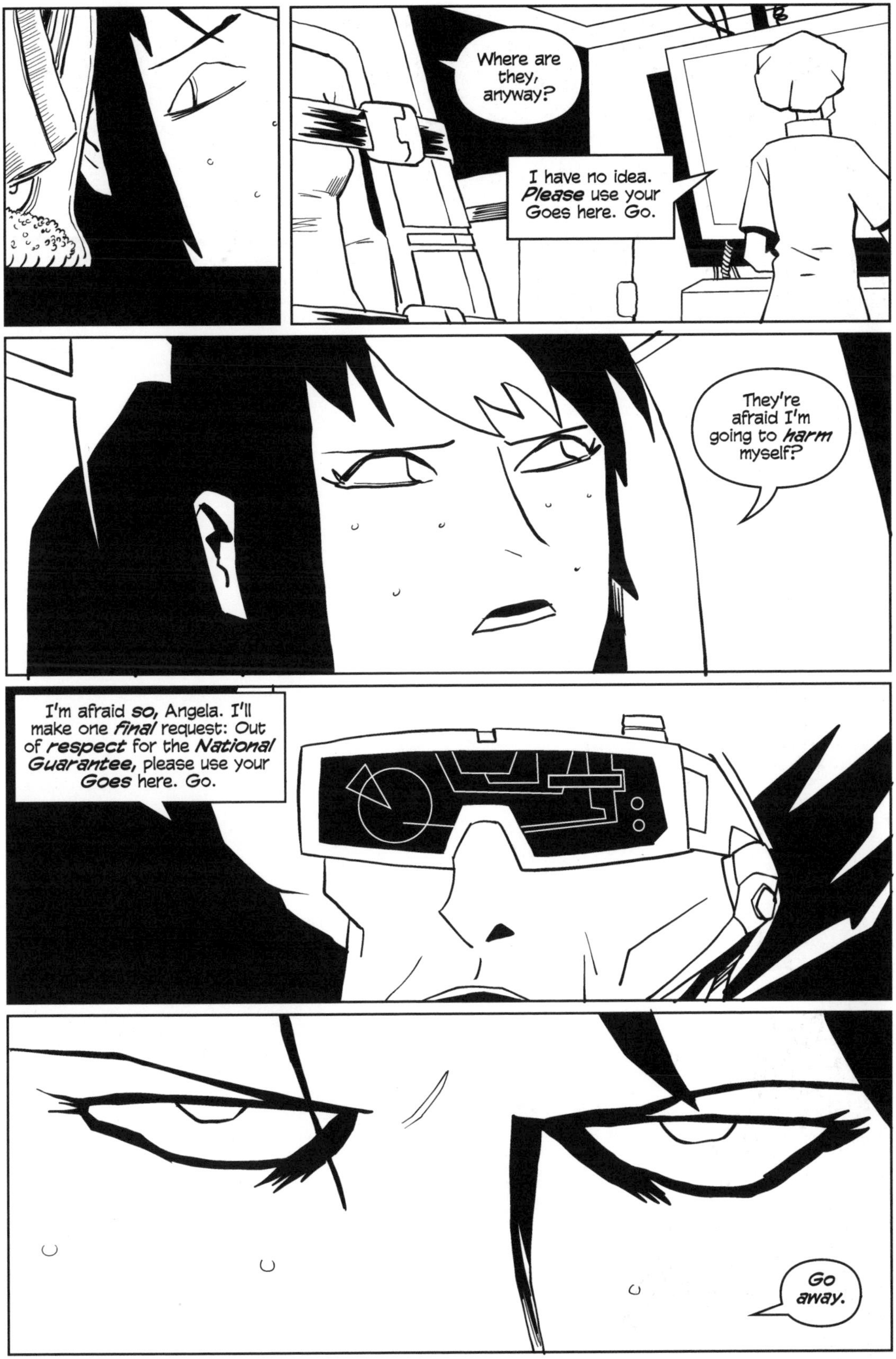
Where are they, anyway?
I have no idea. *Please* use your Goes here. Go.
They're afraid I'm going to *harm* myself?
I'm afraid *so,* Angela. I'll make one *final* request: Out of *respect* for the *National Guarantee,* please use your *Goes* here. Go.
*Go away.*

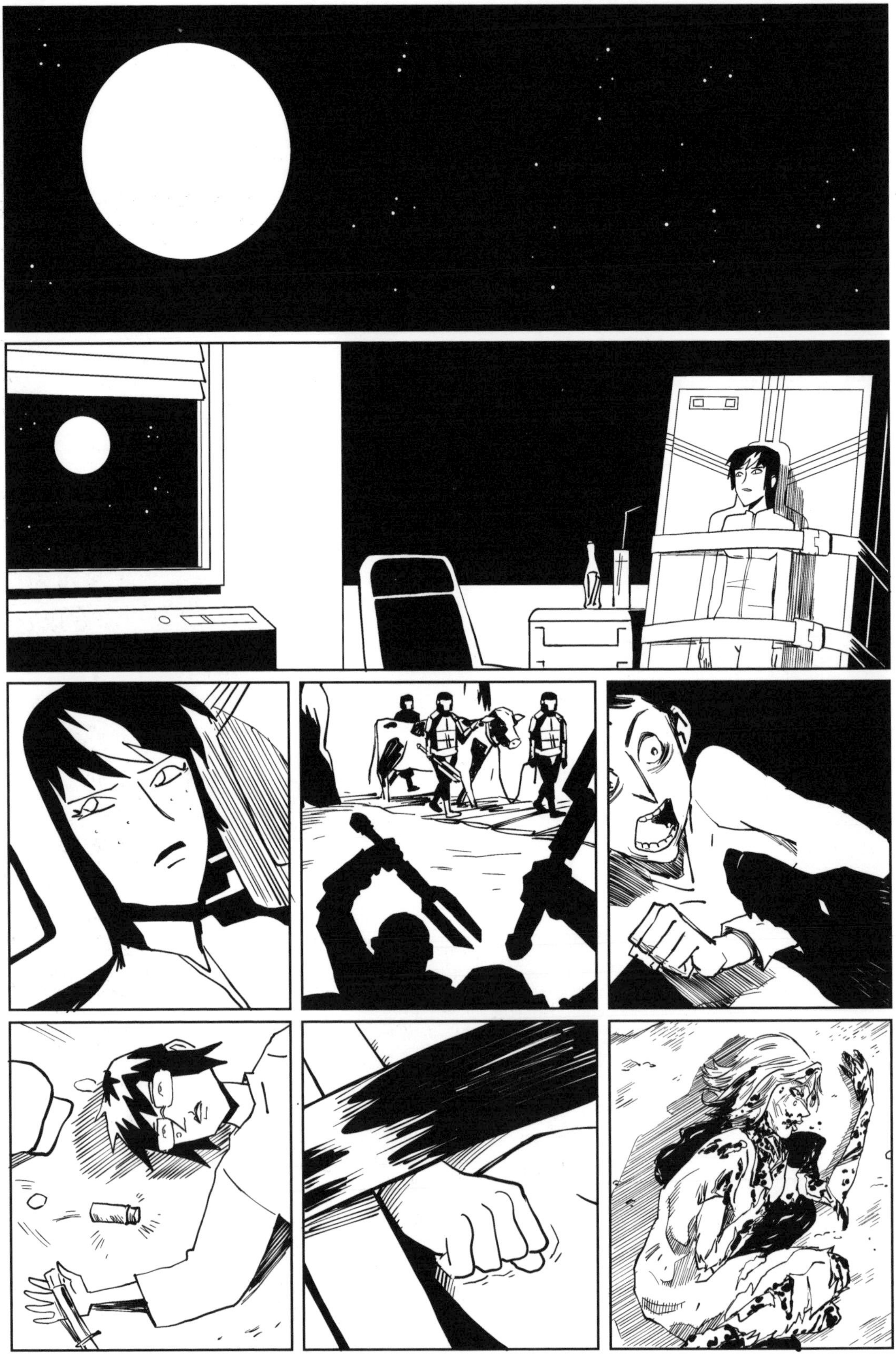

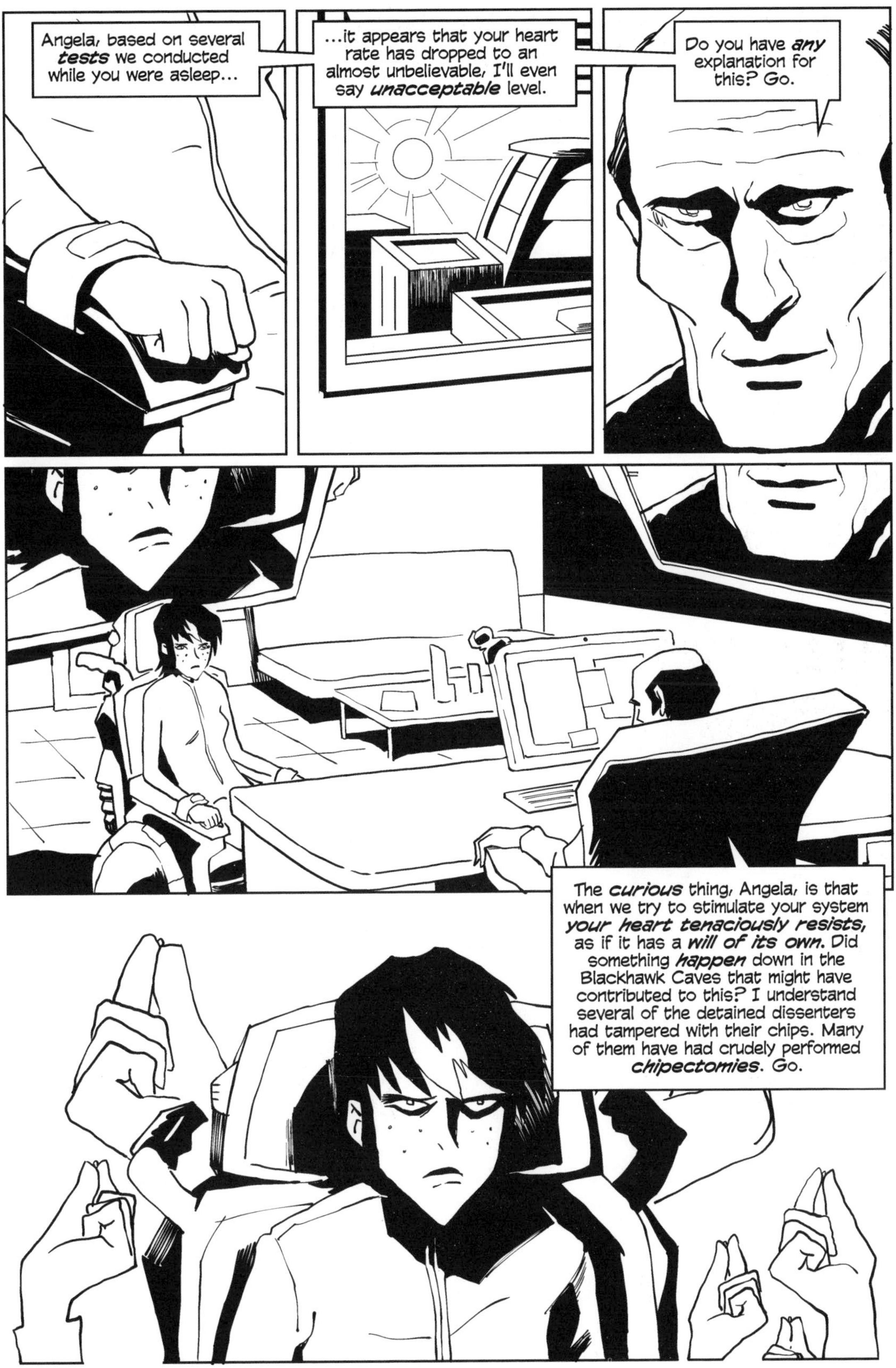
Angela, based on several tests we conducted while you were asleep...
...it appears that your heart rate has dropped to an almost unbelievable, I'll even say unacceptable level.
Do you have any explanation for this? Go.
The curious thing, Angela, is that when we try to stimulate your system your heart tenaciously resists, as if it has a will of its own. Did something happen down in the Blackhawk Caves that might have contributed to this? I understand several of the detained dissenters had tampered with their chips. Many of them have had crudely performed chipectomies. Go.

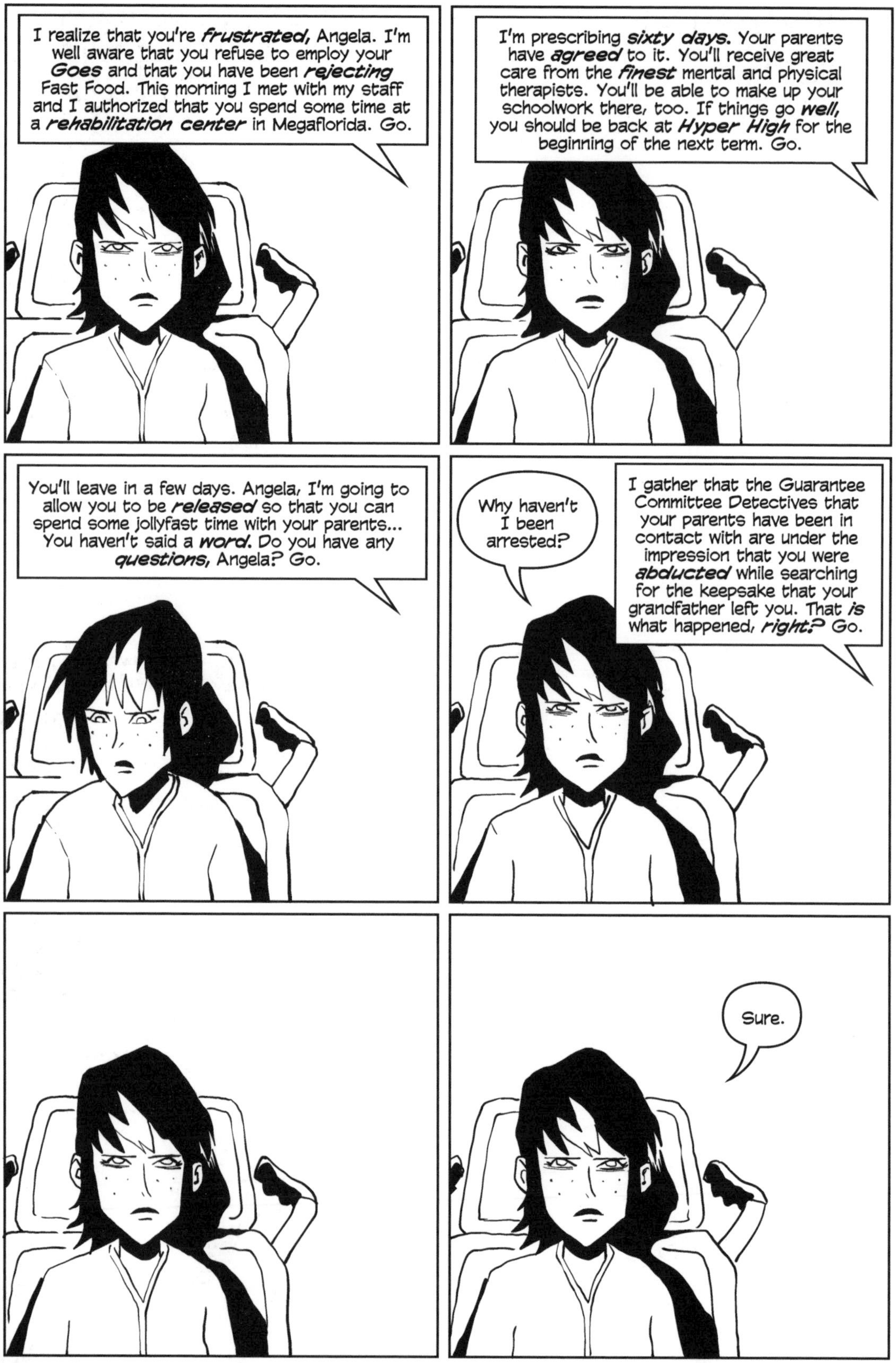
I realize that you're frustrated, Angela. I'm well aware that you refuse to employ your Goes and that you have been rejecting Fast Food. This morning I met with my staff and I authorized that you spend some time at a rehabilitation center in Megaflorida. Go.
I'm prescribing sixty days. Your parents have agreed to it. You'll receive great care from the finest mental and physical therapists. You'll be able to make up your schoolwork there, too. If things go well, you should be back at Hyper High for the beginning of the next term. Go.
You'll leave in a few days. Angela, I'm going to allow you to be released so that you can spend some jollyfast time with your parents... You haven't said a word. Do you have any questions, Angela? Go.
Why haven't I been arrested?
I gather that the Guarantee Committee Detectives that your parents have been in contact with are under the impression that you were abducted while searching for the keepsake that your grandfather left you. That is what happened, right? Go.
Sure.

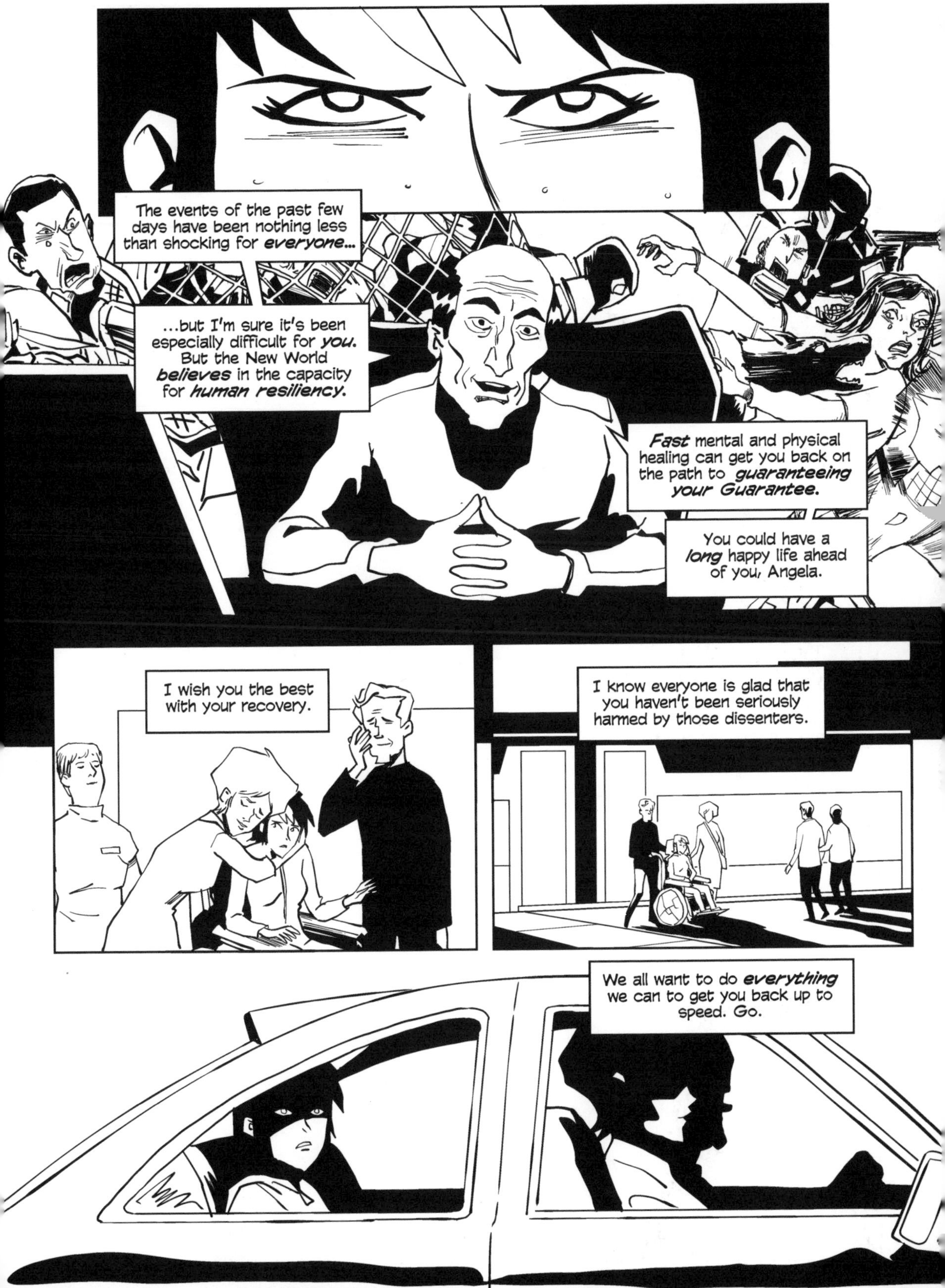
The events of the past few days have been nothing less than shocking for *everyone*...
...but I'm sure it's been especially difficult for *you.* But the New World *believes* in the capacity for *human resiliency.*
*Fast* mental and physical healing can get you back on the path to *guaranteeing your Guarantee.*
You could have a *long* happy life ahead of you, Angela.
I wish you the best with your recovery.
I know everyone is glad that you haven't been seriously harmed by those dissenters.
We all want to do *everything* we can to get you back up to speed. Go.

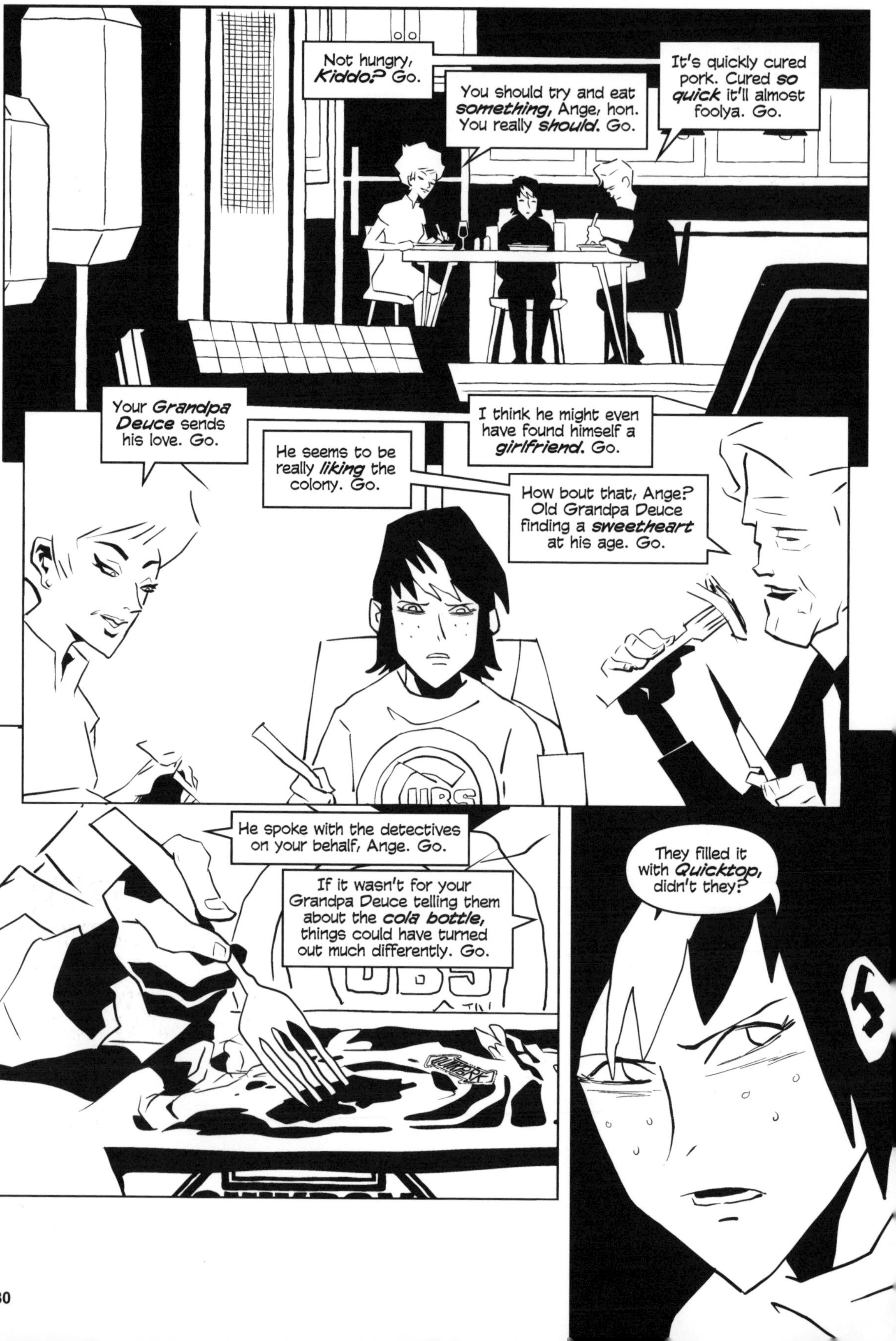

Not hungry, *Kiddo?* Go.
You should try and eat *something,* Ange, hon. You really *should.* Go.
It's quickly cured pork. Cured *so quick* it'll almost foolya. Go.
Your *Grandpa Deuce* sends his love. Go.
He seems to be really *liking* the colony. Go.
I think he might even have found himself a *girlfriend.* Go.
How bout that, Ange? Old Grandpa Deuce finding a *sweetheart* at his age. Go.
He spoke with the detectives on your behalf, Ange. Go.
If it wasn't for your Grandpa Deuce telling them about the *cola bottle,* things could have turned out much differently. Go.
They filled it with *Quicktop,* didn't they?

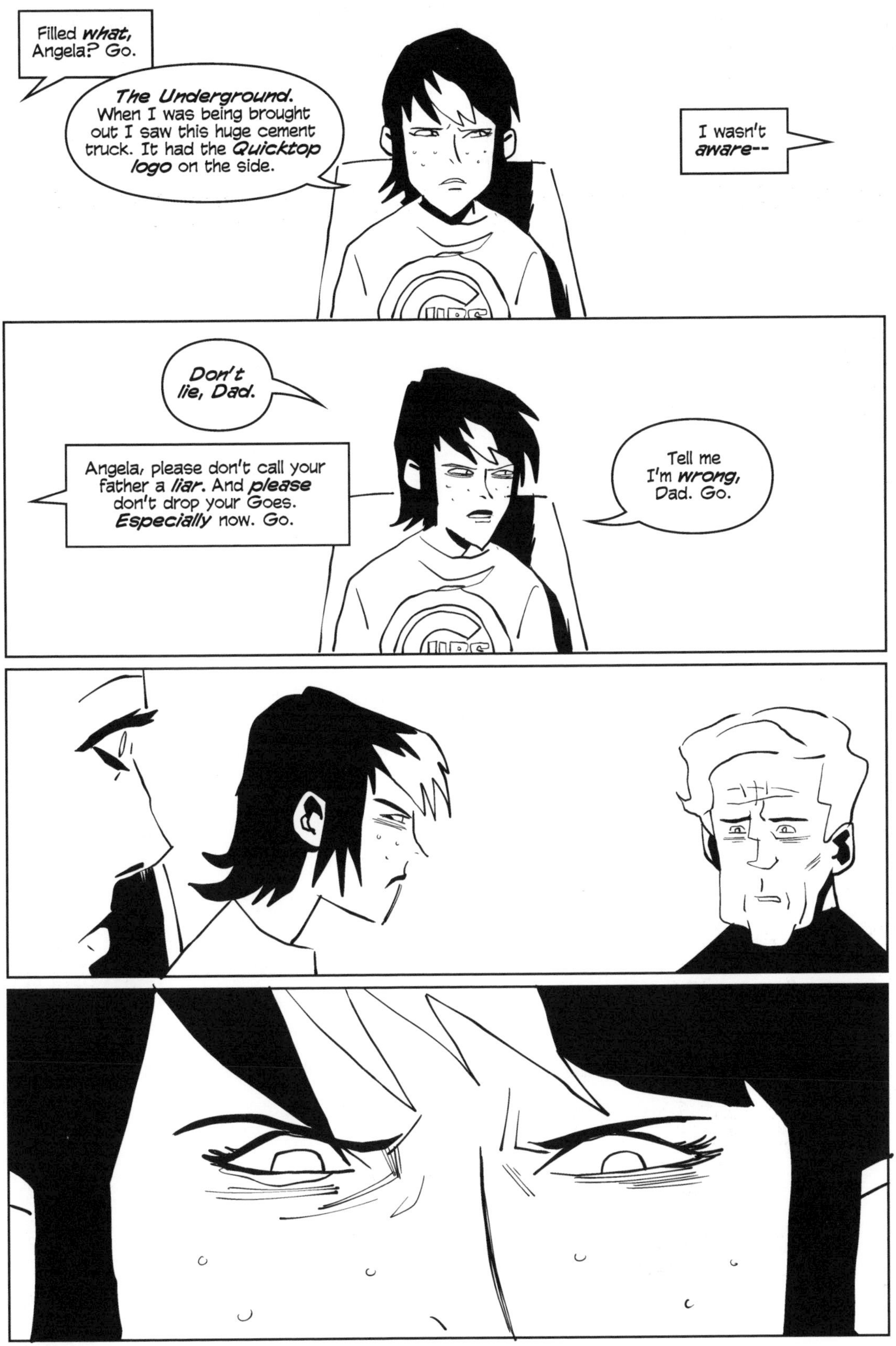
Filled *what*, Angela? Go.
*The Underground.* When I was being brought out I saw this huge cement truck. It had the *Quicktop logo* on the side.
I wasn't *aware*--
*Don't lie, Dad.*
Angela, please don't call your father a *liar*. And *please* don't drop your Goes. *Especially* now. Go.
Tell me I'm *wrong*, Dad. Go.

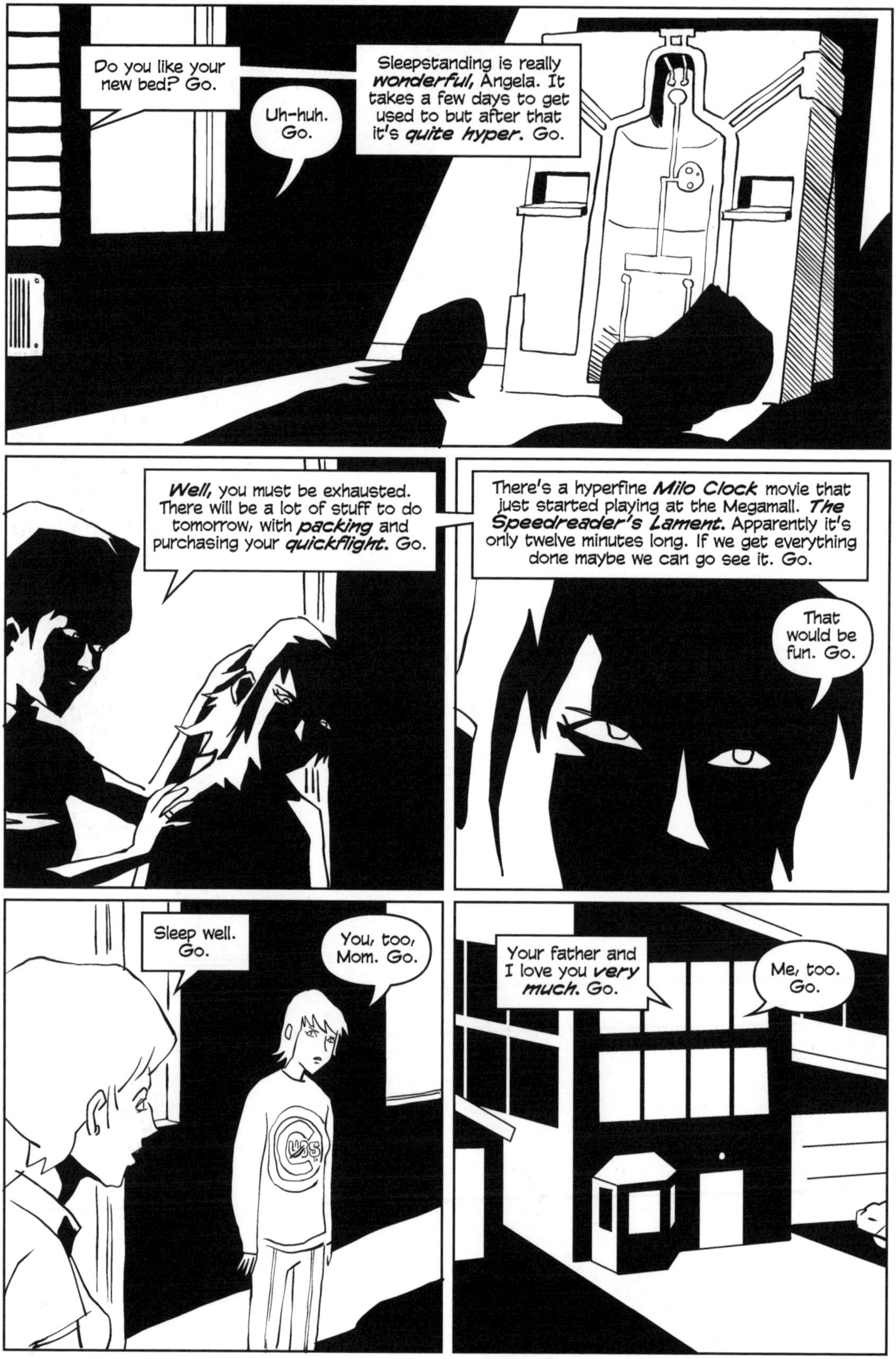
Do you like your new bed? Go.
Uh-huh. Go.
Sleepstanding is really *wonderful,* Angela. It takes a few days to get used to but after that it's *quite hyper*. Go.
*Well,* you must be exhausted. There will be a lot of stuff to do tomorrow, with *packing* and purchasing your *quickflight*. Go.
There's a hyperfine *Milo Clock* movie that just started playing at the Megamall. *The Speedreader's Lament*. Apparently it's only twelve minutes long. If we get everything done maybe we can go see it. Go.
That would be fun. Go.
Sleep well. Go.
You, too, Mom. Go.
Your father and I love you *very much*. Go.
Me, too. Go.

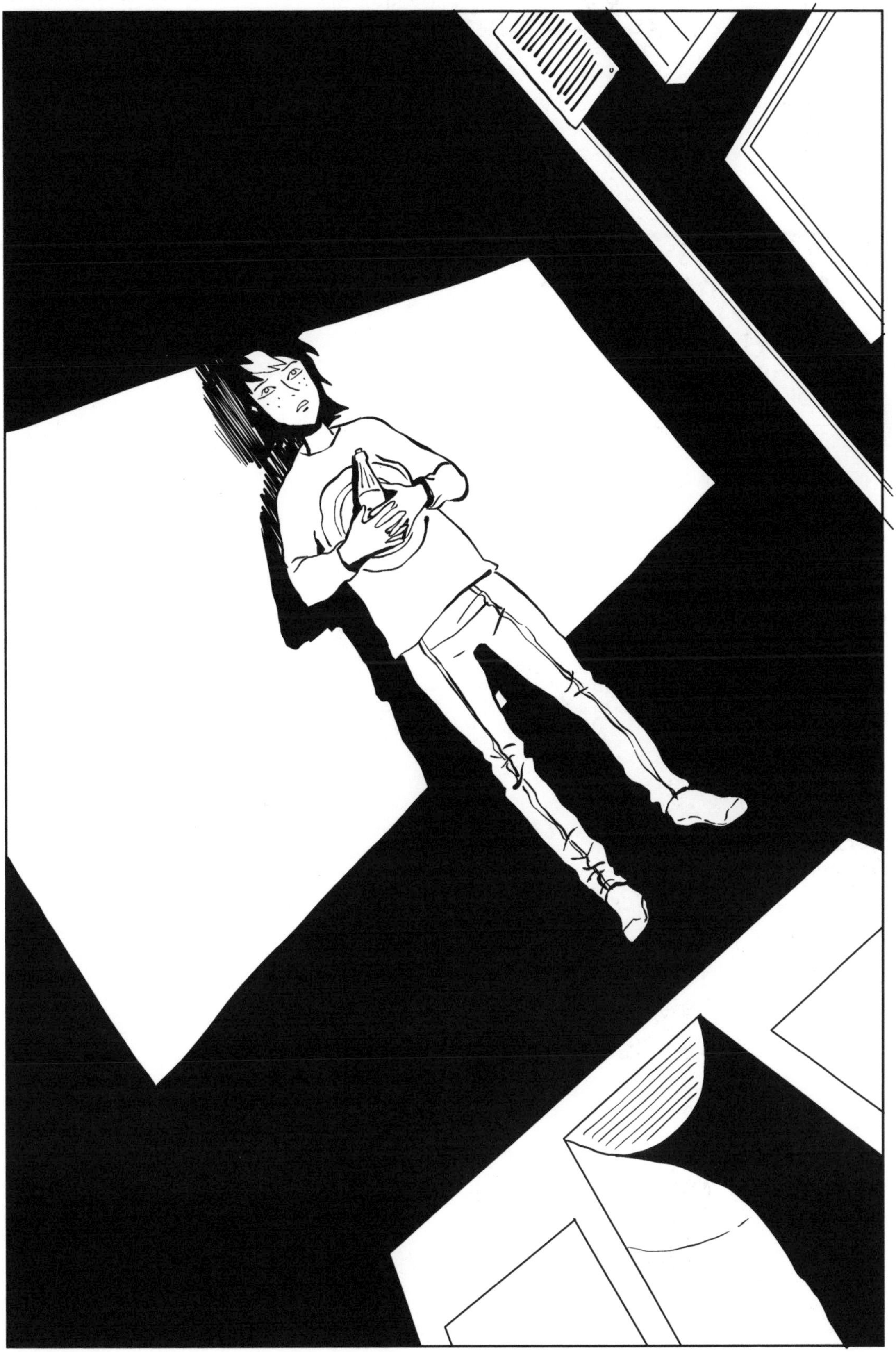

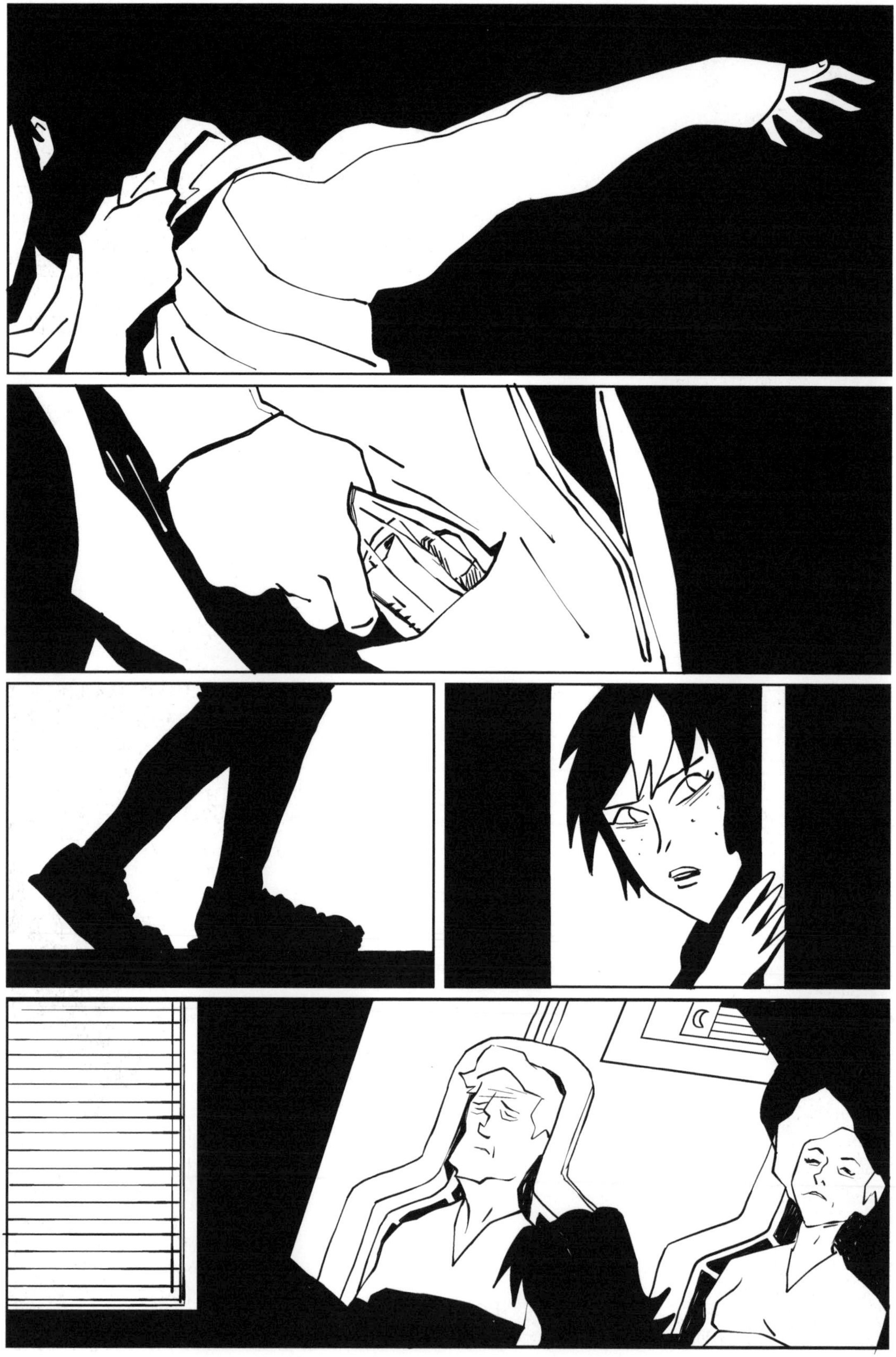

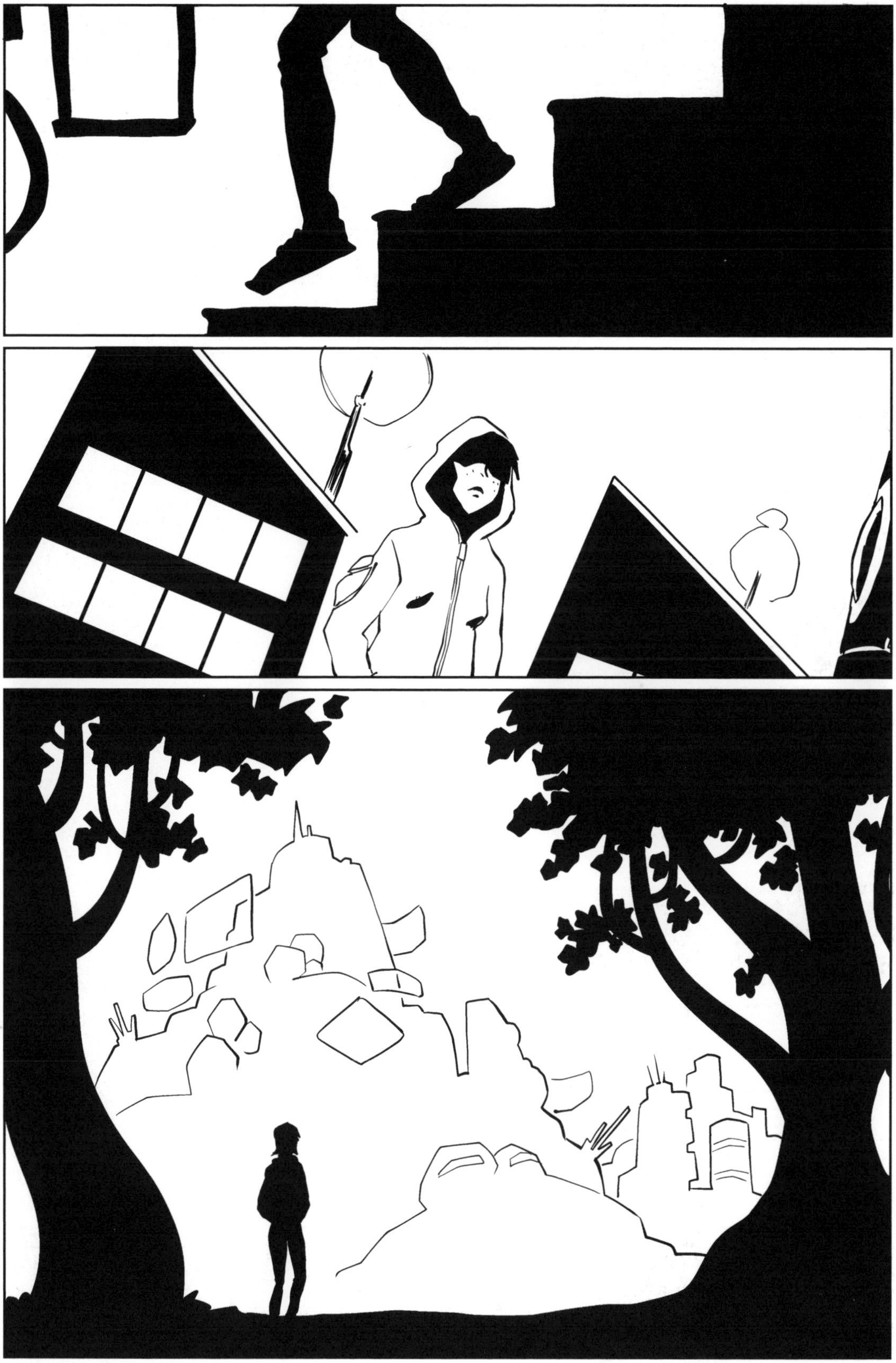

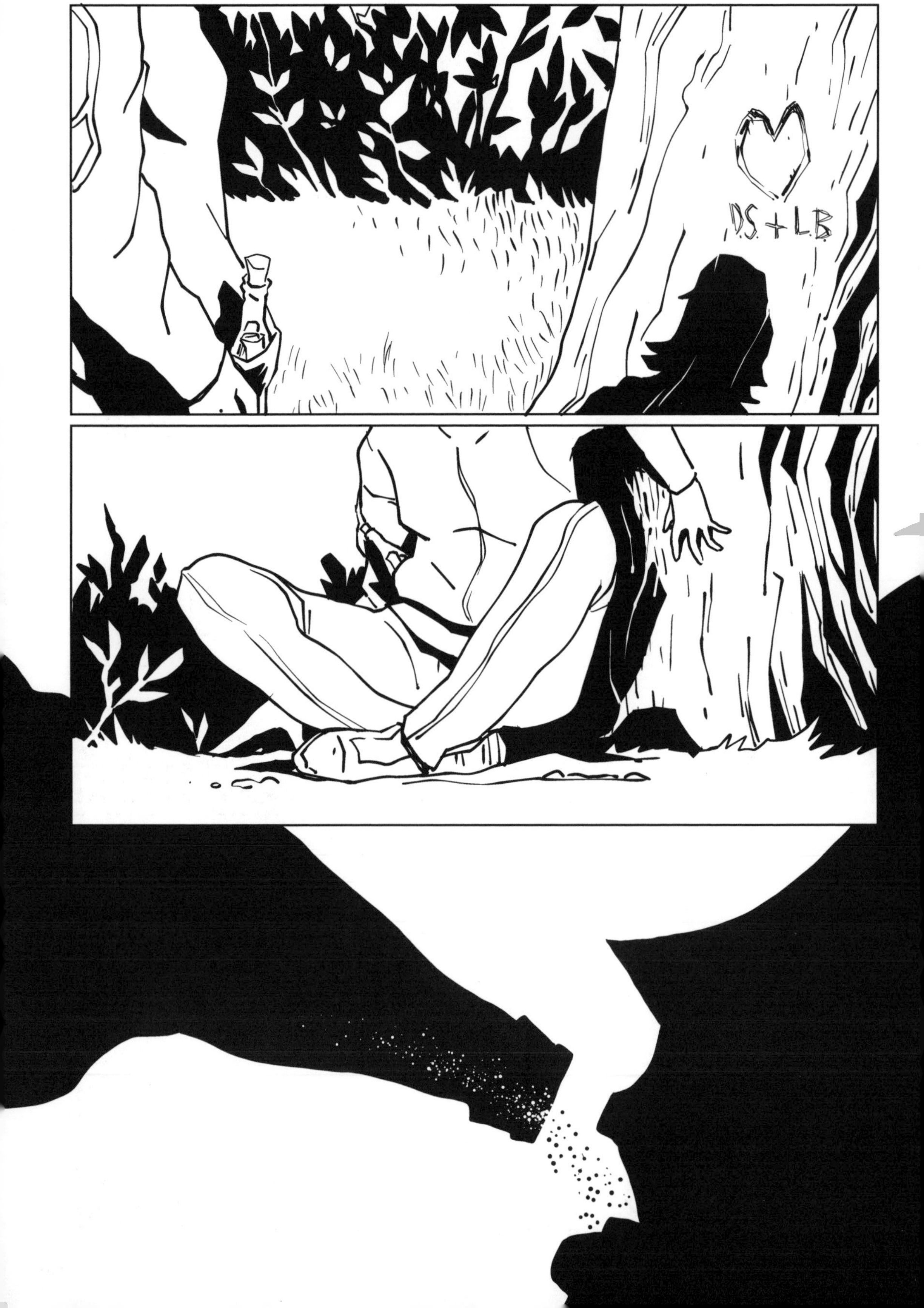
D.S. + L.B.

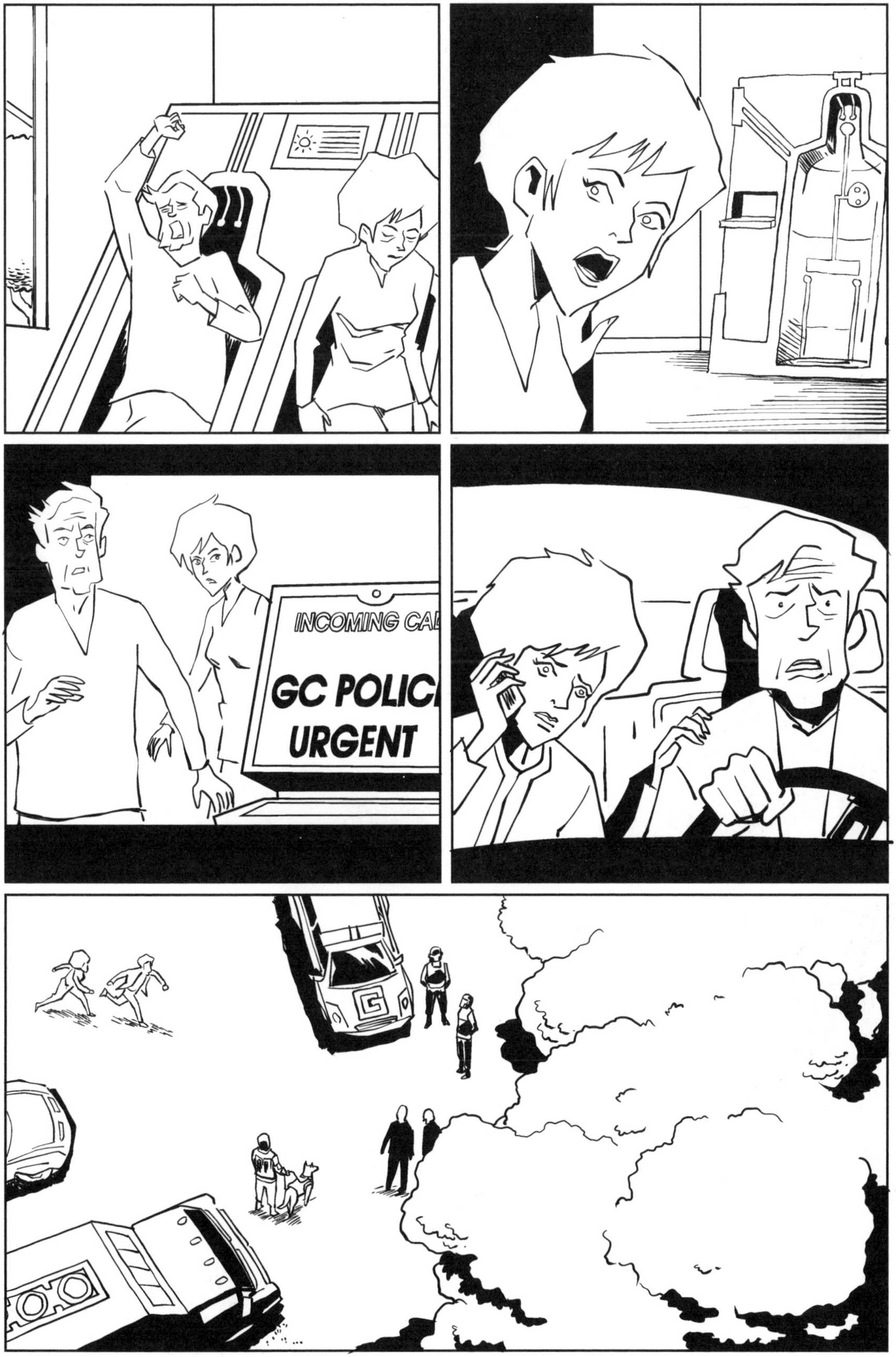
INCOMING CAL
GC POLIC
URGENT

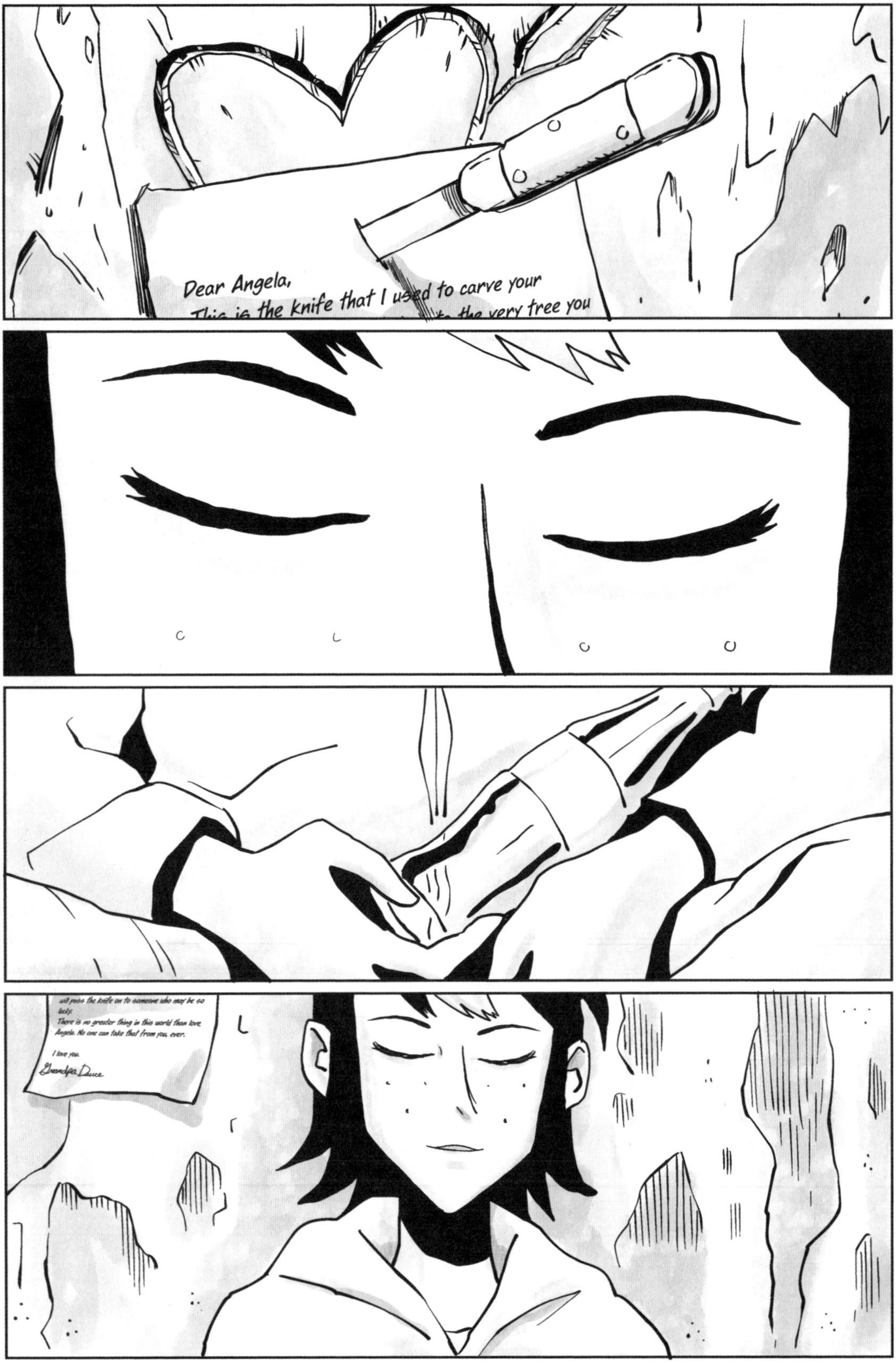
Dear Angela,
the knife that I used to carve your
the very tree you
will pass the knife on to someone who may be so lucky.
There is no greater thing in this world than love, Angela. No one can take that from you, ever.
I love you.
Grandpa Deuce

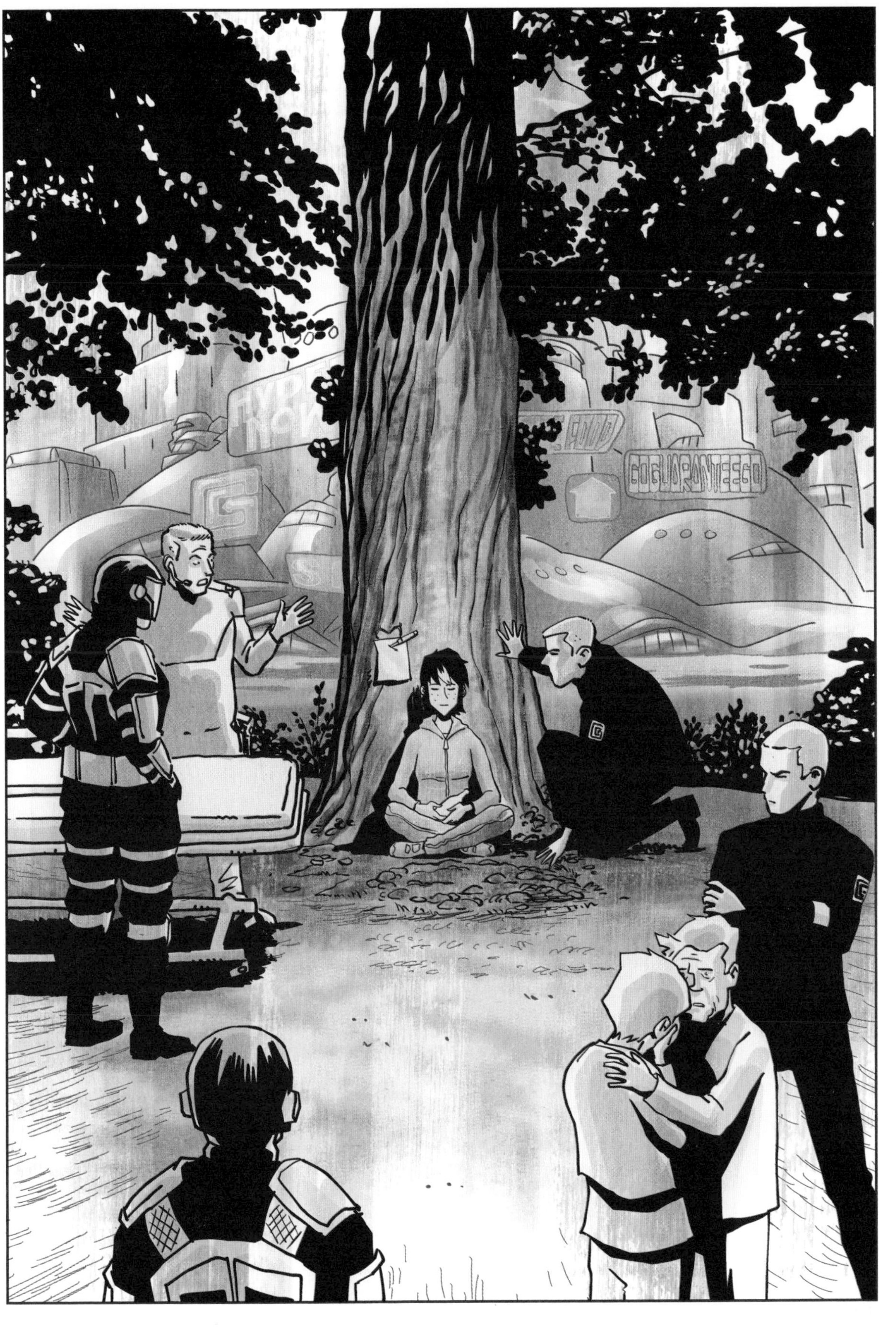
GOGUARANTEEGO

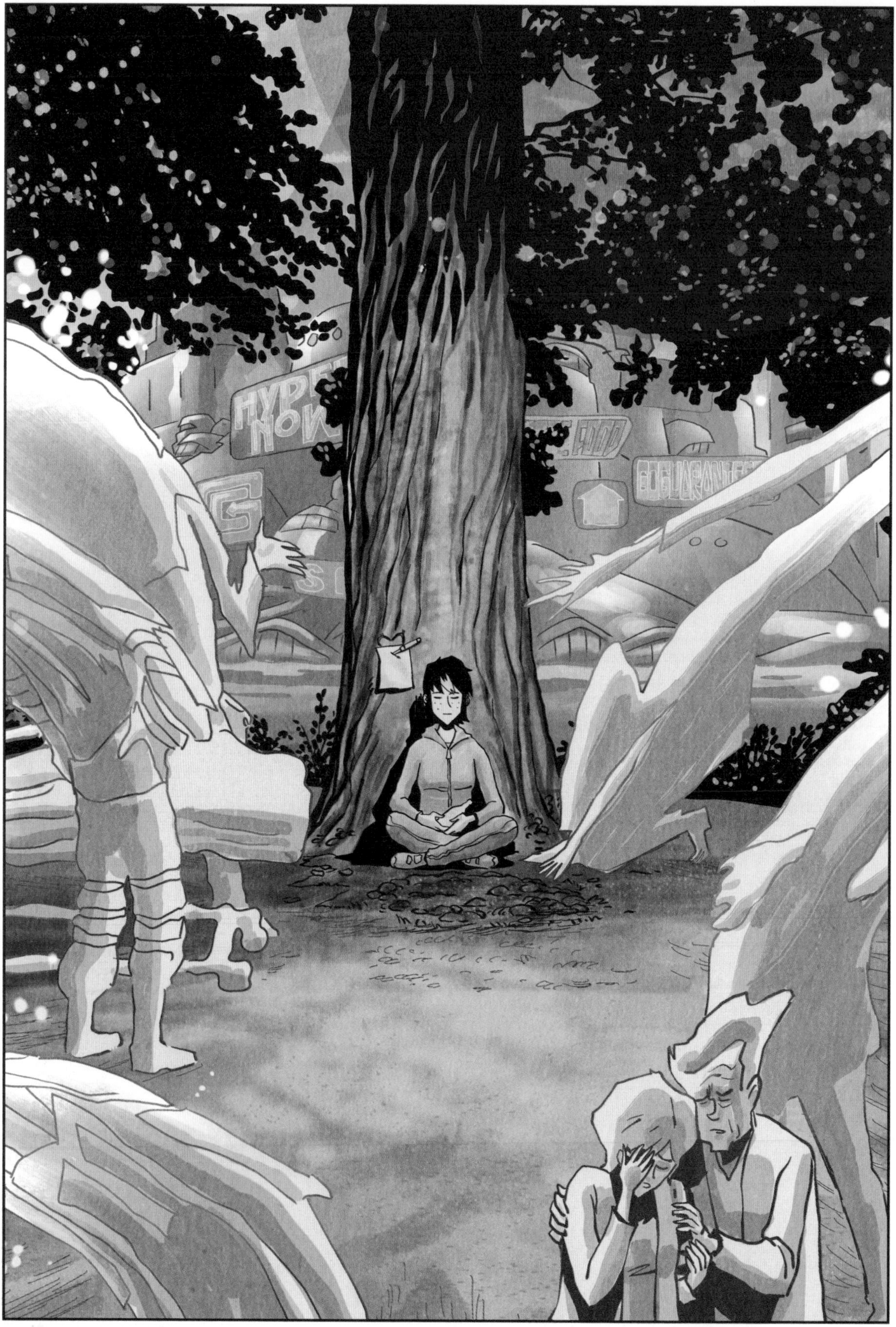
HYPE
NOW

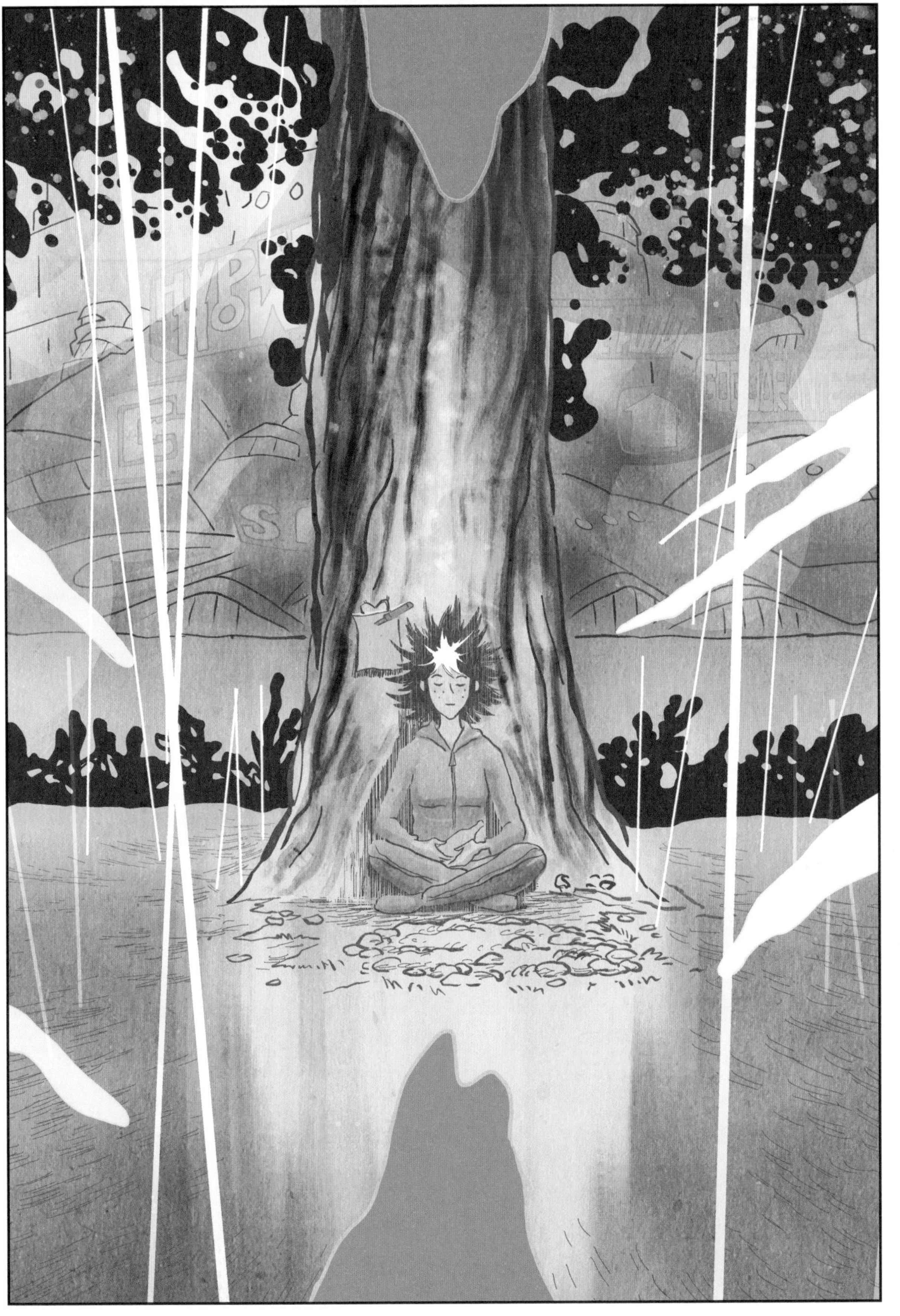

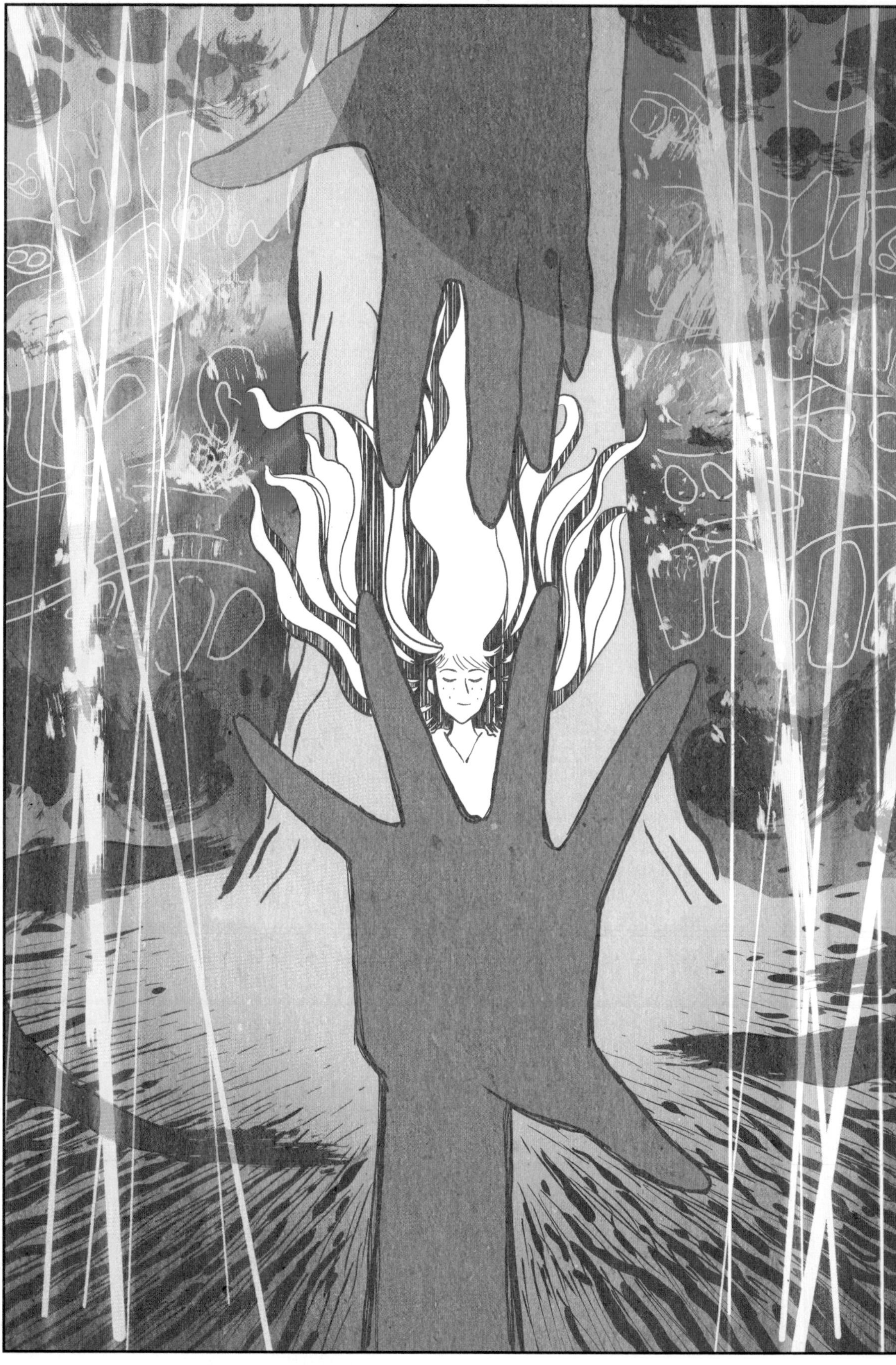

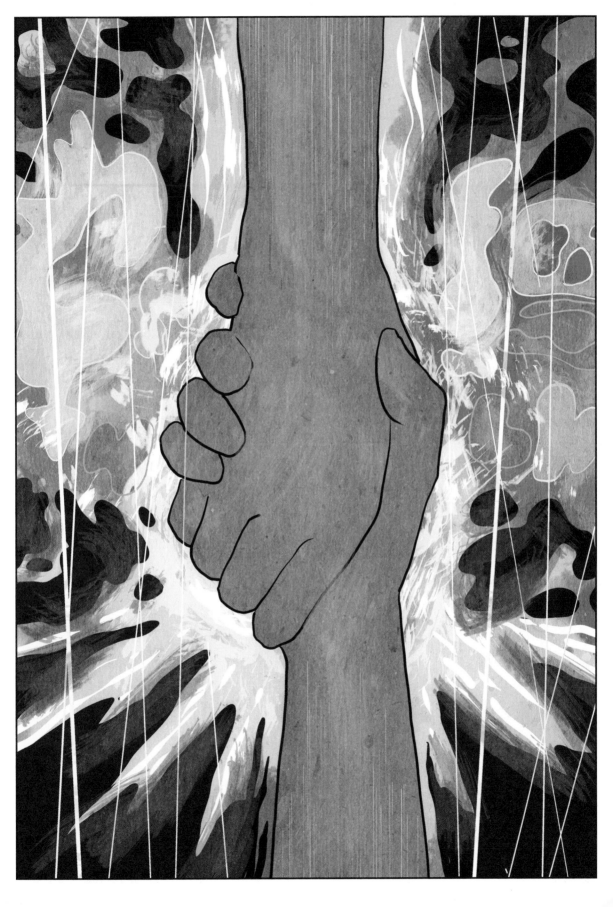

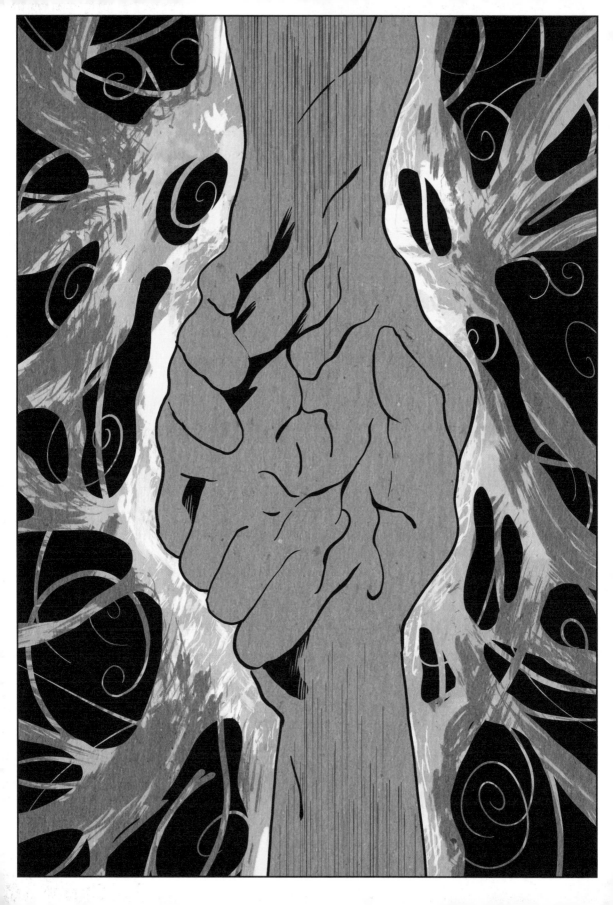

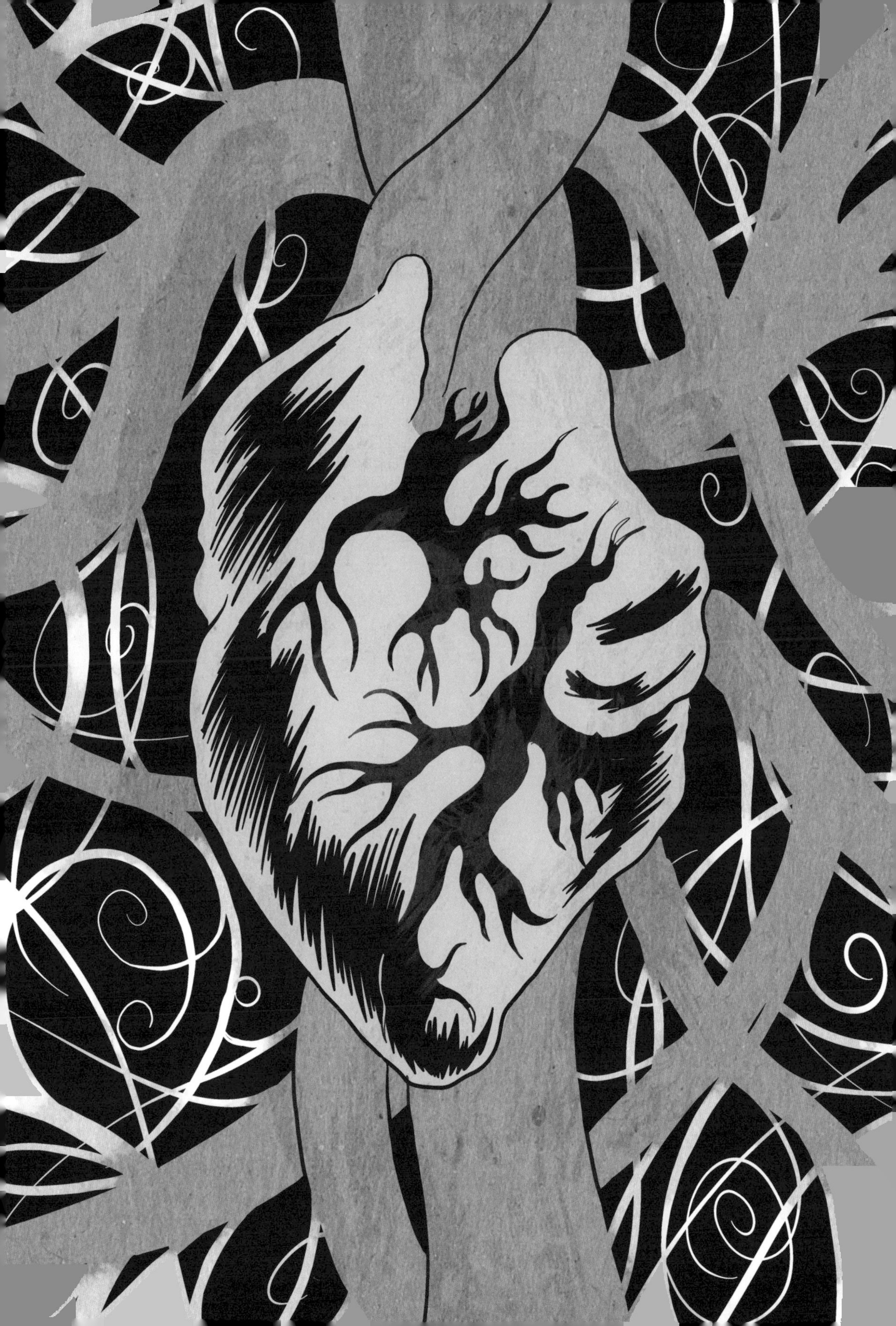

The author would like to thank Mark Siegel for his dedication to seeing this book all the way through. And he would also like to thank Mike Cavallaro for his incredible artwork.

The artist would like to thank:
Mark Siegel, whose patient encouragement made my contributions to this book possible.
Adam Rapp, for having me onboard.
George O'Connor, who happened to mention the existence of this manuscript.
Lisa Natoli, the Heartest Working Artist I know and my main inspiration.

Angela's journal entry

March 4

They're installing more scanner ports over by the mall. In Accelerated Appliances I saw this little boy itching his arm where they install your chip. It looked like he had a rash and the more he scratched the redder it got. His mom kept saying, "Stop that, Edward! Go. Stop that, Edward! Go. The poor kid must have been so confused. All those goes and stops. He was maybe eight or nine but his face was old like an alligator's. It made me wonder if the chip made his face that way or if it was old when he was born.

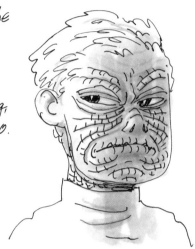

I'm starting to feel further and further away from things. Like I'm on this slow little boat floating out to sea and everyone else is back at shore, drinking Rapid Jo and "going" their heads off. My boat is starting to fill with water and I hope I find an island soon. I'm not a very good swimmer. I always wind up treading water.

Do the seagulls still have their own eyes?

At school sometimes I have this urge to just stand in the middle of the hallway between classes. Just stand there and make everyone bump into me. In Future History Mr. Lambert asked me what I wanted to do with my life. I told him that I had plans of becoming a statue.

"Ambitious," he said. He didn't add a Go. I know he was trying to be funny.

My feet hurt from walking so fast. Those new "super soles" they make us wear only hurt my arches.

Speaking of walking, last night I had this dream that I was walking barefoot through this old dirty field. It started to fill with the guts of old computers and batteries and Old World remote controls. And then there were wolves lurking. Their eyes were so blue. I walked up to a wolf and offered my hand. It started to sniff it. I had this feeling that I was a wolf too. And then I woke up.

No one actually looks at anyone anymore. We're all just looking at what we're supposed to look at.

I think my dad is turning into a robot. Like you could open this little door in his chest and there would be a blob of aluminum foil instead of a heart. Sometimes I think he has more to say to the refrigerator than to me.

And Mom's no better. Everything's Go Go Go. The spaces between her words are shrinking more every day.

All this complaining.

Here's a positivity poem.

Let's walk to the ocean
Walk right on in
We'll meet some incredible prehistoric fish
Who can play the saxophone
And teach us to breathe underwater

That's all for now.

More tomorrow . . .